Of Legend and Lore

A Collection of
Fairy Tale Retellings

The display type was set in Goudy Bookletter 1911.
The text type was set in Garamond.

Published by Rowanwood Publishing, LLC.
www.rowanwoodpublishing.com

First Edition

Introduction

We are the Just-Us League, a group of friends dedicated to the craft of telling stories.

We come from all over the world. We all have different backgrounds and different styles of writing. But we all have storytelling in common. We bonded over our writing, and our love of putting words onto a page to entertain is what makes us truly happy.

For our fourth anthology, we have returned to a beloved genre—fairy tale retellings. Each author has chosen a story to adapt and make their own. Exploring new twists on our favorite tales—some well-known, others obscure—allows us to rediscover the magic of childhood through a lens that is neither rose-colored, nor black-and-white, but somewhere in-between. We hope that through our retellings, you too may do the same.

Without further ado, we present to you the *Just-Us League Anthology: Volume Four*. Please enjoy.

Sincerely,
The Just-Us League

Table of Contents

Seeing Through Him by B. C. Marine...1

Jack and the Storyteller by Matthew Dewar.................................31

Three Nights by Kelsie Engen...63

Cursed Glass by M. T. Wilson...95

Princess and the Frog by Renee Frey.................................131

Swapped by Allie May...167

The Gruffs vs. Dragon by Louise Ross.................................199

Wishes Between Worlds by Sam Waterhouse.................................225

The Charcoal Cat by J. E. Klimov.................................257

Solstice Flames by Heather Hayden.................................279

The Firestone by Elise Edmonds.................................315

Seeing Through Him

B. C. Marine

With every pass of the polishing cloth, the glass cleared, revealing a curving river of dark auburn in the reflection. Rosabella leaned in, rubbing harder, willing the surface smooth. Ocean blue eyes floated lopsidedly in an uneven tawny face. She buffed one last section. With every movement, the distortion traveled around her head. Full but crooked lips tightened into a frown.

She groaned. "Warped again?" Tossing the cloth into a basket, she slumped into a chair.

Six months. For six months, Rosabella had apprenticed under Mistress Elba, master mirrorsmith, and her work was still worthless. At this rate, she would never become a master herself.

Her mentor set down her tools and crossed the forge to inspect the mirror. She gave a single curt nod of approval. "It's an improvement."

Rosabella scoffed. "You're just trying to make me feel better."

"No, really. The ripples are less pronounced than your last attempt."

"But it still doesn't show a true reflection."

Mistress Elba waved a hand. "You're too hard on yourself. Perfection requires time and patience."

Rosabella rubbed her temples. Her Allure could be a

pain. No matter how many times she asked people to treat her normally, they couldn't help but be lenient with her. Being inherently likable made every compliment suspect and all too often softened or erased criticism. Mistress Elba was no exception.

Squinting, the master mirrorsmith ran a hand over the mirror. "Most of the warping appears to be on the surface. The backing seems smooth enough…I can probably salvage this one." She bent down and inspected its profile. A few silvery strands escaped her thick, ash brown braid. Her rugged fingers grazed the glass with a feather-light touch, liquefying the center.

A gentle smile crinkled the corners of her eyes as she straightened and dusted off her hands. "There. See, the defects were only superficial. Once it cools, you can frame it."

Rosabella crossed her arms over her thick leather apron. "But how would I fix it? I don't have Fire."

"I'll teach you the alternate method when you're ready."

"But—"

"You have enough to practice already," Mistress Elba said adamantly.

Rosabella sighed. "Maybe this was a mistake. My Gift is all wrong." It seemed as though all her lessons were the alternate ones.

Mistress Elba put a hand on her shoulder. "None of my former apprentices ever worked this hard."

None of them had needed to, but it would be rude to interrupt again.

"You've worn yourself ragged. Take a break. Go outside."

Of course, running errands. At least she could do that well. "Where do you need supplies from?"

"No, Rosabella, a real break, not a supply run. No

more errands or practice or lessons today."

"It's barely past noon!"

Mistress Elba steered her toward the door. "I mean it. I need you to take a walk and clear your head."

"Mistress—"

She flung the door open and pointed. "Out!"

Rosabella snatched her poncho from a nearby hook and shuffled outside. "I'll be back in an hour," she grumbled over her shoulder.

Mistress Elba smiled and shook her head. "You're not coming back until dinnertime." She closed the door, leaving Rosabella standing agape outside.

Fine, then! If she wasn't needed… Rosabella took a deep, calming breath. Compared to the stifling workshop, the warm, late spring air was refreshing. The street still glistened from the early morning rain. Townsfolk passed by, and Rosabella stepped aside to let a wealthy-looking couple into the shop. To her left, Pablo's bakery opened its windows, and the scent of fresh cornbread wafted out. Her stomach rumbled. Hours of hard, but shoddy, work had built up her appetite. She ducked inside and emerged a few minutes later with a sweet, golden treat.

But now what?

She knew all the shops here at the southern end of town, but she'd never visited the north side before. She'd never had half a day to kill, either, as she usually spent her rest days practicing. It was as good a time as any to explore the rest of Espejo.

After meandering for a few blocks, it became apparent why she'd never had reason to go there. Cedar cabins lined the road one after another, but shops were few and far between. Most were general stores, reselling merchandise from the market squares to those unwilling or unable to walk across town, all priced higher than at the original shops. One window even displayed a few of Mistress Elba's pieces alongside wares from all the top masters in town, from goldsmiths to tailors. Oh, to someday be the best in her own town. But for now, it was merely a dream.

Rosabella could have returned to the mirror shop, but Mistress Elba would have sent her back outside anyway. She wanted to trust in her master's judgment. After moving halfway across the kingdom to train under her, Rosabella couldn't return home unskilled. While few without Fire took up mirrorsmithing, Rosabella had been compelled to seek out Mistress Elba after seeing her work on display at a festival the year before. Copper spruce branches had surrounded a perfectly smooth glass oval. The blue-green patina that had formed over the frame only made the evergreens more lifelike. The shining surface held yet more beauty in its truthfulness.

If Rosabella could create something half as beautiful, she could open her own shop back home. But that wouldn't be enough for her. Having the wrong Gift for her profession meant working twice as hard and reaching twice as high. Yet here she was on a pointless walk when she could be practicing.

The farther she went, the more trees grew between the houses until the houses stopped entirely. She had passed into the forest now, and the sun filtered to the west through the evergreen canopy. Ferns and salal lined the path, weaving between the firs and cedars. Not far down the road, a wall of pink peeked out between pine trees. Curious, she picked up her pace and strode toward it.

Not a wall. Bushes.

Wild roses climbed ten feet high with clusters of blooms in all their five-petaled glory. Between them, a door opened into a cedar log cabin. Next door, smoke billowed out of a shed. Mistress Elba always told her to look for inspiration around her. Perhaps Rosabella could buy a rose cutting from whoever lived there. She poked her head through the cabin doorway but saw no one. She circled the outside and called, "Hello?"

Nobody answered.

Who would leave a smokehouse and an open cabin unattended in the woods? If a fire went wild, it could reach the town quickly.

As she circled the cabin again in search of a bucket of water, a momentary shimmer inside caught her eye, leading her inward. A simple log-frame bed covered in deerskin and a matching wooden nightstand stood at one end, with a river rock fireplace and oven at the other. A large pine table filled the center of the room with a single thick-spindled chair pulled up to its middle. Whoever lived there hadn't bothered to hang decorations anywhere. Next to the doorway, a small, plain wooden table held a silver hand mirror. Its intricately wrought details looked out of place in the otherwise sparse and rustic interior.

She picked up the mirror for a closer inspection. Ornate swirls and vines twisted up the handle and crept around its glossy face. Etching gave the effect of vines melting into the edge. Though she didn't recognize the handiwork, it was clearly a masterpiece.

"Hey!" a deep voice boomed. "What in the world are you doing?"

Rosabella started, dropping the hand mirror. No! It shattered on the floor. The sharp crack of glass pierced the air, breaking a piece of her soul with it.

"I'm sorry. I didn't see anyone. I thought—" She turned around to face the speaker but saw no one. She spun around completely, yet she still saw only an empty room.

The voice snickered. "Stop spinning. You're making me dizzy just looking at you."

She halted and backed toward the doorway. "I'm sorry about the mirror. I would never break such a piece on purpose, I swear."

"What are you doing here?"

She gripped the doorframe behind her and looked

around the small cabin. The velvet voice was definitely coming from inside and decidedly male. He sounded more annoyed than menacing, but that didn't help to loosen her fingers.

"Please, show yourself first," she said in the most charming tone she could muster in her fear. "I'd like to converse in a more civilized manner." She stopped short of batting her eyelashes. Saving her own skin was one thing, but forcing Allure too much felt grimy.

He laughed. "I'm afraid you'll have to settle for uncivilized conversation." Slow, heavy footsteps echoed through the cabin. The chair moved across the room on its own, scraping across the rough wood floor. A deerskin pillow on the seat flattened, and the chair settled with a creak. "Now, what are you doing here?" he asked with less edge than before, letting his baritone warm into near sultriness. Forcing her Gift might have been too much for him. No need to abuse her power—or give him any wrong ideas.

Rosabella had never met someone with Invisibility before. She let go of the doorframe and took a step toward the chair, careful not to add to her natural Allure with a hip sway or sweet inflection. "I wanted to see if I could buy one of your beautiful roses, then I saw your smokehouse and thought your fire was unattended. Why did you wait so long to make yourself known?"

"Most people go away if I ignore them. They don't usually break my things."

"Again, I'm so sorry. I just wanted a closer look. I shouldn't have touched it." She picked up the frame by its handle and laid it on the entry table, then crouched down and began gingerly collecting the largest shards of glass. Such beautiful craftsmanship, destroyed. "I can get you a new mirror. With enough time, I might even be able to replace the glass in this one." She hated the thought of such a lovely frame being discarded.

He sighed. "It doesn't matter. It's just a mirror. I don't need it."

Rosabella raised an eyebrow in the general direction of the chair. "Just a mirror? It was a work of art. It would be a dishonor to my craft not to make it right."

"If it really bothers you that much…" The chair squeaked, and the cushion shifted and inflated. A leather bag vanished from the big table. The floorboards groaned. He was close enough now for her to faintly hear his steady breathing.

Holding her own breath, Rosabella looked for movement. What was he doing?

Shards disappeared from the floor one by one, followed by clinking sounds. With a louder clatter, the leather bag reappeared on the table next to the frame. Broken glass glittered inside. "You can put the pieces in here. There's a broom by the door for the rest."

Relieved, she hopped up and fetched the broom, and the chair creaked again. "You only have one chair?" she asked.

"What would I do with another one? I only have one butt."

Rosabella cleared her throat to mask a giggle. After making quick work of the mess, she wiped her hands on the work apron she'd forgotten to remove. "But what about when you have visitors?"

"I don't have visitors—and trespassers don't count."

How awful! How could anyone be completely alone? She couldn't fathom the idea. "No one at all? I—"

A far-off bell tolled, signaling the end of the day for shops in town.

"You should probably go back where you came from now," he said, disappointment overshadowing a tone of resignation.

This wouldn't do. Not when she could change it.

Rosabella took the bag of broken glass and added the frame. She could use the pieces for mosaic work. "I'll return with a new mirror. I promise." She took two steps out the door before she popped back inside. "I never got your name—mine's Rosabella, by the way."

"Why do you care?" He sounded confused.

She shrugged. "I can call you 'Mister Not There' if you prefer."

He groaned. "No thank you. Call me Leandro."

"I look forward to seeing you again soon, Leandro," she said over her shoulder as she turned back outside.

"Ha. I won't hold my breath."

***

Leandro tossed a branch from the roof, careful not to lose his footing in the process. It was finally dry enough to confidently venture onto the cedar shakes and remove the needles and branches that had accumulated, but the rains had still worn the wood smooth enough to give him pause. If he fell, nobody would come to his aid—they'd have to find him first.

It was a small price for his solitude. Why endure the noise and cramped spaces in town just to be unseen and ignored? People didn't interact with him either way, but at least here he could have a little space to go along with the lack of conversation.

He swept pine needles off in fluttery green and brown clouds. Stray maple seeds followed, twirling over the roses and floating toward the path. In the distance, a tiny figure moved closer, weighed down by oddly-shaped cargo.

It couldn't be Rosabella. It had only been a few days, and she said it would take time to repair the glass.

Maybe she was visiting!

No. Why would she want to come back and visit a

hopeless recluse? He sighed. Probably just a merchant.

Leandro finished sweeping, then dropped the broom in front of the door and inched over to the ladder on the back side of the house. By the time he reached the ground, someone was knocking on his door.

"Hello? Leandro?" Rosabella called out as he rounded the corner. She had tied a basket to the seat of a chair and used the extra rope for shoulder straps to carry it all on her back. The leather apron was gone, and her fitted lavender blouse flattered her more delicate features, though her strong arms still hinted at her trade. Dappled sunlight highlighted the red shimmer of her dark hair. She was downright stunning when she wasn't damaging his property.

"What are you—why—what is all this?" Such eloquence. Thankfully, she couldn't see the accompanying blush that warmed his cheeks. A simple greeting and he melted like a fool.

"It's a rest day. The shops are closed." She grinned. "Want to see what I brought you?"

He tilted his head and opened the door. "I must admit I'm curious." More dumbfounded, really. Maybe he'd fallen off the roof and banged his head.

She reached out and patted the air with her hand before entering the cabin. In a few moments, she had the basket open on the kitchen table, and the smell of warm bread filled the room.

His mouth watered. Hunting and gathering had sustained him for years. The last time he'd had fresh goods from town was almost fifteen years ago, for his birthday. A strawberry-and-cranberry stuffed pastry. The morning of the Gifting ceremony, he couldn't wait for anything. He inhaled his breakfast and ran to the lodge. Had he known what would happen that day, he would've run away from it.

Not that it would've done any good. Invisibility would have found him anyway, but fear and logic rarely get along. Though there was much debate over the age at which a person's Gift became fated, no one ever made it to age thirteen without their Gift, whether through induction on their twelfth birthday or natural manifestation thereafter. Inducing his Gift at the ceremony should have made it easier to control. As he still had no idea how to turn it off, Leandro didn't want to imagine what even less control would be like. Mentors for rare Gifts were hard to come by, and in his case, impossible to find.

Unable to catch a clerk's attention in a busy bakery and unwilling to risk being mistaken for a thief, Leandro had given up on buying fresh bread, and most other goods in town for that matter. He didn't realize just how much he missed it until now.

Rosabella served a portion of bread and raspberries in front of his chair, then sat in the one she had brought and served herself. "I ran out of room for meat in the basket. I hope that's okay."

"I have some in the smokehouse," he said without thinking and made his way there. What was he doing, offering up his food? Just a few days ago, she was a trespassing vandal. But she drew him in, *alluring* him…

Oh no. Could he be more oblivious? It was only the name of a stinking Gift. She must be conning him using Allure. But why? She'd already broken the only thing of value he had. Torn between suspicion and attraction, he returned to the table with a piece of venison.

She reached into the basket, radiant with excitement—or perhaps it was part of her Allure—and pulled out the leather bag she had taken from the house before. She offered it to his chair. "I'm still working on your other one. This one's nowhere near as fine, but I didn't want to make you wait."

Leandro sat and took the bag. The mirror inside had a smooth wooden frame and handle, and the glass bowed slightly. Most likely a reject from the shop.

"I made it yesterday," she said, sitting up straighter. "Mistress Elba told me I could bring it to you, and you can keep it even after the other one is repaired."

He grimaced. Poor quality or not, he couldn't bring himself to insult the mirror when she seemed so proud of it. "Thank you. That's very…generous." He picked up the bread while it was still warm and dug in. Knowing she couldn't see, he ate with abandon, savoring every bite. He'd forgotten bread could be so sweet and savory at the same time.

Rosabella ate in peaceful silence herself for a few moments. Then began the telltale wriggling in her seat of someone uncomfortable with silence. Whatever she wanted, he wouldn't be the one to speak first. Let her squirm all she wanted.

"If it's not too rude to ask…" she said finally.

As if that had stopped her yet.

"What do you need a mirror for without a reflection?" She leaned forward. "Was it an heirloom?"

Should he answer? It seemed like a harmless enough question, but he still wasn't sure what she was playing at.

"I'm prying, aren't I? Was that too personal?"

"No, no. I've just never been asked before." Meh, why not? This particular knowledge couldn't do any harm. He plucked another two pieces from the basket and held one just above her plate. "You're right. I don't usually have a reflection. But I'm sure you've noticed that when I carry something or wear it, it turns invisible like me." He dropped the bread onto their plates, enjoying seeing her eyes widen at the sudden reappearance. "The hand mirror acts as a part of me."

"Does that mean you're not invisible to yourself?"

He laughed. "Thank the Giver, no. It's bad enough that nobody else can see me." He shuddered. "Speaking of nosy questions…"

Rosabella raised an eyebrow.

"Why would someone like you work with her hands?"

"Someone like me?" she lied flimsily.

"You know, someone with your Gift." If he was wrong about the pull he felt and mentioned it aloud, she'd think he was flirting. Better to keep it vague.

She picked at the bread on her plate and said softly, "You noticed that."

"What can I say? I've become adept at observation. It comes with the territory."

Rosabella shrugged. "I need to do something, don't I? And I've always been drawn to mirrors."

"Wouldn't it be easier to use your Allure? You could marry rich or become a popular merchant easily. Why physically work?"

"Do *you* want to be defined by *your* Gift?" she asked, almost flirtatious in her confidence.

"We are. Whether we want to be is irrelevant."

She shook her head. "I refuse to accept that."

Maybe she wasn't a con artist after all. Just deluded.

***

Rosabella wiped her forehead as more droplets snuck down the back of her neck. The forest wasn't as sweltering as the town, but she still longed for the cool shade of Leandro's cabin. The weekly visits had become a welcome respite, especially as the summer heat hit its peak. After Rosabella returned that first evening with a renewed sense of purpose, Mistress Elba had encouraged her to continue to leave on rest days, telling Rosabella that more time spent away from the forge made her a better apprentice.

She smiled as the rosebushes came into sight. Their first blooms long gone, the thorny branches stood sentry over the tiny hideaway.

"Oh, good. You're here," Leandro called out before she had reached the doorway. "I need your help with something."

"Should I be worried?" He never asked for help; he barely tolerated visits. Even when she actively tried to be charming, he remained walled off.

"How adept are you with a pair of scissors?"

Ten minutes later, Rosabella stood behind Leandro's chair, a comb in one hand and shears in the other. "How did you talk me into this? What if I cut your ear off?"

"I'm watching in the mirror. I'll tell you if you get too close."

Sculpting red-hot glass and metal felt less dangerous than this, but she needed to fulfill the trust he'd placed in her, or she'd likely never see it again. She took a deep breath and slowly reached forward with the comb until her hand stopped.

"That would be my neck."

"Oh no!" She sprang her hands up in surrender. "I can't—I have no idea what I'm doing."

"Rosabella, it's fine. Put the comb in your other hand and hold it out for me."

She did as he asked, and a calloused hand wrapped around her wrist. He guided her up and forward, burying her fingers in dense, long hair. It was surprisingly soft and clean. As she ruffled the roots, hints of mint and pine implied a fresh washing, and she resisted the urge to lean closer and inhale the manly scent.

"That's the top of my head." He pulled her hand farther to the hairline, traveling down to his left ear. With a bit more force, he led her a few steps around to the side of the chair and moved her hand back to the apex. "You can start there." As he slid his hand away, he gave her fingers a slight, reassuring squeeze.

For a moment, the air under her hands pulsed in a hazy man-like shape, as faint as a shadow in the corner of one's eye, then disappeared. Rosabella blinked, but the image didn't return. She had seen only what she wanted to see.

After another calming breath, she combed out what felt like an even strip of hair and held it between her fingers. "This is probably going to look silly."

"What do I care? I'm not cavorting through town. As long as it feels cooler and lighter, it'll do."

"All right then." She snipped the shears just above her fingers. Eight inches of wavy, maple brown hair flashed into view on its way down to the floor. She moved to his left and cut again. To the left once more—

"Wait. A little to the right."

She followed his directions. They carried on thusly until the right half of his head felt sufficiently shorn.

"How did you do this alone?" she asked, continuing to cut.

"I gathered it all at the base of my neck and cut that. It wasn't very effective."

"I can see that. I don't know if you're aware, but there are people in town who can do this professionally. We call them barbers."

"Very funny. You know I don't like people."

He was bluffing, but she played along, putting a hand on her hip. "I'm a person."

"You're different."

Rosabella scoffed.

Leandro grunted. "That's not what I meant. Allure has nothing to do with it. You're my only visitor. That's all. My own family hasn't even been here."

"Why not? Did you have a falling out?"

"Nothing so dramatic. I was often overlooked as a child, and when they couldn't see me anymore, it didn't take them long to forget me. After a couple of years, they forgot me for a week solid, and I just left."

At a loss for words, she rested a hand where she

guessed his shoulder to be, and his hand enveloped hers for a moment.

He cleared his throat. "We should finish up soon. I'm hungry, and I'll have to sweep all this hair up before we can set the table."

Smiling internally, she nodded. For a moment, she'd glimpsed the man inside.

***

Rosabella passed her latest work to Mistress Elba for inspection. It was a small piece, but the quality was high; she knew it. Nevertheless, Rosabella always dreaded the flaws her mentor would inevitably find.

"Beautiful repair, Rosabella. If I didn't know better, I'd say it looks new."

She nearly burst with delight. "Thank you, Mistress! I needed to get this one right."

Mistress Elba chuckled. "I'm not surprised. I know how important it was to you." With a wink, she handed back the elegant hand mirror. "I'm guessing you'd like to deliver it tomorrow?"

"My perfectionism has kept Leandro waiting long enough. I hope he's pleased with it."

"He will be. You've come a long way. In fact…" She picked up a drawing from the table. "I saw the design you've been sketching. I think you're ready to create it. There's a festival at the beginning of next month. Mirrorsmiths from all over the kingdom will be here, competing for honors. I want you to enter the apprentice contest."

"You think I can complete it in time?" Rosabella asked. "I've never tried something that complex."

"I'll lighten your list of chores."

"But what about getting your orders done on time?"

Mistress Elba waved the comment away. "I managed just fine before you. I can handle a little less help for a short while. But, you need to do one thing for me."

Rosabella nodded. "Anything."

Mistress Elba put her hands on Rosabella's shoulders. "Make me proud."

***

Leandro fiddled with the red leather ribbon in his hands. He'd dyed the deer hide himself. Invisibility made hunting easier, and he had no shortage of meat and pelts. A cloth ribbon would've been more traditional, but the spirit of the gesture demanded frugality, so leather it was.

He checked out the window. Still no sign of Rosabella, although she wasn't due for another twenty minutes.

He loosened his grip on the ribbon. If he tore it apart before she arrived, it wouldn't be much use. Such a small token—which was entirely the point—but to him, it meant everything. The ribbon of intent. If she accepted the offering, he could woo her openly, as propriety dictated. And if that went well…

Maybe she was right about not being defined by Gifts. Maybe they could have more.

He just had to get this part right first. When he'd left town, he'd been just old enough to know the basic requirements, but young enough to never have tried them. Hopefully, neither his memory nor passing fashions had altered what little he knew.

Footsteps outside broke his reverie. Rosabella bounded through the door, holding a small package aloft and dazzling him with her smile. "Look what I have!" She set it gingerly on the entry table.

"Is that what I think it is?"

"Take a look. I did the work myself."

He unwrapped the coarse ramie cloth to reveal

familiar silver. His old mirror, just as he remembered it. He picked it up to see his scruffy reflection smiling back at him. Maybe it was for the best that she couldn't see his unkempt appearance. At least he bathed regularly. Unwashed man-stink scared away game.

"Do you like it?" she asked, inching closer.

"It's perfect." Could he do this? It was just a ribbon, not a ring. But now that she was here, his resolve faltered.

"Good. Speaking of mirrors, there's a festival in a few weeks…" She traced the wood grain on the table with her finger.

"The Festival of Reflection?"

Her head popped up. "You know about it? I thought you didn't go into town."

"Well, I was born there."

"Fair enough. Anyway, I'm working on a piece to enter." She fidgeted again, moving her hands to the back of the chair she would normally have sat in by now.

"I hope you can bring it by. I'd love to see it." It was more than flattery. The improvement between the first mirror she'd brought him and this one was impressive.

"It'll be too large to just bring out here, I'm afraid."

"Oh. That's too bad. You'll have to tell me how it fares, at least."

She smiled sweetly. "Why don't you come with me? We could have so much fun. I hear there's even dancing in the evening."

"No. I can't." The thoughtless words came of their own accord.

Rosabella frowned. "But—"

"I don't dance. I don't go into town."

"I know. You hate getting lost in the crowd, but I'll be right by your side."

What had he been thinking? He couldn't court her. He couldn't court anyone. That might lead to marriage. Then he'd have to go into town, maybe even live there. And she couldn't live out here in the woods without a forge and a shop, not when the market was on the opposite edge of town. She only visited once a week; she wouldn't want to make that trek every day. He crushed the ribbon in his hand and closed his eyes, wishing away his foolish dream. Why had he let her in? Her presence only fueled desires that could never be filled.

"Leandro, please. Just talk to me." She reached out to him, just shy of his location, grasping empty air.

"There's nothing to talk about." He said it more harshly than he intended.

"Why are you so upset?"

"You're demanding too much of me."

"Demanding?" She rolled her eyes. "It's just an invitation. You're overreacting."

"Why are you even here?"

She tilted her head. "What is that supposed to mean?"

"Why are you here?" he enunciated.

Rosabella crossed her arms. "I'm returning your mirror, and I *thought* we could have a pleasant lunch together."

"No. Why are you here? Why do you keep coming back? What are you getting out of all this?"

She shrugged. "I wanted to be your friend."

"You have no trouble making friends. You probably have more than you know what to do with."

"So what? Yes, I *can* make friends easily. But believe it or not, I choose to do so with people I *want* to be friends with."

"Why me?"

"Because you needed one."

As if he didn't already feel like dirt. "I don't need your pity," he spat.

Her eyes widened. "It's not—"

"You might as well leave." Each word he spoke tore at him, but it had to be done.

"Leandro!" She reached forward with more force, stumbling when he stepped deftly out of the way. Steadying herself on the table, she scanned the room for signs of him, though he did not move.

"You aren't obligated to keep returning here—"

"Please, don't do this—"

"And I don't want you to."

Her shining blue eyes allied with his heart, pleading for him to stop. If he didn't do this now and let things progress instead, it would only hurt worse when everything inevitably fell apart. He opened the door.

She walked through and stopped just outside, turning back to say, "Don't shut me out, Leandro. You don't have to be alone."

He forced himself to say, "Goodbye, Rosabella," and closed the door.

He marched to the fireplace, wadding up the ribbon, prepared to hurl it in, but his arm would not cooperate. The trinket was worthless to him now, and yet he couldn't bring himself to destroy it. No more destruction. Not in that moment. He let go.

As the ribbon fell to the floor, Leandro dropped into his chair, head in his hands, and wept.

Rosabella was wrong. He would be alone forever.

***

The copper strip snapped in two as Rosabella stretched it. "Frog nuggets!" She slammed the pieces on the table.

"Gently this time," Mistress Elba said. "Again."

Rosabella heated and quenched another piece and pulled again, determined to be gentle, but her tense fingers did not obey. It, too, broke under the strain.

Pressure built up inside her chest, spreading into clenched hands and clouding her vision. She closed her eyes. The moisture that escaped between her lashes stung in the dry heat.

Mistress Elba's tools clanked against the table, and a hand squeezed her shoulder. "Let it out," the master said.

Rosabella wiped her cheek with the back of her wrist. "Curse my hands. I'm just so clumsy today."

"That's not it. You've been in a mood for days."

Rosabella put a hand up. "It's personal."

"It affects your work in my shop. That's not personal anymore."

Rosabella's breath hitched. "I'll keep it to myself better."

"No. Trying to hide your pain is the problem. What we do is art. Don't fight the pain. *Use it.*"

She looked at her mentor, confused. "Use it?"

"Follow me." Mistress Elba led the way into the gallery. "Look at these." She pointed to a shelf of poor but salable mirrors that Rosabella had made months ago. "When you started, you were so bent on perfection you could never attain it. Now these." She pointed to a shelf of gleaming glass, simple but smooth. "When you stopped forcing it— when you embraced life—your work flourished."

Rosabella sighed. "Being happy made inspiration easy." Couldn't Mistress Elba leave well enough alone? Why turn the knife?

"Yes, you channeled that happiness into beauty, but life isn't always happy. You must work with what you have. Feel your pain. Quench your scrollwork with your tears. Etch the glass with heartache. Use it. Put it on display."

"For everyone to see?" Rosabella recoiled.

"Our mirrors reflect their makers as much as their owners. If you cannot handle that, you've chosen the wrong profession." Mistress Elba's blunt tone held no contempt.

The spruce-framed mirror shone from the middle of the room, the same one that had inspired her before. "That piece is about renewal," Rosabella said instinctively.

"It was the first piece I made when I moved here, years ago. Never had the heart to sell it."

Rosabella looked at her own hands. What wonders could they produce? She walked back to the forge and took another piece of copper. As the metal warmed, she opened her heart, the raw emotion rising with the steam as she plunged the piece into water. She exhaled. Tears fell down her cheeks as she stretched the copper into a pointed leaf.

***

Mistress Elba smiled. "If you don't win a prize tomorrow, I'll be shocked."

Rosabella feigned a smile in return. "Thank you, Mistress." The clear glass gleamed in its delicately sculpted frame. She rubbed the smooth metal foliage between her fingertips. As pleased as she was with how her mirror had turned out, something was missing—or rather, someone.

She knew Leandro had hurt himself with his outburst. Lack of practice made him a terrible liar. Why did he have to be so stubborn?

She would have traded all her best work to have him back. Even now, she fought the urge to run into the forest. If she poured on the charm as thick as honey, she might be able to persuade him to change his mind. But what good would that do? Affection meant nothing if it was coerced.

Maybe, given a little space and time to think, he'd let her back in. And maybe he was right about her demanding too much. Though she'd never said it aloud, part of her had wanted more; maybe he knew it. For now, she would try to enjoy the festival, even if it felt like dancing with a broken leg.

***

Leandro stared at the ceiling. It was past time to get out of bed, but he had nothing to do. In an effort to keep the emptiness at bay, he'd thrown himself into scrubbing down every inch of the cabin. He'd chopped firewood. He'd weeded his garden. He'd done every chore he could think of, pausing only to collapse in bed each night. Even his meals were eaten while working.

There were no chores left, and he was alone. For the last eight years, he'd resigned himself to that fact, but after knowing Rosabella, Leandro finally knew what he was missing. He could no longer stave off the pain.

He flopped over and lurched to his feet. Shuffling across the room, he yawned and stretched his arms. Although he wasn't hungry, he willed himself to look in the pantry. He took a basket of blackberries and plopped them onto the table, then slumped into his chair. If he left the fruit to rot, he'd kick himself for it later.

He forced down a few handfuls, letting his vision blur out of focus with his thoughts. A rogue blackberry tumbled out of his grasp. It rolled across the table and fell onto Rosabella's empty chair.

What use was an extra chair? It needed to go.

Grabbing the chair by its back, he dragged it away. As he opened the door and swung the chair around it, he knocked the entry table. The silver hand mirror fell. Leandro dove, catching it at the last second. He groaned and rolled onto his side. Hardwood was not forgiving.

A glint caught the corner of his eye. His clumsiness had dislodged a piece of broken mirror from between the table and the wall. He reached out for the shard, part of his beard popping into view on its surface as he took hold.

Leandro squeezed his eyes shut. No! Must everything conspire to remind him of her today? Even now, the far-off voices of late travelers heading for the Festival of Reflection assaulted him. He hurled the shard outside, where it burst on a tree trunk.

Enough foolishness.

After a minute, he picked himself up off the floor. Leaving the mirror out on the table was stupid. He'd nearly broken it again. Besides, if he stashed it away, it couldn't taunt him all the time. He opened the drawer and shoved the mirror inside. But as he went to close it, a tangle of red stopped him cold. The ribbon of intent curled around his fingers as he cradled it in his palm.

If the Giver himself had condemned his folly aloud, he couldn't have felt it more keenly. He'd hoped to spare himself future pain, but nothing could be worse than this.

Before he could second-guess himself, he stepped outside and locked the door. Around him, the cluster roses paraded their second blooms. He stuffed the ribbon in his pocket. If he was going to go far enough to remedy his mistake, he might as well aim high.

***

Leandro hung back against the outer wall of a shop at the edge of the market district. Just a few yards away, crowds of festival-goers filled the streets. On the emptier roads, he could walk far enough away from people to avoid interaction, letting thoughts of Rosabella distract him and urge him forward. But here, he would have to rub shoulders with others to pass by.

He shook out his nerves and bounced on the balls of his feet. It was too late; he couldn't return home—not after coming this far.

A quick inhale, and he dove into the crowd. Dodging elbows and weaving between revelers, he surged forward, into the heart of the festival. Tinsel and glass baubles hung overhead, strung on lines between buildings. As the name suggested, the mirrors were featured at the center of the Festival of Reflection. That's where he would find his own heart as well, if the crowds didn't suffocate him first. Unaware of his presence, person after person ran straight into him, causing ripples of minor, temporary panic in the crowd as the unseen obstacle startled them. Leandro did his best to jump out of their paths, but that often meant backing into someone else. Despite his high endurance, the sheer number of people wore him down as he progressed.

When he thought he could go no farther, the displays came into view. Behind ropes, various tables and stands held up dozens of mirrors, large and small, reflecting everyone and everything but him.

He knew the piece he was looking for instantly.

Wild roses surrounded a two-foot by three-foot rectangular mirror. Some were etched in the glass itself, and others had been formed in metal and cured into the perfect shade of pink. From a distance, it looked like a mirror nestled inside one of his real rosebushes.

He approached the piece, confident that he could still back away unnoticed if he didn't speak. A small card tucked in the corner read, "Apprentice: Rosabella under Mistress Elba of Espejo."

A group of five judges were walking behind the ropes, stopping to inspect the mirrors and marking their cards as they went. Leandro waited until they passed nearby to venture closer for a peek. At least three had marked Rosabella for first in the apprentice class.

Her work had progressed so much. What if he was a distraction? She might be glad to be rid of him.

Behind him, Rosabella's laugh cut through the din. He turned. She sat at a table near the middle of the plaza, smiling and sharing lunch with two men: one young, the other much older. Both were enraptured by her, especially the doe-eyed younger man.

Leandro backed into the rope and sighed. She didn't need him. She could move on just fine. If he left now, she could forget him like everyone else, if she hadn't already.

***

Rosabella nodded politely as Juan regaled her with his triumphs in the forge.

"…lifted the whole sheet myself," he said, flexing his bicep and winking.

It took all her strength to suppress an eye roll. Time to change the subject before that strength wore out. "Master Roberto, you've been awfully quiet."

"You know, I remember my first Festival of Reflection…"

Any other time, she would have eagerly picked the master's brain, but her own mind insisted on drifting away. Where was Mistress Elba? She should've been back from the shop twenty minutes ago. Rosabella began to suspect she'd left her with them on purpose from the way she'd scurried off right after introductions. Why couldn't Mistress Elba keep her nose out of Rosabella's affairs? She didn't need her help; she could find someone new herself if she wanted to.

Rosabella scanned the crowd. Near their mirrors, the rope barricade pulled inward on its own and swayed. Hope welled up.

Leandro?

She watched the area for a few moments, waiting for another odd movement. Nothing. Of course not. She picked at her bread. It could have been the wind. She shouldn't let herself get excited so easily.

"Are you all right?" Master Roberto asked.

"It's nothing. I just thought I recognized someone." She glanced back at the rope.

"Maybe you did," a familiar voice rumbled.

A wild rose materialized in front of her. Around its

stem, a crimson leather ribbon formed a tidy bow. She had rejected many ribbons of intent before, but this one, wrinkled and mismatched with the pink flower, was the loveliest she'd ever seen.

"Leandro?" Rosabella covered her grin with both hands.

"You were right," he said. "I don't want to be alone. Not without you."

She picked up the rose and breathed in its sweet perfume. The ribbon untied easily. "It's beautiful." She tucked the bloom behind her ear.

Juan wrinkled his nose and arched an eyebrow to Master Roberto, who shook his head. Poor Leandro. His public declaration was sweet. He probably wasn't aware of his faux pas and certainly didn't deserve to be mocked for it.

"Excuse us," she said to the fellow smiths and held out a hand to Leandro.

He helped her off the bench and looped her arm through his. "Did I offend your admirers?" he whispered.

She chuckled. "Master Roberto is an old colleague of Mistress Elba, and his apprentice is competing with me."

"They didn't look happy."

"I think they were a little scandalized." She lowered her voice. "Some say it's coercive to offer in public; it doesn't let a woman decline gracefully."

He jerked to a stop. "I'm sorry."

"Don't be. I don't care what they think." She held up the ribbon and wrapped it around her wrist. "And don't believe for a second that I'm giving this back."

He tied off the ends then circled his arms around her. "If you don't care what people think, we could join the dancing later and look completely foolish."

Rosabella put a hand on his chest. "That sounds wonderful."

Beneath her hand, a rough gray tunic appeared,

followed by tawny leather leggings and boots. His body blossomed into view, the maple brown hair and beard bringing out the gold flecks in his icy blue eyes. She thought no sight could ever fill her with more joy; then he caressed her cheek and leaned in closer, proving her wrong. Sliding her hands behind his neck, she closed the distance. His lips against hers tasted like bliss.

As she pulled away, she saw her mirror reflecting their embrace, revealing them both in perfect clarity. With a grin, Rosabella looked into Leandro's eyes and said, "I can see you."

Jack and the Storyteller

Matthew Dewar

Jack swallowed his nausea, and his stomach tightened. He swirled his spoon around the sickly green bowl of pea and ham soup. With heavy eyelids from lack of sleep, his mind raced with fear as the most important moment of his life drew nearer.

"No matter what happens tonight, your mother and I will always love you." Dad smiled warmly, but his eyes betrayed a fleeting flash of concern. "You've trained and prepared for this. You've got it."

Jack's head drooped, and he was unable to meet his father's gaze. The words bounced off his skin, and he scratched at his neck. Did they really mean it? What if he failed? Would they still love him? Would they still be proud to call him their son?

Mom pointed to Jack's untouched bowl of soup. "I know you're nervous, but you must eat. Even though everything will happen in your dreams, you're going to need as much energy as you can get."

On any other night, Jack would have devoured dinner and asked for seconds, but tonight, his mouth was so dry and his stomach so knotted up that it took a mountainous effort to force every mouthful down.

"You remember what to do?" Dad pushed his empty bowl away and rested his elbows on the mahogany table.

"Yes, Dad." Jack sighed. "We've been over it a

million times. I'm going to be fine." *I'm not going to be fine.*

All of Jack's friends were so lucky. They weren't living descendants of a fairy tale hero. They didn't have to climb a massive beanstalk or fight a human-eating giant tonight. They would go to sleep and wake up in the morning like normal. If he succeeded, life would carry on, but if he failed and the giant triumphed, every *Jack and the Beanstalk* story in the world would be magically rewritten, and Jack would become a failure and an embarrassment.

Mom's smile radiated warmth and pride. "We know you'll do well, son. There's no doubt in our minds you'll be a huge success."

Jack's phone buzzed in his pocket. Opening the notification, he found he had been tagged in a meme about rushing an assignment the night before it was due. He couldn't even muster the energy to crack a smile. He wished an assignment was all he had to worry about tonight.

After dinner and washing up, Jack crawled into bed.

"We'll see you in the morning." Mom kissed Jack lightly on the forehead before leaving the room.

His father nodded before turning off the lights. "Make us proud."

***

Sleep took Jack slowly, and once the darkness had fully enveloped him, a tiny speck of white light appeared. It grew bigger and bigger until it took on the shape of an ancient man with flowing, periwinkle blue robes and a long, wispy white beard.

He bowed his head. "Good evening, Jack. Do you know who I am?"

Jack nodded. "I do," he squeaked. After clearing his throat, he tried again. "I do."

"Then you must also know what is about to happen. Take my hand." He extended his long fingers, bony and cold to the touch.

As soon as Jack made contact with the Storyteller, the darkness around him swirled in a vortex of color, until he stood in a large, sterile room with a few other kids. The Storyteller was nowhere to be seen.

A girl stepped forward and shook Jack's hand. Her blond hair nearly reached her ankles. "Hi, I'm Rapunzel."

"Jack." He smiled at her.

"Nice to meet you, Jack," said a girl with wavy red hair and eyes as blue and fierce as the ocean. Her eyelashes fluttered in his direction, making his cheeks warm.

"I'm Hansel, and this is my sister, Gretel," introduced a boy with sandy hair. Apart from the age and gender difference, they almost looked identical.

"Nice to meet you all." He was familiar with most of their family's stories.

Over the next half an hour, the Storyteller continued to bring children in from all over the world. There was an exciting mix of skin colors, accents, and emotions. Jack met lots of interesting people, some he knew a lot about, but many he had never heard of before, including Vasilisa, a young girl from Russia, and Yeh-hsien, a small and shy Chinese girl.

The Storyteller gathered the hundreds of kids around him in a semicircle. "Most of you know why you're here, but unfortunately for some, tragedy has left you without parents to coach and guide you. As the Great Fairy Tale Accords proclaim, every one hundred years, all living descendants of fairy tale heroes and villains must relive their family's story. We do this to maintain peace between good and evil and provide both sides of the story an opportunity to prove their worth."

Jack scanned the crowd. He couldn't see a single face that looked evil. Shaking his head in frustration, he realized the Storyteller wouldn't group the heroes and villains together. The giant was probably in a similar room to this with all the other baddies, ready to plot, hurt, maim, lie, steal, cheat, and kill their way to victory.

Stroking his long beard, the Storyteller continued. "Several hundred years ago, the villains summoned an ancient magic that allowed them to travel back in time to rewrite your family's stories and triumph over good. But good prevailed, and they manipulated that magic into me and my Storybook. The Accords were begrudgingly signed by both sides, and every one hundred years, the integrity of you heroes is tested. Tonight, you will travel into the dreamscape that is your family's story and defend it from your villain. Succeed, and your story will remain unchanged. Fail, and your story will be rewritten as such. Society depends on your stories to teach children right from wrong, good from evil. Failure is not an option. Good must triumph."

Shifting his feet to stop his legs from shaking, Jack stuffed his hands into his pockets. Self-doubt strangled him, and he prayed he had what it would take to make his family proud.

The Storyteller pointed to a fierce Chinese girl with short black hair. "Mulan. You are one of the most inspirational heroes in this room to millions of people across the world. Your story has been one that has encouraged women to shatter gender stereotypes and fight for themselves. Are you ready to prove yourself and face your enemy?"

With bright red cheeks, she clapped her hands together and bowed low. "I have been training for this my entire life. I will not bring dishonor on my family."

"Excellent. Children need role models like you." The Storyteller gazed around the room. "Like all of you heroes. I do not mean to scare you, but I need to remind you all how important being a hero is. There is immense pressure on your shoulders. None of you chose to be here, but you are, and I have full faith in all of you."

Mulan ground her teeth and a vein pulsed over her

temple. "I will not fail."

From the depths of his robes, the Storyteller produced an ancient book. He opened it up in front of them, where words spiraled in a vortex on the pages. Jack caught glimpses of images: Mulan cutting her hair, riding her horse into battle, returning home to her family.

Her outline faded, as if her skin was turning to ink and being sucked into the book. After a few seconds, she was gone.

"Aladdin. Come here." The Storyteller beckoned a small, gangly boy forward. "Anyone reading your story will learn that slavery is an abomination, to be careful what you wish for, and that above all else, it's who you are on the inside that counts."

Aladdin nodded. "Not gonna lie, I'm a little nervous."

"Nerves are good, boy. Turn that energy into something positive." The Storyteller opened the book once more, and again the words swirled, this time with images of a genie, great treasure, a beautiful princess, and an entire Arabian kingdom.

Same as Mulan, Aladdin disappeared within the book. The Storyteller snapped the book shut and spied Jack. "Come forward, Jack."

Taking a steadying breath, Jack obeyed.

"Your villain is one of the largest any hero will face, but do not let his strength and size get the better of you. Your strength comes from your head and your attitude. Those are your greatest assets."

Jack stood frozen before the book. He knew in a short moment he would be sucked into the book and his tale would begin. He couldn't fail. He couldn't. He was born to be a hero.

The Storyteller opened the book and Jack caught glimpses of images from his story: a boy leading a cow, a giant beanstalk, a magic harp, a ferocious giant.

"Good luck, and may your story end happily ever after."

An invisible force yanked Jack from his midsection and pulled him toward the whirlpool of swirling words.

***

Quiet sobs drew Jack from his slumber. He rolled over, grimacing at the stiffness in his muscles from the lumpy mattress beneath him. His eyes slowly adjusted to the unfamiliar dim room. Tiny and bare, there were simple window furnishings and naked walls. A candlestick sat lonely on his nightstand. He grunted as he stood and looked down at his scratchy white shirt and dark pants.

"This is so weird," he muttered. His old life was a distant memory, like a movie he had watched years ago. Memories of a life he had never lived breached the surface of his mind. Sitting in the corner of the room throwing and catching a ball against the wall. Father, angry because Jack didn't like hunting. Hungry. Always hungry. Father's funeral. Mother's tears.

Wiping his eyes, Jack shook his head. He forced himself to distance himself from those memories. They weren't his. They belonged to a *very* distant relative. He was here to be a hero and then return to his old life.

On autopilot, his hand drifted to his pocket. His heart fluttered at the absence of his phone. He had known nothing modern would travel into the dreamscape with him, but he didn't know how much he relied on his phone; he was like a baby without a security blanket.

He padded into the kitchen to find an unfamiliar woman whom he was tempted to call Ma. He didn't know her from a bar of soap, but the memories that weren't his told him a story of a caring mother who never fully recovered from her husband's passing. Compared to the memories, her face was now much more gaunt, dark shadows making her look at least a decade older than she was. Her hair was short and wiry, hanging limply as if each follicle had given up on life.

"What's wrong, Ma?" He draped an arm around her shoulders. It felt both foreign and normal to call her that.

Between sobs, she replied, "Bessie has stopped producing milk. We barely made any money selling what little she did make, and now—" She sobbed. "Now it's all gone." She buried her puffy, bloodshot eyes in her hands.

Jack inhaled. The story was unfolding as he knew it would. "Let me take her to the market. I'll see how many coins I can get for her."

Ma briefly looked up. "Thank you, my boy. Don't bother coming back unless you sell her for a good ten silvers."

With his stomach rumbling, Jack walked outside and tied a rope around the cow's neck. Even though he was in a dream, he was experiencing everything the real Jack did, from hunger, to exhaustion, to pain. He led her toward the market, stopping every so often to let her ancient legs rest. It was weird walking without headphones in. No music to distract him from the natural beauty of the countryside.

After cresting a steep hill, the village came into view. Empty fields ringed the farms, homes, and stores that sprawled out beneath him. High stone walls surrounded a distant castle where the grass was emerald green and the crops bountiful.

On his way down the hill, Jack spied an old man sitting on the ground beside an upturned cart while his donkey lazily ate grass. Rough mumbling and grunting from the old man grew louder and louder.

He glanced up as Jack approached. "You, boy. Will you help an old man out of a pickle?"

Jack eyed the man, wondering if he was the one who would give him the beans. The original story was vaguely written, and the only information Jack had to go on was that the cow was traded for a bag of magic beans. If Jack stopped to help this man and he didn't have the beans, he might miss his opportunity. If he didn't stop to help and this was the man, he would miss the opportunity anyway.

With a heavy sigh, Jack prayed he was making the right choice. "Of course I'll help you."

Jack tied Bessie's rope around a nearby tree branch and walked over to the cart. One of the wooden wheels was wedged at an awkward angle between two large rocks. Even if they righted the wagon, it probably wouldn't roll very well.

With straining muscles, Jack and the old man heaved the cart into an upright position before lying spent on the grass on their backs, panting, staring up into the clouds.

How could a castle of giants float on clouds of water vapor? It was probably best to ignore logic. Logic couldn't explain a goose that lays golden eggs. Or beans that grow to the sky for that matter. Heck, logic couldn't even explain how a mysterious older man came to him in his dreams to make him relive the life of one of his great-ancestors. Logic had no place in fairy tales.

"Look at that castle," the man said.

Jack stared hard through the clouds but couldn't see it anywhere. "Where? I don't see it."

"Look where I'm pointing," the man said impatiently.

Jack's face reddened when he saw the old man sitting up, pointing to the castle on the outskirts of the village. "Oh, right."

"What do you see?"

Jack stared at it. There was nothing out of the ordinary as far as his eye could see. "A castle."

"I'll tell you what I see: walls that separate the rich from the poor; the solution to our hunger and poverty hoarded away from us for people that already have more than they'll ever need; ignorance and pure evil masquerading as leadership."

Jack swallowed. If this man thought they were evil, he had no idea of the evil that lurked in a second castle somewhere high above them.

"So, what brings you this way?" The man clambered to his feet with a grunt and dusted off his pants.

"I'm going to market to sell our cow." Jack stood and walked over to Bessie, untying her from the tree branch.

The man joined Jack and inspected her. "Is she still giving milk?"

Jack hesitated, before lowering his gaze. "No."

"Well, if that's the case, you're not likely to get much for her. You know what? You helped me, so let me help you. I'll save you the journey into town and make an offer on her right now. I have these magic beans. Rumor has it they come from giants. One planted bean will feed you and your family for months."

Jack chewed the inside of his cheek, trying to act like he was contemplating the deal. But inside, he was jumping for joy. "Magic beans? Giants? I might be young, but even I can tell that doesn't sound like a good deal."

The old man shrugged. "Good luck to you then."

"Wait," Jack called out as the man began to walk away. "Fine. You have yourself a deal."

The man smiled. "Of course I do." Retreating to his cart, he pulled out a small pouch before returning to Jack. He pooled the beans in his open hand and then tipped them back into the bag. "Eight beans in exchange for your cow."

"Deal." Jack handed over the cow and took possession of the beans.

"It was a pleasure trading with you," the man said.

"The pleasure was all mine."

***

Jack returned home with a spring in his step. Part one of his tale was complete, and the further he ventured into his story, the more confident he felt. Although, he still had to face the most challenging part. The giant weighed down on Jack's momentary win. These beans would deliver him straight to the giant's castle in the clouds. A giant that wanted to grind his bones to make his bread. Jack shivered at the thought.

Home finally came into view at the base of the little valley. The words of the old man echoed in his mind. He and his mother lived in this ramshackle cottage, with no more livestock and a withering crop of vegetables that would barely see them through the rest of the year. His stomach rumbled painfully, almost as loud as the brewing storm overhead. The fluffy white clouds were turning dark and angry.

Forcing himself to stop, Jack reminded himself that this was not his life. He was reliving a life from long ago, a however-many-great-grandfather that was a hero in the eyes of so many young children around the world. Only a boy at the time, he had faced off against a man-eating giant to save his family from starvation.

Inside the house, his mother was on her hands and knees scrubbing the floors. She beamed when he walked in holding the small brown pouch of beans. "You wonderful boy! How many silvers did you get for her?"

Jack's throat tightened. He knew she wouldn't like what he had to say. He had read it so many times already, but the thought of her anger coming down hard on him… "I traded Bessie for these eight magic beans."

His mother threw the scrubbing brush into the bucket of soapy water with a splash and stood, standing a foot taller than him. "You what?" she roared, snatching the bag from his hands.

She tipped out the beans into her open palm and sobbed. "You stupid, stupid boy. We needed the money to buy a new cow, or a goat. These beans aren't going to feed us for more than a day." In her rage she walked over to the open kitchen window and threw the beans outside before slamming it shut. "It was so simple! How could you mess up so badly?"

Jack's eyes stung as tears threatened to spew forth. For a moment, he lost himself in the memories of the original Jack. He had never been overly smart, athletic, or helpful around the house. And seeing his mother so angry and disappointed in him hurt. He blinked away tears, knowing that this was a necessary horror he had to endure.

"Looks like we're going hungry tonight. You better get used to it." She stormed out of the room, dropping the empty brown pouch on the floor.

Jack clenched his jaw and took several deep breaths on his way to bed. The storm outside intensified and shook the house, eventually rocking him to sleep. When he woke up in the morning, he crept through the dark house. There was no light seeping in through the kitchen window, but not because of the storm.

Leaping into the air, Jack landed and did his happy dance, trying to remain quiet so he didn't wake Ma. His heart pounded with excited relief. The beans had truly grown into the beanstalk from his fairy tale. It was so high it reached the heavens. The only disappointment was that he couldn't take a selfie with it. He had the perfect hashtags to go with it too.

Jack snuck outside and took several deep breaths. This was it. Trading the cows for the beans was one thing. Climbing the beanstalk? The giant? Things were heating up.

The first few feet of the beanstalk were easy. He silently thanked his father for all the intensive physical training he had been put through over the years. Without it, he doubted he'd make it very far at all. His feet occasionally slipped on damp leaves and roots. But it didn't shake his confidence in the least. Every day since he could remember, his father had taken him climbing in all sorts of conditions. He was born to succeed.

"Jack!" Ma's shrill voice sounded beneath him.

"What on earth do you think you're doing? Get down here now!"

"I'm sorry, Ma. I've got to do this. I promise I'll be back soon," Jack shouted. He continued to climb higher until Ma's voice faded.

***

The higher he climbed, the thinner the branches were. The wind swayed the large stalk to and fro. Jack's muscles burned, and his legs trembled with exhaustion. He stopped every few minutes to wipe his sweaty palms on his pants. He hadn't trained for endurance quite like this. He had started climbing at sun up, it was now close to noon, and the clouds still seemed miles away. How did the original Jack manage this climb without any training? A jet pack would be pretty handy right now.

Once he was inside the clouds, he couldn't see past his fingertips. Focusing on each handhold, he slowed down and felt his footings carefully before entrusting his weight on the slick branches. The only thing preventing him from freezing with fear was the knowledge that if he did fall, he would wake up unharmed. A disappointment to everyone, but at least alive. Eventually he climbed through the mist and reached solid land. Worried that if he lay down to rest he would never get back up again, Jack forged ahead.

If he hadn't just climbed above the clouds, he never would have guessed that that's where he was. It was like standing on solid ground. "Hashtag fairy tale logic."

Tufts of grass poked sporadically out of the dirt that stretched endlessly around him. A herd of sheep the size of cars galloped past, making the ground tremble. Jack's mouth watered. Just one of those behemoths could feed an entire village for days. And a video of him riding one of those bad boys would make him a Youtube sensation!

His eyes were drawn to a stone castle that was easily

bigger than the skyscrapers back home and nearly as wide as it was tall.

Jack rolled his shoulders and stretched his neck before jogging toward the villain's lair. Four stone turrets stretched so high into the air he almost couldn't see the tops. The front of the castle looked like a monster, with a large door as a mouth and two large windows for eyes.

Standing before it, the sheer size of it stole his breath away. If the door was an indicator of how large the giant was, Jack had his considerably tiny hands full. He searched for a way in, but there was no room to squeeze under the door, and the walls were too smooth to climb to a window.

Thunderous footsteps and heavy breaths sounded behind him. Jack spun around to see a giantess reach toward him with thick fingers the size of rolled-up carpets. He tried to dodge, but she snatched him and brought him up to eye level. Crushing pressure squashed his lungs, and his scream remained silent. Jack clawed at her hand, but her skin was so thick and tough she probably couldn't feel anything.

"What have we here?" Her breath washed over him like the wafting aroma of a six-month-old dirty trash can.

Jack's heart froze. Cold, brown eyes squinted down on him as sharp, stained teeth glistened in the late afternoon sunlight. His head spun and he saw double for a moment.

"A little human!" Her eyes softened, and she smiled, releasing the pressure around Jack. "I love you precious little things! You look hungry. Come inside and I'll fix you up something."

Jack relaxed. In the original tale, the giant's wife had fed Jack and showed him kindness. Here she was, doing the same thing. The only two people that could change anything were him and the giant. The hero and the villain.

The giantess placed a spoonful of mutton stew in a thimble the size of a large bowl and passed it to Jack. She sat opposite him with a bucket of stew for herself.

Jack put a mouthful of the steaming stew into his

mouth and spat it straight back out. It was so hot! His eyes watered and his tongue burned.

"I know. I'm sorry it's so tasteless." She lowered her eyes, staring distantly into her meal. "Our lands aren't what they used to be, and none of our seeds are growing. Even our sheep barely have any grass left to feed on."

"I'm so sorry for seeming rude. The stew is great. It's just very hot." Jack blew on his stew and slowly began eating small portions at a time. She was right. It was rather tasteless. But given that she could easily snap him in half or step on him, Jack decided to keep that comment to himself.

She glanced to the door. "My husband will be here soon. You'd best be on your way. As he grows more and more hungry, his temper is getting shorter and shorter. He is not fond of your kind."

"Thank you," Jack said, shivering at the fear of being the main ingredient in the giantess's next stew. He walked toward the open door, glancing over his shoulder at the woman. As soon as her back was turned, he darted to the corner of the room where he hid under a rudimentary-looking shelving unit. He folded himself back as far into the shadows as he could, feeling quietly confident. The giant would return home soon, sleep, and Jack would make his escape with the large sack of coins he had yet to find. Easy peasy lemon squeezy.

Jack waited and waited, constantly shifting and fidgeting from boredom and discomfort, but his villain never arrived. Strange.

The giantess paced about the dining room in a floral nightgown and fluffy slippers. "Come on, Larry. It's late. Where are you?" She folded her arms and started toward the door. "If I find you've been talking to that ugly troll in the caves again, I'll—" her threat was cut off by the slamming door, which bounced in the jamb and remained slightly open.

Jack chewed the inside of his cheek. That was a good

question. Where was he? He should have been here ages ago and said his "Fee, fi, fo, fum" line. He was clearly up to something. Maybe planning an ambush by the beanstalk? Maybe he had gone down the beanstalk to destroy the village?

His throat tightened at the thought, until he reminded himself that none of this was real. Nothing he or the giant did would have a lasting impression…unless the giant won. Only then would the story be rewritten. With a newfound urgency, he crawled out from under the shelf and wandered around the giant's castle, searching for the coins.

Jack couldn't imagine searching through the entire castle to find the treasure. It could have been anywhere. Luckily he knew his story well enough and knew the treasure was in a closet in the giant's bedroom.

With difficulty, he opened the large door and marveled at the immense fortune inside. The goose slept peacefully in its gilded cage on one shelf. The golden harp sat silent on the shelf below. Gem-encrusted goblets and chalices were on display, alongside bejeweled weapons and trinket boxes. On the lowest ledge, Jack found what he was searching for: a large brown burlap bag filled to the brim with gold. It was a pity he couldn't bring it back to his real life. He could quit school and never have to work a day in his life. A huge smile worked its way onto his lips as he imagined all the things he could do with the gold back home.

Dragging the sack behind him, he felt like a mash-up of Robin Hood and Santa Claus as he imagined the faces of Ma and the rest of the village when he showered them with the riches. But he didn't let himself get too comfortable. Larry still hadn't made an appearance, and he could be anywhere, doing anything. Just like Jack had been preparing his whole life to be good, Larry had been honing his evil skills.

Under the cover of night, Jack descended the beanstalk. It took considerably longer going down than it did climbing up. He sang every song he knew—some two or three times—in an effort to drown out the fatigue and pain.

The sun had just started to brighten the horizon when he reached the bottom. Relief washed over him as he dropped the heavy sack of coins to the ground with a clanking thud and saw no evidence of Larry the giant down here. His house still stood, and there were no enormous footprints in the soft dirt.

Rubbing his aching shoulders and dragging the treasure behind him, he entered the house and gently shook his mother awake. "Look what I've got."

Ma groaned and rubbed the sleep from her eyes. Then her face fell slack as she took in the treasure. "Oh, Jack! My marvelous boy! I am so proud of you!"

Warmth filled his belly and extended to his extremities. "And that is not it. Tomorrow, I shall return with something even better."

And that's exactly what he set out to do the following day. After a well-deserved rest, he climbed the beanstalk to retrieve the goose that laid golden eggs.

Jack slowed down on his approach to the giants' home. The front door was wide open. It was obvious that Larry had laid out a trap for him. Steal the coins, come back overly confident, and then BAM! One Jack Sandwich coming right up. Or a FlapJack. Maybe Jackghetti Bolognese.

Cautiously peering inside, Jack saw that the giants were nowhere to be seen. Jack scurried in, hugging the walls and keeping to the shadows, aware that at any moment he could be ambushed and eaten.

Passing by the kitchen on his way to the treasure trove, Jack spied an old woman sitting on a small stool in front of a large cauldron. She waved one hand in the air in a circular motion, and a large ladle stirred the contents. She was no larger than him and wore a black cloak over her candy-print apron. Tiny gingerbread house earrings dangled from her ears. With a loud burp, she covered her mouth with her hands and the ladle fell into the stew.

"Chocolate almonds and candy canes!" With a dramatic sigh, her shoulders slumped. "Whatever am I to do now? If only someone was here to help me. But alas, I am all alone."

Jack didn't know what to do. He had never read about this lady in his story, and his father had never told him about her either. She almost reminded him of the witch from Hansel and Gretel's story. He hoped the other heroes were doing well.

"Can I help you?" Jack tentatively asked, stepping out of the shadows and peering about the empty castle nervously. Still no sign of the giants. Yes, it was most likely a trap set by the giant, but he wouldn't be a hero if he didn't at least try to save her.

The old lady sniffed and turned to face him. "Oh, a hero! My prayers have been answered." Hunger flashed in her eyes as she beckoned him closer with long nails painted red and white. "Come here, child, and help this old, frail lady."

"Are you okay?"

"Of course I'm not okay you stupi-stupendously adorable little hero." With theatrical gestures and expressive tone, she continued, "I dropped my ladle into the cauldron, and the iron dampens my magic. I am too old and too weak to reach inside and get it. If I burn the bottom, the giants will surely eat me."

Jack smiled. He liked her. "Are you their slave?"

She nodded, burying her face into her wrinkly hands to hide her tears. With a brief pause in her sobs, she peered at Jack from between her fingers.

Jack's heart ached for the old woman. He was a hero, and it was his job to save those in need.

He walked over to the cauldron and used a stool to pull himself up and peer inside. Chunks of vegetables bobbed about in the water. The ladle had sunk to the bottom of the pot. "There's no way I can reach it."

"Believe in yourself, dearie. Just climb inside and get it." Her voice was fueled with excited desperation.

"But isn't it too hot?" Jack really felt for her. He could just imagine what horrors she'd endured as the giants' slave, but he didn't want to risk his own life or get third-degree burns.

"Just get in!" she yelled. Then, in a calmer and more encouraging voice, she said, "I took it off the flames a while ago. It should be comfortably warm by now."

Jack reached in and tested the water. It was like a heated swimming pool. Hoisting himself over the rim, he jumped into the water and dove to the bottom to retrieve the ladle. When his head broke the surface, the cauldron was dark. The lid was closed!

The old lady cackled, muffled by the thick iron walls of the cauldron.

"Hey! Let me out! What's going on?" Jack sloshed through the stew and used the ladle as a sort of lever to try to lift the lid, but it was too heavy.

"That pesky little brother and sister can be someone else's problem for once. Finally, I can earn my rightful place in the Hall of Villainy!" Her cackling laugh grew louder until it suddenly cut off. "No! Not now. It can't be. No! No! No!"

A fluorescent green mist started rising from the surface of the stew, swirling around him lazily before becoming an impenetrable wall of green. It disappeared in a flash, dumping Jack and the contents of the stew in the middle of a dark forest. Chunks of vegetables lay scattered about his feet as soup dripped from his soggy clothes. The full moon cast its silvery light down on an enormous hedge maze which stood in a clearing not too far away from where Jack now stood.

"What the?"

Twigs cracked. Jack's head snapped around. Leaves crunched. Jack twirled but couldn't see anything.

Footsteps sounded all around him. Hushed whispers carried on the still air.

His heart pounded in his chest. How could he have messed up his story so badly? What had happened?

Through the brush, two pale creatures stalked toward him. Jack backpedaled, stumbling over a fallen tree branch in his haste to get away from the monsters.

"Jack? Is that you?" The young girl from earlier ran forward, leaving her brother behind. "Hansel, it is him. Come quickly."

Hansel jogged over and stood beside his sister. "Please tell me your story was really messed up too."

Jack stood up and wiped his muddy hands on his pants. "Yeah. The giant—the villain in my story—never turned up. Apart from that, my story was going well, until some old witch tried to eat me."

Hansel and Gretel shared a look between them. "Somehow our villains must've traded places then. We were all set to trick the witch into freeing us, but when we got to her gingerbread house, she wasn't there. Instead, a giant chased us. He kept repeating a phrase over and over again." Hansel wrapped his arm around his sister and squeezed her gently.

"Fee, fi, fo, fum," Jack whispered.

"Yeah." Gretel's slight frame trembled. "He was just about to grind our bones to make his bread when this green mist swirled around us and brought us here."

"Any idea why?"

Jack and the others jumped as the bushes rustled, sticks snapped, and dirt crunched, as more and more children appeared. They all had the same frightened, confused look on their faces. It wasn't long before the Storyteller appeared, seeming like he had aged a thousand years since Jack last saw him. His face was etched with deep lines, eyes dark and sunken, and the periwinkle blue of his robes had faded. Even his hands were covered in liver spots.

"Children. I have some concerning news." The urgency and authority remained in the Storyteller's voice, but it was weighed down heavily with fatigue. "The villains did the unthinkable and banded together to steal the Storybook. They are going to ruin everything unless you stop them. Every fairy tale is in jeopardy.

"I am unable to directly interfere with your stories, so I have shaped my power into this maze. You heroes and the villains will have an equal opportunity to find the Storybook hidden within. I am unable to choose sides and assist you more than I already have, but I know you." His eyes fell on Jack. "You have everything it takes to find the book."

He coughed for several long seconds, eyes grimacing in pain as he clutched his chest. He recovered and took several shaky breaths. "I understand if any of you choose not to enter the maze, because once you've entered, you will have only an hour to locate the book or risk being trapped in that maze for all eternity."

Glancing around, Jack noticed some determined faces, and others that were confused or petrified. He knew that if anything happened to him in the dreamscape, he would survive. Dying in the maze would have the same outcome, but unless someone found the book, he would be trapped here forever. The odds were stacked against him. The easy option would be to leave it to someone else, but could he live with himself if he never tried?

He wouldn't, couldn't, give up on his fellow heroes.

"As Grand Storymaster, I am unable to assist you any further. I have already done too much. Please, children, if the villains get the book and rewrite those tales, children all over the world will learn bad lessons. The world will end in chaos."

"You can count on us!" said an older boy in shining armor, brandishing his sword overhead.

"I will bring honor to us all," Mulan cried.

The Storyteller spread his arms. "Go!"

***

Jack was swept up with the swarming mass of heroes sprinting into the maze. A quick glance over his shoulder showed him no one had elected to stay behind. He ran with knights, princesses, warriors, servants, boys, and girls, all with one common goal: reach the Storybook before the villains.

The thick walls of the maze loomed enormously high above them, and the passageways were wide enough to accommodate giants and other horrible monsters that Jack tried to ignore. After the last heroes entered the maze, vines and leaves intertwined, sealing off the entrance.

"We can do this!" yelled a confident voice somewhere to Jack's left.

With a battle cry, Jack sprinted deeper into the maze with the other heroes.

Their group thinned as people spread out with each new fork in the road. The more ground they covered, the better chance they had of a hero getting to the book before a villain.

The threat of remaining trapped in this maze hung heavily over Jack, and he knew the same fear drove every hero onward. But seeing his fellow heroes happy to take that risk gave him hope. Every hero was placing their life on the line, and with that kind of dedication, there was no way they could lose.

"Shhhh! Stop," warned a handsome prince in silver armor. He drew his sword and stepped forward slowly, lifting his visor.

Then Jack heard it.

Soft panting. A low growl.

A wolf stalked around the corner with a menacing snarl on his lips and a strip of crimson fabric stuck between his teeth.

"I finally got Little Red," he said in a growl. "But she only whet my appetite. Who's next?"

The wolf pounced at the prince who parried him away with his sword.

"Go! I've got this!" The prince's sword slashed through the air, barely missing the snapping jaws of the wolf.

Jack and the others sprinted around the corner. He prayed the prince would make it out of there okay.

The air grew colder and colder as they twisted and turned through the maze. Frost crept along the leafy hedges. Their breaths plumed out in small white clouds.

"What's going on?" asked the youngest girl in their dwindling group, who had stumps instead of hands. She stepped forward to the front of the group, investigating the frosted hedge.

"I have no idea," Jack mumbled, but he expected they would soon find out. His mind raced with possibilities, and he hoped it wasn't who he thought it was.

A beautiful woman in a white gown and with a tiara nestled in her platinum blond hair turned the corner. With every step, ice spread out from her silver slippers. She smiled sweetly at them before extending her arms and blasting stump-arm girl with a cloud of frost, turning her into a terrified ice sculpture.

"Heeeeyyaaaaaaa!"

The ice queen went flying, landing face first in the dirt with a sickening crunch of her neck. She didn't move. Behind her stood Mulan, breathing hard. She winced at the sight of the stump-arm girl. "Is everyone else okay?"

Jack and the others nodded.

With a thin-lipped smile, Mulan shrugged. "I just came from the very center of the maze. The book wasn't there. But the villains are still searching, so they don't have it either."

"What if the villains already have it and are just

pretending to look for it to keep us distracted?" Aladdin asked.

"The center is too obvious," Jack thought aloud.

"Well then, where would it be?" Mulan folded her arms.

Warmth spread across Jack's cheeks. "I don't know."

"How far away is the center?" Aladdin asked.

"Not far."

"Take us there."

Howls, roars, screams, yells, and shrieks sounded all around the maze, but the heroes' journey to the center was uninterrupted. They reached the center and looked around the clearing. A circular wall of hedge boxed them in, with a way in and out on opposite ends.

"What are you thinking?" Aladdin asked, staring intently at Jack.

"Where are we?" Jack asked.

"In a maze," Mulan replied as if she thought Jack was losing the plot.

"In the *middle* of the maze," Jack corrected. "And where did we start?"

"At the beginning."

"Exactly. Every book has a beginning, a middle, and an end. We started at the beginning, and now we've reached the middle. Maybe we have to find the end of the maze to find the book?"

Mulan's face widened into the first smile Jack had seen from her. He had wondered if her facial muscles were capable of such a feat. "Excellent idea! Come on." She turned and ran toward the opposite side of the maze, Jack and Aladdin close on her heels.

"We must stick together," Mulan commanded as they ran.

"Good idea." A stitch stabbed Jack in his right side, but he forced the pain out of his mind. There were bigger things going on. If the villains got their hands on the book and rewrote all the great fairy tales, generations of children would grow up without morality. The consequences would be catastrophic.

The three heroes sped around a corner to find a small queen with an axe in her hand chasing a young girl in a sky-blue ball gown. As she ran away from her would-be murderer, one of the girl's glass slippers fell off.

"Off with your head!" the queen screamed as she gave chase.

"Shouldn't we help her?" Jack asked, staring at the lone glass slipper lying on its side in the dirt.

"The best way to save her, and all the other heroes, is to find the book and get out of here," Mulan said. "We don't know how much time we have left. Come on."

"What's that noise?" Aladdin asked between breaths, causing Jack and Mulan to stop in apprehensive curiosity.

Pip-pop-pip-pop. Repeated suction cup sounds came from around the corner, and then she appeared. Jack's spine chilled at the familiar sight of the Sea Witch, with her eight black tentacles extending from her waist and her white hair flowing about her head as if she were still underwater.

Her almost-transparent face widened into a warm smile, and she held her hands up in surrender. "You three. Do not run or fight me. I am on your side."

Jack stepped forward. "Oh, I know all about you. Let me guess, you want to make a deal with us that will end up with you in control of the book? Not likely." He was very familiar with how manipulative the Sea Witch could be.

She crept an inch closer, pain on her face as if he had slapped her. "No, child. There is no trickery." A tentacle reached up and rested over her heart. "You, like everyone else, don't understand the *real* me. Only the version of me that has been vilified with each generation of you *heroes*." She spat the last word. "Please, I beg you, let's work together."

The pleading look on her face lowered Jack's defenses. Maybe there was some truth to her words? He turned around to face the other two, to see if they were buying her sob story, when one of her tentacles lashed out and wrapped itself around his wrist.

She yanked him toward her, twisting a tentacle around his throat and binding his arms to his sides. A crushing force strangled him. Air struggled to enter his lungs, and spots danced at the edge of his vision.

"Let him go!" Mulan yelled, sweeping her leg around and dropping low into a warrior's stance.

The Sea Witch's laughter boomed in Jack's ears. "Hey, I didn't choose to be a villain. My ancestor wasn't the villain that everyone thinks she was. But being nice won't get me anywhere. I'm ready to embrace the character everyone thinks I am and finally achieve something!" Her grip around Jack's throat tightened.

Mulan buried her hand in the wall of the maze and snapped off a pointy stick.

Aladdin rushed at the Sea Witch and leapt into the air, bringing his foot sweeping around in a kick to her head.

She dodged, loosening her grip on Jack enough that he was able to pull himself free from her suckers. Painful, large red welts covered his skin.

Mulan rushed at the Sea Witch and, with a powerful shove, drove the makeshift spear directly into her heart.

Jack froze as the Sea Witch gasped and her eyes widened in shock.

Her body convulsed briefly as she let out an evil laugh. A tentacle twirled around the protruding stick and yanked it out, carelessly discarding it on the ground near Jack's feet. "Oh, honey, I am part octopus. I have three hearts. You can't kill me that easy."

Two tentacles shot out at different angles. One grabbed Aladdin by the throat, and the other latched on to Mulan's arm. Both heroes twisted and tried to pull themselves free, but the tentacles wound tighter and tighter until they fell to their knees.

With raspy breaths, Jack picked up the stick and brandished it in front of him like a sword. "Sea Witch, you have no heart. Or soul. None of you villains do."

"Foolish child. You have been corrupted by the *idea* of good. There is no such thing. Just people who justify their actions in different ways. My hearts all desire one thing. To see each and every one of you heroes suffer for the generations of our families that have suffered at your hands. How is that different to what you desire?"

Jack ground his teeth. "There is always good and evil. Just because you can justify your actions doesn't make them good. You are evil. All villains are."

Jack eyed Aladdin, who was clawing at the tentacle around his throat. Mulan struggled to free her wrist from the Sea Witch's grip. When their gazes met, Mulan nodded.

"I can see the problem isn't your hearts." Jack took a deep breath and threw himself forward. With a sickening pop and squelch, the stick drove through the Sea Witch's eye, burying it deep within her skull. "The issue is in your head."

The Sea Witch fell backward, releasing Aladdin and Mulan. As her body fell onto the grass, she dissolved into a puddle of black ink that melted into the ground.

Mulan clapped Jack on the back. "Excellent. I'm sorry my first attack failed."

Jack squeezed his lips into a thin line. He dropped the stick and shoved his trembling hands in his pockets before anyone noticed. "Let's get this damn book." Even though the Sea Witch was a villain and this wasn't real life, she didn't deserve that.

After running for what felt like a lifetime, Jack had given all he had. His lungs were deflated balloons. His muscles were wet rags. Pain ran through his nervous system like a fireworks display on New Year's. But still, he forced himself to keep going.

After a left turn, they found themselves at the

beginning of a one-hundred-yard straight path to the exit of the maze. The book hovered beneath an arch, gold and green mist swirling around it.

"The end! You were right, Jack, there's the book!" Mulan exclaimed.

Seeing the book lifted Jack's spirits and gave him his second wind. The three of them raced toward the end, but after only a few feet, the ground trembled.

Jack glanced back in time to see a giant round the corner. The giant from his story!

The giant's face contorted in rage as he spotted them. His angry cry rattled Jack's bones, spurring him into action.

Jack's feet pumped faster than he'd ever run before. His muscles burned, lungs screaming for a rest, but he couldn't stop. The sounds of the gaining giant boosted Jack's adrenaline and pushed him beyond anything humanly possible. He was faster than the other two and getting closer to the book with each passing second.

Glancing back a second time, Jack watched in horror as the giant caught up to Aladdin. With a roar, he swiped his arm wildly, and Aladdin was sent screaming through the air with a spine-breaking crunch. His body dissolved before he landed.

A few steps later, Mulan suffered a similar fate, being crushed under the giant's foot.

Hearing her bones grinding down into powder and the scream dying on her lips, Jack sprinted until his vision blurred, head pounded, and he thought he was going to pass out.

When Jack was only a few feet away from the book, the giant roared, "Stop!"

Fear rooted Jack's feet to the ground, and he tumbled forward into the dirt. If he stretched out his hand, he could grab the book, but the pain in the giant's voice froze his muscles.

"You're the real villain!" the giant bellowed from a few meters away. A fat tear slid down his face and splashed on the ground. His voice softened into an almost defeated sigh. "Don't steal this chance from me, from all of us, like you stole my wealth."

"What are you talking about?" Jack was wary after his interaction with the Sea Witch. The giant was either distracting him from something or stalling to buy himself some time.

Jack scanned the nearby areas, and he was confident that there was no evidence of a nearby villain creeping up to steal the book. He had time to hear the giant out, and a part of him wanted to listen.

The giant counted on his fat fingers. "You break into my house, steal my things, and then kill me by chopping down the beanstalk when I'm trying to get it back. How does that make you a hero and me a villain?"

Jack opened his mouth to reply, but his voice choked. He honestly had no idea. It felt like his ribcage was crushing his heart. How had he never seen it like that before? How had no one ever made him question his actions and think about the giant as anything other than a monster? He didn't even know the giant's name was Larry until a short while ago.

"That goes the same for a lot of us *villains*. Not all, mind you, but most. We don't want to be bad. We don't have to be. Don't put us with the real villains when that's not who we are."

Jack glanced between the book and the giant. He could see the pain in Larry's eyes, and every cell in his body knew that what Larry said was true. Jack's ancestor was starving, but he didn't have to steal and kill the giant to save himself.

Jack stood up and squared his shoulders. "Trust me. I'll make things right."

Larry's eyes softened, and his shoulders slumped. "I

pray you do."

Extending his hand, Jack reached for the book.

***

With a gasp, Jack woke up back in the little cottage of his fairy tale. Ma's sobs echoed through the quiet morning. He was back at the beginning of the story again, like nothing had ever happened. Except this time, he had a different ending in mind.

He took the cow toward the market and helped the man with the overturned cart, swapping the cow for beans after their conversation about the king and queen living their life of luxury behind their high stone walls while the people starved. When he returned home, he faced his irate Ma and went to sleep hungry.

In the morning, Jack climbed the beanstalk and found Larry waiting for him inside the castle with his wife beside him, who was nervously glancing between Jack and her husband.

At the sight of Jack, Larry roared and pounded his fists on the table. "You came to steal from me again! I trusted you. Now I really will become a villain and kill you and everyone in your village for your treachery!"

Jack threw his hands up in surrender, which emphasized just how small he was compared to Larry. "Please! Hear me out." His voice was a mousy squeak compared to Larry's thunderous roar. "I apologize for everything my family has done to yours in the past. My ancestor robbed from yours to feed our family. He killed your ancestor, and I am truly sorry. He was starving, and without your treasure, they would have died. But that is no excuse."

Larry opened his mouth in protest, but his wife placed a hand on his arm. "Shh, dear. Let him finish."

Larry grumbled but obliged.

Jack continued, "I do not want to steal your treasure, and I do not want you to die. I have come here to put an end to our family's feud."

Folding his arms over his chest, Larry huffed. "And how do you propose we do that?"

"You have all the seeds but lack the land to grow your crops. Whereas down below, our fertile land is wasted by the true villains: our leaders who live in luxury while their subjects starve. Tell me that's fair."

Larry shifted in his seat. "It is not," he eventually mumbled.

His wife smiled.

"If we work together, we can all benefit. In exchange for you using our land, all we ask is to keep some of your yield."

The giant looked to his wife who nodded her approval. "I think that is a fair deal."

***

Jack woke up back in his own bedroom, wearing his familiar pajamas. His phone rested on his bedside table, illuminated with notifications. Normally, he would have to read each one before getting out of bed, but he ignored it.

Dressing as quickly as he could, he raced into the family room where his parents were sitting side by side on the couch reading his book. He felt like he had been gone for months, but he knew everything that happened had occurred in only a single night.

His real mother looked up with wet eyes and closed the book with a beaming smile. "That new ending is pretty impressive."

His dad stood and hugged Jack tightly. "I am so proud of you."

Three Nights

Kelsie Engen

~ I ~

"I won't suffer any more fools. I have been too lenient on these men," King Effrenatus of Edormisco says to his advisor.

Underneath his feathered cap, Sir Hartwig frowns, and his pen hesitates above the parchment. "Perhaps, Sire, we should increase the reward? After all, a title may not be incentive enough—"

The king throws up a hand in annoyance. "Fine. Give them this ultimatum: if, after three days and nights, they have not discovered where my daughters go and why they return with ruined slippers, they shall lose their heads."

The adviser's eyes round. "And should they succeed?"

Thoughtfully, the king stares across his library, over the mound of twenty-four hole-filled slippers lumped on his desk yet again, and his gaze falls on a row of leather-bound royal genealogy books. An idea recurs to him, one that he has considered—reluctantly—for many months.

Effrenatus sighs. "Then he may have the pick of one of my daughter's hands in marriage."

Sir Hartwig double-blinks, then dips his head in a nod. "I will issue the decree immediately, Sire." In a moment, Hartwig has exited the room, abandoning the king to his thoughts.

Effrenatus sags back against his chair and drags a hand from forehead to whiskery chin. Twelve daughters and no sons. If only his wife were still alive. She would know what to do; she always did. But the last daughter was too much, and she couldn't recover from his beloved Prudens's birth. Even fifteen years later, he cannot put the tragedy aside.

How much I have missed my daughters. But who is worthy to break this curse? What will happen to my kingdom?

He can recall the exact moment when they changed. The twelve had been out for a ride and gotten lost. The entire royal court searched the enchanted woods all day. And then his daughters simply rode out from the tree line at dusk, just when the king was forced to call off the search for fear of the forest and its nightly dangers. Beside himself, he was wide-eyed when they, instead of soothing him as they might have done before, laughed and said, "Papa, we are women now, we don't need men looking after us."

They rode home ahead of the court, and that night the first worn-out slippers appeared. Every night since, the princesses disappeared until daybreak. No matter how hard the king tried, he could not discover where they went. Every morning since, they rose looking more haggard, as though they had not slept a wink. A dozen princesses with dark circles smudged under their eyes, unkempt hair, and gowns hanging from wasting bodies.

But more had changed than his daughters. A year ago, his library would have been littered with the light of a half-dozen faery attendants dusting his shelves and reshelving his scattered books. Now, ever since the Great Fae had argued and attempted to exile one of their own, the minor fae had all but disappeared—from both the palace and the town.

What do they fear? Could it possibly be connected to the curse upon my daughters?

Effrenatus stands and paces to the window. Books lay scattered on tables where he's abandoned them, searching for an answer to this curse—if it is a curse. He isn't sure anymore. All he know is that it is worth a dozen more men's lives if it saves the lives of his daughters.

***

At the end of his patrol shift, Silvanus turns to the town square's announcement board. Plastered over the old sheets of wanted criminals, group gatherings, and an assortment of animals or belongings for sale is a proclamation crisp and white against the others:

By order of the King:

Any able man willing to risk his life to track the princesses will be given three days and nights to make his attempt. Reward: his choice of princess's hand in marriage. Failure will result in loss of head.

Underneath is the slash of King Effrenatus's signature.

Silvanus stares at the board until he's nudged aside by a crowd of shoppers leaving the square.

"Sorry, soldier," one man says in deference to Silvanus.

"Can you believe the new proclamation?" his friend says. "What do you think they'll face?"

"I couldn't imagine. Will you try?" the man answers.

Silvanus half-turns to see a gawky young man with gapped teeth walking past the board with a friend. As he watches the friend dig into his pocket, a gold coin falls out, unnoticed, to the ground below.

"Not on my life! I like my head attached to my body. Over a dozen men have already tried to uncover where the princesses go—and died," the gap-toothed man replies.

"And they didn't have only three nights to find it out."

"Excuse me, sir?" Silvanus says. When the first man turns, confusion on his face, Silvanus holds up the coin. "This fell from your pocket."

"Oh." The man's hand rushes to the pocket of his tattered jacket, then a look of relief floods his face as he reaches for it. "Thank you, sir!"

With a nod, Silvanus deposits the coin into the man's outstretched palm.

Thanking him again, the man turns to his friend with wide eyes. "Did you see that? That's a *king's* guard right there."

Hurrying away, Silvanus half-smiles to himself and lets his thoughts return to the men's discussion and the proclamation. *Become a prince simply for telling the king where his daughters go at night? That seems too easy to be true. It's got to be more complicated than that.*

Silvanus glances at the chiming clock tower as he passes underneath it. He tugs his cloak around himself against the evening damp as he exits the square.

Halfway home, a twinkle out of the corner of his gaze draws Silvanus's attention down an alley. Something bobs in the air, and he frowns. Silvanus blinks against the sparkle as it brightens, beckoning him onward. With another frown, he hesitates, glances around, and turns his feet toward the light. Hand on his sword, he takes one step, then another. The light flashes brightly, as though encouraging him. The hilt heats in his palm. *Should I draw my sword?* It's just a light, after all. But something deeper than his thoughts stills his hand.

A foot from the light, Silvanus blinks in sudden darkness as it flickers and dies.

A voice speaks from the black night. "I was waiting for someone worthy."

Silvanus cannot tell if the voice is male or female, nor whether it is welcoming or threatening. He squints, just able to make out a shape in the shadows: a narrow top and a full bottom, like someone wearing a dress. It shimmers faintly around the edges, as if laced with faery dust. *A woman? With…magic? Not—*

"Yes, I am one of the Great Fae."

Silvanus nearly pulls his sword and flees down the road the way he came. "I didn't say—"

"No, you did not have to. The Great Fae know all."

He frowns. *If that's true, then why have they allowed the princesses to be enchanted by dark magic?*

"We cannot control all," the faery continues, "but that is why I am here."

"Why? To uncurse the princesses?"

"Exactly." There is a smile in the faery's voice.

"Oh. Well…good luck." He straightens and turns.

"No, you misunderstand, Silvanus."

At his name, he halts, eyes wide. *They really do know everything.*

"We want you to break the curse."

He laughs, a low, long chuckle that echoes in the narrow alley. "I'm sorry, but I thought you said you wanted me to break the curse."

"Yes, exactly." The smile is back in her voice again.

He peers through the darkness but can't decipher anything. "Reveal yourself to me then. How do I know you are who you say?"

As he squints, a glow dawns a short distance away. Features of the faery begin to emerge: tight, pearly skin; pale, amber eyes; curled, golden hair; and the fanciest golden ball gown he's ever seen.

"Do you believe me now?"

His eyes widen then narrow. "Well, I'm not sure. You could be just dressed up like this—it doesn't prove you're a faery."

There's a flash of light, and the alley around them disappears. Instead they're in a square room made of wood and brick. His home. He gasps. "How did you—?"

She gives a delicate shrug. "I *am* a faery."

"Right. Of course." He thinks about sitting down, glances at the cold fireplace, then spreads his hands. "What do you want from me?"

"I've been watching you," she says. "And you are exactly what I've been waiting for."

"And what is that?" Silvanus crosses his arms over his chest. His house is chilly after a day's solitude with no fire, and he shivers.

She tilts her head at him, her amber eyes glistening with an inner glow. "I'm sorry. Here." She waves a stick at the fireplace, and Silvanus only realizes it's a wand when a fire bursts to life and instantly warms the small house.

"You shall be the next one to approach the king about the princesses."

Silvanus laughs this time. "No, I won't. I mean, I couldn't— There have been several unsuccessful attempts already, what could possibly make me worthy?"

The faery smiles coyly and waves her wand again. "You will use this." Something sparkles in her hand, a cloak of many colors that reminds Silvanus of a lake reflecting the forest on a still day.

He reaches for the cloak, running his fingers over it. With a shimmer, his hand and the cloak disappear. He snatches his hand back. It shudders back into view, and he casts a wide-eyed look at the faery. "What is this magic?"

Her expression is kind and understanding. "Do not fear. It is good magic, pure, and intended to help others. The twelve princesses are cursed by an evil enchantment, and you must help release them from it. This cloak will make you invisible and allow you to follow the princesses without detection, to see what they see. It will protect you from everyone's sight, even one of the Great Fae's."

Hands tucked in his belt, Silvanus chews on his lip. *This is wild. I cannot fathom taking on this challenge—and losing my head in the process. How could I be any different from the dozen who have tried before?* "But if I do not wish— Why have you chosen me?"

A bemused frown crosses her lips. "You have a destiny, Silvanus. You are different from most. Those who feel that they are owed something, or they deserve my help. But you…you don't expect anything to be given to you. And for that alone, you are worthy of this gift."

Still worrying on his lip with his teeth, Silvanus glances at the fire, which flickers merrily as though it has been burning all day long.

His gaze shifts to the cloak that will make him invisible. *What could I do with power like that?* The thought comes out of nowhere, and he shakes it away the same way he shook the cloak from his fingers.

"You may not think yourself worthy, but with my support and help, you will be successful. All the Fae have faith in you, Silvanus."

He turns to her. "All the Fae want me to do this?"

She dips her head. "You are our best hope. You have the purest heart."

He scoffs. *That's not saying much then, is it?*

A small smile works its way onto the faery's lips. "I did not say it was without fault. And there will be temptations and troubles." Warning appears on her face, deepening her amber eyes to dark honey. "The twelve princesses are enchanted to stop anyone from following them. But with my magic, you shall be successful—if you heed my warnings."

Silvanus inhales and holds it. He is a soldier to the king. *It is my duty to help protect the kingdom of Edormisco. And is this not helping the kingdom?* Looking up at the faery, he finds her smiling.

She extends the cloak to him. "Good luck. We will not be able to contact you within the palace walls. Our faery sister who began this curse is keeping a close eye on it and them, and we would unleash her ire by alerting her to our assistance."

Reluctantly, Silvanus accepts the cloak, unnerved when his hands disappear underneath it. *Is this the right choice? Or do I only have three more days on this earth?*

When he lifts his gaze, the faery is gone, and only the fire and cloak remain to remind him of her presence and his duty.

~ II ~

King Effrenatus stares out from the faery-glass window of his throne room, his soul heavy. Eighteen men. Eighteen men have tried and failed to discover the princesses' whereabouts at night. Eighteen men he has beheaded, all in the name of his daughters' lives. The new proclamation was issued two weeks ago, but no one worthy has come forward yet. *It is worth it. It must be. So why do I feel this guilt? My daughters are worth the lives of the entire kingdom, if it would just free them from this curse.*

A throat clearing interrupts the king's thoughts, and he turns without interest to find Sir Hartwig bowing before him, hooked nose halfway to the white stone floor. The king's sigh echoes off the pearly walls. "Is the court ready?"

"No." Placing his hands behind his back and straightening, Sir Hartwig answers, "A volunteer."

"What? You said there were none this morning." Frowning, the king casts his glance around the empty room as Sir Hartwig steps to the side and a lanky man in a soldier's uniform enters. His hair flops in all directions, and he holds his hat in his hands, but the pale blue outfit of the king's guard exactly matches his eyes and gives him a penetrating, intelligent stare. The effect startles the king. *Perhaps this soldier can solve the mystery.*

"This young man volunteers as the next to attempt the," Hartwig pauses, then says simply, "the impossible."

The king blinks. "I—" He cuts himself off and fixes a stern look upon the soldier. "Yes. Excellent. Soldier, what— Do you know what you are attempting?"

Cap in his hands, the soldier bows his head deeply to the king. "I do."

"And you understand that, should you fail, it will be at the cost of your head?" The king injects his voice with strength, determined to appear strong before any of his subjects, even one who will probably be dead in three days.

"Yes, Your Majesty," the soldier replies, head still bowed. "I understand perfectly well that, should I fail to find out where the princesses go, I will lose my head, as have the others."

The king winces, then sets his jaw. "So be it."

"Thank you, Your Majesty." The young man still does not lift his head, and something about his humility speaks to the king.

"You are a soldier in my army?" he asks.

"Yes, Majesty."

"Are you skilled?"

"I have been taught well, Majesty."

"Then I would be loath to lose you."

The young soldier's shoulders brace at the words. "I would be loath to fail, Majesty."

The king hesitates, wondering if he should ask the young man's name. But he has refrained from doing so with any of the other men, for to do so might make it impossible for him to follow through on the ultimatum should they fail. Instead, he steels himself with a deep breath and, exhaling as silently as possible, says, "Good luck."

***

Silvanus follows Sir Hartwig out of the throne room,

his heart galloping in his chest. It was far easier to be brave on a battlefield than to agree to this madness before his king. *What am I doing? Even with a Fae's blessing, this seems a fool's errand.*

Trailing the advisor, Silvanus pulls his thoughts away from his task and examines the ornate, faery-crafted statues, tapestries, and inlaid designs along the halls. Although it all has a faery glamor about it, there is a thin layer of dust over every item, as if they have been neglected for weeks or perhaps months.

Hartwig stops abruptly. "Here is your room. There is the princesses'." He points him to a door opposite one similar. "Your task begins now. You have three days and three nights."

Silvanus nods, tightening his hands on his sack of personal items, including the faery cloak.

Hartwig inspects him from head to toe with heaviness in his eyes. "Good luck, soldier. May the Fae bless you."

They already have, he thinks as the advisor leaves him and strides down the hallway. *But I'm not sure how much good that's going to do me.*

Alone, he walks into the room, finding it to be simple, yet large, with plush covers and pillows atop a generously sized bed. Beside it sits a bottle of wine and a large glass, from which he pours himself a serving. He drinks it as he inspects the rest of the room, the crackling fire, and the view of the Edormiscan Forest from the window.

Turning away, he runs a hand through his hair and gives a yawn. *I should rest before the night arrives.*

He curls up atop the covers, snuggles into the pillows, and in a moment, he's enjoying the heaviest sleep he has experienced in some time. When he wakes, the room is dark. He blinks, confused. Then he bolts upright. "The princesses!"

He stumbles from the bed, head foggy, his legs not

obeying as usual, and reaches for the door. Outside, sparsely spaced torches brighten the hallway. He lurches to the princesses' door and is about to throw it open when sanity returns to him. *This is the door to the future queen of Edormisco's bedroom.* Taking a steadying breath and straightening, he knocks, first calmly, then, when it remains unanswered, with more force.

"Princesses?" He presses his ear against the thick wood. With no sound from within, he makes his decision. "Dash it all."

He pushes the door open. A curse leaves his lips at the sight of twelve empty beds. He gropes for his sword, as though he sees a foe he can slash down, and finds his hip empty. *It's back in my room.*

"What a fool," he mutters to himself, heat crawling to his face. *An utter fool.*

With nothing more to do that night but wait, he returns to his room and tries to rest.

In the morning, he eats a little food, procuring it from the kitchens himself to make sure it isn't tainted. Still, the warm food in the drafty castle makes him tired, and he falls asleep midday, not waking until past dark to find the princesses' room empty.

"Faery's—" He doesn't bother to finish his curse. Instead, he retrieves his faery cloak and, this time, returns to the princesses' room underneath it. There he sits, until sun begins to peek through the window and a door opens in an expanse of blank wall. It's only his soldier training that allows him to muffle his sharp gasp. *The door wasn't there before—was it? No, it appeared…as if by magic.* Silvanus shakes his head, reminding himself of the Fae and what he's dealing with as, through the door, a dozen young women trickle, looking exhausted but pleased with themselves.

"This one is easier than the others," says a girl dressed in blue with dark hair.

A younger girl laughs. "They're all imbeciles."

Another princess, this one dressed in pink with dark hair that cascades to her waist, casts her sisters a look that is almost reproachful. Her eyes are soulful and conflicted, with smudges of exhaustion underneath them, as if she can see the truth of their situation. He thinks he recognizes her as the second-oldest princess, Bianca.

"Regardless, we must make sure to replace the wine in his room tonight," the first girl says. "We cannot have him following us on his third night either."

The faery's words come back to Silvanus in a rush: *they are enchanted to stop anyone from following them.* Hidden under his cloak, he grimaces and has to force himself to stay quiet. *Sneaky little princesses, aren't you?*

As he watches, the girls remove their worn slippers. He closes his eyes as they disrobe, only to open them again when he hears no more shifting beds or rustling blankets. The princesses are almost instantly asleep under their covers.

Silvanus rises, careful to be as silent as he can and keep himself covered under the cloak. He wanders amongst the beds, staring down at the young women. *Why are they so cursed to spend the nights doing…whatever they do? Cursed to thwart any and all attempts at discovery. Cursed to waste away under this enchantment. A sad way to die.*

His gaze strays downward to the ends of their beds to a dozen pairs of slippers with holes in them. Then to the now-blank expanse of wall, where they had emerged through an arched door.

He runs his hands over the wall. Smooth. He taps it with a knuckle and finds the area sounds the same as that around it. *Curious.*

He turns to the last princess, Bianca. She lays on her side, the blanket on her chest gently rising and falling. There is something about her that calls to him, something that makes him look closer. Her lashes are dark against sallow skin, her dark hair braided back from her exhausted face, and her cheeks flushed from what he presumes was outside air. A yellow jewel the size of a marble has worked its way free from the neck of her gown and lies upon her pillow. He leans closer to inspect the unusual gem.

"I can feel your presence," she murmurs, eyes still closed.

He recoils from shock, nearly stumbling into the next princess's bed. Recovering, he creeps forward and leans over her, not daring to breathe should he awaken her.

Her eyes fly open, and he freezes.

"I cannot see you," she whispers. "But I know you are there."

He bites his lip to keep from answering.

Her dark eyes cast around the space where he stands. *She cannot see me.*

"I know you have only one night left, but promise me that you shall not eat or drink anything until your time is over. If you have not succeeded in following us by then..." She trails off and sighs. "What's the point? I'm just imagining."

He hesitates, then reaches a hand out from under his cloak. A sliver of moonlight shining through the window illuminates it.

At the apparition, she gasps.

"Come with me," he whispers. He grabs a robe sitting on a chair beside her bed, holding it out to her. "And speak with me. Please." He closes his eyes, waiting for her to answer.

There are a few moments of hesitation, then the robe is taken from his hands. Bedclothes rustle and a spring squeaks, then a hand touches his. He leads her out of the room and across into his, and only then does he pull the cloak off himself and stand before her as he is.

Her eyes widen slightly as the cloak returns to its shimmery state, and he drapes it across the end of his bed.

"I apologize for bringing you into the bedchamber, but—"

"It is the only place we might not be overheard," she answers for him. "Do not apologize." Without another word, she goes to the side of his bed and takes the bottle of wine. She sniffs at it and takes it to the window, where she dumps out the remainder. "Do not eat or drink anything you are given. Even if it comes not from one of us." She replaces the bottle on the bedside table, a hand lifted to her throat as if choking. She swallows and adds, "I cannot explain to you why—I cannot—but you must listen to everything and do exactly as I say."

"Yes, of course." He fixes his attention on her and her nut brown eyes, rimmed with red.

"We will leave right after dark. Enter our room while we attend dinner. Do not touch any food or drink, no matter how thirsty or hungry you are until you stand before our father the morning after. Do not sleep. You must also follow us through the—" she chokes again, "—wherever we go. Do not lose sight of us. Not for a moment. Promise me."

"I promise." Silvanus finds himself enchanted by her worry.

"I could not bear it if one more lost their life because of us." Tears brim on her thick lashes.

I ought to say something to encourage her. But all that comes out of his mouth is, "Should you return—before you are missed?"

She takes his hands in hers and presses them tight. Staring deeply into his eyes, she takes a slow breath and says, "You must be the one. I know it."

Before he can answer, she drops his hands and dashes from the room.

***

Silvanus lays atop his bed, finding it difficult to wait for the princesses to leave for dinner. His stomach growls and his mouth is dry. It's only midday, and yet the more he thinks of his hunger and thirst, the harder it is to keep himself from it. He plays with his dagger to pass the time and keep himself awake or stands and stretches, determined not to sleep, eat, or drink. He eyes the sun hovering in the sky over the forest until it finally begins to sink.

He covers himself with the faery cloak and positions himself in the hall. Soon, the princesses emerge in a line, from oldest to youngest. He finds the one that warned him second in line. She keeps her head down, although her gaze darts to his doorway more than once. Her gaze slides to where he stands, and she gives a little smile. *Can she see me?* He eliminates the thought. *She must be guessing. She is smart.*

"Oh, I forgot my shawl," Bianca says, turning back to the doorway. "Go ahead. I'll be right behind you."

Crown Princess Clara gives her sister a scrutinizing look but says simply, "Hurry."

Bianca nods and returns to the room, leaving the door open, while her sisters continue down the hallway.

Silvanus takes his chance and creeps across the hall into their room.

"I hope you're in here," Bianca whispers as she grabs her cloak.

Before he can answer, she slips away again. Silvanus positions himself beside the now blank wall where the door had appeared the night prior. *I cannot fail tonight. If I fail…my life is forfeit.*

The hour creeps by, even though he passes it meticulously sharpening his dagger. The sun has just set when soft footsteps echo in the hallway outside, and the door swings open.

"Have you seen the new man?" one princess asks. "The soldier?"

"No," another answers. "I'll go check his room. He's probably asleep."

In the midst of her sisters, Bianca's face is stricken.

Silvanus winces. *I should have feigned sleep then returned to their room to wait. What a fool!*

But Bianca interrupts his thoughts. "No, I'll go," she says. "It's my turn."

A minute later, Bianca returns to the room and says to her sisters, "He's asleep."

"Excellent," they murmur in response, as if this exchange happens every night.

In a hush, the sisters gather at the wall he stands beside, half of them carrying lit torches. His heart thumps in anticipation, but curiosity drives him to remain calm.

As the eldest princess takes a key from around her neck, the door materializes in the wall. Silvanus inhales sharply.

A frown on her plump lips, Princess Clara pauses with the skeleton key hovering before the wrought-iron lock and looks in his direction.

Silvanus bites his lip until she shakes her head and turns the key in the lock, pushing it open with a small creak. She waits until all eleven of her sisters have entered, then reaches to pull the door shut.

Clutching the cloak around him, Silvanus dashes under her outstretched arm, squeezing inside before she pulls the door closed and locks it. At a soft tug on the cloak, he casts a glance back to find Clara frowning in his direction. His cloak flutters around his ankles, as though the door had caught it.

Eager to put a little distance between himself and the eldest princess, he hurries into a tunnel black as a dark faery's heart after the other girls.

Bianca trails at the end of the line.

Why is she so far back? he wonders as he falls in behind her. He opens his mouth, but shuts it. *I dare not speak with Princess Clara so near.*

Hurried footsteps, soft against rock, are almost at his heels before he hears them at all.

Princess Clara seizes her dark-haired sister by the

arm and says, "Bianca, have you seen anything odd?"

"Odd?" The princess's eyes widen. "No, Clara. What do you mean?"

"I could swear I saw a flash of someone's trousers as I shut the door," the eldest princess answers. Her face, illuminated by Bianca's torch, is lined with worry.

"No, I've seen nor heard nothing." Bianca's voice is firm. "You're just concerned because it's the last night. He'll lose his head tomorrow, like the rest."

"Yes," Clara murmurs, her gaze growing distant. "Of course." She shakes her head and lets go of her sister, then hurries to the front of the line, as if she must lead the sisters on.

Silvanus falls into quiet steps a few paces behind Bianca, who seems to purposely trail her sisters. He follows for ages, through the dark, damp tunnel as quietly as his soldier training has taught him. After some time, the princesses in front of them begin to disappear up a set of stone stairs. As the one in front of Bianca steps up, he presses Bianca's gloved hand with his.

Her breath is sharp at the unexpected touch, but a flash of a smile breaks out before she hides it. Her foot pauses halfway to the step. Glancing up, then back at him, she whispers, "Go up before me, or else you shall be trapped down here."

Not daring to speak, he squeezes her hand in thanks and brushes past. She waits a heartbeat and follows on his heels.

The sisters are impatient when Bianca emerges.

"What is taking you so long tonight?" the youngest demands. "I want to dance."

Clara locks the door exiting the tunnel as she did the door from their room, and the line of princesses hurries off toward a nearby lake. Silvanus falls in beside Bianca and brushes her hand to let her know of his presence. She jumps but smiles.

"Stay close and quiet," she whispers and nods her chin at the half-dozen boats bobbing in the lake. "Enter the boat with me."

He remains silent and does as she asks. The boat sags under his added weight, but no one remarks upon it. It starts with a jerk, and Silvanus has to keep himself from grabbing at the sides. He should have expected the magic, given their enchantment, but it still makes him uneasy.

With no effort from the princesses, they travel across a still lake. As the shore slinks by, trees begin to climb to the sky, limbs and roots encroaching on the shore. Although the leaves on the trees are still, the princesses shiver. He suspects it's not with cold in this warm night, but excitement.

He catches his breath at the sight before him. The forest surrounds them; trees sparkle with dew as moonbeams shine through the limbs and onto the princesses in their boats, illuminating them as though they are subjects of a painting. Ahead in the midst of the trees, a silvery glow issues as bright as fire.

They glide a few moments more upon the water, through a narrowing in the lake, and to a short dock. The boats pull up and fall still, settling into the water like horses awaiting a master's return. He gazes back the way they've come, at a far distant shore barely visible. Escape is not possible now.

Without warning, the princesses give childish shrieks of joy and rush from the lakeside. To his shock, Bianca does the same, darting after the others.

Abandoning caution, he pursues them, as silently as possible.

They race into a clearing with thick pine trees surrounding it. As soon as they enter, the forest comes to life. Music swells around them, lights spark to life in the branches above, and the moon seems to swell to twice its size as it lowers itself in the sky.

Faery magic, Silvanus reminds himself. *This is all faery magic. I must take great care.*

More thankful than ever for his cloak, which the faery said would protect him even from Fae eyes, he tugs it tight around himself and sticks to the edge of the clearing.

The twelve princesses circle in the middle, faces alight with eagerness. A dozen animals emerge from amongst the trees. Without a word, the girls each go to one, one to a fox, one to a beaver, one to a deer, another to a wolf until each princess stands before a different beast. The women bow to their choice, and then the animal lifts itself onto its hind legs and becomes a man.

The men-animals take their princess in their arms and begin to dance.

***

Silvanus blinks owlishly. It has been so long since he last slept, he doesn't know how much more dancing he can endure without rest.

He smothers another yawn, his eyes growing heavier as the night wears on. This time he doesn't need food or drink—the music, the faery dance, the sparkling dew, all lull him into a deep slumber.

Silvanus starts up, his cloak slipping from his head at the motion. What…what woke him? He scowls blearily at his surroundings. He's in the forest.

The forest! The princesses!

Jumping to his feet, he can see his failure in an instant. They're gone, as if they have never been.

Cursing, he drags his cloak back over himself and darts for the forest path, stumbling over rocks and roots that were not there before. The forest changed as he slumbered, and his path has disappeared under roots and trees and rocks. Branches tug at his cloak, revealing parts of him, a finger here, a foot there, an elbow, his hair…

He begins praying to the Fae, wondering if they can

even hear him. *Please get me out of this forest. I can't leave Bianca and her sisters to this fate. I must find a way to free them, even at cost of my life.*

He stumbles through the trees, breaking out onto the shore of the clear lake. The *empty* lake.

He groans. Specks on the water's surface show the princesses floating away—on his only ride home.

Huffing out a breath, he glances around. Back the way he came is dark and the path is…gone. To his left is the lakeshore, as well as to his right. He glances at the water. *No boat in the rushes. And I can't very well swim home. Well…left or right?*

Silvanus turns to the right and pulls the cloak tight before taking a step. Rustles from the forest keep stealing his attention from the path along the shore, pulling it to the trees above. The muddy ground snags at his boots and at the faery cloak, constantly tugging it from his head, but he dares not remove it—not with the eerie presence around. *Were those eyes in the forest? A scratch? Something's watching me. Waiting for me to be visible…*

His heart pounds in his throat. He reaches for his dagger, but his cloak slips from his head with the mud's relentless tug. The eyes amongst the trees brighten and near. Silvanus hastily pulls the cloak back into place.

With a mighty squelch, the mud grabs his ankle. He stumbles, falling to his knees, and the cloak slips off one shoulder into the mud below. Struggling with his boot and the cloak, Silvanus almost doesn't see his enemy's approach until it's too late. Teeth flash in the moonlight, and a low growl makes him react with a soldier's training. He drags his dagger from his hip and stabs in the direction of the doggish teeth just as a smaller set of teeth lunges for his arm. He slashes through the air, catching the large teeth underneath. With a grunt, he slams his hand down on top of the red muzzle clamped on his arm.

The teeth release, and a yelp fills the silent air, then

another growl, this one higher pitched and less dog-like. *Fox?*

He squints through the darkness, one hand clutching the cloak, the other gripping his dagger—both are equal parts of his salvation.

Glints of silver and red catch in the shards of moonlight, and Silvanus's mouth parts. *Fox and wolf. The men from the clearing? Could it be that they're enchanted to protect the princesses, too?*

With a jerk, he brings the cloak up out of the mud and over his head again, desperate to hide from whatever else lurks. He hastens to his feet as the tail tips disappear into the trees. The forest is silent again. *Watching.*

He steadies his breath and, keeping his dagger out this time, resumes his trek toward the distant castle as blood drips from his arm.

It almost happens again several times. *I can feel them circling me.* But he keeps the cloak tight and his dagger even tighter, and, step by step, reaches the far side of the lake. He half-expects the princesses' boats to be bobbing in the water, waiting for tomorrow night's dancing, but the shore is empty.

Even from this side of the lake, the castle is a great distance away. The moon has progressed across the sky as Silvanus walked along the lakeshore, and, now, urgency pricks him, sharp and fearful. Although free from the dangers of the forest, he has miles to walk before daybreak. *Should I arrive late…* He shudders at the consequence of being late on his third morning.

Sheathing his dagger, he pulls his cloak tight and forces his tired feet upon the dirt road to the palace. *One foot after another. Just like a soldier's march.* So he begins to sing a marching song under his breath, just loudly enough to keep himself from falling asleep on his feet.

And muddy, exhausted, and bloodied, he arrives at the castle as the sun crests over the distant hills.

~ III ~

His body aching and bloody, his clothes dirty, Silvanus stands before the king. Three dozen pairs of worn-out slippers lay heaped on the floor between them, with a dozen pairs of red-rimmed eyes watching from either side of the throne room. Surrounding them is a full court of nobles and commoners alike, all present to hear Silvanus's report. Some appear eager to see him lose his head, others watch with concern in their gazes.

"Well, young soldier?" King Effrenatus asks him in a cold, imperious voice. "What have you discovered?"

Silvanus bows low before the king, a mixture of dizziness and exhaustion washing over him and threatening to drag him into darkness.

"Stand and answer. Or if this be your answer, off to the dungeons to await your beheading."

Silvanus stays low for another moment, gathering his courage and strength to speak and tell the king the truth. *What if he's angry that I did nothing to stop them dancing? And what if it doesn't break the curse? How am I to free them?*

Shaking off his thoughts, he stands and addresses the king. "Sire, you are right to worry about your daughters, for they are under a dark faery's enchantment."

The princesses' dresses rustle as they shift on either side of the king's throne.

"And every night, the princesses eat dinner with you and return to their room." He holds the king's gaze. "Where they ready themselves and the eldest unlocks a magic door with a key kept around her neck."

King Effrenatus's gaze flicks to Princess Clara, whose face is whiter than the faery's full moon. As if her expression has verified Silvanus's words, the king returns his gaze to Silvanus and says, "Go on," in an icy, unflinching tone.

Silvanus continues, relaying to the king exactly what

he witnessed in the forest.

"And have you broken this curse?" the king asks, his voice penetrating through the deepest corner of the room.

Dread floods over Silvanus. *Was that part of the arrangement? The king had never said—*

"No, Sire. I have only identified where they go."

"Then they are still cursed!" the king barks. "You have failed—"

"Well done, Silvanus," comes a new voice cutting across that of the king, whose face mottles with outrage at the interruption.

The crowd gasps and looks from the king to the voice and back.

Silvanus whirls to face the speaker and finds the Great Fae standing behind him. Some of the crowd steps back at her sudden appearance in their midst, while others bow or fall into curtsies. With a majestic smile, the faery approaches Silvanus.

"Well done. You have thwarted the curse of my sister, shown us exactly what and where she is hiding—"

"No longer," a second voice interrupts, one as majestic as the Fae's.

At the voice, a tremor travels down the Fae's body before she stills. Silvanus follows her gaze as she snaps her head toward the new arrival. A Great Fae, dressed in a gown of palest blue with a silvery crown of aspen tree branches upon her head, stands with blue eyes glittering in cold fury.

"Ceara." The first Fae's voice is ice. "It is no longer your place here, sister." A wand appears in her hand, sparking as dangerously as her amber eyes.

The new Fae smirks in answer. "I beg to differ, Alva." Ceara motions a hand at the twelve princesses, standing in row, expressions vacant. "It seems quite apparent they remain mine. No thanks to your industrious soldier here." Her cold gaze settles on Silvanus with a quick, narrow assessment.

Alva steals her chance to raise her wand, but Ceara is too quick. She disappears from her spot, only to appear behind the immobile princesses, as the crowd scatters and screams. A blinding light erupts from behind the princesses; the crowds silence and freeze.

Silvanus cannot speak or move. *Why can I only move my eyes?*

Likewise afflicted, his fellow Edormiscans have terror in their eyes.

Behind him echoes the scuffing of feet against the ballroom floor. *The Great Fae*, he thinks with a surge of hope. *She can defeat her sister—can't she?*

Flashes of light blind him from both sides as the burn of magic whistles past his ears. He does not know how long it goes on, only that he clenches his eyes shut against the heat and the sight of the princesses before him.

Bianca.

The whisper rushes through his mind, drawing his eyes open and along the twelve princesses until they land upon the brunette dressed in soft pink. Out of all her sisters, she is the only one with fear in her gaze.

How do you resist it? Silvanus wonders. But there's no time for any more wondering. The ballroom explodes in a shower of sparks as a spell descends next to Ceara. Smoke follows, hiding half the princesses, including Bianca, from Silvanus's view.

As the smoke begins to clear, a glowing orb takes its place. Crisscrossed around the blue faery are beams glowing gold and silver. The trapped Fae's expression sends waves of terror down Silvanus's body from hair to toenail. Her mouth opens and an inhuman scream issues from it.

Silvanus shrinks back, aware that he is able to move at the same time as a great shattering sound joins the scream. He covers his ears, hunkering down to the floor as the glass of the ballroom windows sprinkles down upon him. Sobs and whimpers break the silence of the room. Then a soft whisper of heels crunching on broken glass.

Silvanus lowers his hands from his face to watch the Great Fae stride toward her sister, cold fury on her features.

"You are no longer welcome in this country, sister," the Great Fae says, standing before the cage constraining the blue faery.

Ceara's face darkens, her nostrils flaring in hatred. "You cannot exile me—not without the other sisters' agree—"

"Which I already have," Alva interrupts. She raises her hand and a parchment appears in it, glinting in the unaltered sunlight streaming through broken windows. "We have called for your exile, effective immediately. As you know, the king fully supports this act." She cocks a brow. "Is that not why you cursed his children to begin with?"

The Great Fae steps forth with the paper, now rolling itself into a scroll. With a wave of her hand, the scroll slips through the gaps in the cage and hovers before the blue faery.

The beautiful faery's face turns pale, her eyes sparking at the scroll before her.

"Take your punishment, Ceara, Blue Faery of Edormisco," the Great Fae says in a voice of thunder. "A thousand years' exile."

Ceara's eyes round, but then narrow. "I won't—"

"You will," the Great Fae replies, waving her wand. Ceara's hand begins to rise, until it reaches for the parchment and closes around it. As her fingertips touch her palm, the scroll glows with golden light so strong, Silvanus squeezes his eyes to slivers. She cannot seem to let go of the parchment. Fear occludes all the anger Silvanus had seen before in her gaze.

"You are henceforth banned from Edormisco's borders until a thousand years pass. Your wand will be broken." As the Great Fae speaks, she motions with her wand, and the one in Ceara's hand slips free of her clutch.

The cage shimmers as the wand passes through the gaps, drifting out between Ceara and the Great Fae. Ceara's round blue eyes lock on the strip of pale wood as it glows bright and then fractures into a dozen pieces with a dull roar like a mile-high waterfall.

Another cry fills the air, this one low and guttural, a wounded animal. Ceara's face is pale, as though she might faint.

"Effective immediately," the Great Fae says. As soon as her words disappear into the ether, the Blue Fae's outline begins to shimmer. She looks down upon herself, eyes wide, as she fades. A few moments later, there is nothing left in the cage, not even a sparkle of magic.

The Great Fae stands a moment between Silvanus and the line of princesses, staring at the cage that sits between them. Then with a heavy sigh, she lifts her wand. Agony appears on her features and disappears. With a swirl of her silver wand, the cage evaporates, the glass on the floor turns into whirlwinds that return to their rightful places, and those with cuts are healed. Silvanus looks down at his arm only to find the bite mark from the creatures in the forest gone. He turns his hands over in wonder at all the missing nicks and scrapes he suffered overnight. His skin is smooth and whole again.

The Great Fae turns to the king, lifting herself high, and says, "She is the reason for the curse, King Effrenatus, and now that she has passed out of our borders, her spell is lifted." As she speaks, the princesses stir, blinking heavily at their surroundings and turning to one another with confused expressions.

"It is only because of Silvanus's courage to pursue the princesses into the enchanted woods that I could draw her out and thus exile her. You will give him his reward for his courage, as deserved."

"I-I—" the king stammers.

"Or I will put another on your throne."

"Of-of course." As he speaks, he looks to his daughters and softens.

"But what I don't understand," Alva says, turning to the princesses, "is why your second born could resist?"

Bianca fixes a half-terrified, half-embarrassed expression upon the Fae. "I—"

"Do not be afraid, child," the Fae says, her words as gentle as the glow upon her skin. "Simply tell us what happened, and how you resisted the sway of my sister's magic."

Bianca steps up to her father and spreads her hands. "That day in the forest, we were drawn away from the path. We wandered around for hours and stumbled into this faery's nest. That faery—the blue one—found us there, and she cursed us. She said…" The princess hesitates, giving her father an apologetic look. "She said your agreement to exile her was a great offense, and because of it, we all would suffer for the rest of our lives. Then she cursed us to dance every night forever, and we could speak to no one about it in any way."

"Then how could you help me?" The words slip from Silvanus's mouth before he can stop them.

Bianca's smile has a tinge of sorrow to its edges as she reaches one hand toward her neck and glances to the Great Fae, who watches from beside Silvanus. Out from her bodice she draws the gem that Silvanus noticed before. "Father, I know you must recognize this. It was Mother's, a long time ago."

"Yes, I thought so." The king's brow furrows. "But what does it—?"

"Naturally! It has protective qualities," the Fae answers for her. "The gem was once blessed by a sister of mine, and, while Princess Bianca *was* cursed, she suffered a lesser curse than that of her sisters."

A murmur runs through the crowd in the silence that follows.

"Well, soldier, come here." The king's voice is gruff and demanding, as if ready to deliver another condemnation.

Hope flares and whooshes out of Silvanus at the tone, but he bends his knee before the king.

"Well," King Effrenatus says in a voice like the grating of pebbles against one another, "it appears you did what no duke's son, no prince of Abbattia, and no other aristocrat could do." He motions to the Fae standing in the midst of the throne room, a wide span of space around her, as though no one dares come close. "You even have the blessing of the Great Fae. And so what do I do with you?"

Silvanus dares a glance up at the king, and his mouth falls open to see a small smile on his sovereign's lips. "…Sire?"

"My daughters' curse has been lifted. And they will recover." The king nods, letting his smile go until it beams upon his lips.

The hope sparks to life again in Silvanus's chest.

"And so you choose your reward. For any man with a faery blessing is a man I would be blessed to call my son." The king rises from his throne and descends the steps, until he stands before Silvanus's kneeling form. Then he crouches and takes Silvanus's hands in his, lifting him until they both stand. "Rise, my son. And tell me, which of my daughters would you like to marry?"

"I—" Silvanus had all but forgotten the reward offered to the man who could discover the princesses' nighttime whereabouts.

From the side of her father's throne, Bianca's expression is inscrutable.

Silvanus blinks at the king's expectant look. "I'm afraid there is only one that has interested me, Your Majesty. And she stands beside you." He turns to Bianca. "And if she would have me, I would be honored to call her my wife."

A flush colors Bianca's cheeks as she breaks into a modest smile. "I would be delighted."

A grin breaks across the king's face, splitting his gray-streaked beard with a set of ivory teeth. "An excellent choice, my son. Let us set a date then. Shall we say one year from today?"

In her soft, breathy voice, Bianca answers for them, "I think that will be perfect, Father. After all, my sisters and I could use a long rest from dancing."

Cursed Glass

M. T. Wilson

~ I ~

High Witch Ethleda's soul pounded in her chest as she entered the forbidden cave. It rose above her in an almost perfect dome. Jagged streaks of sunlight flared through cracks in the ancient cavern's roof onto the stone below.

Thirty witches of the Glacela clan gathered behind her at the entrance, fidgeting anxiously. None of them spoke, for the ceremony had been carefully planned. Ethleda kept her back straight and head up, showing no sign of the unease that enveloped her.

The empty glass coffin floated in the air beside High Witch Ethleda. Soon it would contain her dishonored sister. Her soul constricted at the thought. It was an unspeakable punishment for only the most unspeakable of crimes.

Ethleda moved her hand, hiding its trembling in the wide sleeve of her cloak. The glass coffin drifted down onto a raised stone dais in the center of the cave.

Around the dais stood five witches wearing rich green cloaks, with hands lifted above them. Cracking sounds echoed off the curved walls. Pearly molten witchglass glowing with heat appeared around the edges of the cave. As the witches raised their hands higher, the glass spread in a wave up the sides of the cavern to the top of the dome, where the liquid met in the center and hardened. The cracks were sealed, but a distorted light still shone through the glass.

Ethleda took a deep breath and turned to the entrance. Melantha stood outside the cave, mist swirling around her. Glowing witchglass manacles clamped her wrists. The enchanted glass would ensure she could not escape.

Two hundred years had passed since Melantha had been stripped of her witch title and imprisoned for the havoc she had caused in their lands. Her escape from that prison had been a blow to the clan. Such a short time was nothing to an immortal witch, but it had been an agonizing wait for Ethleda to finally see her sister recaptured and sealed away. As much as she believed Melantha was securely in her custody this time, her every sense was on high alert.

Melantha strode through the lines of silent witches, passing out of the misty dawn light and into the dimness of the cave. White hair streamed down her back in contrast with her black robe. The train of her gown swept along the ground, leaving a trail of dead grass in her wake. The witches raised their hands and placed them over their eyes, bowing their heads in a demonstration of Melantha's shame and sacrilege to the laws and customs of the glass witches.

The disturbing blankness in her captive's expression unnerved Ethleda. There was neither smugness nor defeat, neither smirk nor frown from the fallen witch. Melantha bore no emotion, and Ethleda knew her sister was lost. Not once had she shown remorse for the death and destruction she had caused, but neither had she shown satisfaction.

The High Witch saw for the first time that Melantha was drained. Darkness had consumed her soul and left her empty.

Ethleda's sister stopped in front of her. The words Ethleda must speak hovered in her mind, but she could not say them. Her sister had been warped completely, unrecognizable from the girl she had grown up with, but she couldn't seem to detach herself from the Melantha she kept safe in her memory: the one who, although shy, was rarely afraid of anything except herself.

Fascinated by her younger sister's power as a child, Ethleda had encouraged Melantha, in rapture at her unique gifts. The first time, they had been sitting under a great tree a stone's throw from their village, its bark inlaid with witchglass. Six-year-old Ethleda struggled to create glass from nothing, a skill she should have been adept at by that age. She remembered gazing up longingly at the imbued tree cradling the sky above them.

Melantha, only four years old, had closed her eyes and, with no trouble at all, created glass from air, morphing it into the shape of the bird on the bough above them. Then the glass had changed from the usually clear, pearly appearance of witchglass to deep black. Both young witches had stared in awe at the altered glass, neither of them understanding what had just happened.

It was something strange and unknown that had immediately marked the young girl out as different. To Ethleda, it was unique and wonderful, but if she had realized how others would view her sister, and what that scorn would turn Melantha into, she would not have been so encouraging.

Ethleda pushed the memories back. It didn't change what Melantha had done. She could never feel satisfaction in bringing her sister to her eternal prison, but as much as it pained Ethleda, the law of their clan had to be upheld.

Ethleda swallowed. "Melantha, former witch of the Glacela clan, you are hereby sentenced to imprisonment in the glass coffin for crimes of murder, attempted murder, genocide, kidnapping, and treason. You may not speak. You have no voice in our land any longer."

Part of her expected Melantha to disobey the order. The dimple would appear in her left cheek as she smirked, ready to deliver a sharp comment. That part of Melantha had gone a long time ago.

High Witch Ethleda stepped aside, and Melantha walked to the dais where the coffin lay. Ethleda raised a hand, sensing the energy in her bones calling to the witchglass, and the coffin arced upward to stand vertical, the lid swinging silently open. She glanced at Melantha, but there was no hint of emotion in her sister's brown eyes.

The High Witch would have once expected resistance, but today it seemed she would get none. Melantha stepped inside and turned to face the gathered clan members. Careful not to touch the glass of the coffin, Ethleda held her hand aloft a final time and the lid swung shut. The ghastly face of Melantha stared at her through the transparent surface.

"The curse of this glass is that you shall remain entombed in this coffin, immortal as you are, until your soul is no longer dark," Ethleda declared. "Your soul will depart your body, transferred to that of another, and pass through the generations until it returns to the light and breaks the curse."

A screeching sound pierced Ethleda's ears, and a gust of wind tore toward her from the coffin. Melantha's mouth was open in a scream. A wave of darkness burst from her chest and passed through the glass. It morphed into the shape of a panther with glowing white eyes that paused for a moment in the air between the coffin and Ethleda. It flew through the air and disappeared through the mouth of the cave.

Ethleda covered her eyes with her hands, not wanting to see the contorted expression on Melantha's face. To have your soul removed was an agonizing punishment for a witch. It had brought the first sign of emotion to Melantha's face since she had arrived at the cave—pain.

The temptation to move her fingers and see Melantha one last time was overwhelming, but she could not do it. It would be disgraceful to do so. As High Witch, she must lead by example.

Turning on her heel, hands still covering her eyes, Ethleda strode across the cave to the entrance, sensing the space around her. Once she felt sunlight warm her hands, she removed them and blinked at the brightness of the rising sun. The witches followed her out of the cave. Two of them raised their hands, and a sheet of glass formed over the entrance.

Melantha's tomb was sealed.

~ II ~

Fel Blakely-Smith climbed over the contorted root of a tree and paused to catch her breath. The humidity of the forest made her uniform cling to her skin, and she tugged at the sticky collar. A thick canopy of lush green leaves completely blocked out the sun, but a glimmer of light slanted through the branches ahead. She was nearing the tree line. Since the last humans left the Earth two thousand years ago, the ancient woodland had reigned. It was a sight few humans had seen in those thousands of years, and Fel was one of the few to return and see it. To step in the footsteps of their ancient ancestors took her breath away.

Forests were all but nonexistent on Herul. She'd been on a couple of trips to the wild woodland of a neighboring planet, but it was always crowded with tourists. This place was totally natural and undisturbed. Nothing could have prepared her for the beautiful sight of uncultivated woodland that greeted her when their spacecraft had landed.

Unfortunately, the onerous arguments between their team leader and the scientists had completely ruined the ambience of the place. Since Fel had snuck off, barely a sound had disturbed the natural expanse. They probably hadn't even noticed she was missing yet. She was just the assigned, tag-along student.

The others had planned to search the woodland, so if Fel headed elsewhere, she might be able to find a unique and interesting sample. Something that would validate her presence on the team. Something that might change their understanding of the planet their ancestors once called home.

A strange cawing came from somewhere high above, and Fel swung her head up toward the sound. As much as the forest was beautiful, it was also unnerving. The sudden noise made her eager to reach the light ahead and get clear of what now seemed like an oppressive tangle of trees.

Fel weaved through the foliage and emerged from the dim forest. A small mountain rose in front of her, standing solitary amidst the flat plains. Storm clouds dominated the horizon to the left.

She checked her time keeper—half an hour had passed since she'd left the spacecraft. The ship's weather report indicated the storm would descend on the area in two hours.

Earth had become a planet of extremes, with multiple natural phenomena—storms, hurricanes, flash floods, earthquakes—raging across the planet at any one time. Herul was docile in comparison, and while the thought of getting caught in an extreme storm was unsettling, she hadn't come all this way across the universe to just turn back. She strode out toward the mountain until the short grass petered out into rocky ground at its base.

A large shadow rose before Fel. She froze. A few meters away stood a big black cat. Either it was eerily silent, or she had been blithely unaware of her surroundings. Its completely white eyes stared at her with an unusual ghostly intensity. It cocked its head, then turned and padded up the side of the mountain, as elegantly as if it were born to roam the rocky landscape.

Her heart raced, but not only from fear. She was in awe of the strange creature. Nothing in its posture was predatory or malevolent. It paused and turned to look at her with its white eyes. Somehow, she had the distinct impression it wanted her to follow.

Something tugged her toward the mountain, something strange and impossible. Not curiosity or need, nor a want to prove herself. It was something she didn't understand. Whatever it was, it made her take a step toward the waiting animal.

Fel climbed up the steep incline. Before long she began to pant, her lungs protesting at the exertion in a strange atmosphere. It required much more effort than climbing at the human colony on Herul. The creature carried on ahead of her, keeping a distance, but not letting her fall behind.

Finally, the animal stopped, and Fel gasped with relief. Her chest ached from the effort of breathing, and she pressed a hand to her head. She stood on a large, flat piece of ground halfway up the mountain. Some kind of moss and bracken crawled across the rock, overgrown and tangled.

"Why did you bring me here?"

The cat stared at her. Then, with a leap, it disappeared into the bushes. Fel threw her arms up in frustration and dropped them back to her sides. What was she doing? Maybe the creature hadn't wanted her to follow it at all. The atmosphere must be getting to her head. She went over to where the animal had disappeared and pushed aside the bush. There was no sign of the cat.

A glint of light caught Fel's eye. Beneath the plant, a rivulet of cloudy glass or crystal as wide as her hand ran through the rock, shimmering in the sunlight. As Fel pushed more bushes aside to get a closer look, her foot caught on a loose rock, and she jolted as her body fell out from under her. A rough slope scraped at her uniform as she slid down it, reaching out desperately for something to cling to, sure she was about to fall off a cliff edge. She crashed onto solid ground and came to a stop.

Fel groaned and rolled onto her knees, lifting her gaze to the oncoming storm. It seemed much closer than when she stood at the base of the mountain. She looked down at her time keeper, only to find the surface had cracked, obscuring the crucial information underneath. Her stomach lurched, and she looked back up at the looming dark clouds. Without the time keeper, she had no idea how soon the storm would hit.

She dragged herself up from the ground and dusted off her uniform. Dying in an extreme storm wasn't her idea of an adventure, but she had come so far. She must have at least another hour. It hadn't taken that long to climb partway up the small peak. After so many years of waiting for her opportunity to get to Earth, she was going to spend every minute she could on the planet's surface.

Turning back to the cliff face, she pushed aside vines covering the rock.

Fel frowned. That wasn't rock. She tugged down the vines and shoved them out of the way to reveal more of the unnatural material. It didn't look like a natural crystal, rather…manmade.

Pushing more leaves aside exposed the shape of a door. Fel grinned and placed a hand over her mouth. She had no idea what she'd found, but it had to be significant.

In a second, her excitement turned to uncertainty. She pressed the small button on the neck of her uniform. "Anyone there?"

Static crackled from the tiny speaker.

"Hello?"

The communicator signal must be blocked. She hesitated, torn between going back and going forward. Their team didn't know how long the next storm would last. It could carry on longer than their allotted time to investigate the planet, so this could be her only chance to explore her discovery.

The doorway rose several feet above her head. It was such an unusual material, appearing just like glass, but with a pearly sheen. What would it feel like to touch?

She removed her glove and placed a tentative hand on the surface. Pain burst inside Fel's chest, and she keeled forward, her head nearly touching the door. A crack echoed around her, and Fel snatched her hand away. She yelped and stumbled backward.

A jagged line ran from top to bottom of the glass and a red handprint marked the surface like glowing embers. The doorway shattered, and she flung her hands over her face to shield her eyes. When the tinkling of falling shards faded, she lowered her hands. The pieces of glass littering the ground melted and slithered in tendrils away from a gaping black hole in the rock.

Fel stared, open-mouthed. She put a hand to her chest, but the strange pain had dulled to an ache. What she just witnessed was unnatural and mystical. It made her want to bolt from the place and get the others, but something tugged her inside, like someone pulled an invisible string wrapped around her. Maybe it was the atmosphere making her chest constrict and churn.

She glided through the entrance. The same glass-like material covered the surface of the walls and domed roof of the cave. Looking up, she noticed the glass covered cracks in the rock. That must have been what she saw from above the cave before she fell.

A glass box stood in the center of the room. Fel crept forward to peer at it. Why would it be in an empty cave?

As she got closer, the contents of the box became clear. Her heart jolted. A face loomed at her on the other side of the glass. She stayed still, half-expecting a zombie to leap out of the container and attack her, but nothing happened.

Such a silly thought. Zombies only existed in fantasy stories. She edged closer to the stone dais.

The woman's eyes were closed. A strange, old-fashioned robe cloaked her. What was stranger was the perfect condition of the clothes, as if they were brand new. White hair hung around her smooth, pale face. The woman was untouched by time.

As Fel gazed up at the box, she realized it was a coffin standing on end, but the woman's face wasn't pale as if with death. It looked as if she had been placed inside only the day before. Fel even thought she saw a slight rise and fall of the chest swathed in thick fabric. Perhaps she had imagined it. Could the woman have been suspended in time through cryopreservation? The natural cave seemed more like a burial chamber than a scientific lab.

Fel spun around with her hands on her head as the enormity of what she had discovered dawned on her, but the cave was mostly empty. If she'd come across some kind of burial chamber, it didn't look anything like the ancient tombs they had learned about in History of Earth lessons. Her gaze fell on the coffin again. The woman didn't look at peace in death. If anything, her expression looked strained.

"When we followed your tracker, we expected to find a dead body, but instead we found this!"

Fel jumped and turned at the sound of the man's voice booming through the cave.

Davis, leader of their expedition, stomped inside. Orson, a scientist, scurried in after him with his permanently uninterested expression, although his eyes did widen a bit at the marvel that surrounded them. Their archaeologist, Janneke, followed behind, staring at the cave with mouth agape. They all wore identical navy uniforms to Fel.

Orson hesitated by the entrance, looking over his shoulder. "The storm is getting closer. We should be going back."

"This is amazing," Janneke whispered. She

approached part of the glass-covered wall. "With such a big hole in the side of the cave, it's a wonder this place has been preserved so well."

"Actually, there was—"

"It's not what we came here for, but I'm not going to complain," Davis said. "This is far more interesting than rock samples."

Fel clamped her mouth shut again. She had been about to explain about the glass door, but would have little hope getting enough words in before someone talked over her. Davis liked to walk all over everything he got involved in.

Davis strode to the coffin. "We need to get this thing loaded onto the ship before the storm comes. I'm not taking the risk it could be damaged or lost."

"Remove it?" Janneke shot up from where she knelt at the edge of the cavern, examining the glass that covered the rock. "We can't *remove* it. We have to evaluate the cave. This is my field. I need to take over from here."

"What about the storm?" Orson called from the entrance.

"No time for *evaluation*," Davis dismissed. "Right, let's get it on its back so we can carry it."

Fel stared at him in shock, then exchanged a glance with Janneke. She might only be a student, but even Fel knew that wasn't a good idea.

Davis levered the coffin down, and Janneke and Orson sprang forward to assist. They grasped the box with gloved hands, slowly lowering it. Fel started to protest, but bit her lip. They wouldn't listen to her anyway. Through the entrance, Fel could see the storm clouds getting closer.

"Careful," Janneke chastised. "It could be very fragile. We don't know how long it's been here. You have no idea what you're doing!"

"This thing's surprisingly light, considering the corpse inside," Davis said. "Two of us can manage this."

Fel didn't mention the uneasy feeling she had that the woman inside wasn't a corpse. They would dismiss it as ridiculous. Maybe she was being ridiculous.

Orson stepped forward to help, but Janneke moved in front of him. "If anyone's carrying this thing, it's going to be me. It's my job to ensure it doesn't get damaged."

Davis and Janneke lifted the coffin as if it weighed no more than a cardboard box. Fel's day had become strange when that cat appeared, but it was just getting even more bizarre. Perhaps her niggling feeling about the corpse wasn't so outlandish after all.

They made their way down the crumbling steps of the stone dais with the coffin and headed for the entrance. Fel looked around the empty cave one last time, her fists clenched at her sides. The discovery was hers, but she'd be lucky to be mentioned as part of the team. When she'd signed up, she hoped she might find an interesting natural sample. Instead, she discovered something far more spectacular, but was swept under the carpet as soon as the others entered.

Fel unclenched her fists. Her claim on the discovery didn't matter. Sharing it with humanity did. So long as that happened, she shouldn't care if it was her name at the top. She turned away from the cave and hurried after them.

As they hiked down the mountain, the wind picked up, buffeting them around. The trek through the forest was more difficult. Despite the lightness of the coffin, its shape became awkward as they maneuvered around the gigantic trees. Branches and thick, curling roots threatened to trip them and knock the fragile coffin out of their hands. Under the canopy, Fel had no idea how close the storm was, and the dense trees sheltered them from the wind. With their cumbersome load, they could be cutting it close to get back to the ship before it hit them full force.

"Careful!" Janneke yelped as Davis cut a corner around a tree and the edge of the coffin scraped the trunk.

Finally, they emerged from the forest into an open area of land. As soon as they left the shelter of the wood, the wind slammed into them.

Fel grabbed a tree trunk to steady herself while the others struggled to keep hold of the coffin. The cold blast sucked the air from her lungs, and Fel shut her watering eyes against the stinging wind.

Their spacecraft sat in the middle of the clearing, a small, rectangular landing ship with a sloped front. A red number 571 dominated the ship's side. Their pilot, Eider, stood in front of the open hatch at the back of the craft, clinging to the door supports to hold herself steady.

"You should have been back quarter of an hour ago!" she yelled over the wind whipping around them.

As Fel bent forward to push through the gusts, droplets of rain begin to fall.

Davis and Janneke carried the coffin up the ramp and into the safety of the ship. The rest of them followed, and Eider pressed a button to shut the hatch. Fel leaned against a wall and wiped rainwater from her face.

The hatch rose achingly slow as the wind and rain picked up outside. Water hammered down on the ship, sounding like thunder. Leaves and other debris swirled in a frenzy outside.

The hatch was nearly shut when a large branch flew toward them. Fel ducked instinctively as it crashed into the hatch with a bang. The door closed with a clank, and Fel breathed a sigh of relief. Leaves and twigs coated the metal floor.

"I need to get the ground anchors down. There's no way we can take off safely in this weather." Eider bolted away from them toward the cockpit.

The respite was brief. The ship lurched, nearly throwing Fel to the floor.

"We'll have to hope the anchors hold," Janneke said grimly. "If this storm is stronger than forecasted, they might not."

***

After what felt like hours, the storm faded enough for them to walk around the ship without being jostled by the buffeting wind. It was too stormy for them to release the ground anchors, and it would be at least an hour before it would be safe to take off.

Eider had rustled up some lunch, but Janneke had yet to appear from the holding bay where the coffin had been secured. As soon as the weather had died down enough, she'd been off to investigate their finding. Unsurprisingly, Fel, as the intern, was sent off to search for Janneke while their soup cooled.

"Janneke! Come and grab some food!"

Fel approached the holding bay and froze in the doorway. Janneke was slumped on the floor, her breath coming out in rasps. Red skin encircled her watering eyes, standing out from her sallow face. Wisps of brown hair clung to her sweating forehead. Her hands shook in her lap. Black discolored the skin of her fingers like frostbite and ran up her arms like dark veins across the skin, disappearing under her sleeves.

It was unlike anything Fel had seen before. Janneke had been fine an hour before. She knelt beside the archaeologist and started to reach out when she stopped herself. Whatever it was, it could be contagious.

"Pain," Janneke wheezed. "In my chest."

What should she do? She couldn't leave Janneke. As she tried to focus on the situation, she remembered the communicator. She pressed the button on her uniform with a quaking hand and tilted her head to speak into it. "Need..." She swallowed. "Need urgent assistance in the holding area...please come quickly."

She released the button and took a shuddery breath.

"It's all right, Janneke. The others are coming. You'll be okay."

She hoped. It dawned on her that she hadn't tested whether her communicator was working again.

Fel looked up and realized for the first time since she entered the room that the coffin stood on its end nearby, dominating the small space. The woman inside was like a specter watching over the room. Except she couldn't be watching. Her eyes were closed.

A few seconds later, the sound of hurried footsteps came from the corridor outside. Eider burst in, grabbing the doorway to slow her momentum. "What is it?"

"I…found her like this."

"Oh no…" Eider took a couple of steps forward, then stopped. She reached out a hand. "Fel, come here, there's a girl."

Fel hated it when Eider called her "girl," but in that moment, she couldn't care less. There was something reassuring but also terrifying in the older woman's tone.

Her adventure had taken a turn she could never have imagined, and in that moment, she was starting to wish she'd never signed up for the stupid practical module. Fel rose and backed away from Janneke.

"Did you touch her?"

"No."

Eider looked her in the eye. "Are you sure?"

"I didn't touch her."

"Can you stand?" Eider asked the archaeologist. "We need to get you to the med bay."

Janneke put a hand on the wall. "You don't need to pretend. I…know what needs to happen… You need to get me quarantined."

"What's happening?" Davis appeared behind Eider's shoulder.

The pilot blocked the door with her arm. "Don't come in. Take Fel back to the dining area. I'll sort out

Janneke."

Fel followed Davis, who probed her for answers, but she struggled to explain what had happened. Orson's scrawny face pinched with concern when they reached the dining area, and he put his spoon back in his soup. Fel sank down into a chair and let Davis explain. She felt drained, like a weight was dragging her down. She couldn't think, couldn't process what was happening.

Although humanity's scientific capabilities were advanced, no one was able to eradicate illness completely. Contagious diseases, however, had been stopped a long time ago. Whatever was wrong with Janneke, it wasn't familiar. It must have come from this planet. Fel rubbed her temples.

When Eider returned, the pilot's face was pale and her brows were arched in a frown. "She'd felt fine. Then she started touching that blasted coffin. It was that, I'm sure of it. I had a strange feeling as soon as you brought it on board."

"Don't be ridiculous," Davis snapped. "This isn't a sarcophagus cursed by ancient Egyptians."

"It could have been contaminated with some kind of virus or radiation," Orson suggested. "I would need to examine it…"

"No one else is to touch that coffin," Eider commanded.

Davis shrugged a shoulder and pointed at the window. "It could have come from out there. Maybe this planet isn't as safe as we thought. We have no evidence to suggest it came from the coffin."

"Then why are none of the rest of you sick?" Eider pointed out. "Janneke is the only one to touch the coffin. The rest of you were wearing gloves."

A sudden dread enveloped Fel. She wrung her clammy hands together. She hadn't touched the coffin, but she'd put her hand on the strange glass door of the cave. If it was something to do with the coffin and the tomb, would she fall sick too?

Then another unwelcome thought invaded her mind. If the illness had come from the cave, then it was her fault. She discovered it. If Janneke died…

"Pull up your sleeves," Eider demanded.

"You actually want to check us?" Davis said.

"Yes," Eider snapped. "Come on. Her hands and arms were black."

Fel shuffled her feet and toyed with the edge of her cuff. The others grumbled as they pulled up their sleeves to reveal normal, healthy skin. Eider turned to Fel, and Fel reluctantly did the same. She tried not to breathe a sigh of relief at the sight of her ordinary skin.

Orson shook his head. "Whatever it is might take longer to have an effect on different people."

Fel's relief deflated. If he was right, there would be no way to know if she was infected. She had no idea what the others might do if they knew she had touched the coffin. They might quarantine her too, or who knew what else if they became desperate.

She could feel the rising tension in the room and had an uneasy feeling about the situation. The others gave each other narrow stares as they rolled their sleeves back down. Davis folded his arms across his chest and took a couple of unsubtle steps away from the rest of them.

Doubt gnawed at her. If she didn't say anything and she was infected with something, she could pass it on to the others.

Davis tapped his fingers against his arm. "We should get off this planet and go back to the main ship before it gets worse."

"Don't you think it'll look bad if we return without the surface samples we were supposed to be collecting and with a dead woman in a coffin instead?" Orson pointed out.

Eider threw her hands up in the air. "I don't think that's our biggest problem right now!" She took a breath. "I need to check the ship for storm damage before we can fly anyway. So you might as well go and get what you need. If this sickness is coming from the planet, not the coffin, then we might be able to learn about it from the samples." She stalked off down the corridor.

Nobody seemed to have much appetite for what was left of their lunches. Orson and Davis went looking for samples, leaving Fel alone in the dining area staring at the abandoned plates. Normally, the others would have had her do the washing up, but that was probably at the bottom of their priority list.

Fel wandered away from the dining space, considering seeing if Eider needed a hand, even though she knew nothing about engineering and spaceships. Halfway down the passageway, something made her change direction and head toward the holding bay.

Why did she feel so impulsive? It was as though something invisible was guiding her again, just like at the mountain. Except this time there was no cat to follow. She even wondered if she'd imagined that animal. Maybe she was sick and hallucinating.

The holding bay was off limits, and she shouldn't *want* to go there, since it was where she had found the sick Janneke, but she couldn't seem to help herself. The door to the holding area opened, and Fel stepped inside. Nothing had changed in the last half an hour. Her feet glided across the floor toward the coffin. There was something eerie about the woman inside. How it looked like she had only died yesterday, even though the coffin must have been there a long time. How, it even seemed to Fel, like she could be alive. Trapped even. Waiting to be set free…

Fel stood right in front of the coffin. She was the same height as the motionless woman, and there was something familiar about the contours of her face. She reached out to touch the glass.

~ III ~

Melantha breathed. A rattling gasp. Something had jolted her out of the sleep state. That was all she knew for sure. As her body awoke, she felt the glass at her back. Her eyelids snapped open, and she blinked at the harsh light. She wasn't in the cave anymore. Where was she?

She clutched at her chest. It didn't feel right. The past was a hazy fog she couldn't penetrate. As she blinked, she saw a blurred figure staring at her from the other side of the clear glass.

Melantha reached out stiff arms, pressing them against the walls of the box. She had to get out. Her hands found the wall in front of her, and it swung open. Desperate to get out of the claustrophobic space, she blundered out and swayed, stumbling into a wall. The room was still out of focus. When her eyes adjusted, she saw the gaping, horrified expression of a girl.

"Where…am I?"

"On our ship…we're still on Earth…"

Everything was gray. The walls. The ceiling. Strange triangular markings covered the floor. Had she stumbled into a ritual? A strip of glaring lights ran in a line around the middle of the walls.

Melantha spun round. The glass coffin stood empty. She remembered her sentencing. The punishment. The cave sealed. Spending a long time alone in darkness, and finally working out how to fall into a sleep state. She wasn't in the cave anymore.

"What did you do?" Melantha croaked.

"I…I…I…touched it."

Vague memories swirled in Melantha's mind. When she tried to grasp one, it drifted away. The girl hadn't screamed and run away yet. Some distant part of her mind made her feel like the girl should be fleeing, like that had happened many times before, but Melantha couldn't understand why.

"How did you open the coffin?" Words floated in her mind, the last she had heard—*the curse of this glass is that you shall remain entombed in this coffin, immortal as you are, until your soul is no longer dark.* It shouldn't be possible for the coffin to open, unless the curse had been broken.

Melantha put a hand to her breastbone, realizing why it hadn't felt right as soon as she had awoken. No soulbeat thrummed under her hand. She had forgotten. Her soul had been removed as part of the curse. The soul was an essential part of a witch. Without it, she was hollow, like a shell. It was a strange, uncomfortable sensation. She curled her fingers around the material of her cloak.

"I don't know." The girl seemed to have regained her composure, but her gaze was fixed on Melantha, and her body was still twisted toward the door like she was ready to flee.

"How long have I been in that coffin?"

"I…don't know that…either…" The girl's voice quivered.

Melantha closed her eyes, trying to remember, but it was like her mind had been wiped clean. She recalled little from before the ceremony cursing her. She didn't even remember what she had done that was bad enough for her to be given such a punishment, and she dreaded what it might be.

She opened her eyes. "I think I've been in there a long time."

The girl swallowed and nodded slowly. She wore some kind of tight, full-body clothing made from deep blue material. Black hair stuck out in messy angles, and her dark brown eyes still had a shocked, dazed look.

"Who are you?" the girl asked.

"I am Melantha, of the Glacela clan…" She trailed

off, suddenly uncertain. "*Formerly…*of the Glacela clan."

The girl took in a sharp breath. "Right. I'm Fel…"

Melantha remembered one other thing. Magic. Even without her soul, she could still feel it in her bones. *How could I have been so oblivious?* Melantha could sense it now, her own soulbeat, its unique rhythm, beating from inside Fel. Without having to think about what to do, she reached out her mind to her soul.

"Are you okay?" Fel asked. "You look like you're in pain."

Melantha closed her eyes. As her soul was inside Fel, a deep invisible connection ran between them. Melantha followed that thread, using her magic to sense the pathways, until she stumbled into Fel's memories. Images flashed through her mind, seen through Fel's eyes, and the young woman's emotions washed over her.

Earth abandoned long ago. Human colonies spreading across the galaxy. One of these colonies Fel calls home.

Her father sits by the window, his shoulders drooping. Anxiety flutters inside Fel's chest. He looks more forlorn than usual. He speaks, explains how her mother died. There were no complications during the birth, she was completely healthy, but she died the moment Fel was born.

Her father pauses in his recollection and looks at her. Fel collapses into a chair, running a hand through her tangled hair. She waits for her father to continue.

It wasn't the first time, he says. The same thing happened to her mother's father. In just the same way, when Fel's mother was born, he died.

Fel's father looks up at his daughter with sad, dark eyes and says it's like the family is cursed.

Melantha's eyes stung with Fel's tears, and she pushed on to a different memory, away from those strong emotions.

Sitting bored in a History of Earth lesson. Gazing at the globe projected onto the wall at the front of the room. Intense longing, a need to make her dream of visiting Earth a reality, like it is a matter of life and death…

There were so many memories, but Melantha had seen enough, and she pulled away from Fel's mind. She curled her hand into a fist. Fel's family *was* cursed.

The last voice she had heard entered her mind again—*your soul will depart your body, transferred to that of another, and pass through the generations until it returns to the light, and the curse will be broken.*

"I have been in that coffin for thousands of years," she murmured.

"How…?" Fel ran a hand through her already messy hair, just as she had done in the memory.

Melantha fixed her gaze on the girl in front of her. "And you opened it."

"Hopefully I'm not going to regret that." Fel held up her hands and smiled weakly.

"How did you find the cave?" The emotions Melantha had felt while experiencing Fel's memories were powerful, driven by a magic Fel had no understanding of. Melantha was certain Fel's desire to visit Earth must be connected to her soul and the curse.

"I don't know," Fel answered. "I just felt…drawn to it. I can't explain it."

Melantha nodded. "My soul was drawn to it—to me. The darkness must have gone from my soul. That's the only way the curse could have broken and this lid opened."

"There's a curse? Is that why Janneke is ill? After everything I've seen today, it wouldn't surprise me."

"Who?"

"Janneke, she's our archaeologist. She touched the coffin, and now she's really ill and we don't know what's wrong with her."

Melantha turned toward the coffin. "The glass is cursed."

"Can you do something?" Fel's eyes met hers,

pleading. "Can you heal her?"

"When you opened the coffin and the curse was broken, her illness should have ended."

"Let's go see." Fel dove for the door and it slid open of its own accord. "Come on."

Melantha hesitated. The girl seemed unusually trusting. She wasn't horrified to see a witch thousands of years old awaken. Melantha's soul, trapped inside this human, must have something to do with it.

With a deep breath, she followed Fel into a strangely cold corridor. Melantha struggled to keep up; her limbs were rusty from being still for so long. Then, an image burst into her mind, and she staggered.

A barren field. Bodies litter the ground, and fires fill the air with smoke. An injured soldier tries to crawl away from her, but she points her wand at him, the tip glowing blue. A flash of magic strikes him, and he stops moving.

The image faded, and Melantha reached out for the wall to steady herself. That memory—she was certain that's what the vivid vision had been—couldn't have been Fel's. But Melantha couldn't have been in that field of ghosts.

She looked over her shoulder at the door the coffin lay behind. Her mind was patchy, but she remembered the punishment. It was only for those who had committed atrocities. Had she?

"What are you doing?" Fel asked. "It's not much further."

Melantha pried herself away from the wall and followed Fel.

A village on fire. Bloodstained swords. A woman scrambling away, pleading with a broken voice. Soot and dirt covers her crying face and the hands that cling to her screaming child. She points her wand at the pair. They transform into black glass then shatter into fragments at her feet.

Melantha clasped her head in her hands. So much death and pain, and she had caused it. The farther she walked from the coffin, the more images of her past returned. She didn't remember being that person, but she knew she had been. She had killed them. All of them. She had been empty and beyond any kind of humanity.

"I can't. I'm sorry." She took a couple of steps back. Maybe if she returned to the coffin, the memories would go away. She would rather sleep for eternity than remember the abomination she had been all those thousands of years ago. "It's too much. I need to go back in the coffin."

"We need to check on Janneke. You might be able to help her. You know more about this planet than we do."

Melantha lowered her hands. The invasion of images had stopped. "I will come with you, and then I will return to the coffin." She wanted to help the girl, but would more memories return the farther she went from the coffin?

A shudder passed over Melantha. How had she done such terrible things? How had she not cared?

"Why would you want to go back in there?"

Without answering, Melantha followed Fel into another room. The narrow space contained two beds and strange objects Melantha had never seen before. A large glass window spanned one wall, but it was nothing like the witchglass she was familiar with. Strange blue symbols moved up and down one side of the surface. On the other side, a woman lay prostate on a bed. Her face bore signs of sickness, and her hands had turned black.

Fel went to the window. "She looks worse. Why is she worse?"

Melantha stared at the dying woman. "I don't understand. The curse must not be broken."

"Curses." Fel snorted. "Can't believe I actually believed you. Curses. It's not a curse. It's some kind of sickness."

"I have seen it before..."

A witch lying in a tent, sick and dying from accidentally touching cursed glass. Deep, complete sorrow unlike anything she'd felt before, unlike anything she would ever feel again, except in the memory of that moment. Mixing with the sorrow are anger and shame. The fury burns inside her. The emotions are overwhelming. Guilt eats her from the inside, and rage burns her soul.

Melantha's head spun. She covered her eyes with her hands. The recollection hit her like a wave, tears threatening to slip from her eyes. Pain came with it, but also the agony of forgetting. Such intense pain and sorrow for someone she knew was close to her, but she couldn't remember who. This memory wasn't like the others—the ones with images of war and destruction. With complete certainty, Melantha knew the image of the dying witch had happened first, before her soul became dark.

Blinking back the tears, she tried to push away those thoughts and focus on the room around her.

Melantha returned her gaze to the sick woman and shook her head. "Why would the coffin lid open? Unless it opened with the presence of my soul inside you, but the curse is not broken."

"What did you just say? About your soul?" Fel turned away from the glass.

"As part of the curse, my soul was removed and cast into that of another, to be passed on through the generations until all the darkness left it."

"But—"

The door to the room opened, and Melantha sprung away from it. Her hand went beneath her robes before she remembered she no longer had her wand. It had been destroyed when she was captured.

A woman entered and jumped back at the sight of Melantha.

"What...? How...?"

"The coffin opened," Fel babbled. "She said her name is Melantha. She's been in there for thousands of years."

The woman reached into her clothes and pulled out a

strange metal object, pointing it at Melantha, who stared at it and didn't move. Was it some kind of wand? It had a long point to it, with an odd handle.

Standing at the edge of a pool, wand in hand, the blending of wood and black glass so seamless in its elegant pattern. Her wand.

"Wait, Eider." Fel stepped toward the other woman. "She knows about Janneke's illness."

"Fel! You just thought you'd let a zombie or mummy or whatever this thing is run free around my ship?" Eider's tone was filled with anger, but her pinched face betrayed her confusion and fear.

"I am not dead. I've been asleep in that coffin for thousands of years."

They didn't understand what she was talking about. They clearly hadn't come across any other witches. She couldn't sense any witch souls other than the one inside Fel—her own. Not even her sister's—Ethleda's—the soulbeat that she had always been able to hear, no matter how much land separated them. The realization was like a stab of magic. She was alone.

Eider jerked the strange wand and stepped away from the doorway. "Go that way. Now."

"I don't think she wants to hurt us," Fel said.

"And how do you know that?" Eider retorted.

"I just…know. I'm sure."

"Oh, you are?" Eider said dryly. "That's incredibly reassuring."

Melantha wanted to add something to make them understand but had no idea what to say. How could she explain that her soul was inside Fel and that was why Fel knew Melantha didn't mean them harm? They were deeply connected. It was clear the world she knew was long gone, and these people had no concept of the society Melantha had belonged to.

Moving slowly, Melantha stepped through the doorway. "I just want to go back to the coffin."

Bodies. Death. Disease. It came over her in waves, relentless. She wanted to know who she was, but ached for the memories to stop, ached to not remember the terrible things she had done. Knowing terrified her.

"Get the others," Eider ordered Fel.

The woman kept the object in her hands fixed on Melantha. From the way she held it, Melantha guessed it must be some kind of weapon, unlike any she'd seen before.

Melantha did as the woman asked and followed her directions to another room. It contained a table, chairs, and the remains of a half-eaten meal.

"Sit down." Eider gestured to one of the chairs with her weapon.

Melantha did as she was told.

"Who are you?"

"Melantha, formerly of the Glacela witch clan. I wish to return to the coffin."

"Witch clan? What—? Never mind. How are you not dead? Were you preserved? Where are the rest of your people?"

"I'm immortal."

"Right, of course you are."

The door opened, and Fel came in with two men, who blanched when they saw Melantha. One swayed as if he might faint, while the other blinked repeatedly as if he couldn't believe what he was seeing. Then his expression turned into a grin and he clapped his hands together.

"This is spectacular," the grinning man said. Melantha's eye was drawn to a name stitched on his uniform. *Davis.* "This expedition will be famous!"

"If we can even get off this planet," Eider grunted.

The other man groaned. "Please, no more bad news." *Orson,* his label read.

"There's something wrong with the ship," Eider said. "I don't understand it. It's not storm damage."

"Can't you fix it?" Davis snapped. "What's the point

in having an engineer who's better at making soup than fixing ships?"

Eider glared at him, her weapon still trained on Melantha. "Why don't *you* try it? You don't even have any qualifications warranting your presence on this ship."

"Hey, I—"

"What's wrong with the ship?" Fel interrupted.

"I don't know. Half the electronics don't work for some reason. The engine won't run properly, it keeps cutting out. And I found some kind of strange oil…"

"Don't say you touched that stuff," Orson muttered. "This isn't good."

Eider indicated the streaks on her clothes.

"The curse is spreading to the ship," Melantha said. In her past, whoever she had been, she had caused unimaginable suffering. Even now she was causing pain; the curse upon her was bringing problems to these people.

"What curse?" Orson said.

"The one on the coffin, the one on me," Melantha answered. "The only way to fix the ship and heal Janneke is to break it."

"This is nonsense," Davis spat. "What century are you from? Are you some kind of pagan?"

"I'm a witch, actually, formerly of the Glacela clan."

"I correct myself—we've picked up a nutter."

Melantha glowered at him. These people didn't understand. She was a relic of the past now.

"We should listen to her," Fel put in. She moved closer to Melantha.

"Don't go near her," Eider said. "She could be dangerous."

"We're going to be stranded here." Orson sank to the floor with his head in his hands. "We're going to die here."

"Don't be stupid, man," Davis said.

Everyone's voices rose, fighting to be heard over

each other, mixing in a cacophony that made it impossible to tell who said what.

"I can't fix this ship!"

"What are we going to do about her?"

"Put her back in the coffin!"

"I want to go back in the coffin!"

Screams of pain. Tortured faces. Blood. She had done so many unforgiveable things, and she couldn't remember why.

"Maybe if we kill her the curse will break."

"There is no curse!"

"We're going to die here."

"Let's kill her!"

"No, don't! She can help us!" Fel's high voice penetrated the chaos.

So much death and pain. Melantha rocked back and forth in the chair. She should die. They should have killed her all that time ago. Then she wouldn't be bringing pain to these people. She didn't deserve to live. Then she wouldn't have to live with these ghosts of atrocities she didn't even remember committing. She wouldn't have to live alone.

Staring out through the glass coffin at Ethleda. Pain written across her sister's face. Then she'd felt nothing. Now she felt everything. Her soul had been so dark when she was sealed in the coffin that she had been numb to all. Why hadn't she said anything to her sister in that last moment?

"How long before the rest of us get sick?" Orson said. "It started when we brought that coffin on board!"

"So we take the coffin and her off the ship," Eider suggested.

"This is our prize. My ticket to fame!"

Fel took another step toward Melantha. "We can't go anywhere until we fix the craft."

"I can't fix it if I don't know what's wrong with it!" Eider exclaimed.

"Listen to me!" Fel yelled. "She can help us. I know it! Just listen to her!"

"I've had enough of talking." Eider took a step closer to Melantha with the weapon. Her skin was becoming sallow and her eyes were red like Janneke's. The strange oil she had found must have something to do with the curse, Melantha was sure of it. Eider, like Janneke, was dying.

Eider's hand shook.

"Eider, don't. We need to stay calm and talk this through," Fel pleaded.

"We're going to die here," Orson moaned.

Davis stepped toward Eider. "Don't you think it'll look a bit suspicious if we take her out of here with a bullet wound in her?"

"Once she's dead, we get her and that coffin off this ship," Eider snapped. "It started when you brought it on board. This is your fault." She swung her weapon toward Davis.

"All right." Davis took a step back and held up his hands. "Let's not rush into anything. Just put the gun down and we can discuss this calmly."

Eider aimed the weapon at Melantha. "She's going to attack us. She probably put this curse on us."

"It's me who is cursed," Melantha said. They weren't listening.

Anger and frustration boiled inside her. She tried to contain it and took a deep breath. The power in her blood and bones was beginning to hum, threatening to break loose. "The glass in the coffin carries the curse. Killing me won't help. Only breaking the curse will."

"Maybe killing you will break it." Eider wrapped her free hand around the bottom of the gun, gripping it so her knuckles turned white.

Out of the corner of her eye, Melantha could see Fel taking subtle steps toward them from the right. Eider's finger twitched.

Fel moved in front of her, hands outstretched. A bang echoed around the small room, making Melantha flinch. She waited for some kind of magic and pain. A flash of white light engulfed the room. Melantha scrunched her eyes shut.

When she opened them, the light had faded to a glow that hovered at Fel's breastbone. Melantha didn't understand what had happened. What was the strange weapon? It had made a hole in Fel's chest. A white light—Melantha's soul—glowed from it. As she watched, the hole began to heal, muscle and skin repairing itself, covering the beating soul.

The curse of this glass is that you shall remain entombed in this coffin, immortal as you are, until your soul is no longer dark.

"You broke the curse," Melantha whispered. "My soul is no longer dark."

Melantha.

She turned toward the voice. A ghostly woman stood in the corner of the room, like a faded and colorless painting. Her pearly gown hung in elegant waves to the floor. A band of twisted witchglass circled her head—the diadem of the High Witch. Melantha sensed, for the first time since she had woken, another witch's soulbeat. Not just any soulbeat. *Ethleda.*

I knew you could do it. I believed. Your soul is pure again.

"But…how? I don't understand."

Melantha looked around the room. Time had stopped. The others stared at Fel in a mixture of shock and wonder. Eider had begun to lower the gun. Davis was lunging toward them. Orson still cowered at the edge of the room.

Melantha moved around Fel to face her. She could see it now. The eyes level with hers were an exact mirror of her own. She put a hand to Fel's chest and felt her own unique soulbeat.

It has taken thousands of years, but over time, your soul has become less dark as it has passed through the generations. With each person it passed through, it became a little lighter, until it reached Fel.

She was the last in the chain. She made your soul pure. The coffin opened at her soul's presence, with her touch, but now the curse has been broken.

"How? How was she completely pure?"

Ethleda smiled. *Fel was presented with a difficult situation. She was too shy to speak out against her comrades before. Now, in the most dire of situations, she tried stop the inevitable escalation. When the time came, she had the courage to do the right thing. Pure doesn't mean totally faultless. It is impossible. To a witch, pure means being able to defeat your demons and do the right thing, to be the best person you can be. In this case, Fel made her voice stronger, and ultimately chose to sacrifice herself, knowing you were the person whom—she hoped—could help her shipmates and end the curse on the ship.*

Melantha took a shuddering breath. Her past was still a haze at the back of her mind, but her present and future felt just as muddled, like she was detached from it.

"What happened to you? And all the other witches?"

There is all the time in the world for you to catch up on the last few thousand years. As time changed, our place in the world changed.

Melantha didn't understand her sister's cryptic answer, but it wasn't her most pressing concern at that moment. "What happens now?"

You can join us, in our ethereal state. Your soul will live on in Fel until her human life ends, and then it will return to you so you can be at peace.

"Then? When my soul returns. Then will I remember?"

If you want to. Ethleda's voice sounded uncertain.

Melantha's lips quirked into a smile. "It was you who told me once that what you have done in the past is part of you, but what you do next makes you who you are."

You didn't listen then.

"But I understand now." Melantha's gaze fell upon Fel, frozen in time in front of her. "What about the others? The ones who have the glass sickness?"

Healed with the breaking of the curse. Look.

The healthy glow of Eider's cheeks had returned, and the skin around her eyes was no longer red.

"Will they be okay?" She had experienced Fel's memories through her eyes, had felt her emotions, and as a consequence felt a connection she could not deny.

Do you want to see?

A tingling sensation passed all across Melantha's body. She looked down to find her hand transparent and jerked with surprise. Was she like Ethleda now?

A scuffing sound made her lift her gaze. Time had unfrozen. Davis skidded to a stop mid-lunge. The gun fell from Eider's hand and clattered on the floor. Fel stared down at the hole in her uniform and the smooth, healed skin underneath.

"But…I shot you…" Eider stammered. "I…I shot you. What's happening?" She ran a hand down her face. "Fel…I'm so sorry. I don't know why I did that."

Fel raised her head. "You're better!"

"What?" Eider rubbed her eyes.

"You look normal again," Fel said.

Davis put a hand on Eider's arm and turned her to face him. "She's right. Your eyes. Your hands. They're fine."

Eider held her palms up and stared at them.

Orson uncurled from his position in the corner of the room. "What's going on?"

"I have no idea," Eider whispered.

"Where's the witch?" Davis looked around the room.

It dawned on Melantha that they could no longer see her—she was an ethereal ghost like Ethleda. The others spun in circles in confusion. Fel, however, turned and looked Melantha right in the eye. Her lips quirked into a smile. While the others were still stupefied, Fel raised her hand and gave a little wave. Melantha returned the gesture.

Does she know? Melantha asked.

She might have been frozen in time, but she heard our

conversation. Ethleda took a step back. *Come now.*

Melantha reached out for her sister, and the room filled with light.

Princess and the Frog

Renee Frey

The locket slipped from Zirailla's fingers, tumbling over itself as it rushed toward the deep water of the well.

"No!"

In an instant, the dark depths of the well faded and the past resurfaced, trapping her in the worst memory ever.

"No!" she cried, struggling against the chains binding her tiny wrists. The blond soldier holding the chains jerked her back.

A jeer resonated through the crowd.

"Kill her!"

"Off with her head!"

Zirailla's lower lip trembled. Why did these pale strangers hate her family?

Her mother was led forward by another soldier, this one with fiery hair. Despite shredded clothing barely covering her body, Zirailla's mother held her head high.

"Mommy!" Zirailla screamed.

But her mother didn't turn back. Guards gripped her elbows so tightly that their knuckles turned white. She didn't fight them, didn't struggle. She kept taking each step, deliberate and strong, climbing the piecemeal staircase up and away from her daughter and the other prisoners.

Zirailla looked around, wondering where the other Tukolairans were. A sea of angry pink-skinned soldiers clad in cold blue uniforms filled the courtyard.

They can't just stand by and let these barbarians

slaughter us!

Her mother stood on a hastily built set of scaffolding, chin raised in pride. Zirailla reached for her mother, but the soldier yanked the chain again, dragging her to the ground.

"Kneel, queen!"

Zirailla's mother shook her head.

The soldier commanding her twisted his mouth in anger. "Then eat dirt!" He raised his right hand and struck her with a blow so strong the queen's head whipped around and back, and she fell backward onto the wooden platform.

A faint outline of her mother's face winked at Zirailla as the locket fell, open now. She reached out with her hands, just like on that hateful day. And just like then, she caught only air.

"NO!" Zirailla clawed toward her mother with both hands.

The angry soldier grabbed the queen's head and slammed it onto the waiting stump. He held out his other hand. One of his sycophants handed him an axe.

Tears welled up in Zirailla's eyes. She strained her eyes searching the crowd for someone, anyone to help.

Where is Father?

She clenched her fists. The king had gone with the soldiers to defend the city, leaving the palace and all its inhabitants open to attack from the unknown invaders.

"Death to the Wog's queen!" the crowd jeered. They filled the square, spilling from the surrounding walkways and windows.

Zirailla looked once more toward the palace, a mere sprint away, hoping against hope that someone would emerge to stop this madness.

The crowd hushed as the soldier raised the axe. An eerie silence overtook the square.

Zirailla's eyes locked with her mother's.

"I love you," *her mother mouthed.*

The axe came down with a thud.

The locket fell into the water below with a plop. Zirailla's last memory of her drowned in the still water of the well.

A trembling overtook Zirailla's body.

"Not again," she whispered.

Every time she had a flashback, her body shook with the rush of adrenaline afterward. Clenching her fists, Zirailla tried to fight the oncoming shudders—and lost. She brought her knees up and curled her body around, gripping her legs.

You're here, in a garden, not in the town square. She tried to do what the doctor suggested and name five things.

"Impala lilies—pink and red. A thrush—brown with yellow beak. The sun—bright and *way* too hot. A well—old and unused."

Not even a bucket next to it so I can try to fish the locket out. It's gone—she's gone—forever.

Zirailla bit her lip. *I will not lose myself in memories again. Focus!*

"Are you all right?"

The hairs on Zirailla's neck raised. She jumped to her feet.

"Who said that? Who's there?" She looked this way and that, searching.

"Down here, Princess."

Zirailla scanned through the grass and vines. All she saw was a tiny tree frog hanging from a bleeding heart flower.

"I must be going crazy," she whispered.

The frog's chin bulged. Then, defying reason, it opened its mouth and spoke. "Then what would that make me?"

Zirailla's eyes widened. "What?"

The frog's red eyes turned down. "Yes, I am a frog. Yes, I can talk." His gaze found Zirailla's, vertical pupils boring into hers. Zirailla fought a shiver.

"Now, can we stop discussing me and get to your problem?"

The locket. Zirailla glanced back at the well, shoulders

slumped. It was probably gone for good.

"My locket fell in. The clasp must have broken."

The frog hopped off the flower and sat next to her. "Surely you can afford another trinket, Princess?"

I wish… There was no extra money in the kingdom—even ten years after the invasion and subsequent looting. But Zirailla was not about to admit to a frog that she was impoverished.

She shook her head. "It's not the same. That one had a picture of my mother in it. The only picture of her I have."

"She can sit for another portrait. Please stop crying."

Something cold and clammy touched her hand. Startled, Zirailla's gaze shot down to notice the frog sitting on her hand, patting it with his front foot. The large knobby toes were slightly sticky, pulling the skin a bit.

"I'm sorry, Frog. I—I can't. Mother can't sit for another portrait. She's been dead for ten years." *And I couldn't do anything to stop it. I had to stand there and watch.* Her palms grew clammy. *No! No more flashes! Not today!*

With a shrug, the frog said, "Then I guess I will have to fetch it for you."

***

Frog hopped over to the well, climbed onto the lip, and eyed the deep drop into the dark water below. *Piece of cake.* He launched himself down. *Blast, this water is cold!* Reaching for a tendril of magic, he created a soft glowing orb, making sure to keep it below his body so the princess above couldn't see it. After a moment's search, he saw the glittering gold of a chain. There it was. Grabbing the necklace, he doused the light and swam back to the surface. He emerged from the water, wet and shivering, but triumphant, with the locket wrapped around him.

"My locket! You found it!" Zirailla gently lifted the locket off the frog. She grabbed the hem of her purple dress and dabbed at the picture. "How can I ever thank you?"

Now was the time to strike. Frog tried to conceal his glee.

"Princess, as a thank you, I would like to be your companion. None of the other frogs here talk, and I am so lonely. Could you see it in your heart to grant me a place by your side?"

Her hazel eyes narrowed slightly. "My companion? But wouldn't that be—that is to say, wouldn't you feel, well—"

His stomach did a flip flop. He had to get into the palace. "I would like nothing better, kind and beautiful Princess." Frog imitated a courtly bow, amazed he didn't fall into a tangled heap of limbs. He peeked up at her expression.

The ploy worked. The princess fought to contain a giggle.

"Of course, my friend. For you, anything." She pulled braided strands of hair to the side and re-clasped her necklace, then held out a hand for him to hop on. He obliged.

"What is your name, new friend? Or would you like me to call you Frog?"

As if I would tell her my name. "Frog is fine. And you are?"

She smiled, pearly white teeth popping from beneath full cherry lips. "Princess Zirailla, but you can call me Zilly. That's what my father calls me."

The frog climbed up to her shoulder to get a better view. She smelled of lilac and sandalwood. "Princess Zilly. Nice to meet you. Tell me, do you come to the garden often?"

As the princess chatted on about her daily habits, Frog only paid her marginal attention. He was still gloating about his successful entry into Tukolaire's royal house.

The opportunity had been too good to pass up. Zirailla had been daydreaming and tossing stones in the old well. One time when she leaned over, all he had to do was release a puff of magic. A puff was about all he could manage in his current state, but it was enough. The clasp on the locket had opened, and the weight of the charm had pulled the necklace off the girl and into the well.

Calm the girl, check. Retrieve the locket, double-check. Get to the palace to find its weakness—next on the list.

"So how is it you can talk?"

Zirailla's question interrupted Frog's self-congratulation. His mind raced, trying to think of a plausible explanation. *Well, when you need to lie, tell the truth—just not all of it.*

He pulled his lips back in a froggy imitation of a smile. "I was trapped by an evil wizard and transformed. Something about not fulfilling a quest or other. Now, I'm stuck like this for at least another, oh, year, I guess."

She nodded, seeming to accept the tale. "And how do you break the curse?" She arched an eyebrow and added with a drip of sarcasm, "True love's kiss?"

Frog rolled his eyes. "Please, as if an evil wizard would do something that cliché."

Zilly laughed. "Well, then, how?"

Frog stared off toward the mountains in the east. "I wish I knew."

He knew, of course. He would have to finish what his father came here to do ten years ago—destroy this girl and her family. Something twinged in Frog's stomach, but he ignored it. *Probably ate a bad fly.*

***

King Themba of Tukolaire reread the parchment a tenth time. He still couldn't find what he needed—a loophole to get out of bartering his daughter's hand in marriage for financial and political freedom from House Dioulasso. The letter shook in his hand.

…we find it necessary to demand repayment of the borrowed amount within the year. News of Les Conquerants amassing just beyond the borders cast doubt upon your ability to make good on the terms of the loan. We regret to inform you that failure to honor these terms will cost you our alliance and support of your rule.

Themba crumbled up the letter. Surely they knew he hadn't the capital to repay them. He was still rebuilding the infrastructure from the first invasion of Les Conquerants. The invasion that had cost him the love of his life—and nearly his child as well. *But when has House Dioulasso, the richest in the ruling class, cared about anything other than advancing their own prospects?* Themba should just offer them Zilly's hand, and with it the promise of the throne, and be done with it.

The gentle swishing of skirts brought the object of his thoughts into view. Zirailla stopped just inside the door, fussing with her hair. *Probably playing with her locket again.*

Themba sighed. He wished his daughter every happiness, but no matter what he tried, he couldn't seem to cure her of the persistent melancholia that shadowed her since the invasion. He had consulted healers, sent out across the continent for physicians and spirit masters, but no one had been able to help. And then there were the shakes she got every time something happened to remind her of the invasion…

Themba rose and walked to his daughter. He cleared his throat. Zirailla froze.

"Zilly—so glad to see you. We…we need to talk."

Zirailla took her time turning around. She dropped into a perfunctory curtsy. "Yes, Father?"

"I received a missive from House Dioulasso today." The scratching of parchment on his palm reminded him that he still held the letter in his hand. "I know I promised you I would wait, but I can't delay any longer."

Zilly gasped. "No! No! Papa, you prom—"

"—Silence!"

Zirailla's mouth closed. Her fists clenched her skirts.

Themba fought off another sigh. *Why did life have to be so difficult?*

"I'm sorry, Zilly. I have no choice. I must solicit a suitor for you, and soon."

Zirailla's chin quivered.

Themba continued, "I wish it were different, dear. But Les Conquerants' ships were sighted off the coast last week."

Zirailla's eyes widened, and all the color drained from her face. "No," she whispered, the quiver spreading to her shoulders.

"I'm so sorry, my dear." Themba rushed to his daughter and swept her up in a tight hug. "I wish things were different. But they aren't."

Zirailla shoved her way out of his embrace and ran down the hall.

Themba shook his head at the guard's questioning expression. Nothing but time helped when she got like this. He returned to his seat and smoothed open the parchment. He gestured to a nearby footman.

"Fetch me parchment and ink, please." The footman bowed and strode off.

Marriage to House Dioulasso was the best option. *If only Zirailla would see it, and stop fighting me.*

***

Frog clung to Princess Zirailla's shoulder with everything in him. Bopping and flailing, he fought the urge to call out to her. No need for any of the passing servants to question where his voice came from. When she finally stopped running, Frog's face smacked into the back of her neck. He rubbed his nose with a sticky foot. *Well, this is more than I bargained for.* Stars receding from his gaze, Frog looked around.

This must be her personal suite. It was decorated in lavish plum- and cream-hued linens, the stone walls adorned with polished smoky amethyst and quartz sparkling in the sunlight. Plush cushions were scattered across the floor.

Zirailla darted through an archway and into the bedroom, making for the sumptuous mattress draped in blankets.

"Uh, Zilly?" Frog tapped the princess's shoulder. No response.

"Zirailla!" He crawled onto her shoulder, stumbled, and clung to the back of her dress.

The princess launched herself toward the bed. The filmy fabric loomed closer and closer. Frog gathered his legs and jumped clear, landing on the headboard.

"Hey, watch it!" Frog turned about, glaring at the princess. She didn't react—instead, she lay there sobbing. *What is her deal?* First that convulsion by the well, and now this? Didn't princesses live for getting married? Frog hopped across the mattress to get a better view. Yes, she was crying and shaking.

A young maid called from outside the door, "Princess? Are you okay?"

"G-g-g-go away!" Zirailla screamed.

It took over twenty minutes for her body to calm down.

"Princess?" Frog crept closer.

Zirailla sat up. She opened the locket—the one Frog had rescued from the well. Inside was a picture of a woman. Her eyes were a startling golden green against the rich umber of her skin. Long, spiraled black hair flowed around the heart-shaped face with full lips and a proud jaw. Frog blinked. It looked like Zilly, or at least how Zilly would look in about ten years' time, including the light-colored eyes and strong bone structure.

"I can't do it, Frog."

Her eyes were red-rimmed from crying. She still trembled slightly.

Frog swallowed. "What can't you do, Princess?"

Her hand tightened around the locket, closing it. "I can't get married. Not after—I just can't do it."

Frog hesitated. His mission was clear—infiltrate the royal house from the inside. Commiserating with a brat who didn't want to grow up and fulfill her duty was NOT on the list. Frog studied Zirailla again. She looked too pitiful. Frog was no stranger to family forcing someone into distasteful situations. But even he had never felt the complete and utter terror he had just witnessed from Zirailla. She didn't know who he really was, so he doubted it was an act or show for his sake. And whatever Zirailla expected from her father, she clearly wasn't getting it.

Well, maybe helping her now will get me better access to the king.

Frog hopped onto the tear-soaked pillow. "Why not? I don't understand, Princess."

She sighed. "I can't get married. If I marry a man, he'll do…things. He'll hurt me."

Frog's eyes narrowed. "What are you talking about?"

"The last invasion. I was only nine. Father was with the troops. They broke through the barricade. They got us." Zirailla stood and walked over to her window.

"Who did?"

She turned around, eyes wide with remembered pain. "Les Conquerants."

Frog froze. *The soldiers Father sent for the invasion ten years ago had broken through into the capital.* But Frog remembered there had been no great casualties…except…*the execution of the queen.* Frog's chest clenched.

Zirailla continued, unaware of Frog's inner turmoil. "They got me and Mother. And those soldiers…what they did to her…" A small shake shuddered through Zilly. "Now, any time I think about a man touching me, I—I get like this."

"Surely you understand—"

"I know it's not only like that," she interrupted. "But I can't stop. I've been trying for years."

An uncomfortable pause stretched between them.

Zirailla flopped back on the bed with a sigh. "All Father needs is for me to do what every other princess does. Dress up nice, charm a rich and powerful suitor, and marry to create an alliance that will protect our people. But as soon as I think about some man touching me..." Her voice broke off as she fought another tremor.

Unable to take any more, Frog leapt off the bed and hopped across the room. *Best to give her some space*, he thought as he vaulted out the window. Zirailla's muffled sobs echoed after him.

***

Frog emerged from underneath a garden fern early in the morning. His skin felt stretched and tight. He desperately needed water. In the middle of the courtyard, a small fountain bubbled. Frog jumped in and sighed in relief. His skin soaked up the cool, refreshing water. He clambered onto a small lily pad that grew there courtesy of the fountain's murky depths.

Something streaked across his peripheral vision. Frog blinked and looked. Nothing there. He wriggled, trying to dispel the increased tempo of his heartbeat. Something sparkled in the water. *That's new.* It moved. Two specks slowly approached, barely visible among the sunbeams glistening on the darkened water. In seconds, a gaping mouth opened.

Frog lunged with everything in him. The snake rushed behind, plummeting back into the water. Frog jumped across the courtyard, heaving with all his might to race away. He glanced back. *Big mistake.*

The snake slithered out of the fountain. Water coursed off its scales. Slinking toward Frog, it closed the distance with ease.

Frog gulped. *Keep running.*

He took off, launching toward the wall of the palace. His sticky toes gripped the wall. He began scaling it, climbing as fast as he could.

The snake's tongue flicked out, tasting the air. It too began gliding up the wall—and fell down after a few inches. The snake hissed.

Frog stuck his tongue out at it. *Can't get me here, can you?*

Then it began wrapping its way up, weaving through the bricks of the wall.

Frog's stomach sank. *I'm gonna be lunch.*

A pole reached out and tossed the snake away.

"Get away from him!"

Princess Zirailla squared off with the snake.

"Go on, get out of here!" She brandished her pole— a spear, actually—at the sibilating snake.

The snake sneered at her, then turned to leave, clearly deciding to live to fight again.

All Frog could do was stare at the princess.

Satisfied that the snake was well and truly gone, she turned and held out a hand to Frog. "Are you okay?"

He swallowed and opened his mouth—no sound. *She saved my life.*

"Frog?" Her eyes were wide, her lips tight.

She was worried about me!

"I—I'm all right." Frog eased his way onto her hand. "I don't know what to say." *You rescued me when I was sent here to conquer your family from within. And now I don't want to live with myself.*

She pulled him in close, as if cuddling a kitten. "I'm just glad you're still here. I thought—well, I was wrong."

Something about her tone gave Frog pause. He studied her. "What did you think?"

"It doesn't matter." She shrugged. "You're here.

We're together. And you're not on the menu." She stroked the top of Frog's head with affection.

"You thought I left."

Her face paled.

"I guess I can see why you would think that."

Zirailla looked away. "Not many people stay once they see my…my problem." She walked over to a nearby bench and sat down.

Frog leapt off her hand and sat next to her.

Gazing out over the horizon, Zirailla added, "After the invasion, I was fine with my friends when we were children. As we got older…well, I really couldn't stay friends with any boys. Once their voices changed, it triggered my—my thing. And the girls wanted to spend time with the boys." She bit her lip and looked down.

"So you let them go."

She nodded. "It was for the best."

"Except for you." Frog hopped closer. "I hadn't left. I just wanted to give you some privacy."

She smiled at Frog. "I see that. It means a lot to me. Your friendship."

And I'm not really your friend. In all his life, Frog had never felt worse than at that moment.

"Father almost sent me away. Lucky for you I talked him out of it, huh?" She winked at him.

Frog swallowed. "Yeah, lucky. Wait, send you away? Where?"

"To Balmadou. There's a forest there, with a hidden keep. Father built it after Les Conquerants invaded. In case they came again and we needed to evacuate. He drained what little remained in the treasury to make a place to keep me safe." She toyed with an errant lock of curly hair. "I wish he hadn't. We could really use that money now." She blew out a breath.

Despite the hot sun, Frog shivered. *Now I've got it.* The information he needed—how to bring down the ruling family and secure Tukolaire for Les Conquerants. All that remained was to alert his counterpart about the secret base. Once they had King Themba's daughter, the sovereign would readily relinquish the country to Les Conquerants. If this was success, why did Frog feel sick to his stomach?

"So tell me about your family." Zirailla's gold-flecked hazel eyes focused on Frog. He felt himself drowning in their depths.

He shrugged. "There's not much to tell."

Her lips twisted slightly. She didn't believe him.

He sighed. "My father makes me do a lot of work for him. That's why I'm here now. I—" Frog broke off, unable to continue.

"You had to run away?"

Frog didn't want to lie to her, so he said nothing. *Let her assume what she wants.*

"I'm sorry, Frog. I know what it's like to be trapped. To have your family take over, and define everything about you, even your choices and your future."

Frog couldn't contain himself any longer. "It isn't fair! I'm stuck like this because of him. He has to have everything he sees—and it's never enough!"

Frog's heart sank. He had said too much. He risked a glance over his shoulder at Zirailla.

She hadn't made the connection. His secret was safe.

"I know what you mean." Her voice was raw, filling his chest with an ache. "In less than a month, I'll be married to a man who only wants me for a position in government. A piece of property, used and kept or discarded as he sees fit."

"We could escape together." Frog regretted the words as they left his mouth. He had no future with this princess. He was here to usher in her kingdom's destruction.

Zirailla's lips pursed. "Really? Where would we go? How would we eat?" Her eyes narrowed, studying him. "Did that snake bite you? Are you feeling hot?"

She's teasing me, he realized. Frog smiled. "No, I'm just crazy." A bright color caught the corner of his eye. A bird-of-paradise bloom nested in the garden shrubs. He glanced at the princess. She was laughing and watching the fountain.

With a gentle puff of magic, Frog pulled the bloom off its stem and laid it on Zirailla's lap. "Thank you—for saving my life."

She picked it up, studied it, and smiled. "Thank you for being my friend."

Embarrassed, Frog mentioned wetting his skin and hopped back to the fountain.

***

Zirailla returned the blossom to her lap. *I've never been given a flower before.* Her heart thumped a little faster. What was this new feeling?

And when he had mentioned escaping, she had felt hope. Maybe, if she worked together with him, they could find a way out of her marrying the highest bidder.

"If you're done soaking, let's go inside and get lunch!" she called.

A splash answered her. Zirailla laughed. She picked the flower up again. A bird-of-paradise bloom—the symbol of fidelity and commitment. The wet sploshing of Frog returning startled her from her reverie.

"Well, let's see if your kitchen has anything edible." Frog shook, spraying droplets of water everywhere.

"Yes. Let me just put this in water first." Zirailla scooped up Frog and went back inside.

Lunch was perfect. They laughed at the horrified faces of the wait staff, had a flying food-catching contest (Frog won, of course), then slunk away when Cook emerged from the kitchen in a pique of anger.

"That was a close one!" Zirailla puffed, slightly out of breath after running back to her rooms.

Frog shuddered. "I know royal cooks usually have a temper, but…"

Zirailla laughed. "Yeah, I try to avoid her too. We should probably not throw food for a while."

"We might want to reconsider *eating* there for a while. You heard Cook reciting a recipe for *toasted frog legs*." Frog shuddered. "I like being able to move about, thank you very much."

Zirailla tried to hold in a giggle and failed. "You should have seen your face! I didn't think your eyes could get any bigger, but once she said marinade…"

Frog huffed.

"Hey, I'm sorry." Zirailla scooped him up. "I was only teasing—I didn't mean to upset you."

"It's all right. I was just scared, that's all." Frog hopped away, refusing to meet her eyes.

Zirailla tilted her head to the right. "I should paint you."

"That's really not necessary."

"Ah, come on. It'll be fun!" Zirailla was already pulling art supplies out of a cabinet.

"Do you paint often, Princess?"

Zirailla set a couple bottles on a table and shrugged. "Enough, I guess. Father said princesses are supposed to be cultured. I paint in the local style—big, bright colors and shapes. I think paintings are more cheerful that way." She grabbed a few more supplies, then pointed to a small pedestal draped with blue cloth, mimicking a pond. "Well, hop up!"

Frog sighed, then made his way over and with an enormous leap vaulted onto the pedestal.

Zirailla studied her subject. Blue and green—perfect. Except… "Just one more thing." Zilly dug through a small jewelry chest and emerged with a tiny golden crown. She placed it on his head and smiled. "Perfect."

"Uh, Princess—why am I wearing a crown?"

She took up a palette and started smearing paint on a tiny piece of canvas. "To add more color. And because you remind me of a silly story told to young girls. Hold still now."

Zirailla focused on the tiny square of canvas. A miniature would be best—something small that wouldn't make her father ask questions. She picked up a tiny, single-hair brush and began the miniscule details of Frog's eyes. They were almost human in appearance—despite the vertical slit pupil, sometimes when Frog spoke he seemed so human, with emotions pouring out from a wide-eyed, soulful expression. *I wonder where he came from.*

Zilly pursed her lips and studied the painting. "Come and see." She motioned to Frog, who carefully made his way over so as not to upset the precarious crown on his head.

"Well, what do you think?"

Frog swallowed. "It's wonderful."

***

Frog slept on the windowsill, his bed for the past five days. Being the friend of a princess had certain improvements over dwelling in a swamp. A sliver of moon barely illuminated the garden in a pale glow.

A shadow, darker than any shadow should ever be, crossed Frog's vision. He raised his head. A hand appeared out of thin air, bereft of a body, beckoning. Frog hid a snarl. It was the sorcerer. *What does he want now?*

"It's rather unnerving to see your hand and nothing else, you know," Frog grumbled, careful to keep his voice low and not wake Zirailla.

The sorcerer laughed, but it sounded like scraping on a stone. The disembodied hand motioned again. Frog rolled his eyes but hopped off the ledge and onto the outstretched palm.

"Where are we going?" Frog's stomach clenched

itself into knots. There was no good reason for the sorcerer to show himself now. Unless…

"You've had almost an entire week, my amphibious friend." The shadow fell away from the voice like a cloak, revealing Frog's most hated enemy. Black, beady eyes glistened from beneath gray brows, and a wrinkled face, complete with a hard, perpetually frowning mouth. *Sorcerer Bastien—the man who turned me into a frog.*

Bastien snapped his fingers.

The ground rolled, and the sky rushed toward Frog. Instead of staring at Bastien's feet, Frog could now meet the sorcerer's cold, glittering eyes. A familiar warmth uncurled in Frog's belly. His magic was restored as well.

"Welcome back to humanity, Prince Louis." Bastien's voice sounded like a mix between a buzzing bee and an iron file.

Clenching his new hands into fists, Louis delved into his magic reserve. Nowhere near enough to take on Bastien. He lashed out with fire magic anyway. "Give me one good reason why I shouldn't pummel you!"

The magic struck an invisible barrier and dissipated.

"Now, now, Prince. Temper, temper."

Louis bit back a growl.

"If you are ready to cooperate, give your report." Bastien's eyes narrowed. "Unless you want to go back to your lean, green form?"

Flushing, Louis shook his head.

"Good. Now tell me the best way to capture the king."

Louis's heart constricted painfully. As soon as he surrendered this information, he would condemn Zirailla to death.

Bastien crossed his arms and sighed. "Let me remind you, *Prince*, that your contract with me hinges on providing this information. You were in the palace long enough to learn the emergency plans of the royal family—especially with the little outbreaks of violence I staged throughout the country."

"And if I failed?" Louis whispered.

Bastien shrugged. "Then the curse becomes permanent."

"You mean—"

"You'll be a frog for the rest of your life. However long that is." Bastien polished a fingernail, uncaring.

"Bastien, this wasn't what we agreed to. Not what my family agreed to. I've done everything you've asked. Surely I don't need to—"

"Are you questioning your orders?" Bastien clipped. "You know the contract your family signed. What I ask is well within the limits. You were to serve me in any capacity I demanded. You failed once already, hence the need to…alter…your appearance." The sorcerer stalked around the prince. "I do hope that we are past this, *my prince*."

Louis shuddered. Disobeying Bastien was not an option. "Forgive me, Bastien. I forgot myself."

Bastien stepped close, his face inches from Louis's. "Are you certain?"

Swallowing, Louis managed to nod.

After another moment's examination, Bastien grunted and stepped away. "Good. I am happy to hear it, dear prince. It would so upset me to turn around and terminate a ruling family with whom I have such close and long-standing ties."

Bastien studied Louis over his shoulder. "Let's sweeten the deal, Your Highness. Give me the information I need—I *know* you have it—and I will release you from the curse."

Louis's breath caught. "You mean, end my punishment?"

Bastien nodded.

Louis's blood pressure skyrocketed. All he had to do was tell Bastien about the hidden fortress, and he could stay human. His enslavement to Bastien would be over. *Could I really do that to Zirailla? Sign her death warrant?*

"Come now, Louis, I don't have all night." Bastien's eyes narrowed.

Louis thrust his hands into his pockets to hide their shaking, then told Bastien everything—from the secret passage through the catacombs to the end destination. Throughout the recitation, he fought the urge to vomit. *In less than ten minutes, I have sold out one of my only friends.*

Bastien frowned as he studied the map. "Interesting." He picked up a pen and made a few marks on the parchment. Standing, he returned his attention to Louis. "Here's the plan. There is a group of malcontents waiting at a bar in the Marsh District of the capital city. Unite them, and storm the palace at dawn."

"But I thought—"

"You are still bonded to me for the remainder of the year!" Bastien's gravelly voice deepened. "Must I punish you again?"

Louis reached in deep and assessed his magic. It was strong, stronger here in Tukolaire than anywhere else he had been. But if his magic was stronger here, so was Bastien's. There was no way he could defeat the wizened sorcerer.

Louis gave a small bow. "No, Bastien. I apologize for my shortcoming. I am fatigued from the long day."

Bastien examined Louis for a brief moment before continuing. "Attack at dawn. I will lead men up through the escape path. And then Tukolaire and all her resources will belong to Les Conquerants—as I promised your father all those years ago."

Louis bowed, not trusting himself to speak. Bastien motioned him off. Accepting the dismissal, Louis grabbed some supplies and took off, heading toward the city. Bile stung his throat, and his stomach was in knots. That nasty voice returned. *So what? You've only known her for a few days. You came here knowing you were plotting against her. Nothing's changed.*

Then why did Louis feel that *everything* had changed?

Faint beams of light emanated from the tiny windows of the town's seediest bar. Louis pulled the hood of his cloak over his head and strode in. Dust filled his nostrils, choking the prince. Coughing, he eyed the bar patrons out of his peripheral vision. Everyone took extra care to avoid noticing him. This was the place.

Louis located an empty stool at the bar, strode over, and took a seat. The barkeep, a portly man in need of a shave, pushed a dirty rag along an even dirtier counter.

"One ale."

The barkeep nodded and reached underneath the counter for a glass. Someone tapped on Louis's shoulder.

"Are you new around these parts, friend?" A man in a dark red dashiki leaned over the prince.

Louis picked up the ale the barkeeper slid his way. A dead gnat floated in the foam.

"You could say that." Louis set the glass of ale down and reached out with his magic. He tugged on the man's emotions, using Persuasion. "I was told I could find some helpful people here."

The man sat down next to Louis and held up a finger. The barkeeper slid him a glass of ale, minus the bug. Louis frowned.

"Well, friend, maybe I can help you. Why don't you tell me your troubles?" He gulped the ale.

The prince smiled. "My troubles are of a…royal persuasion."

The man slammed the empty glass down on the bar. "Then I think we can help each other, friend." With a malevolent smile, he reached out and shook Louis's hand.

Louis's glass of ale was replaced. "On the house," the bartender murmured.

He glanced into the ale. No dead insects this time.

***

A clash of metal woke Zirailla. Rubbing the sleep out of her eyes, she walked over to the window.

The entire courtyard was in flames.

She whirled around and darted out of her room and down the corridor.

"Father!"

Guards scurried through the hall, knocking her aside with barely an "excuse me." She dashed about, searching for someone who could explain what was going on.

"There you are!"

Zirailla turned and saw her father racing toward her. She ran into his hug.

"I'm so glad you're safe, Zilly."

Zirailla pushed away. "What's happening? The courtyard—"

"We're under attack. You must go. Now. The maids packed a bag for you." He grabbed her hand and turned to lead her away from the front entrance and deeper into the palace, where the catacombs—and the secret exit—were.

Zirailla trotted along beside him. "What about you, Father? I can't leave you. Please, come with me."

"Zilly, we've been over this." His mouth tightened, eyes flashing. "I must stay and defend the capital. I *need* you to go where it's safe. There's no telling what will happen."

Goosebumps rose on Zirailla's arms. "What's going on?"

"There are still Les Conquerants ships downriver. Right now, this constitutes a second uprising, so every city is at risk, not just here and Bignona." Her father's jaw clenched. "I don't understand it—our people know we are recovering from invasions. These rebellions—they just don't make sense." He shook his head. "Anyways, here we are."

A small hole appeared as Themba depressed a notch in the wall. The dark depths of the catacombs beckoned.

She stepped in to give her father one last hug.

Something wasn't right. Themba had said the maids had packed everything she would need. *Then why do I feel like I'm forgetting something?*

"Go quickly and be safe, dear. I love you."

Zirailla smiled up at her father. "I love you too, Father."

Breaking the hug, Zirailla tried to memorize every inch of her father's face. His eyes had the same sparkle when they looked at her as…

"Oh no!" *Frog! That's what I forgot!*

Zirailla ripped away from her father and sprinted back to her room.

"Zilly? Zirailla! Come back here! This instant!"

The king took off after his daughter, a handful of guards following in his wake.

Zirailla ducked behind a fluttering purple curtain as a small group of men ran by. She had to find Frog. What if he had been in the courtyard when the fighting broke out? What if right now he was hurt and unable to move, or squished beneath heavy feet as men fought? Or trapped behind flames, slowly running out of air? Zirailla clenched her fists and ran on. *My only friend—how could I forget him?*

"Frog!" Zirailla searched through her room, knocking over vases and decorations. She fell to her knees and checked under the bed. "Frog!"

"Zilly!" Themba sped into the room, panting. "You need to go. *Now!*"

Before Zirailla could respond, five men charged through the door.

"Well, well. What have we here? I think we found the prize, boys!" The fighter ripped his patched and worn hood down. He smiled, revealing a broken tooth. "The king *and* his daughter." The rebel's voice was high-pitched and whiny. Zirailla fought the urge to cover her ears.

Themba reached in front of his daughter. "Leave her out of this. Your fight is with me."

The thin man threw his head back and laughed. "You're hardly in the position to give orders, *Your Highness*." The laughter echoed in the small room. The courtyard flames reflected off the gleaming swords and daggers. Zirailla swallowed, trying not to panic.

He gestured, and the four other rough men split—two for each prisoner. They grabbed Zirailla's arms and slammed her against the wall. The toothless leader grabbed Zirailla's chin and turned her head from side to side. She willed herself not to shake or tremble.

"Such a pretty morsel, huh, boys?"

The other goons laughed.

"I think I might need to…take a minute here." He reached for her leg.

The trembling began. "No…" Zirailla whispered.

"Hey! You there!"

The man's face screwed up in disgust.

Another rebel approached and drew back his hood. Instead of dark-colored skin, his green eyes glittered from a face only lightly tanned.

"Good! You found them! This will be done faster than I thought!" The man smiled, but his eyes remained cold.

That voice—it sounded familiar, but not. Clearly it had enough authority that the leader of the quintet stalked off.

"Where should we take the prisoners, Louis?" the man holding Zirailla's right arm asked.

Louis? That's not a Tukolairan name. That's a—no. It can't be.

Louis hesitated. He glanced about. "Lock them up with the others. Post an extra guard." Turning to face Zirailla, he winced and hung his head. "I'm sorry."

Zirailla squinted in confusion. "I don't understand—"

Another band of soldiers approached, clad in

gleaming metal armor with a lion's head splayed across their chest. Zilly's stomach tied itself in knots. It was Les Conquerants.

"Perfect job, Prince Louis. We couldn't have done it without you." The captain clapped Louis on the back. Louis's face reddened.

"Thanks to your help, we'll take over Kayode without losing a single soldier. Your father will be thrilled." The captain gestured, and his retinue took over from the rebel soldiers.

Louis tossed the rebels a bag of coins. "As promised—with my thanks." He turned to the captain. "I'll escort the prisoners."

The captain nodded. "They'll be executed at nightfall."

The blood drained from Zirailla's face. *I am going to die—just like Mother did.*

The Les Conquerants soldiers clapped irons on the prisoners' wrists. Louis grabbed each of their shoulders and guided them out of the palace.

"I should have known." Tears swelled in the corners of the king's eyes. "The rebellions—the timing was too perfect. I should have known. I was a fool." He hung his head.

Zirailla's heart skipped a beat. "It's not your fault, Father. I'm the one who didn't leave when you asked—not once, but twice. I—I'm so sorry." Shame consumed her. If only she had listened and escaped when she had the chance.

"Be quiet." Louis steered the captives down an empty hallway.

A wizened old man with glittering black eyes waited by the only door. "Prince Louis. Forever a prince now, I may add."

"Bastien. What do you want?" Louis's voice was cold enough to freeze the sun.

"Just to congratulate you on making the right

decision, my boy. I feared I would be returning you to your amphibious state."

Zirailla's stared into Louis's eyes. He looked at her, then turned away.

"No—oh no—*Frog?* It was you?" Zilly's head spun. A new set of guards grabbed her and her father.

He nodded. "I'm sorry, Zirailla." Louis turned and ran off, booted footsteps echoing after him.

In the prison chamber, the floor rushed up to meet Zirailla as she collapsed, dissolving into sobs. "My only friend…why?"

***

Louis ran, tears blinding his face, to the only refuge he could think of—Zirailla's room. The air hung with smoke from the courtyard fires. Louis fell to the floor. He felt like scum—Zirailla had trusted him, and he had betrayed her.

Nearby, a coterie of rebels joked and laughed as they looted the surrounding rooms.

"…You should have seen it. She yelled 'Frog' and ran right into us. I mean, good thing, because that's how we caught her, but still…"

"Bumir, are you trying to tell me the princess chose a pet *frog* over safety? You had too much at the bar last night, man."

"Maybe Bumir thinks himself the frog, and that the princess was rushing to him. Sort of looks like one, ya know…"

Louis's heart tore in two as their voices faded. *It's all my fault.*

"Oh, Zilly, what have I done?" How could he ever think that being a frog would be worse than how he felt now? And tonight, when they killed her…

Louis squeezed his eyes shut, fingers curling into fists. *She'll be gone—her nightmares and fears will become reality.*

This was cruel beyond measure. Louis slammed his hands down on the floor. Underneath the left one, cool metal tickled his palm. He grabbed it. Bringing his hand up for inspection, Louis recognized the item immediately. Zilly's locket. *She must have dropped it when she was searching for me.* Just when Louis thought it would be impossible to feel worse, he was proven wrong.

Hesitating at first, Louis opened the golden oval gingerly. There, in the right frame, was the portrait of her mother. But in the left frame…a miniature of a frog. Every detail was perfect, down to the slit-pupil eyes. It was the painting from their first day together.

Louis's fingers tightened around the locket. *I can't go through with this. A piece of me would die if anything ever happened to her. And since I made this mess, I have to set it right.*

The prince shoved himself off the ground and headed back for the temporary prison. Now to find out how to save the princess—and outsmart Bastien.

***

Zirailla sat in a corner of the small, dank room, numb to the world. *Frog, my one friend, betrayed me. He was a spy all along. And I, foolishly, let him into my house—and my heart.*

"Zirailla—are you going to be all right?" Themba put an arm around his daughter.

She managed to nod.

He gave her shoulders a small squeeze. "I know it looks bleak, Zilly, but we'll figure a way out of this—I promise."

Instead of answering, Zirailla shrank into herself more. She was going to die, led up on a stage and beheaded, just like her mother. *At least they haven't stripped and abused me—yet.*

The door creaked open. That same wizened old man stood there, dark, loose robes fluttering slightly in the draft.

"It's time, Your Majesties."

Louis and another Conquerant entered the prison and restrained Zirailla and her father. Zirailla glared at her former friend as he clutched her arms. He still wouldn't look at her.

"Coward," she hissed under her breath, anger at his betrayal eclipsing the fear coursing through her veins.

The march through the corridors of the palace flew by. Their footsteps echoed through the eerie silence. Zirailla fought moving, but when the old man suggested Louis inspire her cooperation in a more physical way, she gave up.

Finally, Louis shoved Zirailla out into the courtyard. It was worse than any nightmare or flashback she had ever had. The jeering crowd was the least of it. Shouts of "Down with the king!" and "End the tyranny!" resounded through the air. The block, bloody from earlier executions, and the hooded headsman waited. Polished contingents of Les Conquerants soldiers stood at attention, watching the proceedings. A shiver tore through Zirailla's limbs. *This is it.*

Louis leaned close. "I'm going to remove the shackles. Hold still—don't let anyone know." His voice, instead of the cold, polished tone, sounded more like his frog voice—earnest and open.

Zirailla froze in shock. The weight of the shackles disappeared. She pressed her lips together. Could she trust him? Could she risk *not* trusting him?

Louis whispered to her again. "They are going to read aloud your crimes and the reason for execution. When they ask for you to step up, start to follow, then duck."

Zirailla bristled. "Why should I trust you? How do I know you aren't trying to—"

"What, kill you?" He jostled her, making it appear as if she was fighting his hold. "If I wanted you dead, I wouldn't even be here." A mere second, although it felt like a lifetime, passed. "Besides, I can't let them kill you."

"And why not?" She turned to glare at him. What

she saw in his eyes stopped her dead in her tracks.

"Bring the princess forward." One of the Conquerant soldiers reached for Zirailla.

"Good luck, Zilly." Louis thrust something cold and metallic into her hands, let her go, and reached for his sword.

Zirailla took two steps then dove for the ground. Arrows whistled through the air.

"We're under attack!"

"To arms!"

Zirailla peeked up. The soldiers manning the execution grabbed for their swords and darted this way and that, trying to bring order to the chaos. The crowd, the jeering, taunting crowd, turned lethal, raining bow fire and attacking anyone within range. The princess crawled underneath the execution stage. Safe from immediate danger, she looked to see what Louis had given her. It was a key.

I need to find Father and free him. Zirailla slipped from her safe haven and darted through the chaos, looking for her father. She spied him off to the right, ducking this way and that, trying to avoid the fighting. Zirailla sprinted toward him, legs pumping.

An explosion rocked the ground. Zirailla stumbled, then recovered, reaching her father. She thrust the key into the chain and turned it, freeing him. The king shook off the shackles, grabbed a sword from a fallen combatant, and leaped into the battle.

Zirailla started to retreat for safety. Another explosion saw her scrambling for balance. She looked over and saw smoke rising from two figures: Louis and the old man, locked in some sort of magical battle.

Louis was so focused on the old man he didn't see a soldier with a wicked mace approaching.

I have to warn him. Pushing her already exhausted body, Zirailla rushed to Louis. The soldier with the mace was going to beat her there.

"Louis!" she screamed.

He turned right into the mace—and stopped it with a shield. Zirailla resumed her mad sprint and caught up with him. The hairs on the back of her neck stood on end. *What is going on?*

Louis's face paled and he whirled around, throwing his arms up just in time to dissolve a blast of fire bursting from the old man's hands. The soldier with the mace raised his weapon.

"Oh no, you don't!" Zirailla gritted her teeth and leapt onto the soldier's back, wrapping an arm around his neck and squeezing as hard as she could.

***

"Do you honestly think you can beat me?" Bastien hurled yet another fireball at Louis.

The prince blocked it and grimaced. His magic was starting to run out. He couldn't spare the mental concentration from his own defense to scan Bastien, but the ancient wizard showed no signs of tiring.

Louis gathered his strength and reformed his shield.

Instead of fire, Bastien hurled lightning bolts. "Your father promised me this land, and I will have it, even if I have to kill you in the process!" he screamed.

"Why do you need it so badly?" Louis shot back, filling his voice with Persuasion. *Please, let it be a hint, a clue, something to help me figure out his weakness.*

"Can't you feel the magic, boy? This land is *filled* with it. Mine it all and I will be the most powerful sorcerer in the world!" A deadly purple glow surrounded Bastien.

Louis cast about with his magical senses. The earth *was* full of magic, rich in a way that home had never been. He had to stop Bastien from getting that power. A blow knocked him over.

Coughing, Louis pushed himself to his knees. He

threw his remaining strength into a shield. Bastien just smiled.

"Face it, boy. You took a gamble—and lost." Another glow surrounded Bastien, but this time it was blood-red.

Louis reached into his pocket and clutched Zirailla's locket. He had to save her. Hopefully then she would forgive him. Louis dropped his shield and braced himself for the magical onslaught.

***

The soldier struggled, then fell. Zirailla jumped clear. He wasn't dead, but he was out of it enough for her to get Louis and escape.

She turned to see how Louis was faring—only to see him flat on the ground, next to the dead body of the old man.

"Louis!" She dove down to him, reaching for his head. "Louis, please be alive, please be okay." Her panic overrode the usual fear of men. And this was not just any man; it was her Frog. She stroked his sepia hair back, then dropped her hand to his neck, feeling for a pulse. It was there, but very faint.

Her father limped over, a wound in his calf oozing blood. "He saved us all, sweetie. That sorcerer wanted to steal the magic from this land. I don't know how he did it, but a white light shone all around him. It made the sorcerer's spell bounce back. He sacrificed himself to save us."

Louis started coughing. Blood trickled from the corners of his mouth.

"Louis! Please!" Zirailla clung to one of his hands with both of hers.

Louis's eyes flickered, then closed. Themba shook his head and strode away.

"No. Oh no. I'm too late." Tears welled in the

corners of her eyes. She grabbed Louis's shoulders and shook him. "Please, Louis. You can't die. Not now. You—you saved me."

He didn't respond.

Zirailla dashed the tears off her cheeks. "Please, Louis. Please, please, be okay." She took a deep breath, then caressed his head. "You have to be okay. I—I love you."

Nothing changed. He remained motionless on the ground.

Zirailla ran a finger over his still lips. No breath. "You died to save me," she murmured. Her chest felt torn in two. Now she had lost her only friend—and the first man she had ever loved. Saying goodbye just wouldn't be enough. Steeling herself, Zirailla fought her inner fears, leaned over, and kissed Louis.

Somehow, he kissed her back. When Zirailla sat back up, his eyes were open and his lips curved in a smile.

"You're alive!"

"I'm alive." He coughed and withdrew one hand to massage his temple. "Albeit with a wicked headache." He took her hand in both of his. "You forgave me." His eyes, so cold before, now twinkled with mischief—just like Frog's.

Zirailla smiled. "I forgave you. Provided you give a fascinating explanation for why you attempted to overthrow my father."

He chuckled softly. "Of course—if you don't mind it waiting for a couple days."

Zirailla snuggled into his safe, strong arms. "I'll wait my whole life if necessary."

***

Two months later, King Themba smiled as three loud knocks sounded from the palace door. Zirailla, dressed in a special dress made for the occasion, flicked her eyes to his. He bit his cheek to keep from laughing. The wedding was about to begin. All he had to do was accept Louis's knock.

Themba waited just a second longer. His Zilly could handle a small measure of the anxiety she had so eagerly awarded him over her life. When she began fidgeting in her chair, he finally had to laugh out loud. He stood and walked to the door and opened it.

Louis, dressed in a dashiki instead of his Conquerant's garb, bowed. "Your Highness, I come to you as a man, to ask for your daughter's hand in marriage."

Themba bowed back to Louis. "I accept your offer and accept you as a son in my house. Enter, and marry my daughter." He smiled at Louis and wrapped the younger man in a warm hug.

"Thank you. For everything, but mostly for loving her." Themba escorted Louis into the throne room, where Zirailla stood waiting.

"I wish you both every happiness."

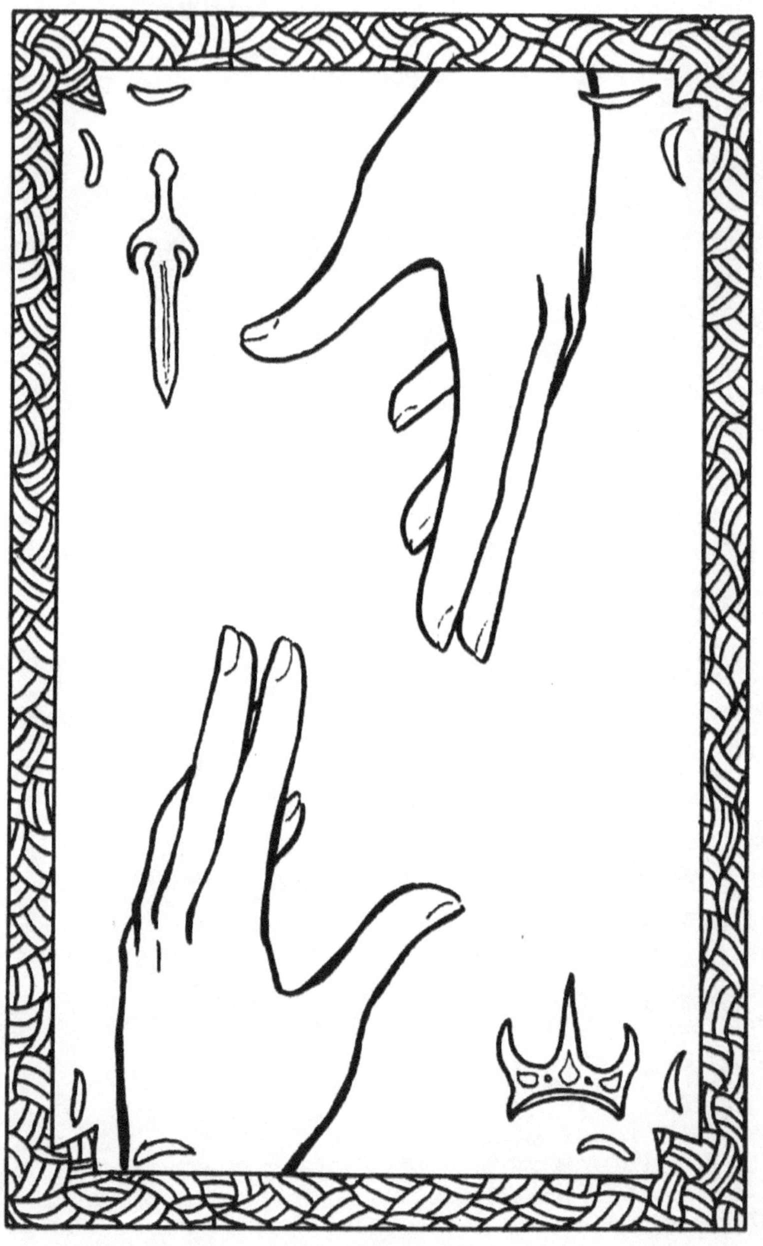

Swapped

Allie May

The door to Prince Rowan's bedchamber burst open, waking the prince from his slumber.

"What…" He jolted up in bed, frowned when he saw his best friend, and lay back down. Reb frequently played pranks, but Rowan drew the line when it came to losing his sleep.

Reb tripped over the chair that had been pulled away from the desk. As he stood, he touched the dark stubble where he bumped his chin. "Out of bed. Come on."

"What do you want?" Rowan rubbed his eyes and rolled out of bed.

"We need to leave." Reb tugged on the prince's arm, pulling him toward the door.

Rowan yawned as he stretched out his muscles, lagging behind.

"I'm sorry about this." Reb struck Rowan on the cheek.

Face stinging, the fog cleared from Rowan's mind. He noticed Reb's brown eyes were panicked, devoid of their usual humorous sparkle. This was not a prank. Something was wrong. "What's going on?"

"The castle's been infiltrated. I need to get you to safety." Reb pushed Rowan out the door.

The prince ran down the hall, his bare feet slapping against the cold floor. "What about my parents?" He paused to peer around the corner, and Reb bumped into his back.

Reb stepped around Rowan to check that the next corridor was clear before waving him onward. "We will meet up with them at the Canty Inn, on the edge of town."

"Isn't that where Princess Emmeline and her royal guard stayed?"

"It is. The owners are loyal to the crown and will get you and your parents out of the capital until it is safe for your return." Reb stopped in front of a large tapestry.

Rowan waved his hand, and the tapestry lifted to reveal a hidden passageway carved into the stone wall.

"Go." Reb nudged him inside. "And don't use your ability. Not until we're sure the intruders are gone. We can't risk revealing Trudeli magic."

The tapestry hovered, then fell back into place behind them, drowning the passageway in darkness. Blinking, Rowan's eyes slowly adjusted. He put his hand on the wall to guide him as he walked. "You're coming with me, right?"

Reb was silent for a minute, but Rowan could still hear his boots against the stone behind him.

"Reb?" Rowan stumbled as the passage banked steeply to the right. He had lost all sense of direction, and he had no idea how far it was to the exit.

"I have to stay here. It is my job to get rid of the intruders."

Rowan scowled, knowing Reb couldn't see it in the darkness. "I don't like that plan." He didn't want someone else fighting his battles. He was no coward.

"I don't care." Reb's words were tinged with annoyance. "These protocols are in place for a reason. They saved your great-grandfather during the War of Thieves when Trudel was invaded because foreigners found out about our magical abilities, and they will protect your life now. You will do as your father, the king, commands. And so will I…" Reb put a hand over Rowan's mouth.

A scuffle sounded.

Rowan held his breath. Was that a rat? Or perhaps his parents?

Footsteps. Silence. Then more footsteps.

A torch flickered to life in front of them, revealing six guards blocking their path. Guards wearing armor emblazoned with the red insignia of Bolea.

Rowan gasped and took a few steps back. His mind immediately jumped to Princess Emmeline, his betrothed from Bolea. He scanned the guard's faces to see if he recognized any of them, but he hadn't paid them much attention when Emmeline was visiting. What did Boleans want in Trudel? And had his parents made it out of the castle before Boleans found them?

The man holding the torch grinned and stepped forward. "Prince Rowan, I presume. I am Tierri, a captain in the Bolean army."

Rowan caught sight of his friend's eyes flitting around the room, probably counting the enemies' weapons. It was Reb's nervous habit. Rowan didn't see a way out. Even with his telekinetic ability and the dagger Reb kept strapped to his hip, they couldn't fight off six men.

Rowan glared at the intruders. "What do you want? My father is a very reasonable man. I'm sure we can negotiate a solution."

The soldiers laughed.

Captain Tierri shook his head as his expression turned dark. "King Osgood cannot be trusted, not when he has been hiding a secret—Trudeli magic. How is it possible an entire kingdom is born with unique abilities, some harmless, others…" He raised an eyebrow at the prince. "Not so much. And not a single other nation knows about it?"

Rowan swallowed. His great-grandfather had used his ability to erase all memories of the War of Thieves from the minds of everyone involved, except Trudeli citizens. The story was used as a lesson for his people to use their abilities with caution. It was always a risk that history would repeat itself, especially now that Rowan was marrying an outsider.

"Trudeli magic isn't fair, not when you're marrying our princess." The captain waved a hand. "Take the prince. This other man? He is useless. Dispose of him."

The guards stepped forward to grab Rowan.

Reb pulled him back, and they both turned and ran in the direction they came.

Rowan could hear the soldiers' boots clomping against the stone as they gave chase. His heart pounded in his throat, filling each step he took with adrenaline.

Between breaths, Reb whispered, "You know what we have to do." He reached for the prince's arm.

Rowan yanked his hand out of his friend's reach. If they didn't touch, Reb couldn't use his ability. "No. I refuse. We can both make it out of here."

"I was given my job for one reason, and one reason only. Go to the inn and stay alive."

"No!" Rowan's foot slipped, giving Reb time to catch up.

Reb jumped forward and grabbed Rowan's hand. A familiar pang ripped through their minds as they closed their eyes.

A second later, Rowan blinked at his own blue eyes and blond hair, now on the figure in front of him. The swap was a success, despite his protests. He was now in Reb's body.

"Run." Reb pushed the prince forward and out of the passageway just as he was grabbed from behind by the Bolean men. He knocked his head back, smacking one in the face, but two more grabbed him.

Fear propelled Prince Rowan to run faster as he watched his best friend taken as a hostage in his body. They had only ever used Reb's ability to play pranks before. The worst thing that had happened while they were swapped was when Reb tripped and cut open his chin, leaving Rowan with a hairline scar.

He rounded the corner to find another way out of the castle. No Boleans pursued. They had their prisoner, or so they thought.

***

Reb only had a second to revel in his victory before the soldiers were on him. He got in a few good punches before his breath was kicked out of him and he ended up on the floor, gasping. Two soldiers grabbed under his arms and dragged him on his knees across the stone floors until Captain Tierri pushed open a door and the soldiers discarded him onto the floor of the king and queen's sitting room.

Pushing himself up, his vision spun briefly, and he forced himself to focus on the gray streaks in King Osgood's bushy blond beard. His head throbbed above his left eye, and his ribs ached.

Queen Cressida, wearing only a nightdress, rushed to his side and laid a hand across his brow. When she pulled it away, her fingers were stained red.

Reb had never seen her without her blond hair expertly pinned up before, and he actively avoided looking at her in her state of undress to avoid violating her privacy.

She fussed over him, trying to clean up the blood, and he worried about the extent of his injuries. But he had done his job. The prince was safe.

King Osgood lunged toward the captain, only to be restrained by two Bolean soldiers. "How dare you?" His voice thundered across the room. "You will all be punished for this. You hear me? I'll have you hanged on the castle wall!"

"Shut him up." Captain Tierri pointed.

A guard punched King Osgood in the gut, cutting off his breath, before the others dumped him on the ground.

"That's better." Captain Tierri stationed two guards at the door and motioned for the rest to follow him out.

Reb wanted to speak, to let the queen know her real son was safe, but he couldn't with the guards listening in.

Queen Cressida's telepathic mind reached out to his. *What have they done to you?*

Before he could answer with his thoughts, her mind recoiled.

She blinked before spreading her consciousness back toward him. *Reb? But where is Rowan?*

Don't worry, Your Majesty. We had no choice but to swap. When they took me, they stopped chasing him.

Reb felt her relief wash over his mind, but it quickly turned to panic.

Rowan is safe, yes, but his body is not. Unless you can escape and swap back…

Uncertainty crept through Reb's heart. *I did what I could to buy us time. I'm not leaving you and King Osgood in danger. I can't.*

Reb, your job is to protect Rowan, not us.

I intend to get us all to safety.

Queen Cressida glanced up at her husband across the room, her lips pressed tightly together. *If they find out you are not him, you and his body will both be killed.*

Reb didn't need her fears pressing on his mind to know the seriousness of the situation. *Queen Cressida, your son and I have swapped bodies frequently enough to trick even you and King Osgood.*

A hint of nostalgic humor washed from Queen Cressida's mind to his. *Yes, you've certainly had enough practice. I will warn the king of what has happened. Perhaps his ability can help with an escape.*

Her mind retreated from his, leaving him alone in the sudden silence of his own thoughts. Did the Boleans know which ability each Trudeli royal had? Surely they couldn't know about King Osgood's, or else they would've left more guards in the room.

But how did they find out about Trudeli magic in the first place?

***

Rowan ran, just as Reb told him. To the edge of the city and into the forest until he came upon a small, two-story inn with a thatched roof. He finally caught his breath while knocking on the door.

A light flickered on through the yellow-tinted glass, and an older woman with silver curls falling out of her bun opened the door.

"Reb?" Her eyebrows scrunched together as she searched his face. "No, I know who you are." She stepped aside and ushered Rowan inside, checking to make sure he wasn't followed.

"How do you know..." Rowan panted, his lungs sore, but his feet grateful for Reb's boots.

"Because he's my son."

Rowan blinked at the woman a few times, her eyes and smile suddenly seeming so familiar. "I guess I never thought about Reb's family before."

"He had to keep us a secret in order to protect this safe house."

Rowan followed her past the stairs and through a doorway, past dried slices of game hanging down, and into a small kitchen. Strong herbs burned his nose, and he caught sight of a mortar full of half-crushed greens underneath the pestle.

"You can call me Isa. Here, let me get you something to eat while we wait for your parents." She sat him down at a wooden table and pulled a pot off the shelf, hanging it over the fireplace.

"My body..." Rowan stared at the red flames licking the soot-covered bricks. Even if it was a secret, why had Reb not told him that his mother ran an inn?

An image of Reb being snatched by the guards flashed before his eyes again, returning Rowan to the present. "My body! I have to get back to Reb! I left him at the mercy of those Boleans…"

"Boleans?" Isa's wooden spoon clattered against the pot as her hand jumped to her cheek.

Rowan could almost feel her fear for her son's safety. "You housed Princess Emmeline during her stay, right? Did you notice anything while she and her companions were here?"

"Your betrothed and her companions left three days ago to return to Bolea. And they kept mostly to themselves while they were here." Isa chewed on her lip. "Why would Boleans attack when we're in the middle of negotiating a peace treaty with them?" She turned back to her pot and began dumping various spices and some suspicious-looking meat inside.

"The soldiers said something about Trudeli magic…" He rubbed his temples to relax his muscles against his impending headache.

"They know?" Isa's eyebrows jumped up to wrinkle her forehead even more. "What about the treaty?"

"They haven't signed it yet. And now they might never sign it. Especially not if they know about my father's ability. They'll never trust that the treaty was negotiated fairly."

"Any idea how the Boleans could have discovered our abilities? Was anyone prying into Trudeli affairs?"

Rowan shook his head. "No one seemed to suspect anything. And when I told Princess Emmeline, she promised not to tell anyone."

The wooden spoon fell from Isa's hand and clattered to the floor. "You *told* Princess Emmeline?"

Rowan folded his arms. "Of course. We're getting married. She's going to be queen one day. She was going to find out at some point. It was better for her to find out from me, and before the wedding, so she wouldn't feel like it was all a trick."

"And you're sure that was safe?" She kept her brown eyes on him while she picked up the wooden spoon and tossed it in a bucket of sudsy water, only breaking eye contact to retrieve another spoon to stir the stew.

"I trust Princess Emmeline with my life. If I didn't, I wouldn't have agreed to marry her."

Isa sighed. "Then someone must have overheard you telling her."

He stood up, pounding his fist on the wooden table. He didn't appreciate some commoner's insinuations about his future wife when she knew nothing about Emmeline. "What matters is that it happened, and now I have to fix it before the situation worsens."

Isa bowed her head and plopped a bowl of the steaming stew in front of him.

Despite its brownish, chunky appearance, the contents smelled delicious, and Rowan found his stomach growling. He humbly accepted a spoon from Isa and downed the contents.

She ladled another helping into his bowl before speaking again. "If Reb has been taken, we have to get you back inside the castle so you both can return to your own bodies."

"It's probably surrounded by Bolean soldiers by now," Rowan responded between bites. "Getting out was one thing, but getting back in?"

"Let me worry about that. You need to figure out how to stop the Boleans while protecting the peace treaty."

"And ensuring Princess Emmeline's safety." If anyone so much as touched his betrothed, he would drag them behind his horse from his home in Trudel all the way to the steps of the Bolean castle for her. "She knew about Trudeli abilities. These rebels may see that as treason. For all we know, she's being held prisoner in her own castle."

***

Two guards leaned against the dark oak doors, one sharpening his sword, the other dozing off.

Reb clenched his fists, eyeing King Osgood. He was expressly forbidden by the king to do anything that could endanger the prince's body. As a trained guard, Reb wanted to fight, but he couldn't disobey the king's orders. He was only to act as a lookout, not a soldier.

Queen Cressida stood.

The first guard eyed her, pausing the steady movement of his whetstone against his blade.

Instead of meeting his gaze, she bent over and massaged her calf, as if sitting for so long made it ache.

The guard returned his attention to his sword, running his finger along the length of the blade before resuming to his sharpening.

The other guard dozed still, his snoring mixing with the rhythmic scraping of steel against stone.

Against his better judgment, Reb nodded to the king. Now was their best shot.

The king focused the strength of his gaze on the first soldier, his blue eyes flashing gray.

The Bolean's eyes widened in submission to King Osgood's will. As his hands froze, he almost dropped the whetstone, but the king was meticulous and deftly caught the fumble so as not to wake the other. After the stone had been pocketed, the king's eyes flashed again as the guard strode toward them on shaky legs, his stumbling footsteps muffled by the plush rug. Once his legs were steady, he swung his sword back and forth in front of him.

Reb watched the sleeping guard while King Osgood tested his control over the first soldier. After another minute, Queen Cressida took her place as the "hostage" while King

Osgood manipulated the guard to place his free hand on her arm and the blade flat against her stomach. One soldier would not typically escort three prisoners, but the king could only control one person at a time, so this was their best solution.

Without disturbing the sleeping guard, the king pulled open the door and they all slipped out, Reb and King Osgood taking their places behind the first guard.

They rounded one corner and passed a couple Boleans. Reb was sure his heart would beat right out of his chest, but he kept his eyes trained on the soldier's back.

King Osgood made sure the guard kept his eyes forward, not even wavering to look at the others. With the queen as a prisoner, no one stopped them.

Encouraged, they turned again and found an empty hall. Reb glanced back toward the king, who wiped sweat off his brow before moving the guard once more. At the end of the hallway, they took the stairway down and turned again.

Another group of guards passed by, heading back toward the king's chambers. Reb recognized the captain who captured him earlier, and his heart stopped.

Captain Tierri paused with an eyebrow raised, his soldiers partially blocking their path. "Where are you taking the prisoners, Gell?"

The king expelled a quiet breath, and the guard spoke a rehearsed line. "I've been ordered to take them down to the dungeon. They were not cooperating."

"I was not informed of this." The captain eyed the sword against the queen's waist.

"Really? I sent Carren down to warn you."

Reb hoped he had heard the sleeping guard's name correctly when he passed that information onto the king.

"Did you?"

Reb heard his pulse throbbing in his ears, hoping the soldier's inflection sounded natural enough, his movements smooth enough.

The soldier, Gell, tossed his head back toward the stairs. "Wouldn't be surprised if Carren was slacking off again. He probably took a nap on the way here."

The captain nodded, his stiff façade broken by a smile. "Probably."

The king took a ragged breath as they resumed walking.

Captain Tierri stepped behind them. "Your Majesty?"

King Osgood turned, his head lowered so he appeared smaller in stature.

"I heard whispers that your power was formidable, but this—" He gestured to the soldier. "This is truly astounding."

Reb bit his lip to hold his breath as he backed toward the queen.

The captain turned to his men. "Take them."

King Osgood's eyes flashed again as Gell released the queen and swung his sword toward the captain.

Queen Cressida pulled Reb toward their escape, prompting him to run. Before he could, another Bolean grabbed hold of the queen's arm and prodded Reb's back with his sword.

Gell kicked down Captain Tierri and trained his sword on the guard holding the queen. King Osgood's face paled as he took another shaky breath. His magic was taking a toll. He wouldn't be able to control the soldier for long.

Behind him, a young soldier charged into the fight, inexperience and fear written all over his face.

"Look out!" Reb lunged forward.

King Osgood turned to face the incoming soldier. Gell raised his sword. But the king's power was too slow.

The younger guard thrust his sword forward. The tip protruded from King Osgood's back, stained red with his blood.

The king's body crumpled to the floor.

The queen screamed and elbowed her captor in the neck, only to fall to her knees in the puddle of her husband's blood.

Gell swayed, then toppled over, now released from the king's magical hold.

Reb pulled the queen to her feet, pushing himself between her and Captain Tierri while she wailed.

The captain blinked in shock as he stared at the red pooling around his boots. A purple vein bulged on his forehead as he turned to the soldier, still holding the bloodied sword. "What have you done?" His voice was quiet.

The young soldier dropped his sword in shock, splattering the blood puddled at his feet. He was barely a man, so young he could easily be mistaken for a child.

The captain grabbed the boy's shoulders and shoved him back against the wall. "What have you done?" he shouted. "She will have your head for this. She will have all our heads for this." He dropped the soldier and spun around, his eyes frantic. "This was not supposed to happen. This wasn't supposed to..." He gasped for air before shoving the young boy again. "What are we going to..."

His guards watched in wide-eyed silence as their commanding officer muttered under his breath. After a minute, he brushed off his clothing and ran a hand through his hair.

"You." He pointed to the guard Queen Cressida had elbowed. "Take them back to the room. And you—" He turned back to the soldier who killed the king and leaned in close. "You get to tell her what you have done." He grabbed the collar of the boy's uniform and pulled him down the hall.

With the soldier's sword pressed into his back, Reb guided the sobbing queen up the stairs. He was too stunned to think until he sat her down on the floor and saw the stains all over her nightdress. The king was dead. Rowan was now the king. But Rowan didn't even know he was the king. Reb was Rowan, and he had to act as the king. His mind spiraled. It had to be some sort of treason to impersonate the monarch. But Queen Cressida was in no condition to take charge. Reb had no choice.

The door burst open. A train of guards poured into the room, followed by Captain Tierri. He chewed on his lip, and his eyes flickered around the room before he pointed at Reb. "You will stand."

Reb followed as he was ordered, still unsure how to act.

"She wants to speak to you."

Before he had the chance to ask who "she" was, she strode into the room.

Dark, curly hair cascaded around her shoulders. A cloak the color of dark wine, matching her lips, was clasped at her collar. Her brown eyes softened when they saw his face.

"P-P-Princess Emmeline?" Reb stuttered before remembering his manners and bowing toward her. Then he remembered that he was supposed to be the prince. No, the king.

"My love." Her expression seemed almost sorrowful as she approached him, tears dotting the corners of her eyes.

Queen Cressida lurched to her feet, and a guard stepped between her and the Bolean princess. "Traitor!" she spat.

Princess Emmeline sighed. "I was afraid that was how you'd see me."

"But…" He stuttered, unable to form any more words. Reb had rarely spoken in her presence, but he wasn't Reb right now. He was Emmeline's betrothed. "Why?"

She stared at Reb, her dark brown eyes almost intoxicating. "My love, I was the one betrayed. By your father. Hiding this great secret from me while our kingdoms negotiated a peace treaty? How am I supposed to entrust you with my life when your people have the abilities to take everything away from my people? I mean, look what your father did." She cast a despairing glance over her soldiers before putting a hand on Captain Tierri's shoulder. "He took away that soldier's free choice. He forced him to attack his own commanding officer. He would've attacked me if that's what it took for you to escape safely."

"No, he never would've…"

"Shh." She placed a soft hand against his cheek. "Your father would've done anything to protect his son, his heir. I don't blame him. My father would do the same for me. Any father would. But I have to do the same for my people. They will never be safe while your people have this magic. It's not fair." She turned away from him, her curls bouncing as she moved.

"What do you plan to do with us?" Reb finally choked out a full sentence.

"You and I will marry as we planned, but you will constantly be under the watchful eye of my guards. Once we unite our people, Trudelis will be forced to stop using their abilities for anything, or else you and your mother will be killed. They hopefully value their royal family more than their magic."

"You're going to hold me hostage for the rest of my life? You'll never get away with it."

Her nostrils flared, and she stomped her foot like a child.

Captain Tierri cleared his throat.

Princess Emmeline took a deep breath, tossed her hair over her shoulder, and faced Reb again with a pained expression plastered on her face. "Your father wasn't supposed to die, my love. And the guard responsible will be punished. I do not want to harm you or your family, but I need to protect my people."

"Princess Emmeline, this is not the way to do things. I assure you, Trudel wishes no harm for Bolea."

"I know you think that is true, but how do you plan

to enforce it? I cannot risk it, my love. I'm sorry." She leaned in close and placed a warm kiss on his cheek before turning and leaving the room, her trail of guards following behind.

***

Rowan gripped Isa's arm as they crept back into the city under the invisible mantle of her magic. Isa decided they had to get in and out of the castle as quickly as possible so that the royal family could make it to safety. Rowan had other plans. He wasn't going to let the coward in charge hide behind the Bolean army anymore.

Bolean guards patrolled the streets with their weapons on display, gathering up Trudeli townspeople and steering them to the square, where the royal family would address the city from the castle terrace. So who wanted to speak to the people now? And what were they going to make his parents say?

"We need to get closer." Rowan pointed to the staircase that led up to the terrace. Two guards stood at the bottom, but he could slip between them.

Isa eyed him. "Your Highness, this problem won't be solved using your ability. That will only add reasoning to the Boleans' anger. Be careful."

He took a deep breath to keep his fury from clouding his judgment. "I have to be until my parents are safe."

As they slipped toward the crowd, still invisible, Bolean soldiers continued to herd the people, Rowan's people. One soldier shoved an older woman forward because she wasn't walking fast enough. She stumbled, and Rowan lunged toward her.

Isa pulled on his arm, reminding him that if they weren't touching, he would turn visible again.

Rowan's heart ached. If he possessed his father's ability, he would've forced the guard to help the woman instead. No one should be treated in this way.

Isa pointed up to the terrace, where more Bolean guards gathered. Rowan immediately recognized Captain Tierri. His blood boiled at the memory of his best friend being beaten in his place.

The captain faced the doorway and stood at attention.

Rowan clenched his free fist as a reminder that he couldn't use his power. If it was spotted while he was invisible, one of his citizens could be blamed. He couldn't risk it.

The door swung open, and Rowan almost dropped Isa's arm in shock.

Out strode Princess Emmeline, her dark, curly hair framing her bronzed face. Without a smile to crinkle the corners of her usually warm eyes, they appeared cold and angry.

What was she doing here? Was she being held with his parents and Reb? Rowan barely had time to catch his breath before she began to speak.

"People of Trudel, I am Princess Emmeline of Bolea, betrothed of Prince Rowan." She turned toward the door and waved her arm.

Guards escorted Reb, as Rowan, out onto the terrace for all to see. He sported a swollen cut above his left eye, along with a few bruises the same color as the prince's sapphire ceremonial surcoat, reserved only for the most special occasions. A gold crown sat atop his blond hair. In the sunlight, the golden stitching that made up the Trudeli crest glistened on his chest and shoulders. Reb eyed the guards all around, and Rowan could practically hear him calculating an escape despite the weapons.

Behind Reb, guards led out Queen Cressida and stood her against the castle wall. Her blond hair had been braided with purple ribbons that matched her silk kirtle. Normally, Rowan wouldn't have noticed what his mother was wearing, but he recognized it from a few days earlier when he approved it at her fitting. It was the dress she had made for his wedding.

"What…" Rowan stared at the door, waiting for his father to appear.

Isa shook her head, still staring at the foreign princess. "I'm so sorry, Your Highness. I didn't want to be right."

"You don't know this is her fault. She could be acting under duress. She could be…"

"I am here to defend the rights of my people." Emmeline pressed her lips in a thin line as she looked over the crowd. "Without magical abilities, I need to guarantee that my people will be treated as your equals, and that requires some new laws."

The crowd started shouting, but Rowan couldn't decipher any of it. It was as if he were underwater, everything cold and muddled. He focused on her face, looking for any tells that might indicate she was lying or being threatened.

Nothing. She remained steadfast and sure. No one was feeding her lines. She never took her eyes off the crowd, even as she held up a hand, directing the Bolean guards to train their weapons on the people, silencing their complaints. "I am as unhappy about this as you are, but something had to be done."

He gulped for air, unable to steady his racing heart. How had he misjudged her intentions like this? He had been so convinced of her loyalty and love for him. Was he that gullible, to fall in love with any maiden's kind words and gentle kiss?

She took a shaky breath and blotted the corner of her eyes with a white handkerchief. "Unfortunately, your king failed to see my side of the situation, and in an act of defiance, he was killed."

Her words stabbed through Rowan's heart, sending

painful shocks out to his extremities and turning any lingering love he felt for her into anger. If Isa hadn't squeezed his hand, he would've toppled over and become visible right in front of some guards.

Noise surged through the crowd. Women gasped and wept while men stepped between their families and the soldiers, ready to fight.

The Bolean guards marched into the crowd, brandishing their weapons, pressing the Trudelis back from the terrace.

He steadied himself on shaking legs and turned back to his mother. She remained stoic and unemotional. Rowan clenched his jaw and forced his pain down. He could not break down, not until this was over.

"Fear not." Emmeline choked out a sob. She dabbed her eyes once more, but Rowan didn't see any tears. After a shaky breath, she took her betrothed's hand, though Reb didn't react to her touch. "Tonight, after my wedding to Prince Rowan, where we will be crowned the new king and queen of Trudel, the soldier who struck down King Osgood will be hanged on the city wall."

Rowan cringed when she spoke his father's name. He needed to talk to his mother, but he needed her mind to reach out to his. There had to be a way to alert her to his presence.

Emmeline continued. "If any attempts to stop the wedding are made, Queen Cressida will be hanged, just as the soldier who murdered…"

He spotted the flower brooch pinned at Queen Cressida's bosom, one he had gifted her for her birthday when he was a child. Concentrating all his energy on the brooch, he reached out using his ability and pushed it so the dangling pearls swung side to side.

Her eyes flitted down at its movement.

Emmeline began listing off some of her new laws. "Any appearance of Trudeli magic will lead to immediate arrest…"

Rowan swung the beads once more.

Queen Cressida blinked as she scanned the crowd, then her mind pressed up against his. *Rowan? Is it really you?*

Yes, Mother. He longed to run to her, to hug her and weep at her side, to properly mourn the loss of his father. But there would be time for that later.

What are you doing here? You were supposed to stay hidden at the inn.

"All Trudeli citizens must report their power for official registration…"

And leave Reb to marry the princess? His attempt at humor fell flat as his anger pulsated. *Is it true?*

I'm afraid so. Her despair washed over him. *She pushed up the marriage so she could implement laws to protect her people.*

Mother, tell Reb that I am here. We have to swap back. I can slip between the guards and get up the stairs…

She disrupted his trail of thought. *And then what?*

He bit his lip as he realized he really didn't have a plan. *I must get you away from here. Isa can sneak you out of the city. I will marry Emmeline, but I won't allow her to use you like this.*

No! You can't marry her! Her tone reminded him of when she would catch Reb and him while they were swapped.

"Any Trudeli citizens outside after curfew will be arrested…"

I am the king now. I need to stop this before things get worse. Our people will fight back, and there will be blood.

Her mind brushed against his, bringing a feeling comparable to when she would kiss his forehead goodnight, then she withdrew.

He edged closer and closer to the stairs. "Isa, use your invisibility to get my mother out of here. She will try to stay for me, but I am now the King of Trudel, and I command you to protect her above everyone else. I just lost my father. I cannot lose her, too."

Isa nodded slowly. "Yes, Your Majesty."

Rowan watched Reb, waiting for any sign that he was ready. The corner of his eye twitched, and Rowan recognized it as his mother's consciousness pulling away from Reb's mind. His father always had the same reaction, which is how he knew when they were keeping secrets from him.

Holding Isa's hand to keep himself invisible, he slipped between the two guards at the bottom of the steps.

One of the guards glanced to the side as Isa passed him, but after blinking a few times, he turned his attention back to the crowd.

"Any business transactions between Trudeli and Bolean citizens must be witnessed by a Bolean guard…"

Rowan used his ability to tug on Reb's sleeve, alerting him to their position. But before the swap could take place, he needed a distraction.

Trees lined the square, barely budding after a long winter. Rowan fixated his power on one and pressed against the top. It bent slightly, then snapped in two.

Rowan released Isa and grabbed Reb's hand while everyone's attention was turned away. The familiar pang stabbed through his mind, and his vision swirled. Blinking away his disorientation, he steadied himself on the stone railing as guards lunged for Reb, now returned to his own body.

With a grunt, Rowan knocked their weapons out of their hands with his ability and scattered them across the terrace.

Behind them, Queen Cressida vanished.

One Bolean restrained Reb while two more ran toward their princess.

She held up a hand to stop them and stepped closer to Rowan. "My love—" Emmeline's voice had a sharp edge to it. "What do you think you're doing?"

"Protecting *my* people." He held his hands out, eyeing the guards surrounding them. "I understand that you feel the need to enforce these rules to protect Bolea, but you are oppressing Trudeli citizens without cause. When has a Trudeli ever harmed a Bolean with their magic?"

She clenched the handkerchief so tightly her knuckles turned white. "Don't you know? Prince Rowan, named for your great-grandfather, the savior and protector of his people during the War of Thieves."

Rowan froze. He heard a sharp intake of breath behind him, either Reb or his mother.

The crowd started to whisper. How did a Bolean remember the War of Thieves?

"How do you know about that?"

She turned to the crowd, speaking louder. "My great-grandmother wrote down what happened during the War of Thieves and hid the letter in a history book. She detailed how Trudel had betrayed Bolea by hiding these powers until it led to war, and how your grandfather chose to use his ability to erase the minds of the Boleans to keep Trudeli powers a secret."

Rowan stuttered. "That's… No… That's not why he did that." He eyed the guards backing up Emmeline. They didn't seem angry like she did. They almost seemed…sad. As if they regretted that these problems had to be resolved with violence, the same way his great-grandfather had felt during the War of Thieves. Could Emmeline understand how his actions were intended to be kind?

"Soldiers kept returning home to Bolea with no memories of Trudel, so my great-grandmother wrote down what happened before her memory was taken, too. She said he was selfish and wanted to keep the Boleans ignorant so Trudeli could overthrow us."

"No, that's not true." Rowan shook his head. "He did it to stop the violence, to protect both sides from harm."

"Lies." She turned to the crowd.

"Is it? Has Trudel once tried to overtake Bolea in the past twenty, fifty, even one hundred years?"

"Just because it hasn't happened yet doesn't mean it won't in the future."

"Emmeline, we only want peace. Why else would we be negotiating a treaty with your kingdom?"

"Why else would you keep your powers a secret if not to use them as a weapon?"

He blinked at her before continuing, his voice quiet. "Are you afraid I might hurt you?"

"You already did." A single tear slipped down her cheek. "By hiding all this from Bolea."

"So you're using my mother as a hostage? Forcing me into marriage? You killed my father. You committed regicide, Emmeline. And now you'll be imprisoned, possibly beheaded. All because you and your father didn't trust our peace treaty enough."

She swallowed, and Rowan could see a glint of fear in her eyes as she scanned her surroundings for a way out.

"Oh." He stepped closer to her. "Your father is not a part of this. Is that why you returned in such a hurry? And pushed up the wedding? So it would all be done before your father found out and arrested you?" His emotions stirred in his stomach, settling into disappointment.

Her brave façade crumbled with a sharp intake of breath. "He didn't believe my great-grandmother's story. He thought your great-grandfather did the right thing, to stop the bloodshed. He said it saved thousands of lives." Her lip quivered, and she eyed her guards, almost pleading with them. "My father will understand once I've secured the future of his people."

A murmur ran through the Bolean guards, and they looked toward their captain. Captain Tierri took a step away from Princess Emmeline, his eyes wide.

Out of options, Emmeline lunged toward Reb and knocked him backward, snatching at the dagger strapped to his hip.

Rowan had forgotten about the knife. "Don't!"

She held the dagger out, pointing it at her guards, at Reb, then at Rowan. With fear in her eyes, she hurled it forward.

"No!" Reb dove between his best friend and the blade.

It froze, the tip pressing into, but not piercing, Reb's chest.

Rowan gritted his teeth as he magically flipped the blade around to seek its new target—Princess Emmeline.

Her eyes widened, and she backed away as the blade wavered in the air.

Isa's warning echoed in Rowan's mind. Using his ability against a Bolean would only anger them more against Trudel and justify Emmeline's actions. This had to be resolved another way. He grunted as he released his magical hold of the knife.

It clattered to the ground.

Emmeline blinked a few times before returning her gaze to Rowan, her brow furrowed. All traces of fear had been replaced with confusion.

Rowan took a deep breath and straightened his shoulders. "This is not how things are done in Trudel. We do not use our abilities to harm others. We use our abilities to aid and defend those who cannot aid and defend themselves." He looked out over the crowd, who all seemed frozen, waiting. Even the Bolean guards watched him with mouths agape. None had retrieved their scattered weapons.

Normally, this was the point when Rowan would turn things over to his father, but he no longer had that option. He was the sovereign leader now.

Reb quietly retrieved his dagger and returned it to its sheath.

"Emmeline, I only wish for peace between our people. I never wanted to keep my power a secret." Rowan held out his hand to Emmeline. "Do you trust me to act in the best interests of both of our kingdoms?"

She inhaled a shaky breath, glanced at her unarmed guards, then expelled the breath. After dipping her chin, she stepped forward and accepted his hand.

His heart ached for her, but he knew what he had to do. "Princess Emmeline of Bolea, you are hereby bound by the laws of Bolea and Trudel and are under arrest for regicide and attempted regicide." He gripped her arms behind her back and watched for a reaction from her guards.

Captain Tierri bowed his head and stepped forward. "Your Majesty, we were unaware that King Galot was not involved. Princess Emmeline gave commands as if he supported her. Had we known that these orders were against our king's wishes, we never would've followed." Slowly, he retrieved a pair of shackles and held them out.

"So you do not object?"

Captain Tierri glanced at his princess with pain in his eyes before shaking his head. "I do not. I will withdraw our forces and escort the princess back to Bolea to face judgment."

Rowan took the shackles and clasped them on her wrists. "I'm sorry things had to end this way."

She looked at her feet, and he wasn't sure if he was disappointed that she didn't reply.

The captain took her elbow and directed his men to gather up their weapons. "We will clear out of the castle by nightfall." He bowed to Rowan and escorted Emmeline inside, the other guards falling into step behind.

Reb leaned onto the stone railing, his expression solemn as the crowd quieted. "The king is dead. Long live the king." He turned to Rowan and dropped to one knee.

The crowd dropped into a low bow. "Long live the king!"

***

Reb stopped outside Rowan's door and raised his fist

to knock.

"Though, how she found out about Trudeli abilities…" Queen Cressida's voice trailed off.

"I told her, Mother!" Rowan shouted. "I move objects with my mind. Reb and I swap places more often than you realize. You can read people's minds! It wasn't fair to leave her unaware. Besides, she was going to find out at some point."

Reb stepped back. Now was clearly not a good time.

The door opened, and Queen Cressida motioned him inside.

He glanced at Rowan, pacing across the room as servants bustled around him, gathering up his belongings to move into the king's chambers.

Reb bowed to the Queen Mother as he passed.

"I will be back to finish this conversation." She tossed her braid over her shoulder and marched out of the room.

"I didn't mean to interrupt." Reb grimaced.

"You didn't interrupt anything important. Just my mother trying to arrange my next marriage prospects." Rowan scowled after her.

"We should probably resolve the last one before moving forward…"

"That's what I said, but she didn't care. I have to guarantee that Emmeline returns to Bolea, but I can't leave Trudel because I have to take care of all the work my father left behind. We have to start drafting a new treaty with Bolea, one that now outlines Trudeli abilities, and—"

Reb interrupted. "I'm going to Bolea with Princess Emmeline's guard. I volunteer to take a squadron."

Rowan blinked. "What?"

"You need a representative who can accurately recount the story and ensure a proper punishment is enacted. I experienced it firsthand, more so than you."

The new king frowned.

Reb looked at his feet. "And I don't know that I can be here right now."

Rowan's brow furrowed.

"I failed you. I failed your father." His voice cracked, and he swallowed back a wave of emotion. "I am a soldier of Trudel. I swore an oath to protect the royal family at all costs, but he was killed right in front of me."

King Rowan shook his head. "You were supposed to protect me, and you did your job. The guard who killed my father is the one responsible."

"It doesn't matter. I can't walk these halls without seeing him bleeding…" He stopped when Rowan cringed. "The Boleans are taking the soldier with them to face justice back in Bolea. No one was supposed to get hurt. They all had orders not to kill, but he didn't listen. I need to see him pay for what he did."

"I understand." Rowan put a hand on Reb's shoulder. "Have you spoken to her?"

"I have. She is now aware of the swap."

Rowan scratched his chin and remained silent.

Reb chewed on the inside of his cheek. "Are you all right?"

Rowan turned away. "I'm not really sure."

"I don't expect you to be."

"I thought she was the love of my life. And now, because of her, my father is dead." He turned to face Reb with clenched fists and blue eyes burning with pain.

He raised his fist and a box on the floor next to him began to shake, then his arm drooped and the box stilled. "I don't know whether to punch the wall or lie in bed for a week. I'm so angry, it's exhausting. And it's my fault. If I hadn't told Princess Emmeline…"

"Princess Emmeline alone is responsible. For the same reason that it's not my fault your father died."

"Logically, I know and accept that, but emotionally…" He ran a hand through his hair and kicked the box across the floor.

"I know exactly how you feel." Reb sighed. He couldn't dislodge that lump of guilt from his chest, and he wasn't sure it would ever go away. Suddenly, it became overwhelming to face his best friend. Reb turned toward the door. "The Boleans are preparing to leave now."

"Reb, wait." Rowan put a hand on his shoulder, then paused, searching for something to say. "Your mother is still here. You should see her before you leave."

Reb allowed himself to smile. "You just don't want me to leave because you're going to miss me."

Rowan punched Reb's shoulder. "Never. Get out of here already."

"Don't worry, I'll be back soon, Your Majesty."

"Don't start with that. It's weird enough that I'm king. I don't need you rubbing it in." Rowan shoved his friend's shoulder and laughed.

Reb bit his lip, but soon enough he was laughing as well. The shaking eased the stress from his back, and the look on Rowan's face reminded him of happier times when they would swap for the sole purpose of playing pranks on friends and family.

Rowan gestured toward the door, and Reb fell into step beside him as they meandered out into the hall. He flicked a finger, dragging a footstool in front of Reb's path.

Reb's foot caught on the bottom, and he toppled over it headfirst. He stuck his arm out and caught Rowan, taking his friend down with him. "Hey!"

Queen Cressida came running from around the corner to find them laughing in a heap on the floor. She frowned, tapping her foot. "You two are trouble."

"We know." They laughed as they helped each other to their feet.

"Rowan, you're the king now." Cressida shook her head.

"No, Mother. Not this lecture again." He turned

back to Reb. "Quick, swap with me. I'll go to Bolea and you can stay here."

"Uh-uh." Reb backed away.

Rowan lunged for Reb's hand. "Please?"

Reb dodged him. "Nope! Not doing it. You're the king. It's your problem now."

"Come on!"

"You can't make me!" Reb took off running.

"Oh yes I can! I'm the king!" Rowan chased after, leaving an exasperated Queen Cressida behind.

The Gruffs vs. Dragon

Louise Ross

Once upon a time, three billy goats with the surname Gruff lived in meadows rarely seen by goats. These three brothers tricked and fought the Gudbrand Brucke troll. Brandt Gruff, the oldest, killed the troll and became a hero. Stories remember the baby brother, Eluf Gruff, as the one who tricked the troll and slipped into the meadows first. Ferdi Gruff, middle brother, neither the strongest nor the one who dared to be first, refused to be forgotten. This is the story of the Gruff brothers and the dragon.

***

Skydda's second eyelid closed, filtering the sharp morning light. He lay with his nose on the grass and scanned the clearing.

A goat stood in the spring meadow.

Skydda blinked, and the goat vanished. He pulled his head back in the entrance to his cave and dozed. Ten minutes later, he opened his eyes and checked outside again. Nothing.

He napped, dozing never long enough for an enemy to cross the meadow. Those moments of sleep never touched the dream-filled nights of his youth, but the brief periods kept him alert to approaching danger.

The sun rose to its zenith. He moved a wing, fighting

the ache in his joints. Over the years, patchy cracked skin had formed on the folds, and the vibrant blues and greens of his wings had faded. Yet moving was too much effort. Even if he had eaten a castle's worth of stone, he could not feel this heavy and tired. He allowed himself five more dozing cycles before swishing his tail from side to side.

From deep in his cave, the river chattered, and he dreamed of a village of dragons and people: folks who washed their clothes in the stream and sang songs about foreign lands, and dragons who crafted and flew just to feel the air currents brush their wings. He drifted off to sleep and woke with moisture on his cheeks and a longing for change.

His eye opened on the meadow, and a goat crept up the edge. He turned his head to watch, but the goat disappeared.

His life was coming to an end. His muscles strained to make even the smallest movements. Perhaps he would let the next champion defeat him. They would get a noble tale, and he would be free.

The goat's brown-and-white coat shifted in long ropes of hair, and between his ears, two tiny horns poked up, no bigger than Skydda's back tooth. He watched the goat, wondering if his imagination had created a mirage warrior, a ridiculous and weak-looking hero who would not tempt him to action. Blinking, he planned to lie still as stone for this unexpected champion.

Across the meadow, the goat stopped. He lowered his head in charging stance and took three running steps before jumping up and to the side. He bleated a long cry, jumped, hopped, and ran away into the trees.

With a huff and sigh, Skydda scorched the grass at the cave entrance. The grass glowed ember bright. With a long inhale, he sucked in the oxygen, and the warmth died before a fire caught. Perhaps he'd see the sun the next day. He dozed again.

In his dream, he imagined the same goat creeping up

along the field, only to turn and run again. He imagined it so many times, he lost track of whether it was during his dreams or while awake. When his mind became bored of the leaping goat, he imagined it running across the field from another direction. Once, he imagined a second goat pushing the first into the field. The day passed into night, and he continued his dozing cycle, happier with the dreams of leaping goats than he had been in a very long time.

***

Ferdi Gruff screamed at his baby brother. No matter how many times he encouraged, cajoled, and shoved Eluf into the field, the younger goat had failed to run up to the dragon. Eluf's foot had yet to step on those rocks that created the cave entrance, which would surely take him to safety and distract the dragon. His baby brother acted like a true kid.

"Some brave and clever trickster you are." Ferdi shoved his brother toward home.

Eluf ran away, taking any possibility of distracting the dragon or verifying Ferdi's great deeds.

Another night lay on the field. If Ferdi was to prove himself the clever and swift hero of a tale, he needed to act now. Surely, Eluf would not keep this adventure from their older brother. Once Brandt learned of the adventure, he would come searching, and Ferdi did not need his older brother stealing this tale. The treasure would have to prove his deed.

Alone, Ferdi circled the edge of the field. Stories said water ran through the cave. While he was not a great swimmer like his older brother, he could swim a long way and would not be afraid to float into the dragon's chamber.

From above, the stream slid like a snake in the grass. It ran through the trees, burbling happily over pebbles and branches. Ripples reflected the moon's light, marking the river among the darkness. Leaping from a rock, Ferdi hiked to the stream.

Up close, the stream was barely a creek. His dreams of floating downriver turned to acknowledgement that the stream would not even wet his knees. Ferdi hung his head. He tore a leaf off a bush and chewed it slowly as he wandered down the brook.

The creek flowed into a small opening. Rocks worn down by water over time stretched wide as a smile and bubbled over the top. An old, toppled-down oak pushed the stream into a narrow channel, forcing the water to flow deeper. He waded into the deepest part until it touched his chest.

Grinning, Ferdi prepared. He tucked his legs up under him and ducked his head, flattening his horns along his body. This would make the adventure his own because his older brother could never perform this entrance. No, his brother was much too large, weighed down by horns and fat with muscle. This tale would truly be about Ferdi, the brother small enough, clever enough, and brave enough to attempt this feat.

With no more than two bumps on the head and a scrape on his forehoof, Ferdi floated into the cave. He bleated with joy as he stood up inside the dragon's lair, a pile of treasure heaped next to him.

***

Brandt raised his head to the sound of hooves and bleating.

Eluf ran into the meadow, knocking Brandt in the side. Because Eluf loved to play, Brandt turned to knock him back and start a mock battle, but Eluf screamed and whined.

"What's wrong?"

Eluf screamed again and ran in a few circles, too excited to speak.

Brandt needed to calm his brother, so he began a game, one to focus his brother's mind and body.

"Trip, trap, trip trap," he called and danced his forefeet in time.

Eluf's leaping stamped in time with the familiar rhyme.

"Come along and see my spears." Brandt turned to show his brother the long horns that curved over his head and paused the rhyme, inviting Eluf to say the next line.

"I'll stab your eyeballs out your ears," his brother sang.

"And with these large curling-stones."

"I'll crush to bits your body and bone." Eluf stamped his feet and ran a small circle, no longer leaping.

With a soft head bump, Brandt stopped his brother. "Now, what worked you up?"

Eluf made wide eyes and looked around. "A dragon." He jumped again.

Brandt nodded, not because he understood, but because he wanted his brother to continue. "What about the dragon?"

Eluf bleated the words so fast, Brandt needed a moment to fish them from the stream of noise and dry them out. To confirm his understanding, he repeated it back.

"Ferdi has gone to the dragon's lair. He wanted you to enter the dragon's cave, but every time you approached, the dragon opened his eyes and frightened you. Ferdi has sent you home, but he did not follow. Is that right?"

Eluf nodded and added, "He's in danger."

Brandt breathed in the clover and dirt of their home. If his brother was in trouble, he would help. They were family, and where one went, the others followed, yet he did not like bringing Eluf into danger. "Will you come with me and stay in the woods nearby?"

Eluf nodded, so together they sought the dragon's cave.

***

Skydda watched the final color slip from the sky and sighed, knowing he'd travel the same path back to the treasure and eat his fill at the cornucopia so he would survive the next day. His legs moved slowly, sluggish to respond when he commanded. His wings dragged along the ground. In the wide entrance, he turned, letting his tail contour to the wall and adjust from momentum rather than any will of his own.

The treasure room was far away. He was no leaping goat to prance back and forth, and his energy failed him. When he was a neck's stretch away, he plopped to the floor and sipped at the stream.

The earthy, cool water washed over his tongue and moistened his lips. It gained a flavor of clover—sweet, yet reminiscent of horse-filled pastures, a scene he had not remembered for decades and one that stoke his anger. A clump of hair brushed over his tongue, giving his anger a target. A stranger was in his cave.

The fire banked hot in his throat. This was no champion come to defeat the dragon. This was a thief, a sneak, a robber. Although his spirit had dwindled during the day, this stealth and deception enraged him. For a moment, he considered letting the thief touch the treasure, but that pushed his patience too far.

He pulled his mouth out of the stream and waited for his intruder.

A billy goat, not the playful short-horned one from the day, but a larger one with talon-sized horns and a beard, floated into the cave.

It stood in the stream and pulled itself onto the dry rock. Its feet pranced, and it bleated. The short and quiet sound died quickly in the cavern, just like its owner would.

Not bothering with a warning, Skydda breathed a stream of fire. The wall of flame rose up between the goat and the stream. The heat boiled the water and lit the goat's fur on fire. Red flames lit the treasure, reflecting light around the cave and creating an orange glow. For a moment, the cave held the beauty of a star and the warmth of a mother's hug. The fire extinguished.

The goat bleated, ran for the stream, and leapt out as the heated water scalded him. His burning fur fouled the air, and wisps of smoke rose from him as he ran past Skydda toward the entrance.

The glow of the room faded and stole Skydda's heart. What he wouldn't give to be back at home or sitting by a fire with friends. He had no desire to chase the goat. The treasure was safe. He'd controlled his anger. The goat would likely live. Everything returned to normal.

***

Brandt heard his brother scream, clear and distinct. A fireball hurdled out of the cave and dropped into the grass. As Brandt galloped toward the cave entrance, ready to block the next projectile with his horns, the bleating cries of Ferdi sounded beside and then behind him. His heart pounded as he turned.

The blackened figure rolled in the grass again. Its legs kicked at the air as it flipped from side to side. Ferdi screamed again.

"Brother!" Brandt rolled him over and checked that the fire had been smothered. "No more fire. It is out."

Ferdi struggled, thrashing from side to side.

Brandt nudged him to his feet. "Safe, brother. It is out. Get to the stream." He pushed Ferdi to the water.

Ferdi screamed. "No! Hot!"

Brandt shoved him more firmly. "Above the cave. It'll be cool."

Zigging and zagging, Ferdi ran toward the stream.

Brandt wanted to run after his brother, to make sure

he was safe, but a mighty dragon lurked in the cave and could come after his family at any time.

"Dragon!" Brandt called into the cave. "I have come for you with my two spears. The end for you is drawing near. Swift and strong I've come to fight. Your fire will die this very night."

The dragon's voice rumbled up through the cave. "Swift and strong you claim to be, but I have never heard of thee. No tale, no saga, no song or rhyme, convinces me you're worth my time. To be a hero strong and brave, you'll have to venture inside my cave."

Brandt narrowed his eyes at the obvious challenge. The Gudbrand Brucke troll had made a similar threat, but the troll had done so out of anger. His voice had echoed through the stones and shook the land the bridge clung to. While the dragon's rumble shook the rocks beneath his feet, it did not charge. Neither the words nor the dragon himself roared up from the depths.

He paused, uncertain. A clever goat sets a trap when force alone will not work. A clever dragon might do the same. So, slowly, one hoof at a time, Brandt entered the cave. The rocks closed over him, dimming the light, and he paused to let his vision adjust.

Inside the mouth lay a cavern large enough for a family of dragons and goats to camp. Along the upper edge, a ledge jutted out. On the ledge, a blue-and-green dragon with translucent wings watched him. There was no trap. The dragon had simply waited for him to come close.

Brandt stepped behind a stone, shielding himself from any fiery blast, and planned his approach. Along the walls of the cave, rocks jutted and climbed step-like. The steps led up and around but never close enough to jump to the dragon's ledge.

He had no throwing weapon, no traps, no lures. So he would cross the cavern, hiding behind the rocks until he reached the other side. Below the dragon and beside the treasure, the stones leapt up to the dragon's ledge in a staircase. If he could survive and the dragon still waited upon his perch, Brandt would defeat the monster.

"You harmed my brother," Brandt shouted.

"Come and fight." The dragon spat fire into the chamber.

The heat spread out and around the stone, but it did not touch Brandt's hiding spot. He ran from his shelter to a closer one.

"Why don't you jump down from your perch? Are you afraid?" he taunted.

After a moment of silence, the air drove down around him, pushing him. It pounded against his ears and left him deaf. Loose stones rolled back along the ground, and Brandt ducked his head to peek into the clearing.

The dragon had jumped down. His wings stretched out, making the giant cavern smaller. The beast stood on his hind legs, belly exposed, and Brandt ran.

His head lowered, tipping his horns toward the beast.

The great beast fell forward, his forelegs closing in for a grab.

Brandt was fast and agile.

The beast moved slow.

With a leap to the side, Brandt avoided the arms. The forward fall aided his thrust as Brandt raised his head and stabbed his horns into the monster's chest.

The dragon's roar filled the cavern. Red shone through the wound, Flames caught and died along the gash.

The beast fell to the side.

"Your brother is avenged," the dragon breathed.

"I am the mighty Gruff, victor of Gudbrand Brucke and dragon slayer." With that declaration, Brandt turned to leave.

Ferdi trotted into the cave. He pawed the dragon's nose. When the great beast did not move, he headbutted it and screamed.

Brandt started to leave.

"Where are you going, brother?" Ferdi demanded.

Brandt nodded to the entrance. "This is done. It's time to go home."

Ferdi whined. "No, brother. We must take the gold. For medicine, for food, to build a home. I cannot carry it as the creature has burned me." Ferdi turned, showing Brandt the black-and-red mottled skin of his back.

Brandt winced at the damage, struck by the injury he could not protect his brother from. What his brother asked, he could do. "One trip. I will take what I can carry now. Nothing else. Our brother waits for us. Go find him."

Ferdi left.

***

Skydda watched the greedy, blackened thing leave, but the warrior goat remained.

The warrior goat crossed to the treasure. He hooked the cornucopia onto one long horn and a collection of necklaces onto the other. He nibbled bits and pieces of jewels before finding a sword. Looping strings of sacks along the sword, he picked it up like a dog with a bone and made his way back to the cavern mouth.

Skydda thought to lie silent, accepting the pain after so much emptiness, but the goat had acted as a true warrior, fighting as a champion and moving to leave without the treasure.

Opening his mouth to speak, Skydda found the words trapped behind his pain. His back teeth tightened, stopping a burst of flames, and he forced one word of warning to the goat. "Cursed." With that, he shut his eyes and faded.

***

Brandt balanced the sword in his teeth and left, unconcerned about the dying dragon's attempt to curse him. Curses needed real power to outlive their caster, and the dragon would soon be dead.

His brothers waited for him in the tree line. Ferdi's voice carried into the meadow. He detailed the scary dragon who had caught Ferdi stealing into the treasure room and a daring fight that ended in fire.

Brandt raised his head higher, upset that his brother had confronted a dragon, proud of his brother's courage, and equally happy that the threat was gone.

Both brothers turned as he approached. Ferdi leapt about and snagged bags of jewels from the sword. Eluf rubbed necks with Brandt and circled him.

"Are you hurt?" Eluf licked the blood on Brandt's horns.

Brandt pulled away, removing the blood from his brother's reach, and set down the sword with its remaining dangling sacks. Blood welled in the corners of his mouth.

"Bring me two branches," he ordered Eluf.

Ferdi lay on the ground and nibbled open a bag. The wounds on his back glistened with wetness.

"We need a healer." Not waiting for his brothers to argue with him, Brandt arranged their treasure into two collections. With the two sticks Eluf had found, he looped the sacks over the ends, gave one collection to his baby brother, and kept the other for himself.

"What about me?" Ferdi picked up the small bag he'd been inspecting. It hung by its strings from his mouth, and he chewed on the ropes lightly.

Brandt shook his head. "You were too hurt to collect the treasure from the cave, so you should not be carrying the extra weight now. When you are better, you may help."

Ferdi nodded but refused to give up his single bag.

***

The closest village spanned the bottom of a valley. Huts, pens, and open land patchworked the town. Ferdi and his brothers walked in to stares. The obvious wealth hanging from his brothers attracted smiles, children, and thieves.

Ferdi bleated at them. When his older brother glared at him, he kicked his head up and bleated louder. The treasure was theirs and no one else's.

The healer lived in a hut. Shelves filled with bottles supported the roof, and clumps of dried flowers and herbs hung from the rafters. It smelled of dried reeds, woven baskets, and weed dust. Ferdi sneezed.

A stoop-shouldered woman with grayed hair appeared from behind a shelf with two pails of water hung over her yoke. A bone necklace hung off her neck and swung back and forth with her steps. At Ferdi's sneeze, she looked up at them. Her eyes grew wide and then narrowed.

"Will you help our brother?" Brandt brayed.

The old woman poked and cut a piece of blackened skin before she agreed to help. In exchange for a single blue gem, she gave them a bottle of gray paste.

The healer scraped the cream onto his skin, peeling back and cutting hair she said was melted. When her nails dug under and into the burn, Ferdi screamed. His brothers chattered at him. Eluf retold the healer about how brave and magnificent Ferdi had been when battling the dragon, and the story gave Ferdi courage to endure her care.

When she released them, Ferdi stumbled with weakness. His body stung and ached, and his stomach grumbled.

"It still burns," he complained and stomped along behind his brothers.

A barn lay on the edge of town. Brandt took pity on him and arranged a barn stall where they could sleep in peace.

"Innkeeper, for a night's safe rest and meal delivered to us, I will let you have one piece of this treasure but not the cornucopia."

Ferdi stamped his feet. Never had a stable master received so much for one night's food and rest. A gold coin alone should provide for a week or more.

"They are helping us in a time of need. We can afford to be generous." Brandt stood patiently as the stable master opened a sack and dug through it.

"But the future," Ferdi whined.

Brandt shrugged. "We lived quite well on the meadows. We can do so again."

Ferdi kicked at the ground and watched as the stable master took a necklace from around his brother's horn.

"Very good choice." Brandt nodded at the man.

They settled in their stalls, and Ferdi shifted. The straw scratched against his side and relieved the pain, so he rubbed his back against the stall wall. When the pain flared, he scratched a little harder.

"Food," the stable master called as he poured out a bucket of grains into bowls and laid out platters of carrots and apples.

Ferdi walked to the table, focusing on a large green apple that he would take for his own. With each step, the apple darkened. He chose another apple, a yellow and red one, and aimed for it, but its skin also had blemishes the closer he came. While the apples may still be good, he'd start with the carrots. The shriveled and split things lying on the tray looking nothing like the bright orange carrots he thought he'd seen.

His brothers came up beside him.

"It's rotten," Ferdi complained.

Brandt chewed on a carrot before agreeing.

Ferdi screamed and demanded new food. The stable master came back and stared at the feast. His hand scratched at his neck. Before Ferdi could scold, the stable master nodded. His attention shifted to Ferdi's back.

"That burn is infected. The food rotted after I left

it." With cold, clear eyes and a confident air, the man nodded as if he made a decision. "You are cursed."

He called out to his wife, and a pretty lady with curly brown hair came to stand at his side. Around her neck, she wore the necklace, a lattice of gold with red stones worked into the pattern. He took the necklace from around her neck and gave it back to Brandt. "You must leave. Take your jewels and leave."

At that, Ferdi bleated. He and his brothers were heroes. They had battled a dragon. They weren't cursed, and there was no reason to be sent out in the middle of the night. The man should be grateful for the gifted necklace and their generosity.

Eluf knocked his head against Ferdi's, but Ferdi didn't want to be quiet or comforted. He bleated at everyone.

Brandt turned and butted him out the back door of the stable. Ferdi fought, dodging around his brother, but the burns slowed him down. Brandt shoved him into the night.

"Brother, how can you let him kick us out? You are more powerful than he."

Brandt nodded but did not relent. "Powerful, yes, but he is right. We are cursed."

Eluf brushed sides with Brandt, making a wider barrier to Ferdi's struggle.

"No." He refused to believe it. He'd battled the dragon. They had the treasure. They won.

"Yes. We have to go back to the cave."

***

Skydda opened his eye, only to find he had not made it to the afterlife. Even in death, he lay in his cave, the walls never changing, the sound of the river a constant noise. He breathed fire against the wall, sending smoke and char up the rock. His chest did not ache as badly, and his voice felt like he could sing if he wanted. The heaviness crept back into his limbs. He had not escaped.

He would continue to live.

If only he had shoved the goat a little further or fell a little faster. Maybe it would have been a killing blow. Maybe it should have been.

Light came in through the opening. Another day began, but he did not pull himself to his entrance. Come what may, he'd sleep if only this once.

***

Brandt huffed and bleated at the cave entrance. Neither taunt nor fire greeted him. He set the sword and its bags of jewels on the stones and stepped in.

The dragon lay where Brandt had left him after the battle. His eyes were closed.

Stepping around the creature's front legs, Brandt stared at the wounds made by his horns. The ember glow shone through its skin, but the openings would no longer fit half his horn. The dragon had healed quickly while his brother became infected and weak.

In a moment of rage, Brandt headbutted the dragon near his wounds.

The dragon roared and released a flame.

Brandt danced back, ready to fight.

"The treasure is where you left it." The dragon's voice rumbled but came out clear, nothing like the strained curse.

"Raze the curse, and I'll bring your treasure back."

The dragon's laughter held the cacophony of stones battered together. "I cannot lift the curse. It is not mine."

"My brother is dying. The curse must be lifted," Brandt demanded. He dropped the necklaces and cornucopia off his horns. "Take it back. Curse and all."

The dragon rolled onto his stomach, ignoring the

zing of pain that shot from his wounds into his wings and neck, and stretched his nose toward the fresh meadow air.

"There once was a queen, a hideous woman with a heart of ice, who bore a son."

"I do not care, dragon," Brandt interrupted.

"You should because it concerns the curse."

Brandt lay on the ground. "Go on."

"The queen did not love her son but wanted him to bring her fame and glory. So she extracted a wish from a witch. The witch demanded payment. She wanted safety, supplies, and a child to raise and teach her skills. The queen agreed. So the witch bespelled the prince to conquer and gain treasures without fail. In casting her spell, she turned the queen's son into a beast so powerful and cunning it could not fail, but the queen became angry at her son's transformation and blamed the witch. She burned the witch's home and incited the villagers to run her from the town. The witch laid a second spell upon the prince. This second spell guaranteed that the prince would never be able to use his treasure. That any piece which left his hand would bring death and destruction upon the recipient. As for conquering, he would succeed but would not be able to keep what he obtained."

Brandt backed up and stared the dragon in his aqua eye.

"Is this the cursed treasure?" Brandt nudged the jewelry he'd dropped from his horns.

The dragon nodded.

Brandt considered the treasure, one held by the dragon who had yet to die. "And what happened to the prince?"

"He could not be defeated. He conquered the lands in the name of his queen. The strongest warriors and the cleverest tricksters could not stop his reign, but it was never enough for his mother. After he conquered, he left. Her armies entered and caused destruction. As he left each town, he took a caravan of soldiers and treasures. One night as he camped beside the road, a thief attacked. It was the first time the prince was not the aggressor, and the thief injured him. He stole a bag from the treasure. The prince tracked the treasure by the pestilence it caused. Driven to despair by the rebellions and death that surrounded him, he came to a conclusion. If his actions brought nothing but death, he would not act. If his treasure harmed those around him, he would not let it be used."

Brandt glanced at the treasure and remembered the pieces he could not carry away. If the treasure had not been spent, then he had little doubt who the dragon was. "Are you the prince?"

The dragon closed his eye. For a long minute, they were silent. The answer when it came floated like pollen on the wind. "Yes."

***

Skydda sank into his memories. The battlefields and rot stank in his nostrils. His own loathing burned acid through his throat. The nightmares danced to the witch's cackle and delight at his eternal torture. He'd heard her only once when he had tracked her down. His own demands to have the curse lifted had not swayed her. It was a feud between the queen and the witch. He was nothing but their whipping boy, his misery inconsequential to them.

"My fate is that I cannot use my strength against others and cannot spend the treasure I collect. I have never known a man who possessed a piece of the treasure to escape its effect. Perhaps if you and your brothers do as I have, you will be spared."

Skydda opened his eye and watched the light glow through his cave. When he was strong again, maybe he would leave. Maybe he would fly away and never know if someone found the treasure. Maybe. And when stories of death and destruction reached him, maybe he would pretend that it did not come from the curse which he allowed to spread.

The goat bleated, whined, and made many noises before responding. "No. I cannot agree. My brothers are smaller and weaker than me. I need to be strong and protect them. I cannot put my strength to the side."

Skydda flexed his wing, feeling the wound on his chest stretch.

The goat jumped at the movement, but he did not run away. This creature bragged that he had defeated the Gudbrand Brucke troll, but perhaps he had forgotten the lesson of his own tale or never heard it from the troll's side.

"You say that because no one stronger has come by yet, but that will not always be true. Do you know the story of the guardian troll?"

The goat shook his head.

"In the land of trolls, there was a guardian. For many years he fought and won battles and challenges. When everyone in the land had agreed he was the strongest troll, they gave him the honor of being the guardian to the gate. As far as trolls went, he was wise, allowing the peaceful to enter while barring the wicked, but he had been the strongest for too long and had forgotten that strength can change in the moments of battle. One day, while he guarded the gate, a peasant wanted to enter. The troll asked why. The peasant swore he was peaceful but danger followed him. The guardian let him in. When a second peasant came, the guardian was more wary, but again when asked why he wanted to enter, the peasant swore he was peaceful and the danger followed him. It was the third peasant who came to the gate. The troll demanded to know why the peasant wished to enter the troll lands. Without answering, the peasant stabbed the troll through the eyes and bashed his bones to bits. So the trolls learned: no matter how strong one is, there is always someone stronger."

The goat bleated. "That's not how it happened! I defeated that troll."

Skydda blew a puff of smoke. "So you have taught the trolls to treasure their strength, but you have yet to learn defeat. Run away. Use your strength to protect your brothers. When they die from the curse and your body is weakened from rotten food and lost battles, may you remember that it is because you could not give up on power and riches."

The goat's head twisted and shook. "No. You don't understand. That troll was the enemy. He'd eat any goat who tried to cross. He threatened to eat my brothers. Even you attacked my brothers. We need our strength to fight off those that would harm us."

Skydda smiled, even though he felt no humor or happiness. "I did not attack your brother. Remember that I cannot fail when I attack. It was your brother who attacked by entering my home. I only scared him off."

The goat chewed on his lip. "But the troll was vicious."

Skydda rolled his head to the side. "So are most men who protect their lands from those without permission."

Skydda closed his eyes, not caring if this goat would run him through again. He was tired.

***

Brandt left the dragon prince and found his brothers under a broad oak tree. Its leaves dappled the grass.

The burn on Ferdi's back had whitened like toadstools spotting a field. Holding a branch in his teeth, he used it to scratch at the toadstools.

"Stop scratching." Brandt took the stick away.

"But it itches." Ferdi laid his head down. "The medicine's not working."

"The dragon says it won't. The treasure's cursed."

Brandt snatched the loose bag from Ferdi's legs and looped it over Eluf's stick.

"Make him take the curse off."

"He can't. A witch set it." Brandt walked along the tree line.

"Fine." Ferdi rocked and tipped as he stood. "You'll make the witch lift it."

Brandt knocked his brother in the head. "Because you know the witch who set it? And she'd be so easy to defeat? With your magic?"

Eluf bleated. "We have to try. Look at Ferdi's back."

One of the toadstools had blossomed and seeped along the wound. The dried medicine cracked in rivulets along the burn.

Brandt stamped the ground. "I don't know where to start."

Eluf chewed on a leaf. After he swallowed, he cleared his throat. "We can ask the healer."

"She cannot help. Her medicine failed."

"No," Eluf shook his head, "ask her about the witch and curse."

"If you think that will help, you may ask."

So together, they returned to the village.

***

"Ms. Healer Lady?" Eluf called into the hut.

Ferdi pushed his way to the door, but Eluf didn't want his brother to upset the healer. Eluf bleated softly.

Brandt stepped up and butted Ferdi to the side.

The healer came from the back, still stoop-shouldered, but much the same as the day before.

Brandt snorted.

"Ms. Healer, can you help us?"

Her eyes narrowed and she swayed. "Help. I helped yesterday, and in exchange, you brought a curse upon my home. A powerful and old curse." She spit over her shoulder. "No."

Eluf looked to Brandt to explain, but he did not.

"We did not know. We are cursed too. Can you help?"

The woman glanced to the bags at Eluf's feet.

Ferdi stomped his feet. "No more. You can't have any more."

Brandt shoved him back farther from the healer. "She is welcome to whatever she needs."

The healer cackled. "You, young goat," she pointed at Eluf, "are innocent. I can lift the curse from you."

Eluf waited to hear the fate of his brothers.

"What will you give me for your freedom?" Her swaying rattled the bones on her necklace.

"You can have whatever you need," Brandt repeated.

Eluf whined, "Can you help my brothers?"

Quick as a leap, she grabbed Brandt's beard and snipped a piece. She shoved it in her mouth. Chewing, she stared at Brandt until he shifted. Spitting the piece over her shoulder, she leapt at Ferdi, who screamed and danced back. Her scissors snipped faster than he retreated. She spit the beard out as soon as she chomped down on it.

"That one," she pointed at Ferdi, "no, but that one," she pointed at Brandt, "maybe. So what do you offer?"

"Anything you—"

"No." The healer struck her hand through the air, cutting off Brandt's answer. "What do you offer?" She stepped up to Eluf.

Eluf wished to be strong like his brother and know what to say, but he didn't and had nothing other than the cursed treasure at his feet to offer. He kicked at the sacks of cursed jewels. The healer had not wanted to help them because of the cursed jewels.

"What do I have that you want?"

The healer pursed her lips. "For you, I will take

another jewel from this treasure and lift your curse, but for him," she pointed to Brandt, "there must be a sacrifice."

"You cannot harm my brothers. I will kill you first." Brandt bumped sides with Eluf and stood nose to nose with the healer, just as he always would.

"Harm me and no curse will be lifted."

Eluf borrowed Brandt's strength and warmth. "I will pay the sacrifice." He raised his head higher.

"You are brave and innocent." She grabbed a bag of spices from a table and crushed them in a bowl, spitting into the mortar as she worked. "You protect your brother, and he protects you. Would you trade your freedom to protect others?"

"Who?" Brandt asked.

"Those who need it. Those who are innocent. Those who do no harm."

Brandt nodded. "I will do this."

The healer turned to Eluf, her eyebrow raised, her pestle gripped in her fist. "You, brave one?"

Eluf rubbed his neck against his brother, feeling his steady muscles and warmth. "Yes. I will."

"What about me?" Ferdi screamed.

The healer spit over her shoulder twice. "May that curse rot at the darkness in your heart and either leave you healed or dead." She spat twice more and returned to her work.

Sweet clover and a spicy tarragon drifted across the room. A single candle heated a bowl. Lard, Brandt's beard hair, and the poultice cooked together.

"Drink it." She shoved the concoction under Brandt's nose.

Without pause, he drank.

Then she cooked the same with Eluf's hair and made him drink.

The hot mush burned his tongue and tasted bitter, but he swallowed.

"Now for the cost." She set the bowl on her table and blew out the candle. "You must go and protect, but make sure you protect that which is good. If you choose to defend the impure," she nodded distinctly at Ferdi, "the curse will return. Choose wisely."

Ferdi screamed. "You can't cut me from my brothers!"

"It's done." She slashed a hand through the air.

Pressure burst inside Eluf, relaxing muscles he did not realize had been tight.

Brandt turned and walked off.

"Brother!" Ferdi bleated.

Brandt looked over his shoulder. "Come with us. Be a protector."

"Why?"

"Because it is right. Because it is the sacrifice required. Because we are brothers and should stick together."

"No."

Eluf danced back and forth, fighting a knot in his throat. He butted his brother in the head. "It's not too late. Be good and find us."

***

"What are we doing?" Eluf asked.

Brandt trotted across the meadow back to the dragon's lair.

"If I have to choose someone innocent to protect, I will protect the dragon. He has done nothing wrong and lives alone, stopping even thieves from being cursed by his treasure." The cave opened into darkness with no dragon.

Eluf jumped to the side and stopped. "But he burned our brother."

Brandt turned to him. "Who was stealing at the time. You do not have to join me. You can travel and find others to protect."

"Are you sure?" Eluf whispered the words.

Brandt nodded and approached the cave. "Dragon," he called from the entrance.

"Goat," the dragon answered.

"Why do you lie there?" Brandt stepped up to the dragon, who stretched along the cold stone wall.

"I am too tired. I am resigned to my fate. Take my treasure, kill me, I have given up."

Brant bleated at him, "Do not give up yet. I have come to guard your entrance and help you." Decided, Brant turned to the entrance. He lay down. Looking over his shoulder, he told the dragon, "Sleep. I will keep watch. When you wake, you can take to the sky or explore the woods. I will be here for you." He kept watch on the field.

A warm burst of air rushed over Brandt, not hot like fire, but comforting as a hug. The dragon's breathing evened out like a beast in sleep.

Eluf crossed the meadow in starts and stops, glancing over his shoulder toward the tree line. When he reached the cave, he lay next to Brandt.

The dragon's breath warmed them. The muscles on Eluf's back jumped, but he did not get up and run away.

"I'll help."

Together they guarded. If anyone came for the treasure, they'd stop them, and while they watched, the dragon slept.

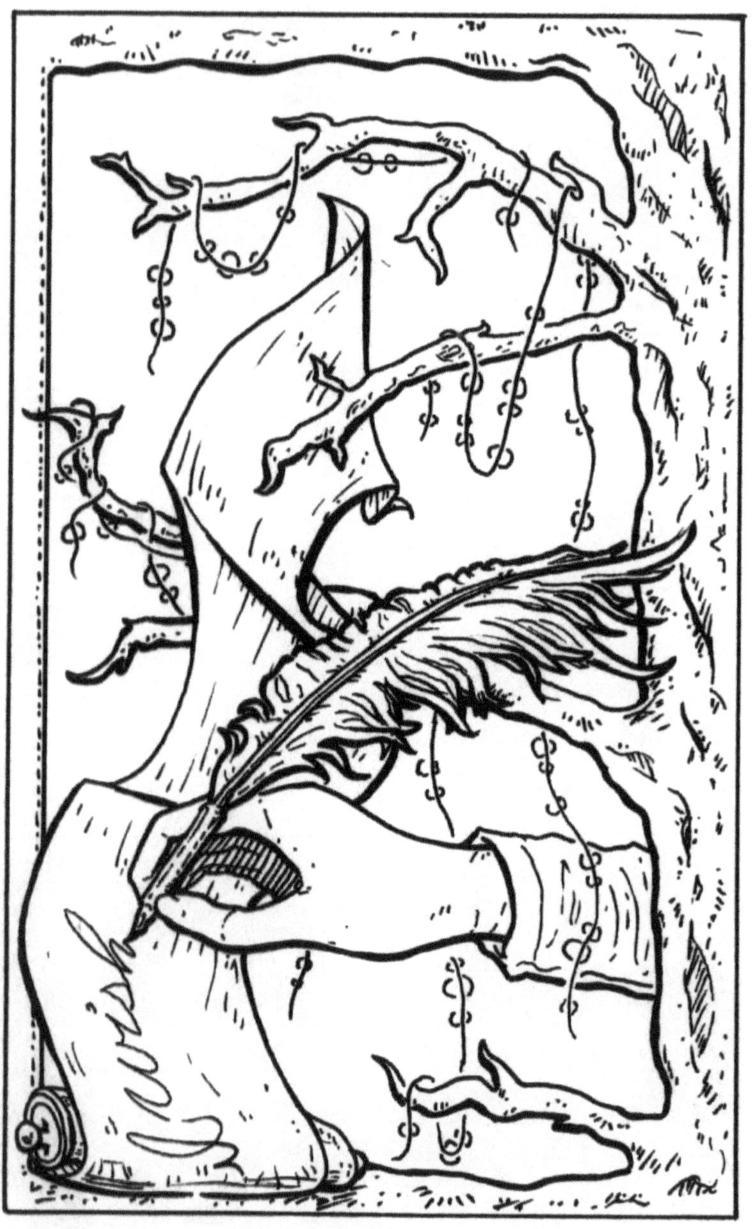

Wishes Between Worlds

Sam Waterhouse

Corvo perched among the skeletal branches of the wishing tree. A warm wind ruffled his feathers, bringing with it the acrid scent of rocket fuel and decay. The thousands of beaded strings hanging from the wishing tree clacked and clattered, a lonely sound in a desolate landscape.

Corvo's eyes strained to see through the smog, watching as the lucky few humans boarded the last shuttle off Earth. Hundreds of such craft had ferried thousands upon thousands of people into space, the culmination of humankind's decades-long plan to evacuate their polluted world. Ignorance, non-action, and the harvesting of Earth's very bones had led to one inescapable fact: within a century, this planet would be unable to sustain life.

He lifted his head, looking up into the polluted sky. Through the hazy daylight, Corvo made out the bright lights of seventeen generation ships hovering on the edge of Earth's atmosphere. They were the hope for ongoing survival, not just for humanity, but for beings like him who had watched the rise and fall of dozens of human civilizations.

"Time to go," came a weak shout from below.

Corvo looked down to the roots of the wishing tree. Old Man River was curled up at the base of a tree, hair lank and eyes closed. His thin face was more gaunt than usual.

Old Man River was dying. Corvo's ability to hold

back the corruption from the wishing tree was waning, as evidenced by the tree's bare branches. Unless they escaped soon, they would fade away as if they had never existed.

"Time to go," Corvo agreed.

He hopped along the branch until he came to a small twig, no longer than his wing, with two tiny buds at its tip. The wishing tree's last growth. Dipping his beak, he took hold of it and twisted, snapping it off the wishing tree.

Gripping the twig firmly in his beak, he launched himself into the air. The wind caught his outstretched wings, raising him high into the sky. Down below, Old Man River had disappeared, his remaining essence sucked through the wishing tree and into the twig. Corvo had promised his longtime friend a way to escape.

Corvo's small shadow passed over the remains of a dead forest and the patchy yellow grass plains beyond. The grass turned to muddy tracks ripped by the tires of hundreds of cars, trucks, vans, and motorbikes, all jammed together like pieces of a shattered puzzle.

Corvo had watched these vehicles carry a horde of humans, all of them denied a spot on the generation ships above, doomed to stay on this dying world. The yelling, screaming masses were even now pressed against the security fence bordering the spaceport, their fury met by jets of quick-setting foam sprayed from automatic defense turrets.

As Corvo flew high over them, he wondered why some humans were chosen to live and others left to die. Did they cast lots and select the lucky ones at random, or were the best and brightest taken? If the second was true, who decided what constituted a worthy attribute?

He shook his head. Humans were a strange species.

The final passenger was about to board the shuttle as Corvo dove down. The passenger, a young man, turned to look back at the world he was abandoning, his eyes brimming with tears. Corvo swooped silently through the shuttle's open door, but not before leaving a white surprise on the young man's shoulder. A small payback against humankind for forcing Corvo to abandon his home.

***

Generation Ship *Odyssey* - Deep space - 122 years after leaving Earth

Sydney huddled in the dark, straining to hear any sound of pursuit. Her heart thumped in time with the whirling server stacks around her, their fans cooling the room and causing goosebumps to form on her arms.

Despite the cold, she waited until her heart had slowed to its normal rhythm. She was shivering as she shuffled forward, as quietly as possible, and bent to peek out from where she was hiding. The room was filled with floor-to-ceiling black cabinets, the supercomputers inside churning through endless digital computations. Sydney tried to watch every corner and every shadow all at once. Paris and Nara could be waiting anywhere for Sydney to reveal herself.

Knowing that she was only putting off the inevitable, she gathered her courage and stepped out into the open. Her eyes flicked left and right. A long minute passed before she allowed her shoulders to fall, sighing in relief.

She'd lost them. She was safe.

For the first time, she turned to assessing where on the ship she was. She had run without thinking of any direction other than away. Padding softly over to the door, she cautiously peered out into the corridor beyond.

It was indistinguishable from a hundred other passages: faded white paint, white illumination strips on the ceiling, and a hundred years' worth of scuff marks. A helpful sign with the words "Train Station" pointed to the left, which was a great relief. The train that ran up and down the *Odyssey*'s thirteen-mile-long spine was her only way home.

There was no sign of her sisters and the way home

was clearly marked. Sydney felt tension flow from her as she stepped out into the corridor and started walking with light footsteps.

Relief was replaced by regret. Sydney should have never listened to her sisters. When they'd approached her with an offer of adventure, she had so wanted it to be genuine. She'd always wished for them to accept her, to stop playing tricks and just be her friends. She had thought that breaking their father's rule against using the train had meant something.

It had all been a ruse. As soon as they had disembarked from the train, Sydney's sisters had chased her away with threats and rude words.

Sydney sniffed and blinked back tears at the memory. They had even blamed her for their mother transferring to another generation ship and never coming back. Nearly a year had passed now and, with every passing day, Father became harder to live with and more likely to punish even the smallest infraction.

That thought made Sydney walk faster. She needed to be home before Father came back from work.

One corridor led to another and another, branching and dividing and joining again, all of them silent except for her footsteps. Sydney worked moisture into her dry mouth. Though the lack of people worked in her favor, it was increasingly strange that she hadn't seen anyone.

Her overactive imagination took this as a cue to kick into action. Perhaps aliens had boarded, capturing everyone else and taking them away on their alien spaceship, leaving Sydney the last person alive on the *Odyssey*. Or even worse, the aliens had eaten everyone and were stalking through the long corridors, looking for her specifically.

Sydney walked by an open door and her eyes flicked nervously to look inside, half-expecting to see tentacled aliens ready to pounce. The room was small, walls lined with vertical pipes, and illuminated by the blue light of a single screen. There was something moving inside and, for a moment, she thought she was about to become dessert. The thing moved again and Sydney's eyes widened as she took in the sight of an Old Earth bird.

The *Odyssey* carried vast historical archives filled with every detail of Old Earth and she had seen pictures of birds from these histories. This bird had black feathers and was tapping at the screen with its beak, navigating through the digital fields of data.

Her feet kept moving as she tried to digest what she had just seen. There couldn't possibly have been a bird using a computer, not just because birds didn't use computers, but because there weren't any unfrozen birds on the *Odyssey*. Seeing a bird was as likely as seeing aliens.

She came to a stop, looking back over her shoulder, staring at the open door. In the silence that followed, Sydney could hear a *tap-tap-tap* coming from the room.

If there wasn't a bird, then what was making that sound?

She was drawn back to the doorway, despite her instinct to run. Sydney sucked in a deep breath and tried to stop her hands from shaking. She had wanted an adventure. She couldn't run away now.

Inching forward, Sydney willed herself to peek around the doorframe.

There it was, covered in black feathers and almost as long as her arm, its beak reflecting the blue glow of the screen as it stabbed and scrolled.

Be brave, she thought as she stepped out from behind the cover of the doorframe.

"What are you doing?" She tried to sound confident, but the words came out all quivery.

The bird whipped its head around at the sound of her voice. "Who the…how…what did you say?"

"What?" she gasped. She hadn't actually expected the bird to reply with *words*, let alone in English. She took a stumbling step backward.

It hopped around to face her straight on. It ruffled its feathers and Sydney got the impression that it was composing itself, as if a talking human was as much a surprise as a talking bird.

"I could say the same thing," the bird said. "In fact, I'm pretty sure I did. What are *you* doing here?" Its voice held a hint of accusation.

"Because I am?" It couldn't know that she wasn't meant to be here. She cleared her throat. If this was an alien, she hadn't made the best first impression. "My name's Sydney."

After a short silence, where Sydney imagined it was thinking about attacking her with that sharp beak, the bird replied, "And my name's Corvo, little human."

"Are you an alien?" The question just slipped out, the first to fully form in among her jumbled thoughts.

It hopped to the ground, talons clacking on the metal floor as it waddled slowly toward her. The bird—which Sydney thought sounded like a "he"—stopped just in front of her and bobbed his head in a bow. "No, I'm not an alien. I come from the same planet as humanity. Also, before you ask, you're also not imagining me. I'm as real as you."

"Then what *are* you?" Sydney flicked a look over her shoulder, thinking that perhaps it would be better if she ran away. She didn't quite believe Corvo was telling the truth about not being an alien. If he meant to do her harm, she doubted he would tell the truth.

"What I am is…look, do you know what a genie is?"

She had no idea, but didn't want to admit it. "Maybe."

"They're creatures from made-up fairy tales that humans told back on Old Earth. They would grant wishes to anyone who asked, which is a silly way of doing business. A very one-sided transaction. Anyway, all of those stories, every single one of them, are based on me."

"Does that mean you do magic?" A hint of excitement crept into her voice.

"Pft, magic is such a human word, used for everything humans don't understand. But, to keep things within your small measure of understanding, yes, I do magic."

"Ah." Sydney wasn't sure what else to say as a smile tugged at her face.

Corvo squawked an approximation of a laugh. "Very eloquent. Now, this chance meeting actually provides us both with a great opportunity. For me, a small distraction from this tedious journey, but for you it's the chance to do everything. However, it would be best if we signed the appropriate documentation in a more comfortable environment. Would you care to come back to the wishing tree with me?"

"A tree?" she repeated, seizing on the one thing she'd understood. There hadn't been a tree for as long as there hadn't been a bird. Yet one was in front of her now, so why not the other? "I'd love to…"

She hesitated as thoughts of Father's displeasure returned. She had no idea how long she'd been gone. He could be home any time now.

"Don't worry," Corvo croaked reassuringly, perhaps thinking that was the reason for her hesitation. "You'll be perfectly safe."

This was a once-in-a-lifetime opportunity. She wasn't likely to ever run into another talking, wish-granting bird again.

"Okay, let's go." She stood up straight.

"Good choice. Now, we don't actually have to go anywhere. Just hold on a second."

Corvo lifted a wing and started tugging at his feathers. After twisting his head back and forth, he yanked out a long black feather. Sydney winced sympathetically as the bird squawked softly around the feather in his beak.

Gingerly, Corvo tucked his wing back down, then hopped slowly toward her. He lifted his head expectantly.

"Do you want me to take that?" she asked.

The bird nodded and hopped even closer. Sydney reached down and gently pulled the feather from Corvo's beak. It was as long as her hand and surprisingly light to hold. She traced a finger through the soft, black fuzz, enjoying the way it felt.

"That's my gift to you, a part of myself and a part of my magic."

Sydney's eyes widened, staring at the feather in awe. "What does it do?" she whispered.

"Anything you write with it comes true. It takes a piece of my essence and uses it to change the course of reality so that whatever you wish to be true had always been so. When you make a wish, the entire universe changes to accommodate it. Understood?"

Sydney didn't, but she nodded anyway.

"Now, take that feather and write exactly these words on a wall: I wish for a door to the wishing tree. You do know how to write?"

"Of course I do," she huffed, stepping up to the wall and pressing the pointy end of the feather against it. She looked down at Corvo. "Do I need any, you know, paint or something?"

"The feather will take care of that."

Turning back, she started to write. Where the feather touched, a red line blossomed on the wall, fading away after a few seconds. She wrote each letter carefully, stepping back when she was done. The last red letter disappeared, leaving the wall unmarked.

Nothing happened.

She was about to look down, to ask Corvo if perhaps she'd done it wrong, when a door appeared. There wasn't any magical flash or burst of colors. It was simply there, as if it had always been. It was almost disappointingly unspectacular. Despite the lack of magic flair, her breath was sucked away. She'd just done magic!

Corvo nudged her legs. "Go on, open the door. I'll be right behind you."

She gently placed the feather into her front pocket. Already, she could imagine showing off to her sisters. They wouldn't dare bully her. She reached out to grip the handle, only to yank her hand back with a yelp.

"It's freezing cold," she gasped, jamming her hand under her armpit.

"I forgot how fragile your bodies are." With a rapid flurry of wings, Corvo launched himself up onto Sydney's shoulder. She staggered under the unexpected weight and made as if to knock him off, but the glinting talons resting just next to her face made her think better of it.

A jolt ran through Sydney's spine. Her fingers and toes tingled and the hairs on the back of her neck stood up.

"What did you do?"

"I'm protecting you against the cold and the radiation now. Try the door again."

"Radiation? Where are we going?"

"Open the door and find out," Corvo encouraged.

With Corvo clinging to her shoulder, there was little choice. She took a deep breath and set her shoulders. Sydney gripped the handle—noting that it now felt slightly warm under her fingers—and pushed the door open. It swung forward so smoothly that Sydney found herself stumbling through.

"Careful," Corvo squawked, battering her head with his wings as he flapped to keep his balance.

"Sorry," Sydney said as Corvo's talons dug into her shoulder. She gritted her teeth and straightened carefully, only to freeze as she saw where she was.

She knew the place right away, even though she'd never been here. Corvo's comment about radiation made sense in an impossible kind of way. She was standing at the edge of the *Odyssey's* vast cargo hold, a chamber so big that it must be what standing on a planet felt like.

It was a single chamber, spanning from hull to hull, two miles across and nearly five miles deep. At the far end of the cargo hold, the indescribably complicated mechanisms of the *Odyssey's* engine could be seen, spewing out invisible and deadly radioactive particles.

It was so big, so vast, that she felt like she was going to float away.

Looking up didn't help the feeling of vertigo. Within the narrow confines of the corridors and living spaces of the *Odyssey*, the reality of artificial spin gravity had never occurred to her. She knew the theories—every child was taught them—but the cargo hold was actually big enough for her to see it in action. The floor curved gently away in both directions until they joined up again directly above. If she turned and walked to her left or right, she would eventually be able to look up at where she was standing right now.

She looked down and squeezed her eyes shut until her head stopped spinning.

"How did people cope back on Old Earth? It's just too…big," she whispered.

"How do *you* cope with being stuck in this metal coffin?"

She opened her eyes slowly, careful to only look straight ahead. "It's not like I have a choice."

She directed her attention to the cargo itself, a gigantic tangle of ramps and walkways, scaffolding and supports, stretching out and up to fill the huge space. Held in by this spiderweb of metal were thousands of cool blue square blocks, Old Earth's legacy brought to the stars.

She took slow, deliberate steps toward the closest block, wanting to see what it held.

"What are you doing?" Corvo asked.

She didn't answer, drawn forward until the smooth blue surface was less than two feet away. The block was easily five times her height, held in place by round metal bars and hand-size bolts. Sydney leaned forward until her nose was almost touching the block's surface and squinted to see through the semi-transparent material.

Two huge elephants were frozen mid-step close to the surface. She'd read about elephants but hadn't understood just how huge they were. Their legs were as big as Sydney's whole body, trunks longer than she could jump and ears wider than her arm span.

"Whoa!" she exclaimed.

"Move away," Corvo said, leaning back while still keeping a grip on her shoulder. "I don't want to find myself stuck to the ice just because you got curious."

She stepped backward, looking up and around at the thousands upon thousands of blue boxes. Each held any number of frozen animals, representing every species that had existed on Old Earth the day humans left. She had a sudden desire to see them all, to know what they were like in the flesh, not just frozen in ice or on a computer screen.

Corvo dug his talons into her shoulder, just enough to make her feel it, but not enough to draw any blood, sharply bringing her back to the moment.

"Focus on why you're here," Corvo said, "or do you want me to leave you to your gawking?"

"Sorry. Which way?" She didn't want to know what would happen if Corvo decided to fly away, leaving her without magical protection from the cold and radiation.

"The wishing tree is in the middle, so just start walking. I'll guide you as we go. It's hard to miss."

She set off at a fast walk. Her eyes constantly flicked between the frozen animals in their cages and the black bird perched on her shoulder. She paid special attention to a blue block containing a flock of birds, each half the size of Corvo, frozen in mid-flight. Sydney tried to imagine them speaking, shouting over each other in an effort to be heard. Was all she knew about animals wrong? Did they talk like Corvo?

The cargo hold went on and on. Corvo occasionally told her to turn left or right, heading ever deeper into the maze. She became hopelessly lost, unsure which direction she'd even come from. She risked a look up, eyes taking in the towers of blue blocks stretching down from the distant ceiling, as if threatening to crash down on her fall at any moment.

"Keep going, little human," Corvo said. "Not much further now."

Sydney kept going. She'd followed Corvo's instructions beyond the point of no return. She walked until she felt like it would be impossible to stop and her legs would keep moving even against her will.

"Left here."

Sydney turned left, walking underneath a low-hanging metal walkway spanning two blue blocks. She stumbled over something, looking down to see that the previously smooth floor was now bumpy and undulating, as if something was trying to push its way through.

"What's that?"

"That means we're almost there. Just keep your balance."

It wasn't long before Corvo announced, "Turn right just up ahead and then we're there."

Sydney turned the corner and saw it. She raised her head up…and up and up until she was in danger of falling over backward.

There were no trees onboard the *Odyssey*. The plants that grew on the *Odyssey* were either mossy coverings or twisting vines, genetically tailored to both oxygenate the air and provide a nutrient-rich addition to the crew's diet. The wishing tree was unlike anything Sydney had seen, thick and brown and verdant. It towered over everything, reaching high enough to pass the point of null gravity and be pulled down toward the ceiling.

"This is my home in exile, my abode on this long

journey," Corvo said, jumping off her shoulder and flapping down to the ground. He lifted a wing to point at the monstrous tree. "You're probably wondering why none of your humans notice it?"

Sydney nodded. The thought had occurred to her. She should have been able to see it clearly from anywhere in the cargo hold.

"Humans are stupid, is what. You never see anything that doesn't fit with how you think things should be. It's clearly impossible for a tree to be growing here, so no one sees it." Corvo cawed a laugh. "I'm constantly amazed that you can learn anything, given how much you ignore. Now, come along. We'll have a good chat next to the tree, but first I've just got to retrieve one thing."

Sydney's eyes widened. "Don't leave me."

"Don't worry, the tree will keep you safe." Corvo flew off, leaving Sydney alone before she could say anything more.

Alone, there was not much choice but to move farther under the towering boughs of the wishing tree. The branches curled, curved, and twisted to cover blocks and gantry, obscuring the blue with lush green. The roots of the tree rose and sunk out of the metal flooring, like a hundred gigantic snakes. She had to step carefully over the leaf-covered floor so as not to twist her ankle.

There was something peaceful about it, to be near something so big and so alive. She reached the base of the tree and placed a hand on its surface, feeling the rough bark against her skin.

Stepping back, she looked up and around for Corvo, but the bird had disappeared into the foliage high above. Something rolled under her foot and she windmilled her arms to keep balance. Kneeling, she rummaged through the dead leaves until she found the offending object.

She picked up the bead between thumb and forefinger and held it close to her face. The bead was transparent and held a white substance that rolled and swirled inside. She peered closer, squinting as she tried to work out what the substance was. She could have sworn that it had formed a face for the briefest of moments.

"I wouldn't do that."

She jumped with a scream. The bead dropped from her hand, disappearing into the leafy debris.

"Who's there?" She whirled around, searching for whoever had spoken.

"Sorry to startle you, but it's just not healthy to look at someone else's five wishes." The voice was coming from a shadowy hollow between two massive roots.

"I'm with Corvo." Her hands moved to the feather tucked in her pocket, thinking to defend herself with a wish.

"I know that. I thought I'd come and say hello. I don't think we've ever had visitors." A tall, thin man appeared out of the shadows, jumping fluidly over the roots to land in front of Sydney with a puff of leaves. Not a monster or alien, just an ordinary-looking person, even if he was dressed oddly.

The man beamed, a smile so warm Sydney couldn't help but smile back. "Hello, Sydney. It certainly is a great pleasure to meet you."

Sydney double-blinked. "Excuse me? You know who I am?"

The man bubbled over with laughter. "Oh yes, I know everyone on this ship."

"You do?" she asked suspiciously, smile fading.

"Come, come. Have a seat while we wait for that dusty old bird to come back." He sat down on a tree root. "Let me introduce myself. I'm Old Man River, a fellow refugee in space on the way to a new world."

Sydney didn't sit. "How do you know so much about me?"

Old Man River winked. "A bit of magic. No doubt Corvo showed you some of what he's capable of."

Sydney nodded.

"I have my own set of unique talents. Sadly, due to the confined nature of the *Odyssey*, most of my talents are going to waste, but I do make sure to keep watch through the water."

"You watch through the water?" she repeated.

"It's not as creepy as it sounds. I don't so much watch as absorb knowledge. It's all very complicated and I don't want to bore you. Anyways, changing topics. Perhaps we can talk about that feather in your pocket."

Her hand pressed against the feather, wondering how he knew about it and worried he would steal it. She flicked her eyes upward, hoping to see Corvo coming back. The bird might be very strange, but it wasn't nearly as creepy as this Old Man River. All she could see above was the vast green and brown canopy.

"What about the feather?" she asked, looking at Old Man River again. "He gave it to me."

"I know he did. Have you used it yet? Oh, I can see by your eyes that you have. Just a small thing, no doubt, to draw you in." Old Man River leaned forward. "Did he tell you the rules?"

A loud caw announced Corvo's return, preventing any further conversation. Corvo landed on a raised root halfway between Sydney and Old Man River. He was holding a piece of paper covered in tiny writing in his beak. He carefully placed the paper on the ground.

"What are you two talking about?" he asked suspiciously.

"I was just about to say that she shouldn't believe anything you tell her," Old Man River said.

"Ha, that's rich coming from you." Corvo turned to look at Sydney. "All this fellow does is talk, babbling on and on. He'll say anything as long as it'll keep you listening."

"And having not had anyone but you to converse with for a century has been nearly unbearable."

They were bickering like Sydney's sisters often did, their words good-natured insults that spoke more of their friendship than any enmity.

"What's that?" she asked, pointing down at the paper Corvo had brought.

"That, little human, is a contract of services, a formal agreement between the two of us on the use of the feather. Go on, read through it and sign."

Sydney moved forward, aware that Old Man River was rolling his eyes. She bent and picked up the paper, scanning it quickly. The words were so small that she had to squint to read them.

This contract is for the services outlined below (see sections 3 through 12) to be granted to the signee of their own free will (henceforth known as the First Party) to be delivered through the capabilities of service provider known by the name Corvo (henceforth known as the Second Party). The terms of Agreement (see section 13 through 18) will become effective at the time the First Party signs this document and freely enters into a binding Agreement with the Second Party. This Agreement shall continue until such a time as the First Party raises a grievance (see section 19 to 20) that constitutes a break in…

Sydney stopped reading. All of this was only a fraction of what was written on this paper. She turned it over to look at the other word-filled side. If she didn't even understand the first part, how was she to understand all of it?

"I think you might need to help her out," Old Man River prompted. "I can see by the bewildered look on her face that she's suffering from overwhelment. And yes, I did just make up that word, but you have to admit that it perfectly captures her expression."

"Hey," Sydney said. "I'm standing right here."

"Ignore him," Corvo told her. "It doesn't matter if you can't read it, all you have to do is take the feather and sign your name on the bottom. Once that's done, the feather is yours to do whatever you want with."

Whatever was written, was it worth paying to possess the magic? She would be able to do anything she could think of…

She took the black feather out of her pocket and sat on the ground, leaves crunching under her knees.

"Are you sure that you want to do that, miss?" Old Man River asked. He made as if to stand up, but Corvo jabbed a wing in his direction.

"You keep still," Corvo said. "She can do whatever she wants."

Sydney put the tip of the feather to the paper and slowly wrote out her name on the dotted line. Once done, she held out the paper to Corvo. "Do you want it back?"

"Just put it down, I'll get it later." Corvo's voice dripped with such satisfaction that Sydney wondered if she'd done the right thing. "As a one-time special offer to celebrate our new agreement, did you want anything from me?"

She laid the paper back on the ground. What could she want? There were a hundred different questions she'd like answered, but she held all the answers in the universe in her hand. She'd sign a hundred pieces of paper to be able to keep doing real magic.

"Perhaps," she said slowly, "you could help me get back? I don't know how long it's been, but I really need to get home."

"You want to go so soon?" Old Man River looked disappointed. "You only just got here and we've barely introduced each other. Please don't leave me all alone with this feathery trickster. He barely even pays me any attention."

"I can send you back to where I found you, little human, if that's what you want," Corvo said, ignoring Old Man River.

Sydney stood, putting the feather carefully back into her pocket. "Yes, please. I don't want to…"

She opened her eyes to find herself sprawled on the floor, the familiar faces of Paris and Nara staring down at her.

"Looks like she's alive then," Paris said offhandedly.

"Probably got scared and fainted," Nara sneered.

"Get off me," Sydney growled up at her two older sisters. She pushed herself to her feet, shaking her spinning head. She was back next to the small room with pipes lining the wall, the room where she had seen a talking bird called Corvo.

She put her hands into her pockets. The feather was soft to the touch and reassured Sydney that she hadn't imagined it all.

What was stopping her from using it right here, right now? She didn't have to put up with this.

Dodging to one side, she slid the feather out of her pocket and hastily scrawled a wish on the wall.

I wish for my sisters to stop being mean.

"What's that?" Paris exclaimed.

"Come back here," Nara growled, reaching out to grab Sydney, snagging a handful of hair. Sydney squeezed her eyes shut, hoping it would work. Her sister's hand tugged painfully, forcing her away from the wall. She stumbled backward, tripping over and falling onto her backside.

There was a sudden intake of breath and Sydney tried to prepare herself for whatever was coming.

"Oh, I'm so sorry! I don't know what came over me."

Sydney carefully cracked one eye open to see Nara hovering over her, hand outstretched. She flinched away.

"You're so clumsy," Paris said, kneeling down to Sydney's eye level. "Are you okay? She didn't hurt you?"

There was concern in Paris's voice. Sydney couldn't remember that ever happening before. She looked down at the feather clutched in her hand, a smile slowly spreading across her face.

It had worked. It had really worked.

Trusting in her wish, she took Nara's hand and let herself be helped to her feet. Her sister actually looked worried.

"It's okay," Sydney said, tucking the feather back into her pocket. "Could you tell me what we're doing? I've forgotten."

"I'm not surprised after what she did." Paris glared at Nara. "We need to get back before Father notices us missing, but we've spent ages looking for you after you got lost."

"Lost?" Sydney remembered Corvo saying something about a wish changing the world around it. Perhaps it could also change what had happened in the past, making it so her sisters had never chased her. "Um…I didn't mean to."

"That's okay, but we really should get going." Paris started off and Sydney followed, Nara a few steps farther back as if worried about tripping Sydney again.

They walked in silence back to the train station. Sydney occasionally looked over her shoulder at Nara, who blushed and averted her eyes. It was like she was ashamed of what she had done. Sydney couldn't help the huge smile on her face. This was just the first step in making her life much better. There were so many wishes she could make. She wanted to get back home so that she could write them all in the privacy of her room.

The way back to the station wasn't long. Sydney had almost made it there before being sidetracked by Corvo. Paris halted to peer cautiously in, Sydney and Nara stopping behind her.

"It's clear," she said.

Sydney started to follow her older sister in when the growl of a deep voice brought her to a dead stop.

"Paris. Nara. Sydney." Each name was snapped out like a curse.

Sydney whirled around to see Father. He moved like a thundercloud, dark and threatening, brows lowered and mouth thin. Sydney knew that look, having been the recipient of its consequences enough times to cringe in fear at what was coming.

Nara was the first to speak. "Father, we didn't…"

"Quiet," he growled. "I don't want to hear it."

This was bad. Father's jaw worked, as if fighting against words he would later regret. Eventually, he managed to say, "All three of you, go stand ready to board the next train."

Sydney did as instructed, Paris and Nara shuffling forward next to her. They waited, quiet and cowed under Father's angry eyes. Sydney touched the feather in her pocket, wondering what wish could make things better. A strong hand gripped her shoulder, derailing any thought of wishing things better.

"Don't do anything unless I tell you to," Father said.

Time moved with glacial slowness, their family standing in awkward silence, until the train screeched out of the tunnel to halt in front of them. Father shepherded them forward into the train's capsule-like passenger carriage.

The doors slid shut and the train accelerated. It only took a few minutes to reach their destination several miles away, but Sydney's knees were close to collapsing from the tension.

"Off," Father directed.

They disembarked, Sydney painfully aware that there were now witnesses to their shame. She could feel their eyes following her as Father strongly guided them the short distance to Housing Chamber 53. The heavy blue door slid noiselessly back into the wall.

Sydney was forced to lead the way, carefully stepping onto the paths between the cultivated vegetation and hanging garden beds. They stopped before the twenty-second door on the left. Their home.

"Paris, Nara, you have homework to do. I expect it to be finished by the time I get back."

Just like that, Sydney's sisters were released. They fled into the house, not even looking back. Sydney watched them with a mixture of anger and jealousy.

Swallowing, she turned to Father. "It wasn't my fault. They were…"

"Enough," Father snapped. "I don't want to hear it. You're grounded, Sydney. Now go to your room and, by all the stars, you'd better be there when I get back from work. I was in the middle of something important when your recklessness dragged me away."

With a final firm push, Father stomped off. Sydney watched him for a moment, fighting back the tears, before slinking away to do as she was told.

***

Sydney sat on the edge of her bed. She stared down at the black feather sitting on her knees, slightly ruffled from its time in her pocket.

She could do whatever she wished, have anything or be anything she wanted. Sydney felt positively buoyant at the endless possibilities. Her next wish should be something big, the most important thing she could ever wish for.

Picking up Corvo's feather, she hopped off her bed and knelt on the floor. She straightened out a couple of the feather's bent bits and, once she was happy with the results of her ministrations, set about writing her next wish.

I wish to live to see the new world.

As before, the red letters faded away. Sydney waited, wondering if she would feel the effect of the wish. Long moments passed and nothing happened. That was disappointing.

Perhaps she should wish for something more immediate. Her family had been happy before Mother had gone to another generation ship. She knew that her parents still talked sometimes, promising that they would see each other soon, but something always kept Mother away. It seemed that the operation of the generation ships was more important than their family's happiness.

Perhaps if there weren't any more mechanical breakdowns or ship-threatening issues, everything could go back to the way it was before. Father wouldn't be so angry all the time, and Sydney would get to see Mother again.

She wrote her next wish.

I wish for all problems with all the spaceships to be fixed and to never happen again.

She sat back, watching as the red letters disappeared, nodding in satisfaction. That should do it. Though, like her last wish, how would she know for sure? She had seen the door come into existence and had experienced her sisters' change in attitude. What she needed to do was see the results of her wishes with her own eyes.

She was about to stand up when her stomach emitted a gurgling noise. It had been hours since she'd last eaten.

She scrawled another wish and, seconds later, a cake appeared in front of her. It was round, coated with cream and chocolate sprinkles, and had a thick layer of jam in the middle. It even smelled like it had just come out of the oven. Sydney dabbed a finger into the cream and put it into her mouth.

She shut her eyes as she savored the taste. Her stomach growled in anticipation.

Digging her hand in, she scooped up a section of cake and shoveled it into her mouth. It tasted better than anything she'd had before, almost like the jam was made from real raspberries and not from synthesized equivalents. She took another handful.

Before she knew it, half the cake was gone and her belly was aching from a sugar overload. Sydney lay back on the floor and closed her eyes. She just needed a minute to let the cake settle before going out.

This little break gave her time to think about the best way to get to Father's workplace. He had told her to stay in her room, so she couldn't be seen by anyone or she'd get in even more trouble. What she needed was a way to move around without being seen.

Sydney rolled over onto her full stomach with a groan and wrote her next wish.

I wish to become invisible.

She lifted her hands in front of her face, but nothing seemed to have changed. Maybe she was only invisible to other people?

Levering herself slowly off the floor, Sydney stepped around the scattered remnants of her cake and over to the bedroom door. She licked a spot of cream off the back of her hand and then opened it.

The small room beyond was a combination of lounge room, kitchen, and dining room. Her home's common area was tightly packed with a small table, chairs, a food dispenser, and a computer terminal.

Paris and Nara were sitting at the table bent over their portable screens, engrossed in their homework. Neither looked up, not even when the bedroom door slid shut behind Sydney. Moving as quietly as possible, she came up right next to Paris and, holding her breath, inched a hand in front of her sister's face.

Paris kept scrolling through whatever she was reading.

Sydney waved her hand around.

Still no reaction. Paris kept reading as if she could see right through Sydney's hand.

A gasp of excitement escaped her mouth before Sydney could clamp her hands over it. She watched Paris and Nara with wide eyes, but neither acted as if they'd heard.

"Hello?" she whispered.

No reaction. Sydney had to stop herself from jumping and shouting in excitement. They couldn't see or hear her. She could go anywhere without discovery.

She walked confidently to the front door and pushed the button to open the door. Sounds from outside flooded through the doorway, people talking, the hum of machinery, and the hiss of hoses as the plants were watered.

"Hello?" Paris called out. "Who's there?"

Her sister must have heard the door opening. Sydney ran through the doorway. It was early evening now and the overhead lights had been dimmed.

She heard Paris call out again, but the words were cut off as the door slid closed.

She was free. Sydney kept to the shadows, not quite ready to completely trust in her invisibility. A few people were out, coming back from their work shifts or tending to the gardens.

She got to Living Chamber 53's main entrance without incident and then waited for it to open for someone else before slipping through. She turned off the route that led back to the train station, heading toward the air filtration system center where Father worked.

There were people about, but she slipped by without incident, neither seen nor heard. Most were too engrossed in their portable screens that Sydney could have been visible and still moved without notice.

It didn't take long to get to Father's workplace. The twin sets of security doors were open, allowing Sydney to peer through. The room beyond was circular, the outside walls covered in screens and the roof a tangle of pipes and blinking sensors.

Father and two other adults were present, dressed in drab overalls. They were standing around a single screen at the far end of the room, facing away from Sydney.

"It just fixed itself?" asked the shorter woman— Sydney had met her before but couldn't remember her name.

"Everything just went green," said the taller woman—Sydney thought her name was Astana—as she pointed at something on the screen. "Washington, you saw it?"

Father shook his head. "I saw it, but I don't believe it. I won't believe it until I've personally checked every system. Are you absolutely sure you didn't do anything?"

"Nothing! I swear it."

Father leaned away and rubbed a hand through his hair, or at least what remained of it. He had told Sydney that he was balding because of the stress of raising three girls on his own.

"If the primary sensors and the backup sensors haven't both failed and this miracle has occurred, then it looks like we're all out of a job. But first we'll have to check and double-check, then triple-check." He raised a finger. "Until we have confirmation, I don't want a word so much as whispered to anyone."

Sydney slipped away. Her wish had worked. Whatever problems were always making Father angry had gone, solved by Corvo's magic feather.

"That has to be some kind of record, little human."

Sydney jumped, a squeaky shout erupting from her at the sudden voice. She would certainly have been heard without the wish. Standing in the door was Corvo, head turned to one side to stare up at her with one black eye.

"How... Where... Don't do that!" Sydney put a hand to her chest, feeling her thumping heartbeat.

"You should be more observant."

"Wait, you can see me? But I'm invisible." Sydney also remembered that she was standing out in the open. She checked up and down the corridor; there was no sign of anyone around.

"To everyone else, but not to me." Corvo blinked slowly.

Sydney took a moment to compose herself. "Why

are you here?"

"You've made five wishes. I can't remember anyone making them as fast as you. Usually, humans take weeks or even years, but to use them all in a few hours is most impressive."

"Five? What do you mean 'five'?"

"The five wishes you got as part of the contract you signed. I was even nice and didn't count wishing for the door. That happened before we entered into any formal agreement, though I did have the legal right to include it."

"I don't get any more wishes?" Sydney dug into her pocket for the feather. Her eyes widened in horror when she couldn't find the now familiar shape. Her pockets weren't empty though. She drew out a white bead, just like the one she'd found under the wishing tree. "Where's the feather gone? What's this?"

"Those are your wishes," Corvo croaked. "That's what happens to the feather when you've used your wishes. If you would like, I can take that bead and hang it on the wishing tree."

A tear escaped and slid down her cheek. She lifted a hand and brushed it away. "But I'm still invisible! I can't stay invisible."

"There's not much I can do about that. You will live for centuries, long enough to see this new world. A worthy trade in my opinion."

"But what about my family? They won't be able to see or hear me." Tears were flowing freely down Sydney's cheeks now. As much as she hated her family at times, the thought of not being able to interact with them was devastating. "Change me back, Corvo. I wish to stop being invisible!"

Corvo turned away. "I can't. It was all in the contract. You signed it of your…"

"I don't care!" she screamed.

Corvo squawked and jumped away. "I'm not here to

be shouted at. Maybe we can talk more when you've calmed down."

Sydney watched the black bird launch himself into the air and fly away. She thought about screaming again, but the only sound that escaped was a hiccupping sob.

Sydney fell to her knees, wishing for it all to have been a dream.

***

Generation Ship *Odyssey* - In orbit around Eden - 526 years after leaving Earth

Corvo flew down one silent corridor after another. As much as he hated to admit it, he had grown attached to the *Odyssey*'s twisting ways. Back on Old Earth, it had become near impossible for him to find a new experience, one of the few problems of living for millennia. This journey through the stars had opened up new sights and dangers, new possibilities and futures.

He swooped through the final door and out into the vast expanse of the cargo hold. Where once thousands upon thousands of frozen animals had rested for centuries, only empty scaffolding remained. The *Odyssey* had been gutted down to its bare bones in the dozen years since arriving in orbit around Eden, as the planet was known. Everything of value had also been taken, leaving the ship a dying hulk, drifting in space alongside its sixteen siblings.

Sydney was waiting there for him. He landed gently on her shoulder, careful not to hurt either the twig he held in his talons or his ancient friend. She was bent and wrinkled, almost blind and nearly deaf, but still alive beyond a normal human lifetime.

"I see you've finally gotten off your perch and decided to leave," Sydney said in a quavering voice.

"There isn't much to do around here. I only stayed

so long because of you."

Sydney laughed, or at least Corvo thought it was a laugh. The old woman hissed out a wheezing breath.

"It seems like you do care. I half-expected you to just disappear in the middle of the night. You must be sick of me by now."

"You're no worse than Old Man River."

"Is he in there?" Sydney touched a crooked finger to the twig.

Corvo nodded. "He and the wishing tree are ready to be planted on the new world."

They fell into a companionable silence, and Corvo thought back to the last few centuries. She had come to him a year after she'd used her wishes, stumbling through the cargo hold to the wishing tree, sickened by the engine's radiation but unable to die from it. She'd collapsed among the roots and her body had slowly healed itself, her wish to see the new world sustaining her.

When Sydney had regained consciousness, she'd explained how she couldn't stand to be around her family anymore, to be unseen and unheard, a ghost in her own home. Old Man River had welcomed her straight away, but Corvo had taken years to warm to a constant human presence.

Once he had grown used to Sydney, they had become inseparable. She never babbled like Old Man River, instead bringing a youthful joy to his life that Corvo hadn't experienced in thousands of years. With Sydney, he was able to see with new eyes and find wonder in simple things again.

Corvo cleared his throat. "Are you sure you don't want to come down with me?"

Sydney laughed again. She did that a lot now, as if living for four centuries made everything funny.

"You'd like that," Sydney said once she'd regained her breath. "The chance to play one last trick on me." She raised a shriveled finger and shook it in Corvo's face. "I've watched you over the years, and I've stopped you from hurting anyone else. I'm not going to be your victim again, no matter how tempting you make it sound."

"Trick? Victim? That's a bit harsh. Weren't your wishes granted? Haven't you lived well beyond your time?" Corvo ruffled his feathers in mock indignation. This was an old argument that had long ago lost its sting.

"I have and don't expect me to thank you for it."

The silence returned. They had said everything that needed to be said a hundred times already. It stretched on as Corvo wondered how best to take his leave.

"Will I die now?" Sydney asked suddenly.

He took a while before replying quietly, "Yes. The wish is fulfilled. Your body's natural processes will soon take hold and make up for the lost time."

"Ah. Good, good. I've had more than my share of years. I've read every book and manual that humanity possesses. I've helped out the people on the *Odyssey* where I could and I like to think I stopped more than one disaster." She gave another laugh. "They say the ship has a friendly ghost. I'm happy with my life, but I'm ready to move on and so should you."

Corvo felt like something was stuck in his throat.

"This is goodbye then," Corvo murmured into Sydney's ear. Strange emotions crisscrossed his mind. Despite living uncounted years, he had never experienced such a close relationship with a human before. Did he feel sad to be leaving her? How could he feel sad for someone so temporary?

He took off across the hangar, willing himself not to look back. A line of people were filing into the shuttle, all looking eager to leave this empty, abandoned ship and go down to the growing settlement on Eden's surface.

None of them saw him, of course. It was a very human ability to ignore what was right in front of them.

The last person, a young man, was entering the

shuttle as Corvo dove through the door. Corvo deposited a white gift on the young man's shoulder.

The last thing he heard before the door hissed closed was an old woman's wheezing laughter.

The Charcoal Cat

J. E. Klimov

Cicadas serenaded the night sky. A comfortable heat settled in the square monochrome room and wrapped around Aoi. He knelt next to a sheet of parchment, smoothing it over the spotless wooden floor. After every few brush strokes, he obsessively rubbed his itchy head. Aoi had never had his head shaved before.

Releasing a sigh, he returned to work. He stuck out his tongue, directing razor-sharp focus past the haze of incense. A pair of lanterns sat on either side of him, flames flickering lazily. His dream of becoming an artist was as fragile as a robin's egg, but he held on to a thread of hope. If only people gave his paintings a chance. He rejected the thought of living like a hermit or an outcast, a fate for people who were useless in society's eyes. An involuntary shiver ran down his spine. Aoi never liked being alone.

"Done," the boy said to himself. He stretched his arms, letting the cotton robe sleeves fall back. "But I think you need a friend."

As he dipped the brush into the bowl of ink, a shuffling whispered down the hall. Aoi froze. Silence. His eyes darted from his current work to a fat, neatly-tied scroll a few inches away. When the shuffling resumed, Aoi scrambled for the scroll and fumbled with the ribbon. Sweat beaded on his forehead. The scroll unfurled over his current work, and the boy winced, praying the ink below didn't smudge. He focused on the dense lines of text.

A shadow appeared on the other side of the rice paper door. It slid open, revealing an elderly man wrapped in a taupe robe. The moonlight reflected off his shiny head. Aoi caught his gaze and glanced down.

"It's late, my son. Have you really spent all this time studying?" A scratchy voice escaped his square jaw.

Aoi clutched his brush behind his back. "Yes, Master Hisao," he squeaked.

The monk swept into the room and knelt in front of Aoi. He hummed softly. "Finally, you're showing promise."

Sinking his head, Aoi blushed. Every day was a living reminder of what an incapable runt he was. At fourteen, he was no taller than a girl on the cusp of womanhood. No matter how much fish and rice he ate, he never gained any weight. By his family's standards, he was useless.

The monk snapped his fingers, jolting Aoi from his reverie. "Son?"

"Sorry, Master Hisao."

"What have you learned today?" He folded his hands in his sleeves and leaned back.

Aoi's brush fell to the floor. Biting his lip, he jerked his head up.

The monk's eyes narrowed.

"I have learned… I have learned…" Aoi peeked at the character-ridden scroll.

"Let's see how you do without it." Master Hisao pulled the scroll toward him.

"No!" Aoi leaned forward with outstretched hands.

Cicadas took over the silence that swept between the two. Master Hisao scowled.

"Well, well, I was wrong about you. Again."

Aoi blinked out tears. "It's what I love to do!" The exposed parchment soaked up each drop.

The two stared at what Aoi had been working on day and night. Every inch of parchment was covered with cat drawings. Cats of various sizes. Some with fluffy tails, others with no tail. Others with large claws, and a few lapping up milk from their bowls. Each cat was intricately designed, down to the pattern of their fur and the length of their whiskers.

A brief fantasy flashed before his eyes: a cat framed on the wall of every home in Japan. Aoi's faint smile disappeared when the monk sighed.

Master Hisao's knees cracked when he stood. Anxiety crawled beneath Aoi's skin as he awaited a response.

"My son, go to sleep. We will meet in the morning, before our meditation." Master Hisao frowned.

Throwing his hands to the floor, Aoi bowed. "Th-thank you, Master Hisao. Good night." He kept his head down until the door clacked against the wall, signifying his master was gone.

With a sigh, Aoi ambled toward the corner of his room. He unfurled his futon, and as he pulled his blanket off the shelf, papers scattered into the air like snow. Each piece fell daintily onto the floor. And each one with a painting of a cat.

An orange glow caught the corner of his eye. The flame from the closest lantern licked at one of the drawings. Aoi gasped and stamped the fire out. Sighing with relief, he bent down and picked it up. The top right edge was blackened. Bits flaked off with each breath. He stroked where the cat's head had been.

"Jin, I'm sorry. You're my favorite cat. I will have to draw you over. Next time you will be bigger, stronger, and even more beautiful."

Aoi blew out the other lantern and snuggled into his futon. Despite his dull days at the monastery, it was much better than spending his nights outdoors. A faint howl resounded through the air. When the wolf cried once more, it was silenced abruptly. Owls hooted and flapped their wings.

Drawing the blanket to his chin, Aoi fought the invisible chill down his spine. He stared out the window, watching the blinking stars until his eyelids were too heavy to hold up. When he thought of his old cat, he calmed. He once had a real cat named Jin, and at times, he could still feel him brush against his ankles. Even though his beloved pet had entered the afterlife, Jin lived through each stroke of ink or any medium he could get his hands on. Aoi drifted to sleep, imagining Jin's fierce eyes watching over him.

The guttural cry of gongs bellowed nearby. Aoi rubbed his eyes, trying to block out the obnoxious assault on his ears. His room was still dark. Master Hisao was always up before the sun, and Aoi hated that. His irritation evaporated as he realized that if he didn't get ready soon, the master would be knocking at the door with punishment in hand. He scrambled to his feet, folded his blanket and futon, and changed into his only other set of robes.

When he sprinted toward the door, his heel slipped. His back slammed against the tatami mat, knocking the wind from his lungs. Aoi groaned as a headache sprouted from a seed to a wrathful vine. Rolling over, Aoi realized he had slipped on his cats. He gathered all the paintings and placed them on the shelf beneath his blanket before bolting for the door.

Aoi thundered down the hall, passing a room filled with golden shrines. Half a dozen monks draped in taupe chanted rhythmically. Bamboo stalks in porcelain pots lined the next room. Scrolls as wide as his fist stood like perfect soldiers on the shelves. Skidding around the corner, he finally made it to the double doors. He held his breath and yanked them open.

"Good morning, Aoi." Master Hisao sat with perfect posture on a plum-colored cushion, his calm countenance unruffled.

Bowing, Aoi huffed to catch his breath. "Good morning."

"Come, sit." Master Hisao gestured to the cushion opposite him. He poured tea into two cups, adjusting his sleeve with his other hand so it wouldn't get wet. Steam curled into the air.

The earthy aroma filled Aoi's lungs, calming him. His hands itched to grab his cup, but he had to wait until Master Hisao took his first sip.

"I have something I want to discuss."

"What is it, Master Hisao?" Aoi's gaze followed the steam toward the indoor courtyard. Rays of sunlight washed over smooth gray stone that dotted the combed sand. Miniature trees with twisted branches swayed in the gentle breeze that funneled through the open roof. Aoi liked those trees. Like him, they were small and unassuming, but they were treasured. He hoped someday he would be just as treasured.

Master Hisao blew on his tea, then took a long, slow sip. "Aoi Uchida. The time has come for you to return home to your family."

The boy's stomach dropped as his heart thundered in his chest. Panic seized him. "But why? I've only been here for a month. My family sent me here to be a scholar—"

"And you will *not* be a scholar!" The master slammed his cup onto the table.

Aoi's chest collapsed as he slumped his shoulders. Tears welled in his eyes.

"Do not act so distraught. You have not learned a thing during this month. Every time I send you off to read, you paint. You draw. You sketch. Cats. And only cats!"

Sniffling, Aoi reached for his tea. His hands trembled, spilling hot liquid onto his skin. He winced. After blowing the steam away, he forced a sip. It burned his tongue and words clogged his throat.

"It's for your own good. You never wanted to be a scholar, did you?" Master Hisao lowered his head to meet Aoi's eyes. The bite in his tone evaporated.

"It is true," Aoi whimpered and bowed. "I'm sorry I have let you down."

"My son, don't be hard on yourself. You are no less of a person just because you are not cut out for this journey. That's why I am sending you home." He made a sweeping gesture with his hand. "This place is not meant for you."

Relief washed over him. Unable to resist a smile, Aoi bowed repeatedly. "Thank you, thank you."

The pair finished their tea in silence. After, Master Hisao insisted on completing their meditation. He assured Aoi it would bring him peace on his journey home. The hour passed swiftly.

When Master Hisao walked Aoi to the exit, he handed him a satchel of pears. "Son, you may be too frail to work at sea with your father, and you may be too distracted for disciplined studies, but you have a gift. Those hands of yours can truly make art."

Aoi's eyes widened, and his heart swelled. "Really?"

The monk broke into a rare chuckle. "Yes. The cats you draw are lifelike. If you can draw, then be an artist. Sometimes humans deny their true talents and desires because they do not fit into the expectations of others. When you return home, speak with your parents and see if they will allow you to train with an artist in a village west of here."

After he finished speaking, Master Hisao dug into his pocket. Aoi stood on his tiptoes and stared. The master fished out a silk pouch. Aoi's mouth dropped. "Wow!"

Master Hisao laughed again. "You haven't even seen what is inside. Go ahead."

Gingerly taking it, Aoi opened it up to find charcoal sticks. The ends were tapered, making them perfect…for drawing cats.

"It is a modest art tool, but—"

"This is wonderful!" Aoi clutched the pouch to his chest.

Waving his hands, the monk shooed him away. "Now go. Return home to your family and seek approval to pursue your dream."

After a deep bow, Aoi skipped down the wooden steps. It was a long road ahead, but the path was wide and clear. The sun shined above without a cloud in the sky.

"Aoi! One more thing!"

The boy dug his feet into the dirt. Swirling around in place, he glanced at Master Hisao.

"Avoid large places at night. If you cannot make the journey in one day, stick to the small."

Aoi cocked his head to the side. "Odd," he muttered, but he forced a wave and continued down the path.

After a half hour of walking, he sat by a tree and pulled out a pear to indulge in its sweetness. He peeked into his satchel. His artwork lay with the pears. Master Hisao had insisted there was no need for the pictures in the monastery. Aoi's chewing slowed as his thoughts wandered. Where would he keep them?

A shudder ran down his spine as memories flooded his mind. Father had repeatedly yelled himself hoarse when Aoi was last home. He was one of five children. Three of his siblings were boys. Two were older, and one was a year younger; however, they were all blessed with height and strength. All the boys were expected to help Father fish when they came of age.

Aoi finished the first pear and reached into the satchel for another. He tried to focus on the taste, but the flavor seemed to dull as memory after memory assaulted him. Aoi had nearly drowned on the first few trips with Father, and each time his brothers had to save him. But that didn't make Father as mad as his drawing. Guilt heated the back of his neck. Aoi had faked illness to stay home during Jin's last days. Once the men left to fish and the women to the market, he would whip out paper and use his father's ink and brush to paint his beloved pet. After discovering the paintings months later, Father forced him to go to Master Hisao's monastery to become a scholar. The last words his father uttered were, "Art will not support you or the family. You're going to a place where you can become useful."

Staring down at the half-eaten pear, Aoi grimaced at the rapid onset of nausea. He had forgotten all the terrible things at home. He flung the fruit across the road and into the woods, along with his short-lived happiness. Father's wrath would crash down on him like an angry wave when he returned. There would be no welcome arms. He would only be regarded as a failure. Again. Aoi's heart shattered like brittle charcoal, realizing the chance of his parents allowing him to study with an artist was near impossible.

Wheels squeaked in the distance. Aoi jumped as a gaunt-faced man driving a horse and cart came into view. He blushed for being so easily frightened.

The man tipped his straw hat as he approached. Tugging the reins, he said, "Are you headed toward the coast? If so, why don't you hitch a ride with me?"

Images of his father ripping the paper cats to shreds filled his mind. He squeezed his hands into fists.

"Are you okay?" The man blinked rapidly. He waved his hand in front of Aoi.

"I'm fine," he blurted. "I am not headed toward the coast, but thank you for your kind offer."

"Oh. Okay, young fellow. Stay safe." The man clicked his tongue and urged his steed forward.

Aoi's heart beat furiously. "No," he murmured. "If I go home, my father will never let me leave. I'll go straight to the village myself!"

Without another thought, he picked up his satchel and veered toward a narrow path, which led farther inland. The expanding town the monk spoke of was located to the west, and it sounded like the perfect opportunity for an up-and-coming artist. He would pursue his passion without anyone's permission. Aoi marched down the road for hours, refusing to stop.

When the sun dipped below the horizon, his chest tightened. The trip was longer than expected. The road narrowed and wound left and right. Overgrown branches caught at his clothes, as if on purpose. He didn't pass any signs.

Wings fluttered in the distance. It dawned on Aoi that the cicadas weren't singing. Bamboo creaked and rabbits darted between bushes. Wrapping his arms around himself tightly, he said, "It'll be okay. I bet it's just around this bend."

After passing a thick bamboo patch, his heart sank. The rays of the sun faded, painting the sky pink and purple. It framed a towering temple, not the bustling town he had hoped for. Weeds overran the perimeter of the stone building. Aoi wrinkled his nose as the scent of stale water wafted by.

Peering past the temple, he realized he wasn't going to make it to the town tonight. He had to find a place to stay. It was dangerous out in the open. Master Hisao had told him of ghouls that haunted the nights. Aoi smirked. "I guess I did learn something."

Throwing his satchel over his shoulder, he approached the temple steps. Pebbles loosened from widespread cracks. When he reached the door, he knocked. No answer.

"Hello? I'm sorry to intrude, but I need a place to stay for the night." Still no answer. "I'm in the middle of my journey, and my luck with the sun has run out."

He peered back at the path. Darkness oozed through the spaces between the bamboo and leafy bushes. A wolf howled. Sucking in a breath, Aoi pushed the door. He cringed as stone scraped against stone. A grand hall with high ceilings greeted him. Rectangular windows exaggerated its height.

"Hello?" Aoi's voice echoed in the vast, empty room.

Taking slow and steady steps, he observed a decrepit desk. Scrolls covered in cobwebs scattered across the floor. The sense of abandonment covered his body with goose bumps, but Aoi shook it off. He was better off staying here than outdoors.

Moonlight poured through the windows as if on cue. Aoi sighed. He wasn't tired yet. Snapping his fingers, an idea popped into his head. He whipped out his burnt painting. Eyes shining, Aoi said, "I'm going to fix you, Jin. You are going to be larger and more elegant than before, and you will make this temple radiate with beauty!"

Moving swiftly, Aoi pulled out the silk pouch and fingered a charcoal stick. He approached the nearest moonlit wall, and he let his arm flow freely. Aoi was almost tickled with laughter. The more he drew, the wider he smiled. When the first charcoal stick was a stub, he pulled out another. "I'm not done with you, Jin. You will have gracious stripes, like a tiger. Your claws will be trimmed to perfection, like a pet of the emperor himself!"

Aoi flicked his wrist up and down. Joy filled his body with warmth as if he had drunk tea fresh from the stove. He didn't pause, and he didn't scrub away any flaws.

"Your flaws will make you unique!" Aoi could barely contain himself.

Stepping back, he puffed his chest out in pride. Jin's features were delicate, yet well defined. His paws graced the point where the wall met the floor, while his eyes stared blankly down at Aoi. It was the largest drawing he had ever made. After observing his work, he yawned. Aoi rolled the blunt charcoal stick between his fingers. His friend Jin needed one last touch. He traced a hint of a smile and two sharp teeth protruding from it.

Aoi stretched. "You look happy, Jin. You look even better than on paper. When I close my eyes, you are more than a black and gray piece of art. I envision a living, breathing reminder of my beloved pet. You have orange fur, and the stripes are white. Your eyes shine like topaz." Placing one hand against the wall, he bent his head in prayer. He thanked the heavens for his gift and hoped that someday others would appreciate it too. When another yawn took over, Aoi decided it was time to sleep. "Jin, you are my favorite work. My favorite cat." His voice wavered. "And my only friend…"

He scanned the room. The wide, open space reminded him of Master Hisao. His warning seemed silly, but Aoi spotted a closet in the corner. When he opened the door, he nodded in approval. There was enough space for him to curl up. The shelves were vacant other than a blanket and broom. The door shut with a click behind him, leaving Aoi in pitch black. His hands traced the walls until his fingers wrapped around the wooden handle of the broom. He slid it underneath the handle and positioned it until the door was secure. Then, he snatched the blanket. Dust billowed into the air, and Aoi sneezed.

"It's just one night," he said as he sat on the slate floor. Exhaustion dragged him deep into slumber.

***

A roar shook the temple foundation, jolting Aoi awake. His breath hitched when something rammed the front door. The walls vibrated. Chunks of ceiling pelted his head. After a deafening explosion, stomping cracked the floors, as if something had entered the temple.

Aoi wrapped his arms around his knees and trembled. He bit his lip to stifle his whimpering. His blood curdled as the creature released a growl. It sniffed the air, then trudged closer to the closet.

The scent of rotten fish and mold seeped beneath the door and choked Aoi. His mind raced. What kind of foul creature could this be? With each step, the ground shook with greater intensity. Aoi's eyes widened in horror as the handle rattled. When the door didn't budge, claws scraped along its length. Aoi cupped his ears at the high-pitched screech.

A growl transformed into another deafening roar. The creature rammed against the door. In-between each assault, Aoi could hear its lips smacking. Unable to form tears, Aoi clenched his teeth. He didn't want to die, but his father's voice echoed in the back of his mind with the words, "It serves you right."

Wood splintered. Aoi no longer had minutes, only seconds. A cackle grated against his bones. Palms slick with sweat, he tore the blanket off and stood. He clenched his fists in front of him. Swallowing a lump in his throat, Aoi convinced himself that even though death was certain, he was still going to try to fight.

The creature sucked in air, ready to release another blood-thirsty cry. Its sheer force bent the door, cracking it bit by bit. When the door was about to give, a high-pitched yowl overpowered the guttural roar. Aoi held his breath. Two monsters?

With a hiss, a body rammed into the creature, colliding with the wall. Flesh ripped. Jaws gnashed. Wood splintered beneath the battle of the titans. They tumbled about the room, exchanging growls. Aoi remained frozen, straining his ears for the victor. He had no idea how long he stood, but glimpses of pale light streaming through cracks in the door signaled sunrise.

A sickening *crunch* snatched Aoi's attention. One of the creatures howled in agony until the sound diminished to a gurgle. The floor shuddered as a body fell. Soft padding footsteps passed by the door and faded into silence.

Forcing deep breaths, Aoi waited for movement. The temple remained still and silent as the rays of the sun strengthened. Day had arrived, and Master Hisao's warnings only spoke of night horrors. Aoi stretched a trembling hand toward the broomstick. He threw it aside and twisted the doorknob. After taking a few breaths to reassure himself, he rammed his shoulder against the door.

Aoi tumbled out as the door snapped in two. He rolled until his face slammed against the floor. His eyes watered as a sharp pain radiated up his nose; the pungent smell was exponentially worse in the room. He raised his head slowly and gasped.

A heap lay on the floor in a pool of blood. When he realized it wasn't breathing, Aoi tiptoed around the body. Patches of matted, black fur had been ripped off. Fine scratch marks marred its torso. The girth was that of a bear, but the head looked like a wolf's. Its blood-red eyes remained wide open. Its teeth were as long as his hands. Aoi's jaw dropped. He always thought ghouls with warped animal bodies were nothing but a figment of the imagination meant to scare kids like him.

"But, how?" He whipped his head left and right, but he didn't see any other presence.

His gaze halted at Jin. His beautiful charcoal cat remained on the wall, but something seemed different. Aoi squinted. His heart stopped. It still looked down at him with a smile. However, viscous red liquid dripped from its two teeth.

"Jin," he whispered. Aoi caressed his drawing. "You saved me?"

The cat stared lifelessly at him.

"Th-thank you."

Aoi picked up his satchel and silk pouch and stared at the dead creature one last time. He leaned forward and strained his muscles, tugging on a fang until a *pop* echoed. He examined the double-pronged tip and then wiped the blood away on a discarded tablecloth. Aoi never wanted to forget what Jin had done. After pocketing the fang, he backed out of the temple. His heart twisted as Jin shrank in the distance. When he reached the outside steps, Aoi turned and sprinted, ignoring the burning in his lungs. He didn't stop to eat or drink. Other travelers passed him in a blur.

As the sun reached its peak, tiled rooftops crept into view. His legs pushed even faster. He skidded down the dirt hill and slowed to a halt at a massive wooden archway. Hands on his knees, Aoi gasped for air. People wove in and out of the crowded village. The smell of freshly baked bread made his mouth water.

Once he caught his breath, he gingerly stepped through the gates. He clung to his satchel. He ducked his head, hoping people wouldn't notice how grimy he was. A body bumped into him, and Aoi immediately bowed.

"Are you okay?"

Mouth agape, Aoi gazed at the man, who smiled warmly. Aoi nodded.

"Where are your parents?" Knitting his brows, the man looked beyond the gates.

Clenching his jaw, Aoi fought for an answer. He jutted his chin up and said, "They sent me on a journey to become the greatest artist in all Japan."

"Oh, really? Let me see some of your works," the man replied gruffly.

Aoi swung his satchel around and pulled his parchments out. As he handed them to the man, he flushed pink.

The man huffed as he flipped through each painting.

Aoi rocked on the balls of his feet, unable to stop fidgeting. He turned his attention to the bustling village center. Red lanterns strung between buildings. Wood chimes serenaded the air. A large mural of a dragon flying through the sky towered behind the man. Everything about this place was the polar opposite of his home by the sea.

Raising a brow, the man said, "How old are you?"

"Fourteen, sir."

"Really?" His eyes widened. "You're so small."

Aoi rolled his ankle. Grimacing at the streaks of pain, he nodded. He didn't mind; it was a distraction from the shot at his already-shattered confidence. "Yes, sir. So I have been told."

The man shoved the papers back into Aoi's hands. "They are amazing!"

"Thank you very much!" Aoi exclaimed. "I'm here to see the master artist who resides in this town." He gulped, fearing rejection for not receiving his parents' permission first.

The man narrowed his eyes. He guided Aoi by the small of his back toward a paved road that branched from the market. "Master Ito lives at the end of this road."

Aoi pocketed his works and ran down the path with the gentle breeze pushing him along. With each step, he felt lighter, as if he could leap into the sky and fly.

A wooden house surrounded by white pebbles stood proudly in front of him. The same trees as Master Hisao's lined up in a perfect row. A large bell swayed idly in the breeze, releasing a rich clang. Aoi spotted a man on the porch with thick ebony locks tied in a bun, leaning into a canvas. With each step Aoi took up the stairs, he summoned more courage to speak.

When he reached the porch, Aoi cleared his throat. The man turned his head and smiled, lifting his plump cheeks. His skin was delicate like porcelain, even with the wrinkles that framed his face. His angular features reminded Aoi of Master Hisao.

"Master…Ito?"

The man approached Aoi. The boy craned his neck to see what Ito had been working on.

"What is a young boy doing trespassing on my property?" He raised a brow.

Aoi bowed so quickly his head swirled. "My name is Aoi, and I was told a master of art lives here. I was hoping to train under you."

Master Ito chuckled, tucking his hands behind his back. His beard tapered down to his breastbone. "You are too young. Go back to your family and return in a few years."

"But…but…" Aoi fumbled in his satchel and pulled out wads of paper. The monster's fang slipped out and clattered on the floor. He shoved his drawings at Master Ito, but the master's eyes roamed past them and fixed on the fang.

Master Ito swept it up to scrutinize it. Color drained from his already pale complexion. Chin quivering, he said, "Where did you get this?"

Cradling his artwork, Aoi bit his lip. Master Ito likely wouldn't believe his epic adventure in the temple.

"Well?" The master tapped his foot.

"I spent the night at an abandoned temple a few miles back. There was a monster…"Aoi trailed off. "When I awoke, I found it dead. Jin killed the monster."

"And who is Jin?"

Aoi swallowed a lump in his throat. "My cat."

Looking both ways, Master Ito frowned. "I see no cat. And no ordinary cat could take down a monster. Where has your companion gone?"

Aoi twiddled his thumbs. "He's at the temple." Swallowing a lump in his throat, he wondered if it was Jin's spirit that had saved him. "He'll make a great guard for travelers seeking safety at night."

The master kneeled to Aoi's height. "Son, this is serious. There is a cursed, murderous creature that roams the night. It terrorizes anyone who is caught outside after sunset."

"It's true!" A shiver ran down the boy's spine. "It was massive! It has a head of a wolf, and a bear's body with blood-red eyes, and it carried the stench of death!"

When their gaze met, Master Ito's eyes narrowed. Wooden sandals clacked against the floor as he sped past Aoi and rang the golden bell. As soon as the rich sound faded, he said, "The legend warns of a cursed beast with double-pronged fangs; however, your story sounds no truer than a fairy tale."

Aoi shrank back until he stood against the wall. His eyes widened as herds of village folk milled down the street, spilling up to the doorsteps.

Master Ito turned and stretched his free arm. The sun glistened behind him. "Come, son."

Aoi hesitantly grasped the master's weathered hand and stood beside him. Before he could blink, the master artist yanked his hand into the air.

"This child claims his cat killed the demon monster that lurks in the night."

Laughter erupted, stabbing into Aoi like daggers. His shoulders slumped as fingers pointed at him. The master flicked his wrist and silenced the crowd.

"I believe he should be held accountable to the truth. I'm taking him to the abandoned temple. Follow if you wish!" The master snatched Aoi's collar and pulled him down the stairs and onto the road.

The thought of seeing the ghoul's corpse curdled his blood, but Aoi was determined to prove everyone wrong. Lifting his head high, he marched ahead and ignored the chatter that trailed behind. Aoi snuck looks at Master Ito, who maintained his perfect posture and wore a neutral expression. Neither spoke the whole way.

By the time they reached the decrepit temple, blisters had formed where Aoi's sandals met his feet. Master Ito floated up the stairs. When Aoi was about to follow, an elbow knocked him forward. A man with a pointed chin and large ears sneered.

"You better be right." His hands fondled a pitchfork. "If not, you will be putting us in danger. There's no way we can return to the town before sunset."

An unfamiliar rage surged up his throat, and Aoi stomped on the man's foot. "If you're so afraid, you shouldn't have come with us!"

Without another thought, Aoi trudged into the temple, fuming. He was fed up with being underestimated, and in a few short moments, he would make everyone look like fools.

A gasp jerked his attention forward. Master Ito collapsed onto his knees before the large, dark mass. The familiar scent of decay filled the Aoi's lungs, but he squared his shoulders and approached. Blood soaked the edges of the master's robe.

"I can't believe it," the elderly man murmured, shaking his head. "This is no regular beast. I've never seen the like before."

Aoi tapped his shoulder. "Pardon me, Master Ito. Please look to your left."

The two turned their heads to the sun-washed wall. A feline drawn in charcoal smiled at them. The blood that clung to its fangs earlier had dripped to the floor.

Master Ito shouted, jumping to his feet. Aoi's heart swelled with pride as he walked up to his drawing. Placing a hand between Jin's eyes, he whispered, "You're going to be famous, friend."

Multiple gasps filled the air as the minutes passed. Aoi remained still, refusing to leave Jin's side.

"It's the ghoul! How hideous!" a woman hissed.

A man cleared his throat but couldn't hide the tremor. "Look at that drawing. There's blood on the wall!"

"Impossible!" a third person exclaimed.

Aoi smiled when the sound of a pitchfork clanged onto the stone floor. When he turned around, he found the crowd quivering by the entrance. Master Ito stroked his beard as he joined Aoi's side. His eyes welled with tears.

"The boy speaks the truth! He and his companion cat have saved our lives!" The master artist's gravelly voice rumbled over the crowds as he waved the fang into the air. "Our village has been freed! Now we can walk the earth at night without fear."

Everyone cheered and pumped their fists into the air. A ticklish feeling swelled in Aoi's chest. When people began chanting his name, his lips twitched into a smile.

Master Ito gently plopped the fang into the boy's hands. "Keep this as a reminder of your bravery."

"And Jin's!" Aoi peeped.

Winking at the wall, Master Ito nodded. "And Jin's. A very brave creature, indeed. As for you, your bravery in surviving the haunted night has shown me your resilience of spirit, which makes you worth teaching."

Aoi's heart thundered as Master Ito knelt.

"I'm working on a painting with a lush forest. A monkey, a hawk, and an owl are perched on tree branches, while a magnificent tiger with glistening stripes lurks on the ground."

"It sounds flawless," Aoi replied. He hoped that he finally proved his worth. His dream dared to expand beyond the protective chambers of his heart.

"Barely. But you know what I have trouble with? I can paint kanji, dragons, and endless clouds of the heavens, but I can't seem to perfect…cats."

Aoi knit his brows together. Even though he couldn't detect sarcasm in Master Ito's tone, he knew he had to be mocking him. "That's silly."

"Oh, is it? How sad. My brother told me about a young man destined to be a great artist." With a wink, he added, "And his specialty was cats."

"Master Hisao?"

Bowing his head, Master Ito asked, "Son, you arrived much earlier than I expected. Regardless, would you like to be my apprentice?"

Aoi dropped his satchel. His heart rocketed to the sky as fireworks erupted in his mind. A warm sensation wrapped around him like a hug, something he had never experienced before. Locking eyes with Master Ito, Aoi grinned.

"Yes, I would like that very much."

"Good." He made a sweeping gesture with his arm. People parted in silence, leaving a path out of the temple. "Let's not waste time. Everyone is going to want a painting from the boy who saved our town from a legendary evil."

Solstice Flames

Heather Hayden

"Merry Sol—"

Ben slammed the shop door shut behind him, cutting off the alchemist's words. Not that the meaning was unclear. After all, it seemed every single passerby was wishing Ben the same thing.

"Hmph." Shaking his head, the young mage stomped down the sidewalk. His new leather boots splashed slushy snow on his favorite wool cloak. Thankfully, he had freshened the cloak's weather conditioning spell yesterday, and the grayish sludge slid right off.

"Merry Solstice!" a group of carolers chorused at him before launching into a well-known song. They were a cheery, red-cheeked group: young and old, tall and short. A small lass with bright blue eyes and a gap-toothed grin held out a worn bowler hat as she trilled the words off-key.

Ben pushed past with a wordless growl and continued on his way. They wouldn't get a penny from him. His money was meant for a better cause than feeding the hungry and poor. The satchel hanging heavy from his shoulder was a constant reminder of that.

There was nowhere to hide from the festivities, not in the heart of Everfeld. Everywhere he turned hung colorful magelights and sparkling tinkers' decorations, celebrating the eve of the shortest day of the year, when the darkness embraced the sun before releasing it, reborn to light another year, on Solstice Day.

Groups of carolers strolled up and down the streets, singing of joy and hope and rebirth, goodwill to all. Pedestrians rushed to buy last-minute gifts. Travelers dismounted horses—and the occasional pegasus—next to inns or the homes of family or friends.

As a major hub of trade, Everfeld burst with life during the holidays.

Ben hated every minute of it.

The crowds thinned as he left the shops behind and entered the artisan district. Workshops sent up puffs of varicolored smoke as masters and apprentices worked overtime to finish their final Solstice orders. A particularly sour patch of dark green smoke forced Ben to cross the street.

As he wiped his watery eyes with a well-starched handkerchief, a hand touched his shoulder.

Jerking away, Ben whirled, one hand already reaching into a pocket for the ward he kept there.

"Ben, it's just me!" Frederick raised his hands and offered a weak smile that creased his stress-worn face further. "Merry Solstice, dear brother. How is life treating you? I haven't seen you in forever."

"I'm fine," Ben said stiffly, cursing himself for not realizing he was near the blacksmith shop where his older brother was apprenticed. "Shouldn't you be at the forge?"

Frederick's brow furrowed. "Master Bran gave me tonight off, and tomorrow, for the Solstice. I wanted to spend more time at home this year, with Anne and Theo."

"Of course, of course." Ben drummed his fingers on the cover of his satchel as they stood in silence.

"Theo is getting sicker," Frederick said quietly, his voice breaking. "Anne and I are doing our best, but…the doctors think this will be his last Solstice."

"Ah. I'm sorry." The words were a formality. Ben had never even met Theo—why should he care if the child was sickly? Perhaps his brother should have married someone better than a poor healer.

"Would you…would you come to Solstice dinner tomorrow? It would mean so much to Anne, having the family together. With Theo sick, we can't travel to visit her parents, and they aren't able to travel themselves." Frederick's deep blue eyes, so much like Mother's, pleaded with Ben.

What would their mother think of her favorite son now, destitute as he was? Ben shook his head. She'd still find something to praise. Frederick had always been perfect in her eyes. *Why can't you be more like your brother, Eben?* The memory of her sharp words wrapped icy claws around his heart. He needed to return to work. Already too much time had been wasted chasing down the last few precious ingredients. "I don't have the time. And I really must be going now." He turned and walked away.

"Merry Solstice, brother," Frederick called after him, his voice thick.

Ben didn't bother acknowledging the farewell.

***

Janey pressed a hand to her stinging cheek, cringing as Pa raised his fist again.

This time, he simply gestured to the door of the tiny apartment they shared with two other families.

"Go!" He was a big man, heavily muscled, and his voice matched his size, a roar worthy of a bear. "And don't come back until you've sold every last flameburst!"

Janey fled, grabbing her thin cloak—more patches than anything—as she escaped through the entrance. She clutched the package of flamebursts to her chest, its hard wooden edges digging into the ribs that stuck out from her thin frame. Where Pa had gotten the cheap fire-starting spells, she had no idea. Asking would have only earned her another slap.

The pain in her cheek faded slowly as she ran, numbed by the creeping cold of Solstice Eve. Far on the horizon, the sun slipped away to its long sleep, taking with it what little warmth it had offered during the day. Streetlamps cast pools of bright magelight against the gathering darkness.

Janey shivered as she paused to tie her cloak around her shoulders. All day she'd spent begging, and Pa had taken what few coins she'd gathered and tossed her right back out again. The roll she had dared to buy that morning with a single copper was long gone, and her stomach released quiet rumbles.

Tears brought the stinging to life again, and Janey's fingers against her skin came away with a faint stickiness. He'd split the skin. She shouldn't have asked for dinner money. Should have kept her mouth shut.

She started walking, her leg muscles stiff from her swift run and the cold. There were few passersby on the sidewalk, and the houses were well-kept mansions. This was a residential district, one far nicer than the slums where she lived. She'd run in the wrong direction without realizing it. It was the heart of Everfeld where she needed to go, where last-minute shoppers might take pity on a poor young girl down on her luck.

Something brushed against her nose, and Janey blinked, then looked up. In the bright magelights, she could make out fat snowflakes floating down. A slow, heavy storm tonight, it looked like. She shivered. Those could get cold. Very cold. She needed to get home as soon as she could.

Looking down at the box of a hundred flamebursts, Janey's shoulders slumped. How was she ever going to sell all of them in one night?

One at a time, she told herself and sat down for a moment to lean against a heavy iron fence. The snowfall grew thicker, and Janey drew her cloak closer around her shoulders. Just a moment to rest her weary feet, and then she'd be on her way.

***

Snow began to fall as Ben turned down the road that led to home, a small but stately house which served as both residence and workplace. Unlike the other houses lining the street, his was dark save for a single magelight lit in the living room and, of course, one in the kitchen, where Bethany, his housekeeper, would be preparing him a simple supper.

His stomach growled at the thought of food and he quickened his pace. Just a quick bite to eat, then he'd continue working on his project. He was close to completing it. So close, at last.

As he approached the short wrought-iron fence that separated his house from the street—and his neighbors—a shape came into view, huddled against the railings. A package? No, he wasn't expecting a delivery. A vagrant, then.

Scowling, Ben looked up and down the street. No sign of a town guard—they were never around when one needed them. Tucking his hand into the pocket with the ward, ready to use it if necessary, he stalked over to the hunched figure. He came to a sharp halt a few feet away, sending up a spray of snow that spattered the person's cloak, sinking into the unprotected fabric.

"What are you doing here?" he demanded.

The person raised her head, revealing a face that might have been pretty if it wasn't smudged with dirt and a faint streak of blood from a cut on her cheek. Unkempt hair that could be dark, or simply dirty, hung in tangled curls down to her shoulders. She watched him nervously, like a mouse eyeing a cat, then jumped a little.

"Oh, sir!" Scrambling to her feet, the young woman dropped into a wobbly curtsy that raised her skirts just enough to reveal bare toes peeking out of heavily worn slippers. "Merry Solstice. Could I interest you in a flameburst or two?"

"What?" Ben stared at her incredulously.

She opened a wooden box with a flourish, revealing cheap flamebursts arranged in orderly rows. "Five for a copper, sir, and that's a right fair price."

He laughed and waved her away. "I'm a mage; I have no need for those trinkets."

Her smile wavered. "Please, sir—"

Before she could continue her fruitless begging, he pushed past her and opened the gate. "Get out of here before I send word to the town guard."

"But—"

Ben slammed the gate shut and stormed down the path leading to his front door. The nerve of that beggar, trying to rip him off like that. Five for a copper? He could make batches of ten in his sleep. That whole box had probably cost her five coppers. Well, she could go take advantage of some idiot do-gooder.

"Bethany," he called as he opened the door. "I'll take my dinner in the living room. Make it quick. I have work to do."

***

Janey slumped against the fence, her face buried in her hands, partly to warm her chilled fingers and partly to hide her tears. She was no stranger to rudeness, but the way that man had just looked *through* her, as though she didn't even exist, as though she was less than nothing…

Maybe that was all she was. Nothing. Pa always said she'd never amount to anything.

Angrily, Janey grabbed a flameburst from the box and crushed it between her fingers, releasing a brief, warming flame. She hadn't asked to be born to a drunkard and a washerwoman who hadn't lived long enough to give her baby a name.

Wind began to blow, stirring the flakes into a mini-blizzard. Janey huddled closer to the fence, not wanting to wander in the storm. It was so cold. She curled her toes up inside the slippers that had once belonged to her mother and pulled the cloak up over her head to keep her ears from freezing.

The box of flamebursts lay on the ground beside her, a dark, mocking shape, and she snatched a handful of them, crushing all of their soft shells into one big mass. If she froze before she sold them all, it would be no better than selling none. The flames flared heavily for a moment, singeing her fingers with bright sparks of pain. Flinching, she dropped the flamebursts into the snow. Their magical fire burned for a moment before the spells fizzled.

Still, the warmth had given her a brief burst of strength. Janey brushed her fingers over the flamebursts. Father would be angry if she returned without any money for them. Perhaps she could ask for a little more apiece, once she reached the market streets. After the storm died a bit, she'd head straight for the heart of Everfeld and sell every last flameburst she had left.

Holding tight to that thought, trying to ignore the creeping fear of what her father would do if she returned with no flamebursts or coins, Janey crushed another one.

***

While he waited for dinner, Ben sat in a comfortable armchair by the living room fire. His satchel rested on the floor beside him. After warming his chilled toes and fingers, the mage sorted through the short stack of mail Bethany had left on his coffee table. Bills for the most part. A few notices from the bank that payments had been delivered for larger jobs he had completed. A Solstice card from some distant cousin, which he tossed aside, unopened. A couple letters from potential clients inquiring about his services.

An amusing one came from a man named Rickard, who apparently had had an issue with a mage releasing his circus's prize possession. Rickard wanted to know if Ben could create a spell to summon a selkie—or a mermaid—to replace the loss. Rolling his eyes, Ben crumpled up the letter and tossed it into the fire. As if any self-respecting mage would pursue control spells like that.

Bethany came bustling in as he set aside the last few letters. The older woman's graying hair was tucked into a smart bun, and her apron was, as always, flawlessly white. She set a silver dinner tray on the coffee table and poured him a steaming cup of tea. Its minty scent mingled with the savory smell of stew and freshly sliced bread.

"Merry Solstice," she said with a bright smile. "I'll be heading out now—my brother's visiting with his son for the holiday."

Ben gave a short nod. "You have tomorrow off, of course."

Her smile rivaled the glow of the room's magelight. "That's very kind of you, young sir. And if you don't think it too forward, you're more than welcome to visit tomorrow for Solstice dinner."

Ben took a sip of piping hot tea and winced. "That won't be necessary. I'll eat leftovers."

"As you wish. Have a wonderful Solstice, Mr. Maiser." Bethany bustled out and he heard the back door open and shut.

After dinner, Ben left the living room and walked down the hall toward his basement workroom. The heavy satchel bumped against his hip.

His workshop was the largest room in the house, as well as the cleanest. Not that Bethany ever came downstairs—she'd been warned when he hired her that his workplace was off-limits due to the delicate nature of spellcrafting. Some mages worked instinctively, gathering magic from their surroundings and building a spell with nothing more than gestures and a few words. Others used a focusing aid, such as a wand or staff or ring. Ben used various ingredients with special properties to mix draughts and potions instilled with magic.

He had many clients, and he had developed several new spell variants over the years, but Ben's masterpiece was not yet complete. He'd spent the past ten years—four in his apprenticeship from ages fourteen to eighteen, six as a new mage rapidly gathering clients—studying every scrap of knowledge he could find related to life after death. To ghosts. To spirits.

Ten years ago, his mother had passed away on Solstice Day. His father and his older brother, Frederick, had had a chance to speak to her before she passed. But he had been sick with the same wasting illness, and hadn't even learned she had died until several days later, when he regained consciousness thanks to the healer's skill.

One by one, Ben laid out the herbs and jars and tiny bottles he'd purchased at the alchemist's shop upon the worn surface of his wood workbench. If all went well tonight, he'd finally speak to his mother, one last time. Prove at last that he wasn't the weak, useless son she'd always seen him as. He would be the first mage in history to successfully summon a ghost.

That would make her proud of him, for sure.

***

Snow coated the street, the sidewalk, the fence, and Janey. Frozen tears glued her eyelids shut, but each gentle flame sent a reddish glow shining through them. Her body shivered violently in the cold, but at least the pain in her cheek was gone.

Half the flamebursts were also gone. Not to passersby—there had been none of those since the storm picked up—but to keep Janey from freezing. She couldn't stay here forever, she knew that. Nor could she go home without coin to offer. Pa would simply send her out again.

"I'll find somewhere else to spend the night," she told herself firmly, rubbing the ice from her eyelashes. She'd passed a church earlier, perhaps shelter could be found there.

As she tried to stand, however, her frost-nipped feet refused to hold her weight. Janey collapsed back into the hollow her body had formed in the drift by the iron fence. A whimper escaped her lips, and she gritted her teeth at the wave of pain sweeping up her legs.

Her fingers brushed over the smooth, rounded surfaces of the flamebursts still tucked into their box. "I just need to warm up a bit more." As she squeezed the little ball of magic to release its flame, something louder popped—a sharp sound, like a brief burst of thunder. Janey jolted and looked around, but couldn't find the source in the foggy white that surrounded her tiny corner of the world.

Flames licked her fingers with welcome warmth, and she huddled toward the flameburst resting on the ground. It gave off a golden glow, at the heart of which she could almost imagine a real fire, crackling in the hearth of a home of a happy family, a whole family, a family who never wanted for warmth or food.

Laughter bubbled through her cracked lips and was swallowed by the wailing winds of the snowstorm.

***

Coughing, Ben waved away the acrid smoke lingering in the air. One of his measurements must have been off by a fraction of a fraction; those ingredients shouldn't have reacted that way.

He surveyed the mess on his workbench with a frown. It was going to take precious time to clean up, and he still had more preparations to make. Everything had to be in place before the clock struck midnight, otherwise he'd have to wait another year.

"Eben Maiser!"

The shout made Ben jump. He turned, jaw dropping at the sight before him: a pale, wavering apparition. There was no doubt about it; he'd managed to summon a ghost. How? He hadn't even completed the final steps of his spell. Yet, here the spirit was, hovering before him, almost insubstantial but existing nonetheless.

"M-mother?" The word stumbled off his tongue as a shiver of apprehension ran down his spine. Had he truly managed to summon her spirit? All that time spent in learning and practice, all those years and accomplishments, and he still felt like a little boy standing before her. He sucked in a deep breath and straightened his shoulders. She'd never had a kind word for him before, but surely now that she could see his power, she would praise him!

The spirit laughed, the sound sharp with amusement, and shook its shadowy head. "Is that who your spell was for?" It laughed again.

Its voice was too deep to be his mother's, and Ben could still make out no features beyond a faint impression of coal-dark eyes that stared deep into his soul. Shaken, he raised a hand. "I didn't intend to summon you. Return from whence you came." He spoke the words of banishment he had developed for such an occasion.

Nothing happened, except that the ghost stopped laughing.

"You have no control over me," the spirit intoned in a sonorous voice. "I was sent here to test you, as you have been found wanting, Eben Maiser."

"Wanting?" Ben snorted. "This is ridiculous. That blast must have knocked me unconscious. I'm dreaming, you're not real, and any moment, I'll awake."

The spirit made a gesture, and a spoon rattled from the table to the floor. "This is no dream, Maiser. I am the Spirit of Solstice, and I am here to show you the truth. Let us first journey to a time before your soul darkened. A time of innocence. A time of childhood long past."

Before Ben could react, the ghost gestured again and their surroundings vanished into grayness. Ben cried out, reaching for a surface, but not even his footing was steady. He fell to his knees on a familiar, worn, hardwood floor. A floor he hadn't seen in years.

Laughter brought his head up, and he watched a young boy with floppy blond curls speed down the hallway. The boy didn't seem to notice him, running past Ben without pause. A second boy, older and with brown hair, chased after him.

"I'm going to catch you!" the older boy shouted with glee, his longer strides eating the distance between the two.

Those words—that voice—

Ben knew where they were. This was the Maisers' townhouse, his family's old home. The dark-haired boy was his brother Frederick, and the young blond was Ben himself. Somehow, he'd traveled into the past.

"What madness is this?" he whispered, watching the boys disappear around the corner, headed—he knew, he *remembered*—to the kitchen for a mug of spiced cider, their favorite Solstice Eve treat.

"No madness at all." The spirit floated next to Ben, as formless as it had been before. Its voice echoed in the empty hall. "Do you remember this time?"

"Of course," Ben snapped. "Why wouldn't I?"

"If you recall the happiness, the joy, that ran through your veins on days like this, why are you so harsh and cold now?" The spirit sank a bit toward the floor, its edges wavering. Despite the brightly lit hall—or perhaps because of it—the apparition still appeared thin and shapeless, more mirage than reality. "Perhaps another scene will help refresh your memory."

"Wait—"

The scene blurred then snapped back into focus.

This time, they were in the townhouse's banquet room, a large dining hall filled with Solstice decorations, tables of food and drink, and merrymakers.

Laughter, a more controlled kind than that of the boys from before but still vibrant, filled the room as voices hummed in merry conversation. Ladies in beautiful satin gowns chatted in circles while men in tailored suits spoke together over glasses of spiced cider and sherry. Frederick's and Ben's younger selves were present, now a few years older, and surrounded by boys and girls their age.

The spirit pointed at the youths, who laughed and chatted among themselves with carefree abandon. "You loved these parties, remember?"

Ben looked across the room in the other direction, where a tall woman with blond hair and a sharp red smile stood. "Mother." He made to walk toward her, but the ghost slipped past and barred his way.

"They can't hear or see or touch you, Eben Maiser."

Ben strode through the spirit, a chill brushing his skin. "Mother!" He reached her side a few steps later, but his outstretched hand passed through her arm. "Mother…" She didn't react, continuing her conversation with another woman.

"I warned you," the spirit said, drifting across the room. It appeared unharmed by his passage through it, just as he had no effect on Mother. "This is a memory, a past that has come and gone. I can only bring you here to see what you've forgotten."

"I haven't forgotten anything." Ben shook his head and waved dismissively at his younger self, who was beaming at a dimpled young beauty with roses in her hair. "These parties were always Mother's way of showing Frederick off, heir to the family fortune. She didn't care what I did, as long as I didn't embarrass her or the family. All those people I'm speaking with, none of them cared to come calling after she died and Father drank away all our money."

The spirit indicated the rose-crowned girl as she laughed at something young Ben said. "Not even Mabel? Are you sure about that?"

Ben turned away. "She lost interest in me, too."

"Or did she think you weren't interested in her? Hm?"

Had it been his fault? The loss of his mother, followed by the loss of the family fortune and his father, had driven him deep into his apprenticeship. He hadn't had time for anyone, not even Mabel. Ben closed his eyes. "It doesn't matter. None of this does. I don't know who you are or why you're doing this, but I insist that you take me home. I'm pressed for time."

"Fortunately for you, we have all the time in the world right now. But that won't last forever…" The spirit's voice faded.

Ben opened his eyes to his empty workroom, table still covered with the results of the explosion. He looked around hurriedly, but there was no sign of the ghost.

"Temporary hallucination," he muttered. "I'll have to speak to that shopkeeper about the freshness of his wares next time I'm there."

Sighing to himself, Ben bent to pick up a spoon from the floor. Memories long-buried jostled for attention, distracting him from his work. Mabel *had* visited after his mother's death. She'd tried to comfort him, but he had ignored her efforts. Ignored her. When had she stopped coming? He vaguely remembered receiving letters at his master's workshop when he first started his apprenticeship. They had been perfumed with roses—her favorite scent. Had he ever responded? Where would he be now, if he had? For that matter, where was she? Likely married by now. Once upon a time, he had hoped it would be to him…

He shook his head. These thoughts of what could have been were pointless. Distracting. Pushing them away, Ben turned his attention to his worktable. To the spell he had yet to perfect.

It was time to try again.

***

"Don't sleep!"

Janey jerked awake, half-crying in terror as she shook off the snow piled over her. For a brief moment, she hadn't been able to breathe. Was this what dying felt like?

The wind whistled in her ears. She thought she'd heard someone speak, but couldn't see anyone. Or anything. Even the hard iron fence she huddled against was invisible in the thick snowfall. Shivers racked her body. Her legs were painfully numb almost to the knees.

"Don't sleep!"

Janey blinked her eyes. For a moment, she saw a shape in the snow, white upon white. She squinted into the storm. Nothing.

As she drew one of the few remaining flamebursts from the box, her chilled fingers trembled and she dropped it in the snow.

"No!" Janey grasped after it, her hand scrabbling in the snow until she found it by sight rather than feel—her fingers could barely move, much less tell soft snow from the firmer, round surface of the flameburst. The pale ball of brewed magic glowed in the storm-dimmed magelight from a nearby streetlamp.

Forcing her stiff muscles to flex, she crushed the flameburst and dropped it in the snow on her lap. Its flames lapped at the white powder, melting some of it. The skin of her palms tingled as Janey held her hands close to the light.

For a brief moment, she heard the thin crackle of flames above the howling wind. If only this were a roaring fire, with a chicken roasting over it, juice dripping down to sizzle in the fire's embers. Her tongue licked cold, chapped lips, tasting the salt of frozen tears. She could almost imagine the flavor of the hot, juicy meat, soaked in gravy, served by loving hands.

When she closed her eyes, she could see the scene, just out of reach of her grasping fingers. A smiling mother and father, calling her name with gentle voices, holding out their arms to embrace her.

***

Ben swept everything from the surface of his workbench, a strangled snarl rising from his throat. "Argh!" Another failure. No explosion this time, just a fizzling of the magic that should have swelled upon the completion of his project.

"What did I do wrong this time?" he demanded of the leather-bound book in which he kept his notes.

"Have you considered giving up this quest?"

Ben whirled around, glaring at the apparition before him. It sounded the same as before, though its form seemed a bit sharper and he could make out a trace of a downturned mouth that twisted around words as the ghost spoke.

"Eben Maiser—"

"Shut. Up." Ben closed his eyes and rubbed them. More hallucinations. Perhaps he should see a healer—no. There was no time. He would have to be more careful with his measurements. This task had to be completed tonight. He had waited so long already. Another year was not an option.

"I am not a dream, Maiser." The spirit's voice grew louder, until it echoed from the room's stone walls. "I am real."

He opened his eyes and inhaled sharply—the ghost was almost close enough to touch. If one could touch such a thing; he'd already proved that wasn't possible. "Go away!"

A chuckle rolled out, dark and ominous. "Oh, I'm going somewhere, certainly. And you're coming with me."

"Not again—"

A swirl of fog enveloped them both.

It faded within seconds, revealing a room he had never seen before. The long table and chandeliers, the fancy plate settings and crystal goblets, told him it was a dining room in some upper-class family's house. The scent of spices and savory meat filled the air. Servants were bringing the dishes in on silver platters, and they took their places in a line against one wall as they finished.

"What is this place?" Ben demanded.

"Wait and see."

A few long minutes passed, then laughter drifted into the room, closely followed by a man and woman, arm in arm, surrounded by three bright-eyed children who looked to be no more than four or five. Golden curls bouncing, the two girls raced each other to their seats. The youngest, a boy, toddled after them on unsteady legs.

"Careful," the woman cautioned gently as one girl almost knocked over a chair. "Dinner isn't going anywhere, my dears."

"What a lovely spread." The man smiled and kept speaking in a light and jovial tone, but his words faded as Ben focused on the man's wife.

He almost hadn't recognized her—how long had it been? Not that long, really—but it was Mabel, plain as day. She looked far more radiant and beautiful than he remembered, a glow filling her cheeks with an almost visible light of joy.

Joy that stabbed his heart, reopening old wounds. He turned to the spirit, fists clenched. "Why are you showing me this?"

"To remind you of what you could have had, and lost." The ghost gestured toward the happy family gathered around the table. "That could have been you sitting there by her side, laughing at the antics of your children."

Ben snorted. "I never wanted children, anyway.

Frederick was the one who did." He scoffed. "And look at where it got him."

"Perhaps we should look," the spirit snapped, its tone sharp and cold as ice.

The gray mist swirled around them, and this time, Ben found himself standing on the sidewalk in one of the poorer parts of town, surrounded by ramshackle houses with peeling paint and tilted window shutters. Snow coated the streets, almost burying his boots. He stomped a few times, wrapping his arms around his ribs as he blew out a steamy breath.

"What are we doing here?"

The spirit floated across the snow, not disturbing a flake—even the falling snowflakes seemed to pass through its misty body. Coming to a stop by one of the houses, the ghost beckoned Ben over.

"Come see for yourself," it demanded, tone still ice-cold.

Shivering, Ben stalked through the snow to stand by the house's small window. A crack in the shutters let him peer inside the dimly lit hovel.

As his eyes adjusted to the low level of light, he first took in the tiny fireplace with a weakly burning fire. A lantern sat upon the small, uneven table, around which three patched chairs stood. Its thin flame lit the faces of those seated around the table, spooning a thin gruel from chipped bowls.

It was Frederick, and the dark-haired woman with him was Anne; Ben vaguely remembered her from his brother's wedding.

"What are we doing here?" he repeated.

"You said to look where the love of his child brought your brother, so here we are." The spirit nodded toward the pitiful scene. "He has poured all of his money into saving that little boy. Look there."

A faint glow appeared where the spirit pointed,

illuminating the face of a child sleeping upon a thin, worn mattress. A heavily patched quilt was drawn up and tucked about him, but still he shivered, sweat glistening on his forehead.

"This is where Frederick's love brought him," the spirit intoned. "Do you understand? No, how could you? You've never felt a love that deep, not for anyone. Not even for yourself."

"How dare you make assumptions about me!" Ben turned away from the window, shaking his head. "Enough. I'm going home." He started down the street, kicking snow out of his way.

The spirit swept by him and halted in his path. "Theo is extremely ill. Even his mother's healing ability can't keep the sickness at bay any longer, and Frederick cannot afford the medicines needed to cure him."

"So?" Ben shrugged but looked away, not quite able to meet the ghost's hollow gaze. He had been sickly himself as a child, but his parents had always paid the best healers in Everfeld to cure him. He could still remember his mother shaking her head as he took ill yet again. *Why are you so weak, Eben? Frederick's never sick. Why can't you be strong, like him?* Ben's shoulders stiffened. He was no longer weak, and he would prove that to her.

The spirit drew nearer. "Do you not have a single drop of compassion in your entire body? Has your endless pursuit of power burned every thread of humanity that once wove through your soul?" The spirit's voice grew softer, more pleading. "Have you no thought, no care, for anyone but yourself?"

Ben opened his mouth to respond to the cutting words, but his surroundings blurred. In a blink, he found himself back in the workroom, once again alone.

Pressing a hand against his throbbing temple, Ben tried to shove the spirit's admonition from his mind. The words stubbornly clung to him, carving pain into his chest.

What was this feeling? Guilt? He had no reason to feel such a thing. It wasn't his fault his brother didn't work hard enough to make money. Ben had thrown all of himself into his studies, while Frederick had wasted time marrying and having a child. His older brother was still an apprentice, while Ben had become a powerful mage in his own right.

Unbidden, an image of Mabel and her family rose in his mind's eye. If he had spent more time with her, could that have been him smiling and laughing while their children played? He wouldn't be where he was now in his studies, certainly, but a part of him that had long been silent asked if that sacrifice would have been worth it.

The clock on the wall struck half-past eleven, breaking through his thoughts. Ben cursed his luck, the press of time pushing him toward his work.

His boots squeaked against the stone floor as he stepped forward to the workbench. Frowning, Ben looked down.

Water pooled around his soles as snow dripped from the leather.

Whoever or whatever his nebulous visitor was, it was no hallucination. A chill ran down his back, but Ben set his jaw and focused his attention on the task before him.

***

She couldn't feel the fence anymore, only knew it was there because it kept her from falling flat on her back. The snow was piling higher, and her half-hearted attempts to sweep it away grew weaker with every passing moment.

"Don't give up!"

There it was again, that strange voice like a bell tolling. Was it Death, come to claim her soul? Janey squinted into the swirling snow but could make out nothing. Her focus returned to the wooden box in her lap.

There were only a handful of flamebursts left. It

didn't matter what Pa would say. She wouldn't be returning home. Janey crushed them one by one, savoring each burst of warmth they offered. In their soft glow, the snowflakes clinging to her eyelashes looked almost like tiny magelights. Her drifting mind daydreamed of a room filled with such tiny, shining lights casting a gentle warmth.

In the room, she decided, would be a huge fireplace always filled with a crackling fire. A soft chair to curl up on. Maybe even a dog to keep her company. Her lips twisted up into a slight smile. She'd always wanted a dog, with a long silky coat and soft brown eyes full of love and loyalty.

The daydream beckoned her mind away from the cold and snow.

"Wait!" For a moment, a white form appeared against the bright backdrop of the lamplit snow, holding out a hand. "Just hold on a little longer."

Not Death, then. Her guardian angel? Gritting her teeth, Janey forced her stiff fingers to reach for another flameburst.

There were none.

The empty box shook in her hands until she dropped it and curled up into herself. She had no tears left. The wisps of sunny dreams faded away, leaving nothing but an emptiness that welcomed her not with warmth, but with a lack of cold. A lack of anything.

She welcomed it, letting it embrace her.

"Come back!" The voice was distant now, the quiet toll of a church bell at midnight.

Death, guardian angel, spirit… Whatever it was, it couldn't help her. No one could. Janey closed her eyes and sank deeper into the darkness.

***

"Yes!" Ben couldn't take his eyes off the long-awaited culmination of all his studies. The simmering blue liquid settled down and turned a deep, vibrant green. Finally, all his work had paid off. Once poured upon the perimeter of the chalk-etched spell on the floor, the potion would allow him to summon his mother's spirit.

Finally, he could confront her and demand she give him the acknowledgement he deserved.

A tiny part of him hesitated as he stared down at the potion. If he hadn't pushed Mabel away, if he hadn't pushed everyone away, would they have acknowledged his accomplishments? Would his mother's praise still be what he craved?

Her voice rose from a memory long engraved in his mind. *Poor marks again? Can't you apply yourself harder, Eben? It's a good thing we have Frederick to carry on the family line. You'll amount to nothing.*

Ben ground his teeth. He'd prove her wrong. Taking up the bowl with careful hands, he paced toward the circle of runes.

"STOP!" The spirit leapt in front of him, waving its arms.

Ben jerked back and almost dropped the bowl. Its precious contents sloshed against the ceramic sides, warning of how close he had come to failing again.

Not that it would have been his fault this time. He glared at the ghost, which seemed more solid than its previous appearances, a ripple of robes accentuating its body and an almost defined hand raised toward him as if to stop his movement.

"You almost ruined my spell! What have I done to earn your torment, demon?" He shifted the bowl to one hand, stretching the other for the ward in his pocket. "I told you to get out of here, and still you remain to interrupt my work. Be gone before I banish you!"

The spirit laughed. "You cannot do that, any more than you can successfully complete that spell you've been pouring everything into these past ten years. Besides, I'm not done showing you what you need to see."

"What's left?" Ben asked sarcastically. "The future?"

"Precisely."

Before Ben could react, the gray fog filled his workroom. It faded more slowly this time, revealing a gloomy, overcast sky and well-kept cemetery. Not far from where Ben stood, a small funeral was taking place. Two gravediggers heaved the coffin into the freshly dug hole, while a single, bonneted woman stood nearby.

"Why are we here?" he asked, his hands falling to his sides. Frowning, he looked down and then around. "Where is my spell?"

"Your spell is safe in your workroom, for whatever good it might do you. As for this, it is the funeral for an unloved master of his craft." The spirit shook its head sadly. "As you can see, only one person is in attendance, and even she is only here out of a sense of duty. Misplaced duty, obviously."

Ben stared at the lonely scene. "Is there really no one who mourns him?"

"Those that might have are busy elsewhere."

"Too busy to attend this poor man's funeral?" Ben demanded, watching the gravediggers toss dirt unceremoniously into the hole. "They must not care much at all."

"Why should they, given how he treated them? And yet they might have, if it were under different circumstances." The spirit turned to him, expression still unreadable. "Would you like to see what their current circumstances are?"

"Yes." Ben couldn't help but feel a little pity for the man; his own craftsmanship had plenty of admirers among those who used or practiced magic. This man had worked tirelessly away at his craft, and yet had nothing to show for it.

The spirit's mouth twitched a bit, almost to a smile.

"Come with me."

This time, Ben was prepared for the exchange of surroundings. He gazed around at the tombstones, these more derelict than the ones he'd seen before.

"Another graveyard?" he questioned.

The spirit nodded. "Yes. Look." It raised its hands and pointed to a small gathering nearby. Two men bent over a small coffin as they lifted it to be lowered. A woman stood nearby, harsh sobs racking her entire body.

"They lost a child?" For a moment, Ben imagined it was Mabel there, heartbroken. The thought made his heart shudder. He reached out a hand, wishing to comfort her, but then let it fall. He wasn't a part of this scene, only an observer.

One of the men glanced up, and Ben gasped. It was Frederick. His brother looked like he had aged, but not from the passage of time—grief twisted his face into a mask of fathomless pain. The last time he had seen Frederick so distraught, it had been the funeral of their mother... The memory brought a deeper ache to Ben's chest, one that refused to be driven away.

"Yes, it is your brother. He is burying his only child. Do you understand now why he couldn't attend the other funeral?"

Ben gave a slow nod. "What connection does he have to the other man? Was he the blacksmith Frederick apprenticed with?"

An odd glint came to the spirit's eyes, and fog began to rise around them, muffling the sounds of Anne's heart-wrenching sobs. "I'm so very glad you asked."

The fog cleared, and once again they stood in the first cemetery, this time in front of a freshly covered grave. A woman stood nearby, her bonnet shading her face and hands folded neatly before her.

The spirit pointed at the gravestone. "Look."

The dim light made it difficult to read the letters

carved into the stone, but Ben peered closer.

Eben Maiser

Ben stumbled back, the air leaving his lungs in a startled gasp. It was *his* grave? But why? He shouldn't have died yet, not so early in his career, his life. "What is the meaning of this?" It had to be a trick, a vision the spirit had fabricated to torture him.

"You focused so hard on your work that it eventually consumed you. Meanwhile, your brother and his wife lost their struggle to save their son. Your nephew died slowly and painfully, drowning as his lungs filled with water. You could have saved him; you could have easily bought the medicine he required. But instead you scorned your brother for choosing love over power." The spirit paused as the bonneted woman walked toward the tombstone.

She reached out and patted the stone. "I hope you're in a better place now, Mr. Maiser. Goodbye."

"Bethany?" Ben stared as she turned and her face became visible.

His housekeeper walked by without noticing him or the spirit. Her face bore a flat expression, no sign of distress or tears. Trick or not, fear sank its claws into his heart. Would his brother have looked the same, if he'd been here? Was there really no one in the world who cared whether he lived or died? Even worse, did he even deserve for someone to care, after how he had treated all those who had ever shown him kindness?

His name carved into the cold stone mocked him. *Eben Maiser.* Only his mother had ever used his full name. *Eben, your table manners are a disaster. Eben, stop wasting time on that drivel and study harder. Eben, why can't you be more like your brother?*

Ever since he had been a young child, he'd wanted to hear those magical words: *Eben, I'm so proud of you.*

Yet, how many times had Frederick told him how talented he was? How many times had Mabel exclaimed over some minor cantrip he performed for her amusement? How many times had Master Cratch praised his spellcrafting abilities?

How many times had he ignored them all? Not just their praise, but their needs, their desires. Master Cratch had wanted him to take over the shop; Ben had refused in favor of focusing on his own spellwork. Mabel had given up pursuing him and found love elsewhere. Frederick's son, Ben's own nephew, was dying.

Falling to his knees, Ben covered his eyes. "Enough! No more, please! I can't take this."

"You can't take the truth?" the spirit taunted. "You still can't understand what you've done?"

"I do understand!" Ben's chest ached as emotions he hadn't felt in years flooded through him. "I know I was wrong. I should have been building friendships instead of power, I should have reached out to Mabel instead of pushing her away, I should have embraced Frederick's choices instead of ridiculing them."

"I'm not sure I believe you."

Gray fog swirled around them, and they were once again in his workroom. This time, though, the spirit remained. It swept across the room to stand within the rune circle. "It's nearly midnight—you can pick up your spell and complete it if you wish."

Ben looked at the bowl sitting on the worktable. All his struggles, all the challenges he'd pushed past to reach this point… They all felt hollow in comparison to what he could have had.

"I don't need it now. I need…" What did he need? Friends? A family? Family… Frederick! Perhaps he could still patch things up with his brother. Help him in some way. The small coffin flashed in his memory, and he shuddered. Could he save his nephew? He had to try.

"If you don't need it, then throw the spell away," the spirit pressed.

Staggering to his feet, Ben crossed the room and picked up the bowl. For a moment, he stared into its shimmering green surface. He could feel the power humming in the spell. It was such a tricky one. He might never get it just right again, even with better ingredients. Even with another decade of work.

"You can't, can you? You still haven't learned your lesson."

"Yes, I have!" Ben hurled the bowl at the floor. It shattered, spilling the potion across the stone. With a hiss, the potion evaporated, leaving behind a dark stain.

"Well, well." The spirit sounded surprised. "Perhaps you have changed, after all." As it spoke, its voice changed from a deep voice to a higher, more familiar one.

Ben turned, eyes widening in surprise. The spirit stood solidly before him in the shape of the woman he had spent his entire life trying to impress.

"Mother?" he whispered, a rush of anger overwhelming him. "Is it really you?"

She nodded and held out a hand as he stepped forward. "Don't try to embrace me, Eben. You cannot touch me, nor should you attempt to do so. I deserve no such thing."

"I wasn't going to!" Every muscle in his body tensed. "I've been trying to reach you for years, to prove to you that—"

"That you are a strong young man with more talent in his little finger than his mother had compassion in her entire body?" Her gaze drifted into the distance before refocusing on him.

The words struck him like a lead weight. She thought him talented? The knowledge should have filled him with joy, but somehow, his heart still ached with emptiness. "Mother..."

"Enough, Eben." Her angry tone softened to one filled with regret. "You don't need my praise, or anyone else's. Don't throw your life away because of me."

He looked down at the broken bowl, feeling as shattered as the ceramic shards scattered across his workroom's floor. "But... I... You..."

"The spell might have worked," his mother said. "Or it might have killed you. You might never know. But you do know what you need to do now, don't you?"

It was difficult raising his head, meeting the deep blue gaze that had long haunted his dreams. And yet, there was no malice in her eyes, none of the frustration or annoyance he remembered. Only pain and sorrow.

"How are you here?" he whispered. "How could you have shown me what you did?"

"I have been watching you for a long time, unable to interfere." She closed her eyes, a single tear running down her cheek. "Suffice to say, a little Solstice magic was involved. This was my one chance, my one opportunity to help you."

"Help me?" he echoed.

Mother opened her eyes but said nothing. No words were needed, not now. He could sense the answer, the truth, deep in his soul. She had come to remind him of love, kindness, compassion, everything that he had lost, neglected, or discarded over the years. Tears stung his eyes. "What have I done?"

"What will you do now?" Mother replied.

Despite her gentle tone, the question shook him, but the answer rose to his tongue without bidding, fueled by a sudden conviction. "I have to find Frederick. Apologize for...for everything." Ben stepped toward the door then hesitated, looking back at his mother. "Will you—"

She shook her head, cutting the query short. "Go, Eben. Live your life in the present, for the future, with all the light and joy your heart and soul can contain." Mother's gaze moved to the clock on the wall as it began to toll midnight. "My time here is done, and I must go." Her form began to waver. "Farewell, my son."

A lump formed in his throat. "Farewell, Mother."

"Live long, Eben. Live well." She faded into a gray mist that swiftly dissipated.

Breathing out a long sigh, Ben surveyed his workroom with new eyes. He could see signs of his obsession with this one spell everywhere, but now he also saw how he could change his work for the better. Spells began to crowd his mind, ones he had previously dismissed as not being beneficial to his goal, all begging for attention.

But there were more important things to do first.

As he stepped out his front door, wrapped in his favorite cloak, Ben found the snowfall had come to a soft end. It sparkled and glistened under the round magelight hovering by his shoulder and spread in an untrodden field across his street and down the yard.

His eyes fell upon a dark shape pressed against the fence. Another memory slid into place—the young woman who had tried to sell him flamebursts. No... Surely she hadn't been out here in the storm.

Ben rushed out the gate. His hope of finding just a deep drift died as he approached the half-buried heap of cloth and limbs. The girl's face bore a faint smile, and her chest moved slightly. He breathed a sigh of relief. She was alive! But for how long? He couldn't believe how unfeeling he'd been. Why hadn't he helped her before?

He moved closer, his boot nudging against a hard object in the snow. The empty box of flamebursts. Ben's heart ached as he bent over her, reaching for her shoulder.

"Please wake up," he pleaded. "I'm sorry I didn't get here sooner."

***

A sharp jerk dragged Janey out of the numbing darkness. A warm hand rested on her shoulder.

Her eyes flickered open, and the faint glow of a magelight hovered by a man she half-recognized, his cloak dusted with snow. Or were those feathers upon his back? Was he an angel, come to take her away at last?

Words tried to form on her lips, but they were too frozen to move. Sounds reached her chilled ears but didn't make sense. She stopped struggling against the darkness again, and this time, the shaking didn't bring her back.

***

The poor girl was definitely alive, but Ben feared it wouldn't be for long if he didn't do something fast. Bending over, he gathered her in his arms. She was lighter than he expected, but still heavy, and he gasped a bit under the weight. He needed a healer, but who?

Anne. Of course.

Spoken magic was not his forte, but there was no time to fetch potions from his workroom. Ben poured his magic into a spell that gave his boots the ability to run across snow. The power rushed from him, tied around his words, and vanished into the soles of his boots. They glowed briefly as he staggered from the exertion.

Gritting his teeth, Ben shoved more magic into a strength spell before dashing out into the street. Black spots danced briefly across his vision; he hadn't pushed his body this hard in a long time. Ignoring the dull ache in his limbs, he kept moving. Right now, it was a matter of life or death. And if this young woman died, that death would be on his hands.

Cradling his limp burden, he raced down street after empty street. There were few people out this late—most were inside, celebrating or sleeping as Solstice Day approached.

If his mother's spirit hadn't shown him Frederick's house, he might have gone straight past it, but thankfully,

Ben recognized the faded green door. He darted across the snowdrifts, set the girl down on the stoop, and pounded on the door.

"Frederick! Anne! Please, open up. It's Ben—I need your help. Please!"

The door flew open, and Ben almost tumbled forward from the unmet force of his knock. Frederick stood in a pair of worn trousers and an age-yellowed nightshirt.

"Ben?" He gasped. "What are you doing here so late?"

Stooping, Ben gathered the girl in his arms. "Where's Anne? This woman needs a healer, badly!"

Frederick stepped back to let him inside then closed the door. Anne rose from the small bed tucked into the back corner of the room. She covered a yawn, but quickly shook off her sleepiness upon seeing the young woman's condition.

"Lay her here," she ordered, spreading a blanket before the fire. "Frederick, stoke up the flames. Ben, get that soaked cloak off her. How long has she been in the cold?"

"I don't know." Ben fumbled with the cloak ties—they were frozen in a knot of snow and ice and his hands were shaking from exertion.

Frederick handed him a knife and moved to the fire. He used a wobbly poker to stoke up the flames. "What do you need, Anne?"

"She's too far gone for herbs and medicine." Anne rubbed her hands together, slowly at first, then with more speed. A soft glow began to form between her palms. "I'll have to heal her directly."

Frederick took Ben's arm and drew him aside. "Where—Ben, are you all right?"

Ben's limbs had begun to shake as the strength spell wore off. He took a step toward one of the chairs by the table and almost collapsed. Frederick supported him with muscles forged into iron from working as a blacksmith.

"I'm fine." Ben sat heavily in the chair, which

creaked in protest. "Just pushed myself a bit too far getting here."

Concern flickered over Frederick's face briefly before his expression became stern. "Where did you find her?"

"Against my fence, on the street." Ben hung his head, unable to meet his brother's eyes. "I'd seen her earlier—she tried to sell me flamebursts. I thought she would have gone home, but for some reason, she was still there when I came out. I was on my way here, actually… I must apologize, Frederick. For everything."

"You have a lot to apologize for." Frederick folded his arms. "Ten years' worth at least, I'd say."

Ben winced. The ache in his muscles was nothing compared to the pain in his heart. "I know. Thank you for letting me in despite that. I didn't know where else to go."

Frederick released a long sigh. "You are always welcome in my home, and you always have been. We're family."

Ben opened his mouth then closed it. What could he say? He didn't deserve his brother's kindness or forgiveness. He hadn't done anything to earn either.

Frederick's stern expression softened, and he rested a hand on Ben's shoulder. "It's good to have you back, brother."

Salt stung Ben's eyes as he blinked back tears of surprise and gratitude.

"Ma? Da?" a tiny voice piped up.

Frederick turned to the bed, where a little boy sat up, rubbing his eyes. Theo's tousled blond curls and blue eyes were bright as he smiled, but his face was pale, almost ghostly, just as Ben had seen him earlier.

Ben recalled the coffin he had also seen, in the brief glimpse of a possible future his mother's spirit had shown him. In that moment, he vowed he would never let such a fate befall his young nephew.

"It's all right, Theo," Frederick reassured him. "Your

Uncle Ben is here to see you."

"You can call me Ben," he ventured. "I'm not sure I've earned the title 'uncle' yet."

"Hello, Uncle Ben." Theo yawned. "Why are you here?"

In a rush of inspiration, Ben replied, "To bring you and your family to my place for the Solstice. And longer, if you wish," he added, glancing cautiously at Frederick. "There's plenty of room in the townhouse."

Frederick appeared hesitant, but a sharp sound from Anne redirected his attention. "Anne, are you all right?" He rushed to her side.

"I'm fine." She gasped a breath, leaning against him for support. "Good thing Father always made me heal frostbite in the sheep." Her weak chuckle was joined by Frederick's stronger one.

"You're amazing," he murmured and planted a kiss on her forehead.

Ben moved closer and looked down at the motionless girl. Water was beginning to pool on the floor as the ice melted from her clothes. "Will she be all right?"

Anne nodded. "With warmth and rest and good food, she'll be fine." She looked up at Ben. "She's lucky you found her—otherwise, her spirit would have taken flight this Solstice."

Breathing a sigh of relief, Ben knelt by the young woman's side. "That's good to hear."

The girl groaned softly. Her eyelids flickered then opened. She fixed her gaze on Ben. "I remember you," she whispered, eyes squinting in concentration.

Ben winced, an apology already on his lips for how he'd treated her.

"You rescued me." A faint, wondering smile spread across her face. "You must be an angel."

An angel? He couldn't hold back his laughter. "Quite the opposite, I'd say. My name is Ben. What's yours?"

"Janey." Her eyes slid shut, but she forced them open again. "Where am I?"

"Safe," Anne assured her, leaning forward and patting the girl's cheek. "Is there someone we should contact for you? Family? A friend?"

Janey shook her head, her eyes darkening. "No. I don't have anyone."

Anne squeezed the young woman's shoulder. "In that case, you can stay with us."

Frederick nodded his agreement, then shot a quick glance at Ben, a question in his expression.

"Yes," Ben agreed. "Welcome to the family, Janey."

"You *are* an angel," she murmured as her eyes drifted shut. "All of you."

In the distance, bells began to toll midnight.

"Merry Solstice!" Theo shouted from the bed. He waved his hands over his head in excitement.

Ben smiled at his young nephew, then at his brother and Anne, and the now-sleeping Janey. For the first time in a very long while, his heart was light with cheer. "Merry Solstice, everyone."

The Firestone

Elise Edmonds

Long, long ago in Wulfran, wild creatures roamed the forests while men cowered in remote settlements. Bare-branched trees stretched to the sky like old witches flexing their fingers. Holly grew thick and bright, its berries tempting squirrels and birds alike.

Icy wind whipped down from a mountain peak, gusting the soft snowflakes into a frenzy. In its shadow lay Haryngai village, where a grim, gray-walled castle built into the rock loomed over squat stone cottages.

Katya Rusakova hated the winter. Her parents' cottage had numerous cracks and crannies, and the central chimney never quite removed all the smoke. She spent the winter with stinging eyes, a raw throat, and a perpetual shiver.

One afternoon, not long before midwinter's day, Katya finished her chores early. Her weak arm ached from scrubbing, and she massaged the muscles to ease it. The cottage walls seemed to close in, leaving her restless. But in the village, people's vision always strayed to her scars; staring crowds made her uncomfortable skin prickle. She craved the open space of the outside world.

Katya pulled on her worn overcoat. She slipped around the back of the cottages. The dirt road was empty, and her pulse quickened. She'd be back before anyone knew she'd gone; Father disapproved of her solitary walks.

After crossing the frozen stream, she climbed over a low wall. A view of the deserted village entrance gave her courage. Most villagers, including her mother and younger brothers, were at the market. Holding her breath, she strode up to the wooden gate. She lifted the bar, hesitated for a moment, but steeled her nerve and stepped through.

She stood, breathless, with her back to the gate. Wind whipped her long blond braids around, and Katya pulled up her hood. Her coat offered little protection, and her toes felt like ice, but the silence of the nearby forest called. She'd return before the night guard's shift began.

Katya walked backward, using her feet to scuff the snow and cover her footprints. When she reached the tree cover, she shuffled behind an ancient fir and let out a sigh of relief, drinking in the clear air.

The forest smelled cold and damp. Katya rubbed her fingers on pine needles, the fresh scent rising. The wind dropped under the canopy, and her breath condensed in clouds. Snow slid off a nearby branch, the plop disturbing the peace.

She trekked through the trees, following a narrow path. Away from her family, the constant band of tension in her head released. Her parents' sympathies with her injuries had waned over the year, after it became apparent Katya wouldn't regain full strength in her arm. Her father couldn't afford a large dowry to compensate, yet he wanted her married in the spring. Last week, he'd started negotiations with the tanner and his sly son. She shuddered to think of it.

But did she regret saving the baby? *I'd make the same choice again.* Katya ducked under a snowy branch, recalling the day when fire sealed her future.

The village leader, Lord Chayka, had been making his monthly round, listening to disputes. Many of Katya's neighbors had attended while she remained home with her younger brothers. A strong burning smell had caught her attention—the one-room cottage opposite had caught fire!

Flames licked the thatched roof. Wailing floated on the breeze. Katya had dashed inside. Her neighbor lay unconscious. She dragged the woman out and went back in for the baby.

A pile of firestones—rocks which sparked when struck—ignited. Stacked kindling burst into flame. Wooden supports smoldered. Katya rushed out, the babe in her arms, the roof collapsing behind with an almighty crash.

Other neighbors arrived. Someone took the infant, and Katya sank to the ground, arm blistered and face sore. Gentle hands lifted her up. Barely conscious, she felt a delicious coolness on her scorched skin. Bandages wrapped and tightened around the pain. She cried out in agony and opened her eyes.

A tall young man stood over her. He pushed his shaggy blond hair back, smearing ash across his face. "I've done what I can. Your arm is clean and dry—make sure you keep it that way."

Before Katya could even speak her thanks, a strident voice called, "Korin, get over here! Leave the wounded for the women to deal with."

Korin gave Katya a grin before hurrying off.

It was only later that Katya realized Korin was the village lord's son. She'd spent many a day since then daydreaming about him and recalling his smile.

What would Korin think if he saw her here, in the seclusion of the woods? She shook her head. *Why would he remember an injured peasant girl?*

Twigs snapped in the distance, and steps pounded closer. Katya jumped and stared wildly from side to side. A tree with low branches stood a few feet away. She grabbed a bough with her good arm and managed to scramble up. Rustling bushes propelled her higher, and she gritted her teeth as her weak limb trembled.

Panting, she lay across a branch and gripped it. She kept still as stone, waiting to see what horrible beast roamed the woods. *Maybe a wild boar—or a bear.*

The steps approached, accompanied by deep wheezing, and Katya flattened herself against the bough. A man pushed through the bushes, and she stifled a cry. He clutched his shoulder, scarlet seeping between his fingers. He stumbled and tripped, sinking to his knees with a groan, reddened hand staining the snow.

Katya swallowed an exclamation. She glanced around, straining her ears for any further sound, but no pursuing animal appeared.

She climbed down from the tree and darted over to him. His blue uniform and empty scabbard didn't belong to any local village.

The unarmed soldier started, relief in his eyes. "You... I need..." He had dark skin and an odd accent. "My arm..."

It didn't matter who he was—she had to help him. Perhaps she could stop the bleeding. Bites from wild animals weren't uncommon in Haryngai. Katya shifted around him to see the wound, but her heart sank at the extent of raw flesh. He'd lost a lot of blood. Bile rose in her throat.

The man wrestled his backpack off, grimacing. "I...must give..."

Katya laid a hand on his arm. "We need to bind your wound. Keep still." She grasped the bottom of her skirt, intending to tear off a strip.

He spoke frantically. "No, take this." He pulled a pale green neckerchief from his bag and handed it to Katya.

She took it, puzzled.

"You must...hidden caves...Zelonuth. Great treasure..." The soldier grabbed her hand. "Do not fear. Token...neckerchief." He closed his eyes, exhausted.

Is he raving? His wound had induced a fever. Yet, he seemed determined. Mount Zelonuth was a short journey south. She had never heard of any caves, but the soldier haltingly described passing through an evergreen hanging curtain and entering a crack in the mountain.

"Don't let the secret die…young lady." He squeezed her hand and fell back into the snow.

Katya bent over him, trembling. His ravings had been a last-ditch effort to fight impending death. The soldier's face stilled. He was gone.

*****

Katya closed the soldier's eyes and murmured a blessing. For now, that was all she could do. She stood in silence, head lowered.

Then she tucked the neckerchief into her pocket. *Why not honor his last wishes?* It might be a fool's adventure, but it was the last one she'd get before marrying some village lout. Not to mention a satisfactory, if minor, defiance of her father. She'd get home before dark, and he'd be none the wiser.

She turned south and headed through the forest, keeping one ear open for wild beasts. An uneventful hour's trek brought her to the base of Mount Zelonuth. The forest petered out, and the vast mountain blotted out the gray sky. Greenery covered the lower slopes.

Katya wrapped her thin coat tighter. What could this fabled treasure be? *Perhaps gold coins?* Gold would probably be commonplace to someone like Korin, but Katya had never owned more than the odd copper.

Following the soldier's instructions, and conscious of the sun's descent, she hurried past a large boulder and two trees wrapped around each other. An ivy curtain hung down the rock face. Her feet had warmed with the walk, but her cold fingers moved stiffly.

With trembling hands, she lifted the plant and gasped. A narrow crack extended into the mountain. *It's too well-hidden to be an animal lair.*

Katya swallowed her nerves and slipped into the dark

fissure. The leaves fell behind her, and gloom hid the way forward. Water dripped from the unseen roof in a steady rhythm.

She stumbled along, hands grazing the damp stone. Fuzzy moss clumps lined the walls. The passage turned sharp left.

Up ahead, a bright green glow shone from an opening. Katya slowed down, hesitating. All manner of myths abounded about the creatures that lurked in the depths of Wulfran's unexplored lands. What if the soldier had sent her into danger? But the urge to see what lay ahead overcame her fear.

Katya passed through a rounded arch in the wall that led into a low-roofed cave. She halted, feet rooted to the floor, heart pounding.

A green-scaled beast, with a lithe, sinuous body, curled on top of a huge wooden chest.

A baby dragon!

The beast was the size of a large hunting dog. He had a long snout and curved forelegs with thick claws spread around the chest. Bat-like wings extended from his shoulders, and a furred ridge extended down and around his body.

Katya sucked in a quick breath. Dragons were the stuff of legends and fireside tales. But the dragon merely gazed at her, his emerald eyes luminous in the phosphorescent glow. Blinking rapidly, she half-expected the beast to be an illusion. She rubbed her sweating palms down her coat, fighting the desire to run. What was that lump in her pocket? She drew out the soldier's neckerchief. *The token.* Tentatively, Katya raised it.

The cloth caught the dragon's eye, and he extended a pointed claw. Katya tiptoed forward. She fought to keep her hand steady, her shoulders tense.

The dragon opened his mouth and spoke in a guttural tone. "Welcome, my lady. You may help yourself to the contents of the chest as you please." He unfurled the coils of his scaly body and climbed off the wooden box. Claws clicking on the stone floor, he settled in a corner of the room, curled up, one eye on Katya.

Her jaw dropped to hear the dragon talk. Never had she thought she'd see a dragon, let alone survive the encounter. She dug a fingernail into her palm and winced. It wasn't a dream.

Not daring to question the dragon, she heaved up the chest lid. It was full of fur-lined boots and gloves. "I didn't expect that," she muttered.

She rifled through the contents, reveling in the soft fur and supple leather. Feverishly, she stripped off her thin-soled boots and chose a sturdy new pair. She added gloves of softest rabbit fur. Now this was a useful kind of treasure. *Bless that soldier!*

Katya closed the chest and curtsied to the dragon. "Thank you, my lord." She had no idea how to address a dragon, but politeness couldn't go wrong. The dragon merely blinked and settled on the chest again.

She walked back through the arch. Farther up the passage lay another opening. Emboldened, her new boots supporting her cold, weary feet, she entered the second cavern.

Another dragon guarded a similar chest. He was larger—about the size of a small mud hut. Red scales gleamed and dark bronze eyes shone. Katya gulped but held the neckerchief out, fingers quivering. As before, the dragon greeted her and courteously invited her to help herself from the chest.

Brimming with anticipation, Katya threw open the lid. She gasped. It was filled with beautiful clothes: coats and skirts, tunics and shirts, and more, crafted from leather, wool, linen, fur, and richer materials in colors she had never seen before in cloth.

Feeling the necessity of remaining practical, she

pulled on a woolen skirt over her own, a warm tunic, and a deep brown fur coat. Unusual warmth flowed into her bones. She stroked the glossy fur with quiet awe.

Once more, she thanked the dragon and left. The light showed one further cavern before the passage ended in a blank wall. She hesitated to step through the arch. A vast golden dragon, as long as the castle tower was high, rested his huge snout on one more chest. His claws encircled the box, and his body twisted and turned inside the length of the cave, golden scales twinkling in the light. He turned amber eyes on Katya.

Light-headed and dizzy at the spectacle, she held out the neckerchief. Once more, she had no reason to fear as again the dragon invited her in.

What amazing thing will this chest hold? Katya opened the lid and nearly dropped it. The chest was filled to the brim with gems and jewelry. She bent forward and ran her fingers through the vast wealth, mouth gaping. She dropped necklaces and brooches and earrings in one pocket, and uncut gems in the other.

A fleeting thought passed through her mind—maybe Korin would notice her, despite her scars, if she were a rich lady. A smile flickered on her lips.

Katya scanned the contents of the chest, letting gems drip through her fingers. She pushed through the jewels, and her fingernail grazed a catch on the chest wall. She pressed it, and a secret compartment opened. A gold chain fell into her hand. She lifted up a beautiful necklace with a fiery orange pendant. She twirled it around in the dim light. It looked like a polished firestone. Flames seemed to emanate from its surface. *Fire ruined me. Now fire may save me.* She hung it around her neck and tucked the gem under her shirt. It lay warm on her chest, oddly comforting.

Rising from her knees and weighed down by her heavy pockets, Katya again thanked the dragon and exited the chamber. She tied the soldier's neckerchief around her own neck. Dazed, Katya made her way out of the tunnel. Back in the gathering gloom and cold forest air, she shook her head, hardly able to believe what had happened, before hurrying home.

***

Katya rushed back as dusk fell. She'd delayed too long in the caves. *I have to hide my new finery—I'll make a plan to account for it later.* She'd be in trouble if she didn't make it home before the night guard arrived.

Her new boots gripped firm as she jogged along in the wet snow. The gate lay ahead, casting a dark shadow. *Nearly there.*

A man strode out of the gloom, a heavy spear at his side. His familiar build made a weight settle on her chest. *Father.* She hadn't realized it was his turn on duty. A second guard took a stance by the gate.

Numb, Katya stopped short. How angry would Father be?

He marched up and shook her arm. "Where have you been? A neighbor said he saw you run off." His brows lowered. "You're in trouble now, my girl."

Katya drooped her head. "I'm sorry, Father. I didn't mean to worry you…I…" She wasn't sure how to explain what had happened without sounding crazy. But her father wasn't listening; he was eyeing her coat.

"Where did you get this?" He held her at arm's length and frowned. "Your coat…your boots. They aren't yours. You'd better not have been stealing."

Katya furrowed her brow. Did he think no better of her than that? "I wouldn't steal. I found them in the woods." The lie tripped off her tongue.

Her father snorted. "Let's get inside. We need to talk." He pushed her through the gate, speaking to the other guard. "Back soon. Cover for me?"

The guard rolled his eyes. "Hurry up."

Katya's feet dragged. She lowered her eyes, hoping no one noticed her as they walked. Imagine if Korin saw her now, in disgrace? *I should have had a better plan.* Thankfully, the slush-lined paths were empty, and they quickly reached the cottage.

Inside, a bright fire burned, and the smoky atmosphere made her cough. Wood crackled, and the rich scent of venison stew made her stomach growl.

Her mother jumped up, mouth tight. She raised her hand and slapped Katya, who stumbled back. Katya cradled her face, the sting radiating across her cheek. *I guess I deserve it.*

"How dare you run off like that?" Her mother glowered.

Katya bit her tongue. Pointing out she'd finished all her chores wouldn't help.

"Look at the girl's clothing." Father gestured to Katya.

Her youngest brother, Rayaul, came and put his arms around her. "Katty, I missed you."

She hugged him back, grateful for the distraction. He leaned into her, then drew back. "Ow, your pockets are hard." He slipped his hand in her pocket and pulled out a handful of jewels. They trickled through his fingers, scattering in the firelight. "Pretty beads."

Her mother picked one up. "That's not a bead." Eyes wide, she ran her hand over Katya's fur coat. "Where did this come from?" She undid the coat buttons and took it off Katya, together with the gloves. Katya scowled behind her mother's back.

Father rifled through the coat pockets and gasped as he pulled out more jewels. "Tell me where you got this stuff. I must know it's not stolen before I sell it."

Katya frowned. Her father assumed anything she owned was his. She thought quickly. "I came across a dead soldier in the woods. I found all these things in his backpack and pockets. They weren't doing him any good."

Father drew his eyebrows together. "Tell me exactly where you found him."

Relieved that he'd believed her, Katya described the soldier's location, and her father rushed off.

Mother piled all the jewels up, a self-satisfied grin on her face. She pointed at Katya's boots. "Take all the finery off, young lady. We can sell that, too. Really, Katya, I expect more of you. You need to grow up. We'll never get you married if people see you running off like that."

Katya hunched her shoulders. She didn't want to keep everything to herself if it could help her family, but it would've been nice to keep the warm clothes. Not to mention that her father had a tendency to gamble money away as quickly as he gained it.

She peeled off the leather boots and heavy woolen dress, leaving her own thinner, ragged dress beneath. "I'm sorry, Mother," she forced out.

"You should be. Go to your room and think about your responsibilities. I expect to see you up early tomorrow to attend to the fire."

Katya, now barefoot and shivering, took a candle and stepped over to a stout wooden door. It led to her tiny bedroom. She placed the candle in the holder before throwing herself on the straw mattress. *What a waste that was.*

Her own small linen chest reminded her of the caves. But now, her delight at finding the dragons and the treasure felt like something that had happened to another person. Would she ever get the chance to go back? She scratched her neck and realized she still wore the soldier's neckerchief: her symbol to the dragons. As she untied it, her fingers touched something metal. *The firestone necklace!* At least she had one thing that was hers. She'd hide that from her parents.

Katya lifted the chain off her neck and stared at the smooth firestone. It shone gently in the candlelight. She rubbed her thumb over it.

A strange low crack sounded, and a puff of green smoke appeared. The linen chest creaked. When it cleared, Katya's mouth dropped open. The green dragon from the cave sat on the chest.

***

Katya covered her mouth. Her eyes felt like they would pop out of her head. The dragon's tail narrowly missed the candle holder, and he wobbled on the compact chest. Katya held up the necklace and the stone spun, glinting in the candlelight. "I…you…"

"My lady, how may I serve you?" The dragon bowed its head.

Katya gaped at him. "Serve me?"

The dragon's green eyes widened and his snout drew back. "Yes. That's why you took the Firestone. Isn't it?"

"Keep your voice down. My family might hear. They'd try to capture you," Katya whispered, still not quite able to believe a wolf-sized dragon crouched in her room.

"No one captures a dragon." He huffed, and smoke columns rose from his nostrils.

Katya picked up the precious stone, turning it over in her hand, thoughts spinning. "What does the Firestone do?"

He pointed a scaly claw at the necklace. "He—or she—who possesses the Firestone can wield its power. Rub it once for me, twice for my red friend, and thrice for the golden. We can bring you anything you require from the chests in the caves. In addition"—the dragon puffed up its chest—"you can command us to transport you anywhere you require, my lady. Following which, one touch of the stone will return you."

Katya stifled a giggle. She'd gone from a poor girl to a lady too many times to count today. Perhaps she should test the power of the stone. "In that case, please can you bring me a pair of warm furred gloves?" If her parents spotted them, she'd say she forgot they were in her skirt pocket.

"Your wish is my command." The dragon disappeared with another crack and puff of smoke. Katya glanced at the door, afraid her mother would hear, but no call came.

A moment later, he returned, a pair of gloves in his claws. "My lady, do you require anything else this night?"

Katya stroked the gloves, marveling at their softness. "No. My thanks."

The dragon bowed his head and disappeared once more, leaving Katya to her thoughts. Completely by accident, she'd picked up the richest treasure of all: the ability to command three dragons. She could have untold wealth now, for all the good it would do her—her grasping parents would have that off her without a second thought. Or they'd have her arrested for theft.

What about the transport option? Could she get the dragons to take her somewhere else? *But where would I go?* She knew little of the world outside Haryngai and the immediate woods and mountains. The neighboring tribe was a few hours away, and to go there would be pointless. They would simply capture her and confiscate her riches. She needed a long-term plan.

Korin.

If she combined her newfound wealth and her ability to transport, it might work. Could she persuade Korin to fall in love with her if she presented herself as a lady, despite her disability? He'd seemed compassionate and friendly. Then she would be able to remain in this village, enjoy her wealth, and marry the man she desired.

Katya sighed to herself. With nothing to lose, she may as well dream big. She put the Firestone necklace back on, wrapped in the soldier's neckerchief. First, a good night's sleep was in order.

***

The next day, Katya woke early to do the chores. Butterflies swirled in her stomach, and she had to bite her cheeks to ensure her growing excitement didn't spill out. She planned her evening and daydreamed about Korin while her hands were busy scrubbing, sewing, and cooking. Even her arm didn't ache as much as usual.

When evening finally came, she declared herself tired and in need of an early night. Her mother made no objection, seemingly pleased with Katya's diligence.

Alone in her room, she set to work. She summoned the green dragon and explained her idea.

Her room was too small to contain any dragon except the green, so Katya neatly arranged some old clothes on her bed, covered with a thin blanket. Should anyone poke their head around the door, she'd appear to be asleep.

She smiled nervously at the green dragon. "I'm ready."

"Touch my claw." The dragon extended a scaled foot.

Katya took it, marveling at its smoothness, then gasped as her room disappeared. A moment later, she stood in the green dragon's cave. Her mouth opened and closed.

The dragon's snout extended into a grin. "It takes one's breath away at first."

She nodded, unable to speak.

"Help yourself to what you need, my lady. Now you possess the Firestone, you no longer need the neckerchief. You may come and go at will."

Katya met the red and golden dragons again as she dressed herself like a fine lady. They greeted her kindly.

This time, she did not choose clothing for practicality—she chose for beauty.

She arrayed herself in a deep purple satin dress with

full skirts and layers of tulle and lace underneath. She found long lace gloves and delicate white boots to accompany it. The gloves covered her scarring. A skein of gems was layered into her hair, and around her neck she wore an intricate amethyst necklace. The Firestone she hid in a small leather pouch around her wrist, to ensure she didn't touch it unawares.

A gem-studded looking glass in the third chest helped Katya arrange her hair: she draped her blond curls over her left cheek to conceal the blemishes.

"My lady, you are charming," the golden dragon half-growled at her.

Katya laughed. "Thank you." She was getting used to Greenie, as she called the green dragon, but the golden had a fearsome undercurrent, even though she knew he would not harm her.

Greenie came in to watch the final proceedings. "Are you ready, my lady? Shall I transport you to the castle?"

Katya clasped her hands. "Yes, please."

"Very well." He extended his claw, and once more, she grasped it.

Her head spun and the cave disappeared. Katya reappeared in a high-ceilinged stone room. She nearly stumbled but caught her footing.

A fire burned low in the grate, and a few cozy chairs sat in a circle. In one of the chairs, a young lad sprawled. *Korin.* A few leather-bound books lay on a three-legged table next to him.

Katya's heart stopped. Then she realized his eyes were closed—he was asleep. She tiptoed forward. It was hard to believe the man of her dreams lay in front of her. Sleep gave Korin a look of innocence, and she longed to reach out and touch him. Fingers clenched in lace gloves, she crept closer. *How can I wake him without scaring him?*

An open book, marked by a slip of parchment, caught her eye. Distracted, she peered down. Her parents didn't own any books. Could people really make sense of the black squiggles?

She gasped as a firm hand shot out and circled her wrist. Firelight reflected in Korin's green irises. He sat up straight, steely gaze fixed on her.

"Who are you?" He held her arm tightly. "One false move, and I'll call a guard." His voice was low and musical and held no trace of fear.

Katya's mouth turned dry. "I...I..." She wasn't sure what to say. "I have seen you from afar, my lord, and I wished for the opportunity to talk in private."

"How did you get here?" Korin glared. "I could've sworn you appeared out of nowhere. I suppose you bribed the guard."

"I...transported here..."

Korin narrowed his eyes and released her wrist, sliding back in his seat. "Sorcery? Is that your game?"

Katya bit her lip. She'd forgotten how suspicious of sorcery the villagers were—it had always fascinated her. "I have a magic artifact which enabled me to appear here." She may as well be as honest as she dared.

"You have possession of a magic artifact, and you wasted it by sneaking up on *me*?" His glance remained wary, but a ghost of a smile hung on his lips.

Katya flushed and then laughed. If he could joke, he wasn't that fearful of magic. "My reality is dull. I needed something to liven it up."

Korin cast his eyes over her, and Katya squirmed. He tilted his head. "You...seem familiar. Who are you?"

"I cannot say." She lowered her eyes.

"Are you from a neighboring village? Did we meet when my father took me to see eligible young ladies? Or did your family send you?" Korin raised an eyebrow.

Katya hugged herself. So, she wasn't the only one who had troubles with marriage. Funny, she'd thought it was a concern of the lower classes, being stuck with someone undesirable. "I'm here of my own volition. I'm destined for a dull, loveless marriage, and I'm at my wit's end."

Inadvertently, she pushed her hair back. Too late, Katya realized she'd exposed her scarring.

Korin's eyes widened and recognition flashed over his face. "The peasant girl from the fire." His mouth dropped open. "You—"

Not waiting for his condemnation, Katya's fingers slipped into the wrist pouch, touched the Firestone, and the scene disappeared into blackness.

***

The next morning, Katya struggled to keep her attention on the chores. All day, her mind lingered on Korin. Seeing him in the privacy of his home had made him real. Her memories of the awful day she'd been burned spun around her head. *He recognized me.* Had she been hasty in disappearing? Her nerve had failed at the last moment. Now, ignited desire mixed with feelings of guilt. She should return and explain.

The day dragged; she could barely wait for evening. Her little brother, Rayaul, helped her split wood and prattled about his chores, and she listened in silence, amused and comforted. Rayaul represented all that was good about her family life. But now that she'd talked with Korin, her discontent with her uncertain future had grown.

Later that night, alone in her bedroom, she summoned Greenie once more. He took her back to the caves.

"What is your wish this evening, my lady?" He stretched his wings out.

Katya clasped her hands together. "I want to see Korin again."

Greenie nodded, an amused glint in his eye.

Katya's cheeks reddened.

Greenie, Red, and Golden watched with interest as she chose different finery: a silk dress of leaf-green with matching satin slippers. She added gold silk gloves and the Firestone in its wrist pouch. This time, she chose a ruby and gold necklace and a gold filigree tiara. After some hesitation, she coiled her hair on top of head, leaving her face visible. *No point hiding what he's already seen.*

When Katya was ready, Greenie extended his claw. As before, she disappeared into darkness before reappearing in Korin's room. Prepared this time, she steadied herself. The fire burned higher than before, the room warm and stuffy. A faint haze of smoke made her blink. Korin stood a few feet away, facing the fire, hands behind his back. He wore a white embroidered shirt and black trousers.

Katya clenched and unclenched her fists. This time, she wouldn't lose her nerve. "My lord—Korin."

He flinched and spun around. "You're back." He strode over to Katya and lightly clasped her shoulders with his hands. "I thought…I thought I dreamed you."

Katya swallowed. "I'm real. And I came to apologize for disappearing."

"I'm glad you returned." Korin released her shoulders, and a flush crept across his cheeks. "Won't you sit down, please?" He gestured to a nearby couch.

Katya sat, smoothing her skirts over her knees with sweating palms.

"That day after the fire, I wanted to check your injuries again, but my father wouldn't allow it." Korin sat next to Katya, knees angled toward her. "I'm relieved to know you're in good health."

"It's been difficult. My arm has a permanent weakness." She took a deep breath and peeled off her gold silk glove, fixing her eyes on the pitted skin beneath. Would he turn away in disgust?

Korin touched her arm with his fingertips. "It's healed well."

Katya stared into his green eyes. His gentle touch sent a tingle through her. "Doesn't it revolt you?"

He shook his head. "I see the scars of a heroine. If other people don't see that, I feel sorry for them."

Sudden lightness filled Katya.

"Tell me about yourself." Korin pushed his blond hair off his face.

Katya, her nerves dissipated, began to talk. She told him stories about her family and neighbors, anecdotes about her brother, and her struggles with her undetermined future.

Korin listened closely, nodding in sympathy. He then shared droll tales of his visits to other settlements and the difficulty of living with an overbearing father. "He's only interested in me as his heir, not as a person."

She felt a kinship with him. "My father treats me like a chattel. He doesn't see beyond that."

They turned to lighter subjects, laughing about last year's summer festival when a boy's prank had backfired, his donkey throwing him in the village pond. She told Korin about the Firestone's power, and he marveled, curious about the magic. They talked until the fire burned low and dawn lightened the windows.

A lull fell, and Korin shifted nearer to Katya. He took her hand. "I haven't enjoyed a conversation so much in a long time."

She laughed. "Nor I."

Korin gazed into her eyes and drew closer.

The room door burst open with a crash. In dashed a bearded man in a robe. A gold circlet sat on his hair. "Intruders!"

Katya jumped up off the couch, heart thudding. *Lord Chayka.* He'd kill her.

"Son, what on earth are you doing, entertaining a young woman at this hour? This is highly inappropriate." He relaxed his stance and wiped a hand on his brow. "I woke and heard low voices. I thought I'd find a thief."

His gray beard flowed over his chest, and even in a night robe, he had a commanding air. He frowned at Katya.

Korin stared at his father, mouth agape.

Katya's lips trembled. She stumbled back, tripping over the edge of a rug. Without thinking, she thrust her hand into the Firestone pouch, and the room faded. Korin's longing face and the lord's fierce brow remained imprinted on her mind. She reappeared in the dragons' caves, hair askew.

Greenie looked at her curiously.

Katya blinked back tears and shook her head. In all her daydreams, she had forgotten the reality of the situation—how would the lord ever accept a peasant girl? She undressed soberly and put her ragged clothes on again, before returning once more to her pitiful bedroom. *Was this a terrible mistake?*

***

The next day, Katya was washing clothes in their small backyard, trying to keep her eyes open, when a cornet call floated out. The sound continued, loud, sweet, and clear—the signal for everyone to congregate.

Katya stood, suds bubbling over the tub, fingertips wrinkled. The Firestone and neckerchief hung around her neck once more. She walked out to the street, straining her ears to hear the conversations around her. *What's going on?*

When everyone was assembled, the messenger stood on an upturned box and spoke loudly.

"By order of Lord Chayka, all are to assemble in the main castle courtyard at midday."

Murmuring began among the people as the messenger departed and moved on to the next set of streets.

Chills ran through Katya. It had to be about her intrusion last night. How could it not be? She heard her parents converse in wondering tones behind her. They had no idea what the message represented. She went back to the washing with a heavy heart.

Within the hour, her parents called her and her brothers. Rayaul slid his hand into hers, and she welcomed his chubby, childish touch, drawing strength from it.

Katya and her family arrived at the main courtyard in a press of people. Every sound magnified in her ears, from the crowd's babble to the tread of feet. She longed to flee.

A large wooden dais stood on one side, where various festivities took place throughout the year. But today, it looked decidedly unfestive. The lord stood there in his best robe, hair and beard neatly braided, scabbard at his side. One pace behind him stood Korin and his mother, also dressed in rich clothes. Men in shining armor guarded either end of the stage, adding to the tense atmosphere. Korin wrinkled his brow and cast his gaze over the crowd.

Katya squeezed Rayaul's hand tight. His eyes settled on her, wide and fearful. The villagers were rarely summoned *en masse*. Last time, over a year ago, Lord Chayka had a man publicly whipped for continual theft. She shuddered at the remembrance of his bloodied back.

The entire village population filled the courtyard. The higher born families stood nearest the castle, not mingling with the poorer folk, like Katya's family, who scrambled for room near the gate.

Lord Chayka paced forward, and the crowd fell silent.

"Folk of Haryngai. I have called you here today on a serious matter. Deception and seduction have been taking place under my very nose!" His voice quivered.

Katya's stomach churned. It was as she had dreaded. She'd thrown away her reputation for a wild, hopeless plan. What would her punishment be? Dare she own up? In her mind's eye, a leather whip whistled through the air.

The lord continued. "An unidentified young woman has been visiting my son without permission."

Katya glanced at Korin, but he stared at the floor. He must be mortified.

The lord's voice echoed around, overcoming the murmurs of surprise and rustles that came from the crowd. "This woman was attempting to gain my son's favor by use of sorcery."

A gasp ran around the crowd. The suspicion of unknown sorcery ran deep—although Korin had quickly lost his doubts after she explained her power.

Lord Chayka's fierce stare traveled over the crowd. "However, I am prepared to be generous. Let her confess herself, and if I deem her worthy of my son's hand, she will be under consideration as a bride; I may overlook this flagrant deception and misuse of sorcery. But if she is unworthy, I will decide on her punishment. And if she does not confess, the village tax will be doubled this coming winter."

Katya gazed into the wide blue sky. She had little hope of being considered worthy, but could she face the consequences of owning up? What if she kept quiet now and ran off later, leaving a note to absolve the villagers? Lord Chayka was unpredictable, though. He might double the village tax in his rage.

She couldn't let her family go hungry because she was too cowardly to own up to her misdeeds. *Imagine Rayaul suffering from lack of food because his sister couldn't take what was coming.* She smiled down into his bright, wondering eyes and then let go of his hand.

Lord Chayka was scanning the nobility at the other end of the courtyard.

People around Katya gasped as she pushed through the crowd. She entered the open space at the front. Her thin boots sounded loud, every footstep echoing her heartbeat.

The lord glared down at her. Katya ascended the dais. Her skin prickled knowing the eyes of the crowd rested on her.

Korin's face lit up, supplanted by a worried frown. The lord visibly shook, eyes bulging.

Katya walked up to Korin. "I am sorry, my lord, for the trouble I've caused you." She lowered her gaze.

Korin reached for her hand, but Lord Chayka shoved him away.

Katya fell to her knees. *Perhaps he'll be merciful.* But the lord grabbed her hair and yanked her head back. Katya bit back a groan, pain radiating through her scalp.

Lord Chayka screamed, spittle flecking out from his mouth. "How dare you! You…unsightly peasant girl! You—"

"Father, please." Korin pushed forward and tried to release the lord's hold on Katya's hair.

Katya stiffened. Her hair would come out at the roots if he didn't let go. She groaned as the pressure tightened. A core of rage built in her stomach.

"Father, stop it. I don't care if she's a peasant. She's intelligent and beautiful, and lively and fun."

The lord spat in Katya's face. Scowling, she wiped the dribble off her scarred cheek. He let go of her hair, pushing her forward. Katya smacked onto the wooden dais, muscles quivering.

"Don't be ridiculous. That crippled peasant isn't worthy of your attention." Lord Chayka raised a foot to kick her.

Katya scuttled back, narrowly avoiding his foot. The gawping villagers stung her pride. *Will he have me killed?* Her breath caught in her throat.

Lord Chayka gestured at her. "This girl is banished from the village. Guards, throw her out."

Korin rushed forward and pulled her up, placing himself between Katya and his father. "I won't allow it. She's injured because she saved a baby. Please, Father…"

Guards descended, and Korin tried to shove Katya behind himself. Quick as a thought, she ripped off her neckerchief and brandished it in a guard's face. It distracted him for a second—long enough to grab the Firestone necklace out of her dress and rub it three times. If she had to depart, it would be on her own terms.

The golden dragon flashed into being with a giant roar. Even Katya's heart quailed as he sailed above the courtyard, his lithe, scaly body mesmerizing. He swirled and spun in the air, filling it with a scent of sulfur and smoke.

Golden hovered in midair, his long snout close to Katya's head. Korin gaped but stayed at Katya's side.

The crowd below ran and scattered, many screaming and vacating the courtyard. The lord dropped to his knees in fear. The guards backed away.

"Where to, my lady?" Golden said.

"I've been banished. I can't stay here. Take me somewhere safe, please." Katya's clear voice carried. She turned to Korin. "I'm sorry, I truly am."

He grasped her hands impetuously. "Take me with you. I don't care what my father says. You have the monsters of the air at your command. What can he do to me?" He leaned down and kissed her.

Katya melted under Korin's kiss. A pleasant shiver ran through her. He filled her senses, and she gazed into his eyes. How could she leave him now?

The golden dragon chuckled, a long low roar. "Korin Chayka, I may only take my lady, due to the magic that binds me. But if you remain constant in love for a year and a day, I can return for you."

"Get the beast, you fools!" Lord Chayka yelled and cursed at the guards.

The armed men pulled themselves together and advanced hesitantly on the dragon. A spear bounced off his shining scales. Golden fixed a smoldering glare on the guards, who retreated.

"Climb on, my lady." Golden lowered his head.

Katya could hardly bear to tear herself away from

Korin. "I will come back, I promise." She climbed onto Golden's neck, grasping a spine at the base.

Taking one last lingering grasp of Korin's fingers, his touch sent tingles up her arm. She smiled down at him. "Wait for me."

His cry echoed. "I will wait for you…"

The dragon shot into the air, its long body spiraling upward, wings outstretched and gleaming in the sunlight. Katya screamed, fear turning to exhilaration, as they danced through the skies. The village lay far below, Korin a speck in its midst.

***

The golden dragon didn't fly back to the caves. He flew on and on into the sky, Katya too exhausted and overwrought to ask where they were going. She lay against his neck, only the cold air and fear of falling keeping her awake. Trees, mountains, and villages passed far below, but still they did not stop.

She squeezed her eyes shut. The enormity of what she'd done sank in. How could she survive outside the village for a year? What would Korin say when she returned; would he stay constant? Would she ever see Rayaul again?

Katya spoke to Golden. "Why do we not transport somewhere instead of flying?"

"Our destination is a secret and shielded from magic—you will soon see why, my lady." Golden glided onward, catching the wind currents.

As dusk fell, the dragon flew between a narrow mountain pass that Katya had never seen before. Her mouth dropped open. A ring of mountains whose peaks disappeared in the clouds enclosed a lush valley. A river led to a wide, azure lake. Grass carpeted the ground, a light dusting of snow over the surface. Evergreen bushes flourished and trees abounded.

Dragons of all colors and sizes wheeled and called in the wide valley. Roars and echoes filled the air. A two-headed purple dragon whipped by overhead. Clusters of baby dragons tumbled and snorted tiny fireballs. Katya laughed and felt alive once more.

Golden landed at the mouth of a large cave. "Enter, my lady."

Katya entered the cave to find Greenie and the red dragon in front of a roaring fire, over which a whole sheep was roasting. Her mouth watered.

"My lady." Greenie bowed. "Our home is your home."

"You don't live in the treasure caves?"

The red dragon chuckled. "Nay, we are merely called there by magic from time to time."

Katya dropped to the rocky floor, the bleakness of her situation sinking in. A myriad of questions ran through her mind, but she didn't have the strength to voice them.

"Do not worry. We will care for you," Greenie said. "There is food, water, and shelter here—all you need." He indicated a bed of dried grass in the corner.

"And in a year and a day we will return to Haryngai." The golden dragon curled up in the cave entrance and promptly went to sleep.

***

Katya settled into her new life. She missed her family in many ways, especially Rayaul, but her newfound freedom meant she no longer worried about other people's opinions. Korin was never far from her thoughts, though.

She improved her fishing skills in the glittering lake and hunted for small game among the trees. Berries and nuts were ripe for picking. As spring came, fruit trees blossomed, promising fall harvest. Katya wandered through groves for hours, reveling in her liberty and the solitude of the vast valley.

Greenie taught her to care for her dragon friends: cleaning their scales, paring their claws, and polishing teeth—a job that scared Katya at first. But she was more than willing to repay them for giving her a home. Clothing caused no problem with the magical chests. She wrapped herself in furs in winter, and chose leather boots and sturdy fabrics for hunting. Every day, she flew on Golden, inspecting the valley and getting to know the other dragons. At times, she felt she could speak to them without words.

Soon, this peaceful life became the only life she needed—except for the Korin-shaped hole in her heart. She replayed their conversations over in her head, reflecting on every nuance of Korin's voice, recalling the way he'd gazed at her. Would he really wait for her? Or would she return to find him married to another woman?

Greenie sat by her on the cold nights, a roaring fire burning at the rocky shelter's entrance. He knew when her thoughts turned inward. "Do not worry, my lady. Have patience and all will be well."

Katya stared into the flames, hoping he was right. *Is the fire in my heart a curse or a blessing?*

On midwinter's eve, a year and a day after Katya left, she awoke early. She could barely quell the churning in her stomach, and her hands trembled as she prepared for her journey.

Golden flew her to the village. The year rolled back in her mind. Katya had changed while the village had stayed the same. She wore her hunting clothes and felt at ease in herself, although her stomach tensed uncomfortably as they approached.

The dragon wheeled above the village. Below, Lord Chayka and Korin stood on the dais, surrounded by guards. Katya leaned close to Golden's neck. *Those guards look unfriendly.* The lord barked instructions as Golden swooped and dipped down.

Spears flew through the air, which the dragon lithely avoided. He opened his jaws, and a warning fireball erupted from his mouth with a roar. It passed over the heads of the people.

Golden descended to the courtyard. Little pockets of villagers screamed and cowered in the corners. He made a neat landing, powerful wings creating a rush of air. The guards backed away, terror written on their faces.

Katya slid off Golden's back. She spun around as light footsteps pattered close. Rayaul dashed up and threw his arms around her. "Katty, I knew you'd come back. I told Father you'd come."

"I missed you. I'm sorry I couldn't send a message." She hugged his thin body, a warm feeling spreading through her. "Just remember, whatever happens now, my dragons will take care of me."

Rayaul nodded, scrubbing his dirty, tear-stained face with the heel of his hand.

Katya's father marched up, one wary eye on Golden. The dragon tilted his head toward him. Her father grabbed Rayaul's arm and dragged him off Katya. "Get away from her." He backed away, his scornful face tinged with fear. "You are no daughter of mine. You've disgraced us all."

A low growl rumbled deep inside Golden. Katya's father turned and ran, dragging Rayaul behind him. Rayaul gave Katya a longing glance and she smiled at him. But a view of her father's stiff back made her muscles twitch. A flicker of pain ran through her—he'd never accept her. She had to move on.

She threw her head back and faced the dais. Lord Chayka caught her eye, and she held her gaze steady, no longer fearing what he could do to her.

Korin's eyes held a sense of awe, but he didn't hesitate. He jumped off the dais and ran over, taking her in his arms. "I counted the days until your return."

She buried her face in his shoulder. The *something*

missing inside her evaporated under Korin's warm embrace. Greenie had been right. He was worth the wait. Strength flowed into her limbs.

The lord stepped down from the dais and sidled closer, glancing fearfully at Golden. His face crumpled. "Please don't take my son. He's my heir, my oldest boy."

The urge to rip Korin away from the village filled Katya, the intensity taking her breath away. She'd fly off on Golden with Korin. They couldn't stop her.

Korin couldn't take his longing eyes off Katya. "I cannot live without her. Father, please, can't you agree to us marrying? We can live in the village if you don't want us in the castle."

Lord Chayka's jaw dropped open and his brows drew together. "Marry a sorceress who flies on dragons? She'll never be content; she'll stir up the peasants."

Katya stood tall. Hadn't this man learned compassion now he faced losing his son? "Lord Chayka, I cannot give up my dragons, but if you consent to our marriage, you have my word I will cause no trouble. I am not here to challenge you."

Korin's eyes softened and then he turned to his father. "Yes, let us do this. I want to fulfill my responsibilities. Don't force me to abandon my people."

"If you wed a crippled peasant, I will be the laughingstock of the surrounding villages," Lord Chayka snapped. "And no one will come here to trade in fear of those dragons."

Golden stretched forward and huffed smoke into Lord Chayka's face. He backed away, succumbing to a heavy coughing fit, fear etched on his brow. Korin slapped him on the back.

Katya clenched her jaw. This man cared more for his reputation than his son's happiness. "Lord Chayka, I ask you once more. Will you allow me to marry your son? Think carefully before you answer."

Silence reigned in the courtyard. It felt as if the village itself held its breath.

Lord Chayka drew away from Korin and hardened his face, steely eyes glaring at Katya. "I will never allow my son to marry a common peasant."

Korin's face darkened, and his hands curled into fists at his side.

Rage built inside Katya. Her muscles shook. "You do not deserve a son if you cannot see where true worth lies." She stretched out her hand to Korin. "Fly away with me."

Korin cast one disgusted look at his enraged father, before turning to Katya. He took her hand in his. "I am yours."

Tingles ran up Katya's arm, and Golden whisked his wings, causing a breeze to race around the courtyard. His tail flicked around Lord Chayka, who ducked in terror. "Lady Katya, Lord Korin. Your wedding feast awaits in Dragon Valley."

They climbed on Golden, Korin holding tight to Katya's waist. The dragon spiraled upward, sun glinting off his scales, the villagers staring after him in awe.

So Katya and Korin flew away to celebrate their love and dwell with the dragons. Months flew by, until Katya held a small bundle in her arms, and Korin gazed down with pride at his son. As the years passed, they raised a family in peace, caring for their dragon friends. Greenie returned to Haryngai Village each year to gather news in secret, until one year they learned Lord Chayka had passed away. His death was mourned by few.

Korin and Katya returned to the castle and were welcomed as the rightful heirs. Rayaul, now a young man, joyfully reunited with his sister. A softer rule came to Haryngai under Korin's line, as he had learned much wisdom from the dragons.

And every year at midwinter, Korin and Katya summoned Golden and flew away to honor their fiery saviors in Dragon Valley, feasting, dancing, and riding dragons through the skies until dawn heralded the new day.

Story Index

"Seeing Through Him" was inspired by Beauty and the Beast

"Jack and the Storyteller" was inspired by Jack and the Beanstalk

"Three Nights" was inspired by The Twelve Dancing Princesses

"Cursed Glass" was inspired by The Glass Coffin

"Princess and the Frog" was inspired by The Frog Prince

"Swapped" was inspired by The Prince and the Pauper

"The Gruffs vs. Dragon" was inspired by Three Billy Goats Gruff

"Wishes Between Worlds" was inspired by The Enchanted Quill

"The Charcoal Cat" was inspired by The Boy Who Draws Cats

"Solstice Flames" was inspired by A Christmas Carol and The Little Match Girl

"The Firestone" was inspired by The Tinderbox

Author Biographies

B. C. Marine – Seeing Through Him

B. C. Marine's Ballads of Carum Sound are heavily influenced by the beautiful Pacific Northwest, where she lives with her husband and two sons. The scenic views of Puget Sound and the Cascades provide plenty of inspiration for her superpowered romantic fantasies. A Western Washington University alumna and former cosmetologist turned work-at-home mom, she writes in between family life and work for A4A Publishing. She loves knitting and spends far too much time researching for her stories.

"Beauty and the Beast" has long been a favorite tale, and she was thrilled at the chance to update its romantic allegory in "Seeing Through Him," using the more modern courtship model of dating instead of an arranged marriage. Look for her other retellings in *From the Stories of Old* and the upcoming *A Bit of Magic* as well as her debut novel *A Seer's Daughter*. For information and updates on future stories, visit her website (www.bcmarinebooks.com) and connect with her on Twitter (@Meriverian).

Matthew Dewar – Jack and the Storyteller

Matthew's passion for reading and writing developed at a young age. Fascinated by all genres, enthralled by the endless creativity of imagination, and captivated by foreign worlds and intriguing characters, Matthew makes time in his busy schedule to write every day. If he's not reading or writing, you might find Matthew working as a physiotherapist, teaching group fitness classes, entertaining his dog, or dreaming of travelling to an exotic destination.

In May 2017, Matthew published *Nightmare Stories*, a collection of young adult horror fiction where twelve young teens discover that happily ever afters only exist in fairy tales. His short stories have appeared in *From the Stories of Old*, *Between Heroes and Villains*, *Whispers in the Shadows*, *The Seven Deadly Sins Anthology: Gluttony*, and *The Seven Deadly Sins Anthology: Wrath*.

You can connect with Matthew on Twitter (@WriterDewar), Facebook (Matthew Dewar Author), or at his website (matthewdewarauthor.wordpress.com).

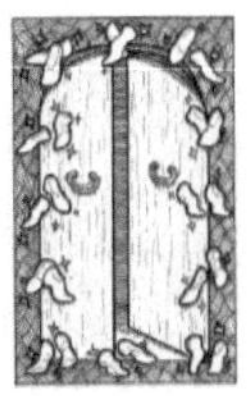

Kelsie Engen – Three Nights

Kelsie Engen is a part-time editor and author, and a full-time wife and mom. She grew up in North Pole, Alaska, where the winters are harsh but beautiful, and Santa Claus was only a five-minute drive away. (Those winters may or may not have inspired her fairy tale world of Canens and the Seven Kingdoms.) In her spare time, she huddles in front of the fire and reads fairy tales to herself or her two children--if they'll listen. If the weather's -20F or above, she might be found outside on a run, listening to an audiobook.

She can also be found through her website for writers (KelsieEngen.com), Instagram (@KelsieEngen), Facebook, (www.Facebook.com/kelsieengenauthor), and Twitter (@KelsieEngen), or hunched over her laptop working on her fairy tale series, the Canens Chronicles, set to release in 2019.

Current information on her newest releases can best be found at her author website: KelsieEngenAuthor.com.

M. T. Wilson – Cursed Glass

M. T. Wilson recently graduated from university, where she studied English Literature with Creative Writing, and now works in marketing. It has been her dream for many years to see her writing published, and she intends to never lose sight of that goal. She has been writing novels for more than ten years. Although she has branched out into science fiction and experimental literary fiction, her first love was fantasy. From a young age, she would plan out epic fantasy series and draw maps of her expansive worlds. She particularly loves dragons and has a large collection of dragon figures. Outside of this anthology, her main project is a young adult science fiction trilogy, which she hopes to publish in the next few years.

Inspiration for retelling "The Glass Coffin" came from the original tale's intriguing imagery and concept. However, many of the plot elements were very typical of a fairy tale and also quite clichéd and outdated. The protagonist stumbles across the woman in the glass coffin, and once he has freed her, they happily marry. This common thread, a woman being saved by a stranger whom she then marries, is seen often in fairy tales. M. T. wanted to put a new spin on the story.

Renee Frey – Princess and the Frog

Renee is both an author and the Chief Operating Officer of Authors 4 Authors Publishing. When not writing or publishing, she teaches dance classes and choreographs musicals. She lives in the 'burbs of Philadelphia (Go Eagles!) with her husband and their two-pound puppies: a puggle named Ziggy who may have eaten your lunch, and a chihuahua mix named Megatron who definitely didn't growl at you just now. She is excited to collaborate with Rowanwood Publishing for this and other anthologies, which spotlight up and coming authors in the fantasy, science fiction, and other speculative fiction genres.

Always fascinated with the story of the Frog Prince, Renee wanted to explore the themes of war, colonialism, and betrayal within the framework of a fairy tale. She wanted the story to focus on the development of romance between the two protagonists, so the harder and more complicated themes take a backseat instead of overpowering the narrative. Renee would like to thank her editing partner, B. C. Marine, anthology producer, Heather Hayden, and everyone in the JL writer group for their help and support with this endeavor!

Allie May – Swapped

Allie May is a dog lover, mom, and Dr. Pepper addict who turns her caffeine-fueled dreams into believable fiction. She fell in love with the impossible at a young age and has been telling stories (some fiction, some mostly nonfiction) ever since. In high school she won two poetry contests, and in college she started the blog Hypergraphia to combat her uncontrollable impulse to write. Her first fiction publication was a Sleeping Beauty retelling titled "Rose & Thorn" that was released in December 2016 in *From the Stories of Old*.

She married her high school sweetheart because he takes her to Disneyland (oh, and because she loves him). Together they have a dog child and a human child. On the weekends, you might catch a glimpse of her in the shadows as a lightsaber-wielding superhero.

"Swapped" was inspired by a dream, as is most of her writing. It wasn't until after she started the outline that she realized it was actually a retelling of *The Prince and the Pauper*.

You can follow Allie on Facebook (@AllieMayAuthor), Twitter (@AllieMayAuthor), Goodreads (Allie May), and her blog (alliemayauthor.blogspot.com).

Louise Ross – The Gruffs vs. Dragon

Louise Ross is a writer from the greater Kansas City area. When not quilting and working, she lives in a fantasy world where ordinary creatures build everyday lives outside the major battles and politics.

"The Gruffs vs. Dragon" is a continuation and play on "Three Billy Goats Gruff". As a kid, Louise loved fairy tales, but she was often drawn to fairy tales that featured animals. Both of her favorite nursery rhymes and fairy tales were animal-centric. So for this second anthology of fairy tale retellings, she chose "Three Billy Goats Gruff".

You can connect with Louise Ross on Facebook (@ALouiseRoss), Twitter (@A_Louise_Ross), and her blog (83louross.wordpress.com).

Sam Waterhouse – Wishes Between Worlds

Sam Waterhouse is a part-time writer with a full-time imagination from Hobart, Tasmania. "Wishes Between Worlds" is his second published story, a futuristic retelling of "The Enchanted Quill" fairy tale. He enjoys writing unusual characters, so a trickster, genie-esque crow was an opportunity too good to pass on.

Sam also contributed to the previous Just-Us League anthology *Between Heroes and Villains* with "Like You," an original story where superpowers are treated as a disease to be eradicated.

You can follow Sam on Twitter (@SW_Wordologist).

J. E. Klimov – The Charcoal Cat

J. E. Klimov grew up in a small suburb in Massachusetts. After graduating from Massachusetts College of Pharmacy and Health Sciences, she obtained her PharmD and became a pharmacist; however, her true passion was in writing and illustration. Ever since Klimov was little, she dreamed of sharing her stories with the world. From scribbling plotlines instead of taking notes in school, to bringing her characters to life through sketches, Klimov's ideas ranged from fantasy to thriller fiction. She has two short stories published in the Just-Us League anthologies: "The Guardian's Secret" in *From the Stories of Old* and "The Fate of Patient Zero" in *Between Heroes and Villains.*

Her debut fantasy novel, "The Aeonians," was published by Silver Leaf Books on November 13th, 2017. It follows the adventures of tomboy Princess Isabel as she races against time to recover parts of a family heirloom—gems that grant elemental powers.

You can follow Klimov's updates and other posts on Facebook (@KlimovAuthor), Twitter (@klimov_author), and her blog (jelliotklimov.weebly.com).

Heather Hayden – Solstice Flames

Though a part-time editor by day, Heather Hayden's not-so-secret identity is that of a writer—at night she pours heart and soul into science fiction and fantasy novels. She is currently working on *Upgrade* (the sequel to her first published novel) and an as-yet-untitled series of fairy tale novelizations.

"Solstice Flames" was inspired by two stories: *A Christmas Carol* (which Heather loves) and *The Little Match Girl* (which she doesn't). In writing her own version of the two stories, Heather sought to create a happily ever after for a character she once cried for. She dedicates this story to her sister, Heidi Hayden, who loves Christmas almost as much as they both love reading.

You can follow Heather's writing adventures on her blog (hhaydenwriter.com), Facebook (@HHaydenWriter), and Twitter (@HHaydenWriter).

Elise Edmonds – The Firestone

Elise Edmonds is an author from the South-West UK. Reading and writing have always been her doorways into another world—a way to escape and spend time walking with wizards, flying with fairies, and dealing with dragons. By day she is a finance professional, and in her spare time she pursues writing as a creative outlet, to put the magic back into everyday life. In addition to reading, Elise enjoys watching movies, playing the piano, and going to Zumba classes. Her greatest loves are God, her husband, her family and friends, and her two beautiful cats.

As a child, Elise enjoyed listening to the fairy tales of Hans Christian Anderson on audio cassette (yes, she's that old!), so when the anthology opportunity arose, "The Tinderbox" was her first choice. Her fascination with fantasy gave her the idea for a twist in the tale—by swapping dogs for dragons! Elise's debut novel is a young adult fantasy titled *Where Carpets Fly*. You can follow Elise on Facebook (@elisemagicwriter), Twitter (@WriterEdmonds), and her website (www.magicwriter.co.uk).

About the Illustrator

Heidi Hayden was raised in the forests of Maine and graduated from the Maine College of Art as an Illustration major. A bookworm by nature, she reads copious amounts of questionable fiction by unpublished authors, in the few moments of spare time when she is not writing and illustrating her own books. She works in gouache, ink, pencil, and fabric, and enjoys repurposing materials for her art.

She drew inspiration for the anthology's illustrations from a variety of old fairy tale books, such as those depicting the tales of the Brothers Grimm. The medium—ink on paper—was chosen in order to capture both the essence of the retellings and the timelessness of black-and-white illustrations.

You can see more of her work on her website (haydenillustration.com).

About the Just-Us League

Hailing from all corners of the globe, the members of the Just-Us League share a common passion for words and worlds.

The League can be found on Facebook (@jlwriters), Twitter (@JL_writing), and our website (jlwriters.com). Follow us for updates, giveaways, and new releases.

Also by the Just-Us League

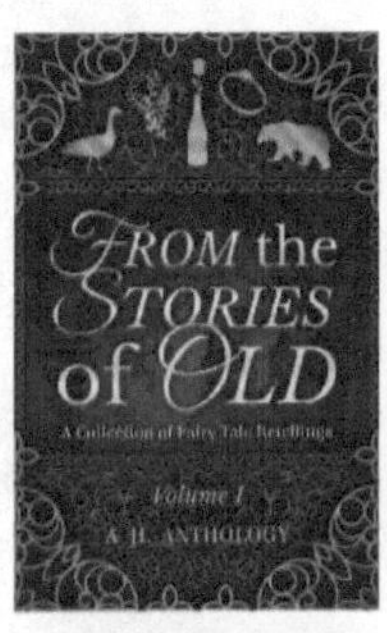